The Love of Stones

TOBIAS HILL

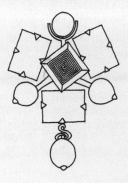

Picador

New York

Acknowledgements

Thanks are due to: Walid Atiyeh, the Kufa Gallery; Felix Graf, the National Museum of Switzerland; Tessa Chester, Bethnal Green Museum of Childhood; Kay Staneland, the Museum of London; Anna Kay, Hampton Court; Jennifer Marin, the London Jewish Museum; Liz Wilson, Sotheby's; Jeanette Cannon, the Jewish Historical Society of England; Lesley Coldham, De Beers; Haled al Fayad; Pip, Hannah, Caroline, Xandra, Victoria and Julian; the Arts Council of England, and Edward Lear.

www.picadorusa.com

Picador ® is a U.S. registered trademark and is used by St. Martin's Press under license from Pan Books Limited.

For information on Picador Reading Group Guides, as well as ordering, please contact the Trade Marketing department at St. Martin's Press.
Phone: 1-800-221-7945 extension 763
Fax: 212-677-7456
E-mail: trademarketing@stmartins.com

Library of Congress Cataloging-in-Publication Data

Hill, Tobias, 1970–
    The love of stones / Tobias Hill.
        p. cm.
    ISBN 0-312-28773-9 (hc)
    ISBN 0-312-31131-1 (pbk)
    1. Jewelry, Renaissaince—Collectors and collecting—Fiction.
    2. Istanbul (Turkey)—Fiction. 3. London (England)—Fiction.
    4. Tokyo (Japan)—Fiction. 5. Jewelers—Fiction. I. Title.

PR6058.I4516 L68 2002
823'.914—dc21   2001050038

First published in Great Britain by Faber and Faber Limited

First Picador Paperback Edition: January 2003

10 9 8 7 6 5 4 3 2 1

For B –
Also to Shimon and Elazar,
Different brothers

A face that toils so close to stones is already stone itself

CAMUS, 'The Myth of Sisyphus'

1
Sterne

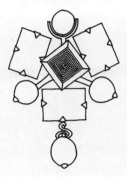

Years before his murder on the Bridge of Montereau, Duke John the Fearless of Burgundy commissioned a jewel called the Three Brethren. It was the shoulder-knot of a cloak, a triangle of stones connected by crude spurs of gold. It was wide as a piece of armour across the collarbone. The jewel gained its name from its three balas rubies, which were identical in every way.

If I close my eyes I can see them, always. The balases are not true oriental rubies. Instead they are a certain colour of the mineral spinel, the shade lying between rose and blood. These rubies, the oriental and the balas, are both formed of oxygen and aluminium; but spinel also contains a single atom of magnesium, and this reduces its hardness and lustre. In India, where the ruby is the Lord of Stones, there are caste systems of jewels. They are as old and intractable as the orderings of people. In the castes of rubies, the balases are *vaisya*, the third rank of twelve.

The origins of most medieval jewels lay in Asia, and the source of the greatest balases was Badakshân, on the banks of the Shignân, a tributary of the Oxus. There is no record of how the stones came to Burgundy. Keep going back into the history of stones, and the people begin to fall away. Go back far enough, and there are only stones. There is nothing written of who brought the rubies to Burgundy.

The Brethren of John the Fearless were table-cut gems, big flat stones, the size and shape of tiles in a game of dominoes. Set with three pearls around a central diamond, with a fourth pearl hung from the triangular form, the Duke's jewel was broad as the palm of an outstretched hand. The diamond was flawless, five-eighths of an inch square at the base. It was cut by the Belgian jeweller Louis de Berquem, and became known as the Heart of Three Brothers. The Heart was the model for De Berquem's new lapidary design. It was faceted like a pyramid, echoing the growth of a raw diamond.

I close my eyes. I see it again. The beauty of the complete jewel

3

lies in the quality of its stones, the spaced balance of its setting, and in the slight asymmetry of its radial structure. It is strikingly modern in its bold lines and functionalism. It is all gold hooklets and wires and claws. But the Brethren also looks archaic. There are the natural cuts of its jewels, as if the crystals are still alive and growing. And there is the jewel's geometry. I see the outline of a talisman in the alignment of pyramid, triangle, surfaces, planes.

John the Fearless was the second Valois duke of Burgundy. He was a loose-skinned man with the eyes of a chess player. Of the four dukes, he was the only one who knew how to manipulate an army. At the age of twenty-four he was captured on the bloody fields of Nicopolis, and held for a ransom of two hundred thousand ducats and twelve white falcons by Sultan Bayazid. He learnt caution from the experience, and a degree of cruelty.

Even in paintings, posed, John always looks as if he is planning. He was a political man, an employer of assassins. A wearer of great jewels. Hard to pity, even knowing what waits for him when the sitting is finished, and the painter gone.

In John's lifetime, no commoner in Europe had ever worn a diamond. He lived in an age when jewels were the international currency of power. The display of stones had more to do with muscle than desire. A great ruby might be beautiful, but the beauty made it functional. It was the means to wage wars, after all, or the motive for waging them. The dowry to avert invasion, or the sacred mystery that justified it. Jewels were still Mysteries, then. It was less than three lifetimes since Louis the Ninth had built the Sainte Chapelle to house the Crown of Thorns. A jewelled relic in a jewel-chamber of stained glass and lancets and spandrels.

When I read the inventories of the Valois dukes I recognise something in myself. The care of the scribes, the precise writing, which is a kind of passion. Love of things, love of power. I see it in the catalogues of John's uncle, where Valois jewels are recorded carefully, without error, as if they might be weapons or the names of lovers.

> *Item six; fourteen named rubies.*
> *Item seven; fifteen fragments of the true cross.*
> *Item eight; an ostrich's egg.*

Item nine; a porcupine's quill.
Item ten; an elephant's molar.

John Valois was born into a dynasty that accumulated a great number of jewels. His own father had been a vain but practical man: Philip the Bold had married Margaret of Male, whose habits were thought ugly (she was fond of whistling and sitting on grass), but who inherited Flanders and its merchant ports. Burgundy was already rich with wine and salt. John's father had added wealth on an industrial scale. His ornamentation was famous. To meet an English envoy he once wore a velvet coat with a running embroidery of broom, the pods worked in sapphires, with rosebuds of pearls and twenty-two blossoms of rubies.

It was the first decade of the fifteenth century when John Valois commissioned the Three Brethren. His Burgundy had become a lean, mercantile state. It strengthened every year, and every year its neighbour, France, seemed to weaken. The kingdom was unsteady, with its child dauphin and lost wars. Whereas Burgundy was all strength. All wine and jewels. Burgundy looked as if it might last for ever.

Weakness attracts. The neighbours of France began to lean against it. From England, Henry the Fifth ferried men to the port towns of Calais and Boulogne. In the east, John began to acquire what was there for the taking. He spent years in Paris, joining in its machinations and assassinations. His mercenary armies fought westwards across the marches of France.

He took Paris but never held it. He won battles but not the wars. He could have succeeded, and the history of the Brethren would have been quite different. The jewel might never have been lost. Nevertheless, by 1419 the French dauphin Charles Valois had reached the age of sixteen and not lost his country or his life. He asked to meet his cousin John, and the Fearless Duke accepted. The rulers were to converse on neutral ground. For this purpose they agreed on the bridge at Montereau, where their forces could be divided by water.

A split enclosure was built on the bridge, a structure which could separate the rulers both from those outside, and from each other. The dauphin's men emptied the bridge houses and crossing. Jehan of Poitiers was with the French as they waited for John to arrive. In his journals he describes a conversation between the future Charles the Seventh and one of his knights, Robert Lord of Trèves:

> We noticed, from the behaviour of the said lord of Trèves, that he wanted to detain the king and to speak with him more at length and, as it seemed to us, he was contradicting what the king said. Then the king left him abruptly, and had the said lord of Trèves summoned two or three times to follow him. But he would not go, and remained in the room with us and several others whose names I forget. As soon as the king, then regent, had left, we saw the lord of Trèves flop onto a bed, so we went up to him and asked what was the matter. He replied in these words: 'Monsieur of Valence, I wish to God that I was in Jerusalem without money or belongings, and that I'd never met this lord here, for I'm very much afraid that he's been wickedly advised and that he'll do something today which will be very damaging both to him and to his kingdom.'

There were rules to the meeting. Charles made them, and John kept to them. Only unarmed advisers were allowed into the enclosure. The doors were locked behind them. It was dim inside, and cool. There was the smell of tallow. The sound of water. The sound of curlews.

John was a middle-aged man who already looked old. Charles was a king in the skin of a boy. It was forty-two years before he would starve himself to death, unable to eat through fear of poison. For now, the two Valois rulers were equal in every way but rank. It was the Duke who went to the barrier, opened it, and knelt at the feet of the child.

Charles took John's hand. There are records which say he gave a signal with his eyes; and records which do not. He began to raise his cousin, but the gesture was never completed. One of the dauphin's men, Tanguy de Chastel, began to move. He took a step towards the kneeling figure, and another. He took an axe from his robes as he came, the haft cut short. He hefted it.

He struck down across John's head, splitting the bone open. A cry went up, spreading to those outside. The Burgundian army lined the river, but when it tried to reach the Duke it found French crossbowmen hidden in the abandoned buildings. The knights were pushed back, leaving the Duke behind, with the King.

6

Of the Burgundians inside, only John himself was armed. Now he tried to draw his sword. He was badly wounded, or half-dead, or dying; the blood in his face where the skull was broken. The hand on the sword was thoughtless, I think. The instinct of the body to protect itself. It was only one sword, and much too late. To shouts of 'Kill! Kill!' from the French, Robert de Lairé held John's arms back by the sleeves (of black velvet, with pods of broom and rosebuds of pearls), and Tanguy de Chastel axed him again across the crown of his head.

It took four blows to kill the Fearless Duke. After his murder, his carcass was given up by the French. It was taken back to Dijon, where the body and heart could be buried in the church and the soil.

And the Three Brethren went with them. With the great cloak it was unknotted from the shoulder of the dead man. It was unfastened from the cloak and put away in the vaults of Burgundy, with the fragments of the Cross and the molars of elephants. The jewel had outlived its first owner. It was still perfect in itself. Still unmarked by ownership.

茶

'They say that God made men from clots of blood.'

He has a smooth voice, smooth hands, and the critical eyes of a pawnbroker. Now he can see the stones I've brought, he looks at them instead of me. I relax. Not too much. His name is Ismet, and he is in the business of jewels.

'Clots of blood. May I ask where you bought these, Miss Sterne?'

'No.'

'I didn't think so. You know, you remind me of myself.'

When I don't answer he goes on talking. 'Yes. You look like you have done this before. Will you drink tea? I can have some brought down.'

'Not now.'

He talks a lot, I think. More than he needs to, certainly. Just talking as he works, comfortable with the knowledge that he is in his own place and I am not and that he can say what he likes, here. He is wrong about us. We have nothing in common, except jewels.

Spread out between us on the desk is a sheet of paper. On the paper are three rough red stones. They are small as the seeds from a pomegranate. The jeweller picks them up and holds them to his monocle lens, one by one, as he talks.

'Clots of blood, yes. So they say. I'm not religious myself. I don't mind if God is a Christian or a Muslim or even a Jew. Still, it's a pity he didn't think to work with these. We might all have been so much . . . more . . . perfect.'

I wait. Outside the noon muezzin begins. The sound shimmers like a heat haze over western Istanbul. The room has a fan on the ceiling and frosted-glass doors in three walls. On the wall without a door there is a chipped washbasin. Above it at face height is a calendar advertising the Golden Horn Shipping and Air Corporation in English and Turkish. August is a tanned blonde draped in fishing nets and diamonds.

Ismet the jeweller puts down the largest of the rubies and clicks his teeth. 'This one has fouls. How much did you pay for it?'

'Enough.'

He grunts. 'How did you find me, by the way?'

'Küsav's.'

'Küsav's!' Derisively. 'They spend too much time talking.'

While he works and talks, I look at his shoes. I look at his watch, his clothes and his hands. The face. The last thing I do is listen to what he says. It's harder to lie without words.

Under the desk's mid-section I can see his legs, spread to support his bulk. The shoes are imported leather, with an expensive shinelessness. The parallels of his trousers are sharp. He wears a good watch, Patek Philippe, nothing loud. An evening watch. The gold is a little heavy for daylight.

Without making a show of it, he looks successful. He is good at what he does, and what he does involves old jewels. It is why I am here. I have been in Istanbul for five days. On two of those five I have been to the Küsav auction house on Has Firin Road, watching the buyers, talking to the warehouse men. When they are not busy working or clockwatching, they tell me about the jewel dealers of Istanbul.

They tell me about Ismet. They say he does well, he buys and sells works from all over the world. Reliquaries from Russia, Mogul necklaces from India. How they are found and how they cross borders are not his problems. If he was a legitimate dealer I

8

would have found him quicker. He would be well known, big in the high street. But then he is not that kind of dealer.

Flight paths thunder overhead. When the vibrations have lessened, Ismet takes miniature electronic scales out of the desk. One by one, he weighs the stones I have brought him. Three times for each stone.

'Of course, the trade in rubies – the market – what can I say? The bottom has fallen out of it. Last month I had a stone from the wife of a Burmese general, my God, I never saw anything like it. Four carats and no fouls. The colour of pigeon's blood. A piece like that, pardon me, I could make love to it. But sell it? No. Now it sits in my bank, making nothing. Now I have it round my neck, it weighs not four carats but four thousand and four.'

He peers at the scales' digital display. I know he wants the rubies. The warehouse men say they are his favourite stone. Even after cutting has removed half their weight, these three gems should be nearly two carats each: a fine size, for rubies. The best of them has no fouls, and their colours are good. I bought them in Sri Lanka from a man much like this, in a room like this. I have been here before, at this point, many times. I have never been here before.

I am following in the footsteps of a great jewel. It has been in Istanbul at least once. A stone from the artefact was sold here three centuries ago, when the shoulder-knot itself was already as old as that again. And great jewels have a way of returning to their past. Anywhere they have been – anyone they have been with – is somewhere they can be again. I sit in the place which is not mine and listen to the slow *shock, shock* of the ceiling fan.

Ismet switches off the scales. 'Pretty little things, aren't they? I'll give you the best price I can.'

'I don't want money.'

He looks at me with his assessor's eyes, picks up the smallest ruby and examines it again. Even uncut, it winks in the light. A fragment of ruby matrix still clings to the pure stone. For a while Ismet says nothing, only smiles up at the jewel. As if he is holding nails in his teeth. 'You don't want money. So what are we doing here?'

'I'm looking for something. It's been in Istanbul before, some time ago. I've heard that your field is antiquities.'

Shock, shock.

'Maybe. I have several fields. Maybe. Just don't tell me you're looking for the Tavernier blue diamond.' His teeth are small and white. 'I already sold it last week to an insurance firm in Tokyo.'

I wait for his smile to pass. He puts the ruby down. Picks it up again. When he's not talking, he's a nervous man. 'So, antiquities. Are you looking for objects, or just information?'

'Either.'

'And you'll pay in rubies?'

'If you like.'

'You have something particular in mind?'

'I'm looking for the Three Brethren.'

He lowers the ruby and looks at me, poker-faced, through the monocle lens. 'The Three Brethren. I see. Why do you want it?'

'Why don't you?'

'Ah.' He concedes a smile, the one eye twinkling. 'Of course I do. Already you know me a little well, Miss Sterne. But I was right.' He leans forward. 'We are alike. We understand each other. Yes. I know your kind.'

I stop myself turning my head away. It is an instinctive reaction. As if he has moved too close. He barks a laugh.

'The Three Brethren. Well, who wouldn't want it? How long have you been looking?'

'What do you have on it?'

'As it happens, quite a lot. Concrete too, very concrete. It won't come cheap. How much can you afford, Miss Sterne? Or perhaps you are buying for someone else. Japanese or American? You can tell me.'

'American,' I lie. It's what he wants to hear, I think: what he expects. He looks me up and down.

'American. Right. And they have money, of course.'

I nod. Ismet gets up without speaking. He looks at me again, without expression. Then he goes through the left-hand door. I watch his shadow move beyond the frosted glass. There is the sound of footsteps going upstairs. Distant voices. When he opens the door again his hands are full. In one he has a box and in the other the arm of a younger man. A retrograde image of Ismet, thirty years stripped away. Nephew or son, a gun holstered at his belt. He nods, taking me in, and goes to stand by the exit. Ismet sits.

'Just a precaution, you understand.'

'Does he have a licence for that?'

'The gun? Of course. I never touch them myself.' Ismet puts the box down. 'Think of him as a security guard. If it helps.' With both hands, he opens the box and pushes it across the desk to me.

Inside is a cut jewel, more than half an inch wide, clear and brilliant on black velvet. It is the shape of a halved raw diamond, as if a growing crystal has been split down the middle into twin pyramids. But the facets are not those of a natural growth. The skin is too polished, too caught up in light.

His voice goes soft. 'This might interest you. I have had this stone for nearly twenty years. The cut is very old, fifteenth century. It is called the Heart of Three Brothers.'

I pick it up and let it rest in my hand. It feels heavy for its size. Like a bullet, although this is an illusion. Diamond has less weight than metal. Across the desk, the merchant sits quite still.

I close my eyes and concentrate on touch. The stone is too warm to be a diamond. I can feel it now. The thermoconductivity is wrong. A diamond draws heat out of its surroundings, giving nothing back. It is a quality that is characteristic of the jewel. Other stones lack that clear, acquisitive iciness. I think of it as a kind of integrity.

I close the stone in my hand, then open the fist again. Letting it go. 'This is not the heart I am looking for,' I say. Carefully, I put the jewel back in its box.

Something vicious rears up in Ismet's eyes. The young man waits behind us. I see the merchant's fingers jerk. Then his eyes clear, the desire is gone. He begins to move again, as if he has woken from a trance. He shrugs. 'What a pity. But you see how it is. I deal in real jewels, Miss Sterne. Not an object that has not been known for centuries. I deal in the rock-solid. You want a heart? I can get you a cock with a good heart on the side. The cock will be so good to you all night, you will forget all about your Brethren. Yes? No? Ah, but you are in a hurry. Rami, let her go. Some other time, some other time.'

They wait smiling while I pick up the rubies. Without looking back I walk down the three flights of stairs to the street. By the time I am halfway down the despair begins to rise up inside me and I push it away.

The air is cool in the shade of the entrance hall. I breathe it in, the smell of dingy offices and men. When I am ready I step out into the heat and noise of Istanbul at noon.

☒

Love of things, love of power.

I see history through the eyes of the Three Brethren. It is the way a pawnbroker might look at things: as if everything has a value and a price. Sometimes these things can seem the same. When John the Fearless was murdered by the child dauphin in 1419, France gained as little as Burgundy lost. The kingdom acquired some time, the dukedom lost its duke. And dukes are easy to replace. Cheaper than great jewels.

But of course they are not the same, value and price. Death is always extraordinary. I wonder if his wife would have given the Brethren to have John Valois back. I know I would not, writing five hundred and seventy-nine years later. The balance of my desires falls differently. At least, I think, his killing made sense, in a time when death was terrifying in its senselessness. In England, apothecaries prescribed powdered ruby for diseases of the heart. In Dijon, the salt merchants wore emeralds to protect themselves from plague. Pressed pomanders against their mouths, like fists.

An ordinary, extraordinary death. I am trying to see it lovelessly now, only in terms of price. The duke was replaceable. The jewel was not. When John Valois was killed with four strokes of an axe, Burgundy wasn't left without an heir. The duchy passed to John's son, Philip, who in time became known as 'the Good'.

Philip learnt from his father's death. If he thought of adding to his territory, he kept the idea close to his heart. More than his father or son, he was a patient man. Over the years, the third of the Valois dukes built up Burgundy into the greatest of duchies. Philip made his state a kingdom in waiting, and he did this by doing nothing. While England and France emptied their treasuries to pay for their wars, Philip waited in Dijon. Counting his banked strengths. The rubies and diamonds, wine and salt. The molars of elephants in their roots of gold.

In the year his father died, the young heir had an inventory made of his father's estate. The document runs to over a hundred pages. Its vellum sheets are still white along the spine, like milk. In the underlit rooms of an archive in Beaune, I transcribe Item XXIII:

> *A very good and rich clasp, adorned in the middle with a very big and great diamond, pointed, and around this are iii good and big square balass rubies called the iii brethren, set in openwork, and iii very big and fine pearls between the said balasses. On which clasp there hangs a very big and fine pearl shaped like a pear.*

A decade later the shoulder-knot is described as 'My lord's brooch', and rests alongside 'the largest balas-ruby in France'. Philip possessed the Brethren until his death in 1467, when the jewel passed to his own son, Charles the Bold, the Foolhardy, last Valois duke of Burgundy.

Charles had a love of order and a hatred of women. His skin was exceptionally white, like vellum. He modelled himself on Alexander the Great, son of another Philip, conqueror of Badakshân, and like Alexander he left no certain heir when he was killed in battle.

Conrad Stolle, a German parson, once heard Charles the Foolhardy say 'that there were only three lords in the world, one in Heaven, that is God; one in Hell, that is Lucifer; and one on earth, that will be himself.'

His jeweller, Gerard Loyet, was a great artist – his gold statuette of Charles kneeling with a crystal reliquary is a masterpiece. Loyet reset the Brethren several times, but it always retained its basic form. On one bill, Loyet is paid £14 for 'an ornament of three great guns arranged in a triangle and adorned with three large balas rubies in lieu of flints, with great flames of gold shooting out all around like the sun'.

For eight years after Philip's death, the duchy of Burgundy was richer and more powerful than any kingdom in Europe. It encompassed Belgium, Luxembourg and half of Holland to the north, and much of both Switzerland and France. It was a medieval empire stretching from the North Sea to the Mediterranean. Charles dressed the imperial part. He rode a black horse in battle harness, covered with cloth of gold and violet. He wore polished steel armour and a martial cloak, clasped with the Three Brethren

His jewelled hats were renowned. Panigarola watched Charles on his way to church in April 1475, wearing *'a black velvet hat*

*with a plume of gold loaded with the largest balas rubies and diamonds
and with large pearls, some good ones pendent, and the pearls and gems
were so closely packed that one could not see the plume, though the first
branch of it was as long as a finger'.*

Charles's obsessions were political power and material wealth.
Jewels were the essence of both. He took them everywhere he
went – to churches, feasts and battlefields – like talismans. His
wealth included twelve gold basins, tapestries of the conquests of
Alexander the Great, a sword with a hilt of unicorn horn, birds
modelled out of scented Cypriot clay in six silver cages, and a
hanging embroidered with a thousand flowers. Aconites and bor-
age, convolvulus and iris and narcissus.

And most of all, he owned stones. By the time of its downfall,
Burgundy possessed three of the finest diamonds in the world.
The flawless centrepiece of the Brethren called the Heart of Three
Brothers. The wine-yellow stone of one hundred and thirty-
seven and a half carats known in some centuries as the Tuscan
and in others as the Florentine; and a jewel of a hundred and six
carats, one half of which became known as the Sancy and which,
centuries after the fall of Burgundy, was cut glistening from its
hiding place in the stomach of de Sancy's most faithful servant.

The fall of Burgundy began in 1476. Without warning, with no
plot or premonition, the balance of power swung away from the
dukedom, and it never came back.

Nothing angered Charles like the rise of the Swiss city states.
For years, Basel and Berne had carried on running battles against
the greater force of their western enemy. Enraged by their independence, the Duke began to plan outright war. He set out by
besieging the castle of Grandson on Lake Neuchâtel. When the
few hundred Bernese defenders surrendered they were all
drowned, or hanged on the walnut trees by the water's edge.

Charles was fastidious in his assembly of armies. The knights
of Burgundy were well dressed and well drilled, and their spectacle was backed up with all the force money could buy – four-
barrelled cannon, English longbowmen, Italian free-lancers. The
greatest weakness of Burgundy was Charles himself, whose
atrocities and arrogant advances united the Swiss into an army
larger and better supplied than that of the Foolhardy Duke.

A few miles from Grandson, the Burgundians met the Swiss

14

forces. The spectacle of the duchy turned out to be greater than its substance. Outnumbered and disorganised, the Burgundians were routed almost before fighting had begun. Retreating in disarray, the Duke left behind all his tents and possessions – bronze guns and Spanish swords, the armour of warhorses with their colander eyes, tapestries of ancient wars, the ducal seals and pennants; and Charles's chests of jewels. The Sancy, the Tuscan, the Three Brethren.

In the broken tents, a Swiss foot soldier found one of Charles's famous, ludicrous hats. It was plumed with ostrich feathers and tipped with a ruby spike. But the soldier threw it away, saying he wouldn't swap it for a good helmet.

The spoils of Grandson were one of the greatest booties in history – comparable to that of Alexander when he defeated the Great King of Persia. It is the only time the life of Charles the Bold really echoed the grandeur of his predecessor.

For a year Charles fought on, losing more disastrously each time. Finally, at Nancy in 1477, the Burgundians were broken, scattered and slaughtered in their thousands. It was days before the body of Charles was found among the dead.

The agreement of the Swiss was to hold the booty in common, and for any profits of sale to be shared among them. But the cities were not rich, the jewels were like nothing they had seen before, and the hands they passed through were very numerous. Stone by stone, the greatest treasures of the *Burgunderbeute* were lost, stolen and broken up, sold on the black markets of Europe and Asia.

But there is a record of the Three Brethren. In the year Charles the Bold died and for twenty-seven years afterwards, it was held by the Magistrates of Basel and Berne. In 1477 the Bernese had a miniature watercolour made of their booty.

It is the earliest picture of the jewel that survives. In the miniature it is curiously inert, a pendulum weight hung motionless from a plain wooden backing. It is an object of value, not an ornament. Its diamond remains unworn by the common people. The Swiss were merchants, not dukes, after all. They had no desire for crown jewels: only for money. The Three Brethren was put up for sale. It was a generation before anyone could afford to buy it.

来

It is a dead-end street where Ismet has his business. A boy hauls black sacks from a kitchen service door, and the smell of rot gets into my mouth and stays on my skin. This isn't what I'm looking for, I think; and in thinking it I sound like someone else. Someone angrier, my sister or some idea of my mother. *Is this what you're looking for? What are you doing, Katharine?*

A woman hangs out washing below the jeweller's offices. No one stands at the windows above her. It is a long way back to the old town and I walk for the sake of it, putting distance between myself and the man with the gun. Trucks groan on the coastal road. Beyond the traffic are drive-in night-clubs and theme bars. Beyond them, the Sea of Marmara. It feels better to be outside, at least. The air is fresher. I breath in its smell of sewage and oil tar, the human mixed with the inhuman, all of it close and familiar.

I dig for the rubies in my pocket. They are something to believe in, a kind of proof. With the rubies I will always have a chance. They can buy me anything, time or information or a plane across the world, my little brethren, my jewels, carried from Colombo to Istanbul inside the folds of my clothing. I think of all the Ismets I have known, with their imitation stones and their mercantile eyes. If I had asked him, I think he would have quoted me a price for myself.

It is hot today, the humidity rising. On the side streets the shopkeepers sit out, worrying at beads, waiting for business. The costermongers sell lottery cards and pretzel bread. Quiet men, thin, waiting to function. Children play football in an empty lot, shouting in Turkish, in English. *Pass, pass. Goal!* They remind me of home, the men and boys. Of England's east coast, and its empty seafront towns. There are lives which could have been mine which are not so different from these. Ordinary working, waiting lives. I think of these things only sometimes; and with regret, less than sometimes. Regret is no help to me. There is little I could let myself go back to now.

It is an old city, Istanbul. You can hear it in its names: Constantinople, Byzantium, Chalcedon, each built over the last, roofs broken down into foundations, subways into tombs. A city of cities, as much as a metropolis of people. Untouched by the Second World War. By the next junction there is a dusty shopfront displaying calligraphy brushes, plastic flowers, a scroll with the characters *Ah, Love!* written in bold sweeping strokes. Next door is a Mister Donut café. Sixties girl-group music drifts out through the entrance, the Shangri-Las or the Secrets. Plastic décor and plastic music. To myself I can admit that I find it reassuring. The modern world, a relief from the past.

I go in and order coffee and two crullers from one of the women behind the bar. Above the stereo hangs a blue glass eye, small and vacant, a ward against devils. There is an empty table by the door and I sit down and look out. Even in here it is hot. My hair feels longer than I would like it. I tie it up with its own pale braid, feeling the breeze against the back of my neck.

The food comes and I eat it. I'm not hungry but it gives me time to think. I take out my notebooks. The pages are stuffed with flyers for sales and jewellers. There are two auctions this afternoon, twelve lots of lapidaries at the Antik Palace on Spor Road, and a Bazaar of Ottoman Jewels, to be held at the municipal auction rooms in the Covered Market. The Antik Palace lots sound more promising. There are texts concerned with medieval jewels, Oriental and Occidental, nothing I'd bid for. If I go it will be to see who buys. While I remember, I write down the details of the Golden Horn Shipping and Air Corporation. It isn't much to have, the name of a shipping firm from a soft-porn calendar in the office of a black marketeer. There is never much.

A new track starts up, something old and vinyl-smooth, nothing I recognise. I listen to it while I pay and leave. On the street an old man is selling blackcurrant ice cream from a metal churn. He smiles at me sweetly, like a grandparent. I buy a cone from him and eat it as I walk. The words of the song follow me. They make me think of the Brethren. But then everything does.

> *Some day, some way, you'll realise you've been blind.*
> *Yes darling, you're going to need me again,*
> *It's just a matter of time.*
> *Go on, go on,*
> *Until you reach the end of the line.*
> *But I know you'll pass my way again.*
> *It's just a matter of time.*

There are two kinds of lapidary. One is a professional, a worker of precious stones. The other is a book, in the same way that a bestiary is a book of animals. At the Antik Palace I walk through the galleries with their Ottoman candlesticks, silver bibelots and meerschaum pipes to buy and take home to Blackburn or Stuttgart. Upstairs the atmosphere is dryer. The sale is already under way, the auctioneer taking bids on the expensive volumes of Leonardus's *Speculum Lapidum* and Emmanuel's *Precious Stones of the Jews of Curaçao*.

No one is making a killing here. There are too many antiquaries and not enough desire. The main buyer is a money-fat woman, western Turkish rather than Middle Eastern, with a face like Henry the Eighth. The last lot of the day is at four-thirty and I bid against her, gauging her interest. She puts down her hand and frowns at me, as if I have interrupted a private pleasure. For $60 plus export tax I'm left with an obscure study of the Tudor crown jewels. The auctioneer smiles with faint commiseration.

Downstairs the shop is closing. I go out by the back door. The Antik Palace service yard has walls topped with broken glass, brown, green and white, as if the owners are drinking their way to security. The air tastes of soot and on Spor Road my head aches with it, and with the need to drink. There is only the calendar company to visit. Part of me eases at the expectation of failure. The clean break of another dead-end day. I stand at the kerb, waiting for the moment when I find I have given up.

Rush-hour traffic hoots at the stoplights. I walk through it to the nearest taxi. The driver's free hand and cigarette tap rhythms on the door as he waits for green. I give him the address from Ismet's office and he nods and I get in. He is younger than me, graceful in the shoulders and hips, with a moustache grown too thick to hide bad teeth. We crawl south towards the Karaköy district. Old Galata, the ghetto of merchants.

As we get nearer the docks the streets become quieter. Two gaunt young men sit in rotting armchairs. The car coasts past warehouses and plank-fronted building sites. There are fewer apartment buildings here, fewer windows that might belong to homes. Less care and human brightness. Along the waterfront are thirties administrative buildings. Now they are full of cargo companies, their windows piled with fake Ming vases, chandeliers, glittering arrays of bathroom fittings. The crown jewels of Kemankes Road.

The Golden Horn Shipping and Air Corporation shares a building with two other freight concerns. Across the strait, Asian Istanbul is faded by smog. Ferry horns echo up from the Bosphorus. I pay the taxi driver and cross a small car park to the company entrance.

Conditioned air curtains the doorway. Inside, weeping figs shrivel in the cold. There is a lone receptionist with the hard face of a retired air hostess. Behind her is a portrait of a businessman, all smiles. Two guards wait at the far end of the lobby. Their guns are prominent, machine pistols, the holsters pushed forward around their hips.

'Yes?' The receptionist is looking up at me. She doesn't smile. The portrait smiles for her.

'Golden Horn Shipping?'

'Yes.' She hardly pronounces the 'y'. The vowel has no sound at all.

'I have some goods to be shipped.'

'What goods?' Her hands and face are tanned a chemical brown, though there is paler flesh on the right wrist and the wedding finger: the colour must be natural. I try to imagine what kind of ring it is that she doesn't wear.

'Stones.'

Her stare remains blank, the whites of the eyes discoloured yellow.

I try again. 'Precious stones. Ismet Atsür recommended you. The jeweller. I'd like to talk to someone—'

She points to a row of chairs. 'Wait, please.'

I go over to the seats. The leather creaks under my weight. There are papers on a low glass table, yesterday's *Herald Tribune* and some Turkish gossip magazines. The front page of the *Tribune* covers an air crash. A Swissair flight, Washington to Geneva. Two hundred and eighty deaths. Two top UN officials. The article also reports that there was a historical diamond on board, en route home from an exhibition at the Smithsonian Institute. I try and think which stone it could be, that would be returned to Geneva.

I stop myself. The tragedy is the loss of human life, of course. Two hundred and eighty people. Not the stone.

Even so.

A small man comes in and starts to talk with the receptionist, leaning forward across the counter. She answers wearily, shaking her head. I look at the portrait above them. Not interested, now. Killing time until the receptionist tells me I can go, that I can't be seen today. As if I am invisible..

Under the painting a title plaque reads: Mr Araf, President of Golden Horn, in three languages. President Araf is wearing a brown suit that makes me think of military men. His hands are folded low across his chest, fingers clasped above the elbows. His hair is black and remarkably thick and it has the flat uniformity of a toupee.

I look closer. On the owner's right hand are two rings, expensive and vulgar. One is set with a red gem, cut cabochon. The other is blistered with rows of jewels in the style of Constantine Bulgari: rubies set together invisibly, like tiles in a bathroom.

The third ring is on Araf's left hand, the little finger, also called the toucher. It is thick gold, granulated in whorls, with a flat blue signet. Something is carved into the stone, a suggestion of humanoid figures. I push myself out of the low chair and go nearer.

The man doesn't interest me. It is the jewellery. The third ring looks medieval, fifth century, perhaps English. The signet looks like blue jasper or jade and it is older, late Roman. The man looks like a collector of jewels, a buyer with more money than taste; and the third ring looks like a black-market antiquity. It is something a collector could buy at a major auction, but only if he wanted to compete with national museums. It is the kind of work, perhaps, that one could purchase from Ismet the marketeer.

Lucky Katharine, I think, although it is the smallest of connections, nothing to be proud of. It is evidence of desire, of a shared field of experience and emotion. The man in the painting knows about more than just shipping. I stand under his image and feel a sensation of motion, unexpected and vertiginous. It leaves me dizzy and I look away.

The small man has gone. The receptionist is examining me. I walk back over to the desk. 'I'd like to talk to Mister Araf.'

'You have no appointment.'

'I was hoping to make one.'

She purses her lips. The movement takes the place of a smile, an expression of satisfaction. 'I'm sorry. To make an appointment you will have to talk to President Araf.'

As far as I can tell, I keep the frustration out of my voice. 'You said I need an appointment to talk to him.'

'Yes.'

I look out through the entrance doors. Across the road are other cargo firms, the wooden slats of a work site. A café bar with plastic tables outside, a window opaque with net curtains and condensation.

'Miss? You will need to speak with President Araf.'

I look back into her yellow eyes. 'Thanks for your time.' She nods very slightly. The guards are looking our way now. I walk out into the last heat of the day. There is more traffic now than at four-thirty. A row of scooters and a taxicab are parked by the café bar. Two old men are sitting at one of the tables, playing backgammon. They snap at one another and drink raki alcohol, milky with iced water. Between drinks they slap the backgammon pieces down hard and swear in whispers.

I go past them into the café. The air smells of cooking oil. There are plenty of customers, drinking apple tea or Efes beer. A woman with hennaed hair and thinned lips is wiping down the chrome counter with a rag. I order a tea from her and take it over to a seat by the window.

I raise the net curtain and look out towards Golden Horn Shipping and Air Corporation. The entrance is clear from here. I can watch but not be watched. It is not an unpleasant sensation. The tea is good. I sip it steadily, feeling its hot fog on the Duralex glass. At the next table a man is eating a doughnut in syrup, wiping up the residue. His face is set in a permanent frown. On the table beside him are a Galatasaray football club programme and two Renault car keys on a Ferrari keyring. They match the taxicab outside. I lean over. Not too close.

'Excuse me. Excuse me, please.'

He looks round. His eyes are hard, dark, like bruises. I point through the net curtains at the car parked outside. 'Is that your taxi?'

He lowers his head in a half-nod. I try to put together the Turkish for what I want. The man watches me, effortlessly chewing, until I fall back on English. 'I need a taxi. From now until about seven o'clock. I can pay.'

There is a soft sheen of syrup on his lips. I get a pen out of my jacket and lean across the table for his football programme. He stops chewing. I write: Taxi 17.30-19.30?, and smile. As if it might help, and perhaps it does.

'Thirty dollars.' His voice is guttural with syrup and dough. I get out the money and he folds it away into hopsack trousers. 'Where do we go?'

'Not yet.'

He nods again, swallows the last of the pastry and goes to the counter. When he comes back he has coffee and baclava for both of us. I try and thank him and he grunts dismissively, going back to the football programme. Turning over the page I have defaced.

I go back to watching the window. No one at Golden Shipping clocks off early. At six-fifteen the driver gets up for more food. When I look back again, two men in blue nylon suits are coming out of the shipping building. Neither of them looks like President Araf. They drive away in their company cars, blaring their horns at the gate.

At five past seven the old men outside finish their backgammon. There is still no sign of Araf. My driver is beginning to pity me, I think. He talks to the woman with the hennaed hair and she brings me over coffee laced with rosewater. It's dark outside now, and there is only one car left in the lot. From here it looks executive. I can only see two lights on in the building. At least one of them marks the security guards.

President Araf comes out abruptly, walking fast. There is a briefcase and a leather document file under his arm and he is searching in his suitcoat. He doesn't look up as he goes towards the car.

'There he is—' I turn to the taxi driver. 'There. Now.'

Already he is folding the newspaper away and heaving himself out of his chair. He moves with the short bursts of a fat man, all muscle and effort. At the door he raises a hand to the owner and the last customers, then we are outside. The only car in sight is a pair of red tail-lights, heading inland.

We get into the taxi. The meter comes on and the driver turns it off and starts the engine. The car smells of Turkish flatbread pizza and imitation leather. The driver is breathing hard, short outward puffs, *boh, boh.*

'Are you okay?'

'Okay.' He turns the car north in a single movement, without needing to repoint. He drives beautifully. By the time we reach Karaköy Road the Mercedes is clear ahead of us, street lights rippling across its back. The Galata Tower looms up, its observation platform lit against the deep rose of the urban sky.

'What is your name?'

'Katharine.' My voice comes out harder than I mean it to. The driver nods.

'Everyone asks you, of course. It is the Turkish way. To be friendly.'

He is still breathing fast. I take my eyes off the Mercedes for a second to look at him. There is sweat on his upper lip. 'I'm sorry. What's your name?'

'Aslan.' He takes one hand off the wheel to shake mine. His eyes don't leave the road. 'Your friend. Do you want to meet him sooner or later?'

'Wherever he stops. Thanks.'

He goes quiet. I look out. Around us is Istanbul at night, hills of light dissected by the dark lines of water. Seas, straits, estuaries. The car dips down. Under a flyover are dozens of bicycle shops. Their racers hung overhead in torchlit rows, like sides of meat.

We turn up Independence Avenue. Ahead of us, the Mercedes is all polished speed, pedestrians parting around it. It isn't far to Taksim Square. Ahead are the high-rise hotels, a glitter of lights and glass.

A block before the square the Mercedes turns right, and by the time we round the corner into the side street it has already parked. The taxi driver passes it without a pause, pulling in at the far end of the street.

As I look back Araf is turning away from the car. The file and case are under one arm, the suitcoat and jacket over his shoulder. Without their fine cuts his physique is clearer, the broad chest matching his belly. There is a red neon sign on the building nearest him. He descends down basement steps.

'Restaurant,' says Aslan the driver. He reaches up behind the mirror and takes out another football programme and a miniature packet of Oreos. 'Expensive. Good fish.'

'Thanks. I owe you some extra.'

He shakes his head, starts to read.

'Thanks, really. How long will you stay here?'

He looks around the street. 'I already made some money. If you like, Katharine, I will be here for maybe an hour.' For the first time he smiles at me. It softens his face, sweetens it.

I walk back to the restaurant. The basement steps lead down to an open door, a cloakroom attendant playing a mobile phone computer game, a curtain of red velveteen half-open to a long dining hall. The attendant doesn't look up at me as I go through. The tables are set back into individual booths, upholstered in burgundy plastic leather. It looks expensive and vulgar, like Araf's rings.

There are waiters serving at two of the tables and I walk up the aisle behind them. In the fourth booth on the left is the President of Golden Horn Shipping and Air. A menu is still closed on the table, as if he has just ordered. He is leant forwards, lighting a cigar. Opposite him sits a girl in a white summer dress. She has dark eyes, the skin of a sixteen-year-old, dark hair with a large white bow. She has a fixed, absent smile, as if someone has just told her a joke she doesn't understand.

'Mister Araf?'

He glances up. The girl turns her head on its Audrey Hepburn neck. In person, Araf has a jerky energy which his portrait painter didn't capture. The document file is on the seat beside him, but not the briefcase or suitcoat. I wonder what kind of work it is, that a man like this takes home at night and keeps so close.

He is wearing cufflinks made of gold krugerrands. If he was twenty years younger he would look like a drugs dealer. He clicks his lighter shut and pulls the cigar out of his mouth. 'I don't know you.'

'I don't mean to interrupt your evening–'

He shouts past me. I look round and two waiters are coming. One has eight plates balanced in his arms. The other is larger and his hands are free. I take the rubies out and put them down on the white table.

Everyone slows down. There is a space of seconds while they all look at the jewels. The foodless waiter says something and Araf waves him away with the cigar. They unload the plates and go. The girl in the white dress tries to pick up one of the stones. Araf slaps her hand back and she tuts at him. The jewels glitter between the plates of doner kebap and oil-baked aubergine. The President looks at me sideways. 'What are these supposed to be?'

'Rubies.'

'And what am I supposed to do about them?'

'Talk to me.'

The girl turns her heart-shaped face up to me. 'I can speak English too. Very good. What is your name?'

'Leyla, go to the bathroom.'

She whines. 'I don't want to.'

Araf leans across the table. 'Five minutes, my love. Why don't you go and brush your teeth?'

'*I don't want to.* I want candy.'

He hisses with impatience. From his jacket he takes a leather billfold, extracts an excess of notes and waves them at Leyla. A scrap of paper falls out, landing delicately on the crowded table.

There is a sulky sneer on the girl's face. Now it develops into a smile. She takes the money, gets up and walks past me, not looking back. Araf motions me into the booth. The plastic is hot where Leyla was sitting. He watches her go. 'Lovely, isn't she? You know what the Italians say?'

'No.'

'She still smells of milk.' He grins. Wrinkles his nose. 'I hope I don't disgust you.'

'I'm not interested in you.'

For a moment he looks surprised. It isn't the kind of thing men like him hear. It knocks the wind out of him and I'm glad of the space. He looks down at his food. 'So you want to talk. I'm listening.'

'You own a freight company. What do you transport?'

'Golden Horn Shipping?' He starts to eat, hacking into the kebap. 'Whatever we are paid for. Fish, cash, old rope.'

'Black-market jewels.'

He stops eating and watches me. His eyes are rapid, with the same energy as his body. 'You don't look like police,' he says. 'Are you tax?'

I shake my head. He shrugs. 'It's no great secret anyway. I would be lying if I said we have never freighted jewellery.' He picks up the scrap of paper. It is a ticket, black numerals on chemical blue. He turns it in his fingers, absently, as he talks; 68. 89. 68.

25

'It is good business. Clean business. There are worse things. Do you have a special cargo in mind?'

'I'm looking for an old jewel. Something called the Three Brethren.'

'Three what?' *68. 89.*

'Brethren. Brothers.'

'Three Brothers.' Araf furrows his brow, but his eyes are wandering, down the aisle after the girl. 'I know the name. Remind me.'

'It's a kind of clasp. Medieval. From Burgundy.'

Interest sparks in his face. He puts down the ticket and points at me, at his carafe of wine. 'Sure. You want a glass?'

'No. Listen.' I take a breath. Keeping my calm. 'I want this jewel. Very much.'

'How much very much?'

'This is seventeen hundred dollars.' I touch the largest ruby. 'If you can stand me for a few more minutes, it's yours.'

He considers it. There is a line of sweat along the President's lip where he shaved this morning. I catch a whiff of it, a smell like mustard, sweet and acrid. Given the heat he sweats very little. For a second I think he is going to call the waiters back. The money is just enough to stop him. He relights the cigar. 'Four minutes.'

'The Three Brethren. The name comes from its three rubies, but it was also set with a diamond and several pearls. Two hundred and ninety carats between eight jewels. It became a crown jewel of England. Tavernier had the three rubies from it when he died.'

Araf's face clears and he eats again. I watch him spoon aubergine over his prominent lips. 'Okay. I've heard of it.' Eventually he cleans his mouth. 'Let me tell you a secret,' he says. 'I like jewels.' He winks. Eats. Now he is all friendliness and complicity. 'I follow the market. What gets bought and sold. All the markets, open, not so open, very not open. I've been doing this for thirty years. And I have never seen a jewel like this, bought or sold. A medieval piece this big, no. Nothing like it. You should listen to your Uncle Araf, because I know what I'm talking about. You're on a wild ghost chase.'

He starts on a plate of minced lamb flatbreads. I watch him roll them up and drown them in lemon and stuff them into his mouth. 'The Middleham Jewel,' I say, and he almost chokes up. He grunts and swallows.

'Ng?'

'The Middleham Jewel was found in England fifteen years ago. It was late fifteenth century and in good condition. Sockets suggesting missing pearls. A central sapphire engraved on the front and back. Sotheby's auctioned it a year or two after it was found.'

'For how much?'

'One point three million.'

'Pounds? Sterling?'

I nod.

'Sure, but that was the eighties, you know? Heh.' I wait again while he pretends not to be interested. 'This Brothers. Tell me about its stones.'

'There are three balas rubies, each seventy carats. A thirty-carat diamond. Four large pearls.'

'How large?'

'Large. Ten to eighteen carats. Good baroque forms.'

'What date exactly?'

'Early fifteenth century, first decade.'

'Mm.' Al Araf puts down his fork. 'You think it still exists? Why?'

I don't answer. He chews thoughtfully. 'Pearls. Well, now that you mention it, I have one customer. In Turkey, but not Turkish – a bit cold for my liking – a north European, you know? You are American, yes? English? My apologies. My condolences. This customer, she loves pearls. The older the better. I've seen her buy only antiquities, always the best. Her family have been rich for centuries. If anyone knows, I think she would be the one. You know, I used to take lessons from an English girl like you.'

'Really.' The seat is becoming damp with sweat.

'Really.' He nods. 'Apple and pears stairs. Trouble and strife. You see? Now I wonder if you are causing me trouble and strife.'

'All I want is information.'

'And information takes time. I have a company to run and many bills to pay and more children than I like to remember. Now, Turkey is a big place – great as three, maybe four of your Great Britains. But I'll tell you where she is, for a cut. One per cent. One per cent of that in advance.'

'I have no interest in selling the jewel.'

'No interest?' The President laughs. It makes him ugly. 'All this shit you are giving me. I listen to you, I get shit from every angle. You want the jewel, you want money. What's the difference? You want to wear it? Either way, I want my cut. How much would a thing like that be worth?'

'It's impossible to say. Whatever someone would give for it.'

He stubs his cigar out in his kebap. 'Come on. Let's assume good stones, yes? They alone could be worth three, four million dollars. Then there is jewel value, and the thing's history. The Queen of England is always fashionable. I would give it six million dollars plus. The trouble is, my cut of that would be sixty thousand, and – forgive me – but you don't look like someone who has sixty grand in their pockets. Am I wrong?'

The rubies are still lying on the table. Bright red between the ruins of the meal. I pick them up. 'I have these. The smallest is worth four hundred dollars. I'll give you that now and the largest later. If your information is good.'

He sighs, crooks a finger at the waiter, motions the writing of a bill. The heavier man brings it in a worked-brass dish. Araf waves a gold card at him and waits for him to take it and be gone. He leans towards me, quiet and serious. 'You won't get anything from me if I don't get a percentage.'

'I can't sell it.'

'Can't or won't?'

'You're asking for a cut of nothing. I'm offering you two thousand dollars.'

He shrugs. 'Of course you can sell it. You can sell it through me. And there is no price high enough for the right information. Listen, I'll give you the name and address. I can put you on a plane tonight – Eh?'

The waiter is at Araf's shoulder, whispering in his ear. The gold card half-hidden in his hand, like a conjuring trick. The President's face hardens gradually, as if it is freezing over. He stands up, reaching for his billfold. Their voices combine into a deep mutter of Turkish.

'I brushed my teeth.' Leyla is back. The men don't look round. She smiles for me instead. She has small canines, very white. In her hand is an ice-cream cone with three garish scoops. The rubies are still on the stained tablecloth. The scrap of paper next to them.

I stand quickly, before my nerves can stop me, and take it all:

28

the three red stones, the one blue ticket. Leyla licks her ice cream, her eyes on the men. Araf glances up as I back out of the booth. He sees nothing. 'Your mistake. We could help each other.'

'I'm sorry to have wasted your time.' I start to walk, away between the busy tables. The skin of my back feels taut. The nerve endings waiting for the voice or hand, so that when Araf calls out again I stop hard, the breath jarring inside me.

'Hey! My dear!' He's grinning, angry and malicious. He winks. 'Watch out for wild ghosts.'

The curtain to the hall is drawn up. I let it fall behind me, cutting off the restaurant's noise. In my hand the blue ticket is already damp and soiled. The cloakroom attendant is asleep. He has a sallow, late-night face. When I wake him he looks at me with the expression of a man who has been cheated.

I give him the ticket. He retreats into his alcove. In the restaurant someone laughs so loud it sounds like shouting. The attendant comes back with armfuls of objects: the briefcase, the Burberry suitcoat, and an unbelievably soft pale scarf, a small fortune in cashmere or shahtüsh wool. The man sighs when I tip him. I hear him whisper goodnight as I go up to the street.

My feet walk me a block before I know what I am doing. I come to a stop only gradually, the adrenaline ebbing out of me. The air is cool. I close my eyes and stand listening to the city. A cruiser hoots, way out on the Bosphorus, turning towards the Mediterranean.

When I open my eyes again the street is empty. I look down at the possessions in my hands. I am a scavenger tonight, taking the leavings from a rich man's table. Not the document file, which is what I would want: only stealing what I can get. It is a small price to pay. There is no price high enough for the right information.

The basements here are locked up and grilled over. I drop Leyla's scarf down the nearest steps, bundle up the suitcoat and case and start to walk back with them. The taxi is where I left it. The cab-light on, Aslan the driver's head silhouetted against it. He is still reading, his face calm with concentration. I tap on the window and he rolls it down. 'You liked the restaurant?'

'I didn't eat.'

'You must be hungry.'

'Tired. I'll get something to eat at my hotel.'

'There is a kebap place. The best in Europe. Not far.' His eyes are gentle. They don't match his face. He is younger than I realised, under forty. The fat ages him. He has the face of someone who is used to being alone.

'I'd like that.'

He smiles again. There is a lever beside his steering wheel. He presses it and the passenger door clicks open. I get in as he is starting the engine. The case and the coat gripped tight in my lap. We turn in the narrow street and cruise up past the restaurant and the Mercedes. No one stands in the basement doorway. Aslan turns into Independence Avenue and picks up speed.

'You found your friend?'

'Yes.'

'Good.' He nods. Watching junctions. 'It is good to have friends.' For a moment he says nothing else. It is warm in the car. The tiredness washes over me again. My eyes begin to close. His voice jerks me back. 'He gave you these things?'

'No–' I look at him. His eyes slide to the bundle, back to the road. I shrug. 'No.'

He goes quite still at the wheel, understanding, his face dull with surprise. He is not like me, this man, not like Ismet the merchant. Aslan knows nothing about me, after all. Not that stones are their own reason, certainly. That jewels, like money, are their own motive. That I want the Three Brethren in the way he might want to sleep or fall in love, and that, given time, I will do anything, almost anything, to get what I want. He looks at me with his small eyes, understanding nothing, and I glance away.

He drives fast but not too fast. Across the Atatürk Bridge, following the road all the way through town to the Sea of Marmara. There is still heavy traffic along the seafront. Aslan turns off and follows the railway.

'Where is your hotel?'

I tell him the address. Suddenly all I want is for him to take me to his kebap restaurant, the best in Europe. But his voice has changed, it sounds dull and old. In the busy tourist streets around the Aya Sofya cathedral he pulls up. I get out with the belongings under my arm. When I turn back I have to shout over the noise of bars. 'You have been very kind. I wish I could give you something better. Here.'

I hold out thirty dollars. In the light of the hotels and bars, his face looks garish, full of colours and shadows.

'I don't want your money.' He doesn't look at me as he speaks. The taxi starts up and I have to step quickly out of its way. The money is still in my hand. I stuff it back in my pocket.

My fingers touch the rubies. I take them out. Three little stones. There is nothing to be ashamed of in them. There is nothing human about threes. We don't have three of anything. It's always the sacred number, the alien one. Three is the odd one out in a crowd.

Someone jostles against me. A woman's voice whispers an apology in Turkish. I am still looking at my stones. To anyone in this hubbub, in this dimness, they will look like nothing. Only one person in a thousand could estimate their value. No one in this city can know what they are worth to me. They are my little treasury, my three wishes. There is laughter on a balcony above, and I turn away from the sound into the hotel.

I go up past the nightman to my room. I undress in the dark, the neon coming in across my back. When I am naked the rubies are still in my hand, wet with sweat. In this light they look bloody and crushed. I put them under my pillow, like teeth, and I sleep.

茶

City Document 2604. Sale between Basel and the Fuggers of September 16th, 1504:

> *This shall be the transaction. Namely that we, the Attorneys, sell to Herr Jacob Fugger four jewels as hereinafter properly described. And I, the same Jacob Fugger, have bought these same jewels in the name of myself and Ulrich and Jorgen my dear brothers. And this is the purchase that has been made for forty thousand two hundred guilders, Rhenish, good and sufficient . . .*
>
> *Item; the second jewel is called the Three Brethren, there are three large balases, square, thick and free of fouls, each weighing seventy carats and in their midst stands a pointed diamond, pure above and below, which weighs thirty carats, and further around are four pearls: one stands at the top, two broad ones at the sides drilled where they sit, each weighs from ten to twelve carats and*

further a fourth pearl hangs below, and it weighs eighteen to
twenty carats . . .

   And each item, the money and jewels, will be given to each
party on the next Monday after the day of the raising of the Holy
Cross in the autumn of the year as is counted from the birth of
Christ our dear Lord, one thousand five hundred and four.

Jacob Fugger citizen of Augsberg recognises the
abovementioned thing.

Michel Mayer citizen of Basel
Hans Hiltbrand citizen of Basel
Johannes Gerster city clerk of Basel recognise the
abovementioned thing.

I want to gain while I can was Jacob Fugger's motto. It suited
him like his own face. There is a portrait of him by Dürer. In it,
Jacob has the features of a professional wrestler. He is all flattened sinew and small features. There is nothing to grasp or to
lose. He sits at ease, without posture, knowing that he is not
defined by how he looks. Only by the price of the painting, the
richness of its frame.

Fugger was the greatest merchant of his time, the prototype
capitalist. Born into a trading dynasty in smalltown Germany,
Jacob's family business came to influence the whole of Europe
and beyond. The spice trade. Mercury mines. Imperial loans.
Precious stones. He was a patient man, and he bought the Burgundian jewels as investments, working secretly to avoid an old
Papal claim to the Fugger profits. Along with the Brethren, the
purchase involved three other named jewels: the White Rose, the
Little Feather, and the Girdle. All three came to be separated into
their constituent stones, which were many and minor, by Jacob
or his successors. None of them was ever heard of again.

Only the Brethren kept its form. It was too famous to be dis-
mantled. Fame gave it value. Fugger kept the jewel until his
death in 1525. He was succeeded by his nephew Anton, who
learned severity from his uncle. Anton's motto was *Pecunia*
nerves bellorum: 'Money is the sinews of war.'

By now the Three Brethren had been unworn for almost half a
century. Anton was its sixth owner. To the Fuggers, the jewel

was a measurement of power, as it had been to the Valois dukes. But to Jacob and Anton it represented something to be locked up. A secretive wealth. By the time Anton began the sale of the jewel it was 1547, and seventy years since Charles the Bold had been slaughtered on the fields of Nancy.

Anton's buyer was Henry the Eighth of England, and he would have worn the jewel, if he could. The King's appetite for the knot had been whetted for years by reports of its beauty. His own sickness didn't weaken his desire. By the new year he was dying, but in his January accounts, Anton recorded the payment received from England. Weeks later the King was dead.

The Brethren would have suited Henry. He was the Tudors' Minotaur, a bull of a man in a political age, losing through lack of subtlety everything he gained from strength. His brute hunger comes through in portraits: he looks as if he is always about to bite. Henry was photogenic three centuries before the invention of the camera. Like the Brethren, he had a crude and effective power.

He was a man characterised by hungers; for alcohol and progeny, meat and land. His appetite for jewels was inexhaustible, and after the Catholic Church was sacked he had the wealth to buy at will. The heaped gold and silver Henry extracted from the monasteries weighed in at 289,768 and seven-eighths ounces, and he spent as if his health depended on it. By the time of his death, jewels and wars had reduced England to the brink of bankruptcy.

It took five years for the Fugger dynasty to complete the sale of the jewel. Aged fourteen, it was Edward the Sixth who committed the Brethren to the Lord Treasurer in June 1551. Within two years, the Child King himself was dead. The Brethren was delivered to Bloody Queen Mary on Hallowmass Eve 1553, and on her death five years later – pregnant with tumour, praying for it to be a Catholic child – to her younger sister, the Protestant, Elizabeth Tudor.

There is a painting of Queen Elizabeth in Hatfield House, Hertfordshire. It is called the Ermine Portrait, after the stoat which sits on the Queen's arm. It is a political portrait in the old style, the Queen surrounded by her treasures. A show of potency to the powers across the water. In this picture the Brethren is the brooched centrepiece of the Queen's black jewelled skeleton.

Elizabeth's maid of honour, Elizabeth Brydges, appears in a similar portrait by Hieronimo Custodis, painted three years later. In her parure of jewels, she looks as insignificant as the water vessel in a still life. The jewels cover her like flowers and butterflies and moths. The human figure has faded, its character smothered in those of the stones. It is a mannequin in jewels.

The Virgin Queen is more substantial. Her eyes are small and quite hard, like those of the ermine poised on her sleeve. It is nearly three decades since she gained the throne, the assassins sent for her from Europe finding themselves, inexplicably, assassinated. It is two years before she orders her cousin to be killed. Elizabeth, like the Brethren, grew into herself with age.

When Elizabeth gained it, the Three Brethren was a hundred and fifty years old. It took this time, five generations, before a woman owned the jewel. Bloody Mary was the first, but Elizabeth was the one with the leisure to enjoy it.

Five generations, in an age when jewels were worn by as many queens as kings. I wonder why it took so long. It seems to me that the character of the Three Brethren is masculine. The shoulder-knot of a cloak, worn for battle. A jewel plain as a piece of armour across the collarbone. Functional as the blood-groove of a sword. It is beautiful in the half-ugly way that certain men are beautiful. Angular, muscular, dulled. It has that hardness.

There is a sexuality to it. The rubies warm to the skin, the diamond cool. I know this is a fallacy. There is nothing human about the Brethren. It is eight stones connected by a single metal element. Still, I wonder how it felt, when Elizabeth wore it. Its heaviness on her breasts. Physical. Like a hand.

It suited Elizabeth. The monarchy of England was growing rich on trade and piracy, and the Queen's jewels gauged and reflected its strength. Elizabeth's possessions came to include the Sancy diamond, and a rock-crystal bracelet from the workshops of Emperor Akbar which is now the earliest surviving piece of Mogul jewellery in the world. In Elizabeth's 1587 inventory it is described as *of rock crystal sett with sparckes of Rubies powdered and little sparckes of saphiers made hoopwise called Persia worke.* There were jewels on her fingers, jewels in her hair. In her coiffure Elizabeth wore 'a spinel the size of a baby's fist'. This was the Black Prince's ruby, which is now set in the Imperial State Crown of England.

34

Under Elizabeth, England had become a repository for jewels. They were pure power. Armies held in waiting. Fleets of ships in the making. And at their heart was the Three Brethren. It was already old, even then. Its inch of pointed diamond remained harder than anything the world could discover.

※

The hotels I live in are always cheap. In their plain rooms I never oversleep. These are the advantages of my habits. For hours I lie listening to the traffic picking up outside, a lovers' argument through the thin walls, the muezzin testing his microphone at dawn. When he begins to sing one mosque joins in with another, and another, like birdsong. In hot countries this is my favourite time, when the sky is light but the air is still cool.

At eight I put on a gym shirt and a pair of chinos and go downstairs to pay for another day. The chipstone steps are cold against my feet. Outside the building the neon sign says: Sindbad Tourist Hotel, but by the time you step into the lobby it has been reduced to *Pansiyon,* and the bargain promises are simplified to three prices in changeable peg-board digits. There is a bar in the courtyard where they serve flatbread pizza in the evenings. No one is out there now. My stomach is taut and empty.

I think of other courtyards, other nights. Sindbad the Sailor, giving meat and gold to Sindbad the Porter. Telling him his old man's stories: *I collected some large branches of Chinese and Comarin aloes and, laying these on some planks from the wrecked vessels, bound them with strong cables into a raft. This I loaded with sacks of rubies, pearls and other precious stones, as well as several bales of the choicest ambergris. Then, commending myself to Allah, I launched the raft upon the water.*

The receptionist is busy with a TV soap opera, her mouth hanging open. When she sees me she smiles and mutes the volume.

'Hiya! You must like it here.'

'It suits me. Is the room free for another night?'

'Sure.' She speaks English with an Australian accent. I've been here long enough for her to recognise my face, my voice. No doubt she knows the belongings in my room, and that I sleep alone.

I pay the cheapest of the three prices, counting out soiled lira

35

notes. There's a photo on the desk. A young man with sideburns, smiling with the sea behind him. 'He's handsome.'

'Oh, that's my boyfriend. Fiancé.' She touches the photo towards her. 'We're getting married. He's really cute. At first I thought he was kind of a wuss but then he grew on me and now I love him.' She shrugs and smiles, her eyes wide. I have to smile back.

'Congratulations.'

'What else can I do for you?'

'Breakfast would be good.'

'Hold on.' She goes into the office. There is the hiss of a hot water reservoir being depressed. She comes back with a glass of apple tea and a handful of pistachios. 'These are really great. And healthy too. I'm Cansen.'

'Katharine.'

'So how long are you staying?'

'I don't really know. Thanks for these. Good luck.'

I put the nuts in my pockets and go back to my room with the tea cradled in my hands. The briefcase and the suitcoat are on the floor. I sit on the bed, open their pockets and locks and spread everything across the one sheet and two pillows. The nuts are good, fresh, and I eat them all at once, gorging myself. The sun falls across the papers and stays there.

There are a lot of bills. The briefcase is full of demands, black and red arranged in thick ringbinders. The coat contains another, crumpled into the hip pocket. In the case's main cavity are the President's treasures. An obscenely plump, ribbed silver pen. A cobra-top Motorola phone with the signal switched off. A tin box of Sobranie cigars with a butt stubbed out inside. Used envelopes.

'Nothing.' I feel my muscles tightening at the sound of my own solitary mutter. 'Fuck. Fuck. Nothing.' I try and think what I expected. A diary at least, perhaps an address book. Some detail of a woman who collects pearls. I remember the document file, never out of Araf's sight.

I flick at the briefcase's broken locks, thinking. The external leather is marked with the tracks of old capillaries. I go through the papers again. Under the envelopes is a *Playboy* Playmate of the Month pull-out and a polaroid of five children, four girls and a boy. A woman smiling with bruised dark eyes. I look back at her absently. The sun is getting hotter. A vacuum cleaner starts churning around the room upstairs. Already it is past check-out time. I take my top off, lean a pillow against the wall, pick out the envelopes.

Not all of them are empty. Two contain shipping orders, though they are incomplete, torn off, downloaded printouts in English, French, Turkish. I make out something about a shipment of DDT production waste in one document and a receipt for five items in the other. A cargo transported for a fee of five thousand Swiss francs. Someone has initialled the payment, 'EvG'. The tea cools on the bedside table as I read the fragments.

Nothing else is comprehensible. I upturn the briefcase and shake it out. Something falls across me. It is a fax, folded twice. The print is already fading and I turn it to the light. It is an invitation to a private jewellery sale in Basel, addressed to President Araf.

The company name is familiar. I read it again. *Graf Schmucke, 3 Museumstrasse.* I have been there. Not recently, not for over a year, but more than once. It is a private auction house and sale room, dedicated to jewellery and jewels. The world of stones is small, after all – claustrophobic, even. I try and remember the auctioneer's name and face. Felix Graf. A young man, ambitious to lead the family firm. A voice polished as a Swiss watch. I would never have guessed he dealt with a man like Araf.

I close the case. It is past noon. I dress for the heat: gym shirt and chinos, Gohil sandals, cotton jacket. In the corner of the room there is a small basin and mirror, stained by rust. I roll up my sleeves, run cold water and press it against my face. Look at myself.

I have blue irises. Here in Turkey they are bad luck. Evil eyes. My hair is turning blonde in the sun. My top lip is swollen on the left side. When I was five I had stitches there. My mother, Edith, woke me up to photograph an eclipse of the moon. She lifted me to the Leica's eye and whispered in my ear. Her arms held me, then let me go. I was still half asleep when I stepped backwards off the garden steps, falling eight feet. Afterwards I blamed her and she tried to make a game of it, an exciting story: *Katharine, you've been touched by the moon! Come here. Come. My little moon face.*

I remember the stitches. I liked them. The photos Edith took of me show me grinning, gap-toothed. I forgave her because of the stitches. They hung down, huge against my tongue, like the roots of plants.

There is a white hair. I turn my head to the right and it is clear, above my left temple. I comb it out with my fingers, feeling its coarseness. My first white hair. I don't pull it out.

'Hallo? *Pardon.*' Someone knocks twice at the bedroom door. I dry my face on the bedsheet, bundle up the briefcase and coat, and open the door while the cleaner is still struggling with her keys. She glares at me as if I have stolen her job. I go past her, down to the street.

It is a beautiful day. A breeze moves across the awnings, and the air smells of the sea, not clean, but real. A rush hour of tourists fills the pavements. Over them the Blue Mosque looms. Its domes grow one out of the next, like bulbs of malachite. Two small boys run past, the first jumping up to tear a leaf off a street tree, the second tearing off the branch. They twist through the crowd to the next junction, between telephone kiosks and away.

I push against the crowd, down to the telephones. There are tokens in my wallet and I pile them on top of the machine. It takes a while to dial and longer for the line to click open.

'*Guten tag.*'

'*Tag.*' I slip into German. After Turkish it comes with a sense of relief. 'I would like to speak with Felix Graf.'

'May I say who is calling?'

'Katharine Sterne. He might remember I bought some documents from him, eighteen months ago. Photographs of the *Burgunderbeute.*'

'One moment.'

There is a snatch of music. A string quartet, Mozart, the anthemic sound of Germanic Europe. Then the line opens again and Felix is there. 'Miss Sterne! Such a surprise. How long has it been, eighteen months?'

'Eighteen months.'

'Ah.' There is a pause. Our capacities for small talk are both limited. 'And you are well? Perhaps you have found your great jewel, your *Trois Frères.* I would be happy to hear that.'

'Thank you, Felix. I'm still looking.'

'Good luck.'

'Thank you. I have a question for you.'

'Please.'

'I am ringing from Istanbul.' The token runs out. I feed in a handful. 'There is a freight company here. Golden Horn Shipping and Air. Do you know it?'

'I think – no.' He answers too quickly. Too smooth. I push harder.

'They deal with black-market antiquities.'

Without losing its polish, his voice cools. 'Miss Sterne, I'm not sure what you are asking. You know we run a reputable business–'

'I didn't keep your telephone number. I have it in front of me, on an invitation. It is for one of your private sales. It's addressed to Mister Araf, President of the Golden Horn Corporation. I haven't asked you the question yet. Would you like to hear it?'

There is a longer, uncomfortable pause. When Graf speaks again his voice is short, clipped down to the edge of rudeness.

'What is it?'

'Araf has a customer who buys jewels. Maybe you know her also.' A police car goes past behind me and I lean into the kiosk, shielding the briefcase with my legs. 'She is an old woman, a north European–'

Laughter. 'Curiously enough, northern Europe is full of old women with jewels.'

'This one lives in Turkey. And she loves pearls.'

'Pearls?'

'You know her?'

He hesitates. 'Maybe. There is someone, a Dutch or German name, I don't remember. She has only bought here a few times. But always pearls. An obsessive taste, and very expensive. From us she has bought only old pieces.'

'What kind of old?'

He sighs. 'There was an early Carl Fabergé, I think. A set of ornamental dice, black coral inlaid with gold pearls. And the Mycenean brooch, I believe that was also bought by her. Two gold hornets encircling a fourteen-carat pearl. An unusual piece, not really to my taste–'

The tokens are running out. I cut in. 'I didn't know you dealt in Mycenean antiquities. When was this brooch exported from Greece?'

'It was perfectly legal. And it was a private sale, on private property.' Graf's voice is pained, quiet. 'Miss Sterne. Katharine. I'd rather not talk about this at work, if you don't mind. Perhaps, if I found you a name and address, I could telephone you tonight...?'

I give him the callbox number. He says he will ring back at six-fifteen, seven-fifteen Turkish time. I put the phone down and pick up the briefcase. The coat I leave, pushed up between the kiosks.

I climb up the cobbled roads, under the avenue of chestnut trees. Past the Aya Sofya, with its ziggurat of domes and launch-pad of muezzin towers. A young man sits on the pavement with a pair of bathroom scales. I weigh myself to see him smile, the information itself I could do without. Next to him is an older man selling pistachios. He waves. 'For you, little sister!'

I thank him in Turkish and he nods and nods. In his ear is the greyish-pink button of an antiquated hearing-aid, like a pearl in an oyster. I buy two hundred grams of nuts and eat them as I walk. If I can, I will eat nothing else today but pistachios.

It buoys me up, the sense of momentum. I am not used to it. I put my hand in my pocket and feel the cache of rubies there. My three little brethren. It is time I spent a little.

Another block and I come to the streets around the Covered Market. Outside, costermongers yell at one another between the tourists. The streets smell of carpets and fish. Split kavun melons. Fresh cardamum, the pods still on their long stalks, the flowers white with thin blue veins. I spend hours, looking for lapidaries. Jeweller's Street is no use to me, with its boutiques full of imitation Tiffany bracelets and Ottoman earrings. It is on Fur Merchant's Street, in the shadow of the Pigeon Mosque, that I find what I am looking for. There is a row of workshops, jewellery makers inside, *mücevherci* in gold-lined rooms.

For the best of the rubies I get a good price, eighteen hundred dollars in crisp high-denomination American notes. The poorest of my stones I trade for a conch pearl. It weighs little more than a carat, but the shape is good. Smooth, with the deep pink of raw salmon. It is the best thing I can find. After all, the woman I am looking for is not interested in rubies.

At six o'clock I am back at the telephone kiosk, waiting in the warm evening. The coat is gone. A parturient man in a leather jacket comes up and points at the phone. In bad Turkish, I explain that I am waiting for a call, and he bows his head, gently, and wanders away.

It is another half-hour before Graf rings. He is nervous and out of breath and I am glad of the advantage. 'I must apologise. We had a late customer, a Japanese lady. In fact she reminded me of you. She is looking for her father's sword. He surrendered it to the Americans in the war. His daughter has been looking for it for almost thirty years. Imagine.'

'No thanks.'

'Ah. I am sorry. Well, I have researched your pearl woman. There is good news and bad news. Which will you start with?'

'Good.'

'Her surname is von Glött.'

'Where is she?'

'Unfortunately, that is the bad news. We have a lawyer's address in Amsterdam, although I would say the name is German. And apart from that and the name, I can find nothing else.' His voice purrs with pleasure. 'All our transactions were via the lawyer. I am so sorry, Katharine. It doesn't seem to me as if I am being much help. Would you like the lawyer's address in Holland?'

'No.' I turn around in the kiosk. Now I am looking back up the street. Neon blinks along the shopfronts, over the Sindbad Tourist Hotel. 'I don't need it. Thank you.'

'My pleasure. Now I will be grateful if you could leave me alone.'

'I'll see you in Basel, Felix.'

I hang up and walk back to the hotel. At reception Cansen has been replaced by a man with a flat cap and a wide whiskered face. He is sullenly licking envelopes, a Cheshire Cat without the smile. He puts down the envelopes to give me the room key and I go upstairs. The windows have been shuttered at both ends of the room, and I open them all wide.

Turkish pop echoes up from the hotel's courtyard. There is a boy down there, cleaning the fountain. He looks twelve or thirteen, slender as a dolphin. A beautiful child. As I watch him he looks up and I wave. He glances away shyly. I go to the bed and sit down. From the case I take out the used envelopes. The receipt for five items, paid in Swiss francs. The initials, 'EvG'.

It is on unheaded paper. The writing is damaged where someone has laid a cup on the cheap paper. The script is delicate, spidery, written in nibbed ink. The stamps on the envelope are Turkish. The postmark is 21000 followed by another two

41

characters, HH or 88. The postal ink is very faint where the paper has bent away from the stamp.

I put the envelope in my jacket pocket and pack quickly. The briefcase I leave behind. Downstairs Cansen is back with a friend or sister, younger and prettily plump. The wide-faced man is chatting them up charmlessly. The television flickers overhead. Cansen waves to me. 'Hey, Katharine. How are you doing?'

'Good.' I put down my bag and take out the envelope. 'I need a favour. Do you know this postcode?'

They crowd around. The new girl says something, a name, and the man agrees. He nods at me. 'Diyarbak'r.'

'It's way out in the east,' says Cansen. 'You can fly there. I've got some nice jewellery from Diyarbak'r. Really fine gold wire.'

The other girl leans forward. Her English is thick and guttural. 'My brother went there. It was for him to—' She looks over to Cansen for help.

'National service,' says Cansen. 'You know, it's a long way. It's like a different country, in the east. Are you thinking of going there?'

'Maybe.'

'But there are much nicer places in Turkey. Western places. You can go to Bodrum.' She smiles. 'I love Bodrum in the summer. Why do you want to go to Diyarbak'r?'

'Maybe I have friends there.'

The wide-faced man cocks his head towards Cansen. She translates for him. He shrugs and mutters in Turkish. I fold the envelope away.

'What did he say?'

Cansen smiles again. Eyes wide. 'It's just Ersan's joke. He says you'll need friends out there, because in Diyarbak'r your enemies will cut out your tongue and throw it in the Tigris.' They laugh together at Ersan's joke. I laugh with them until they stop.

'Cansen, do any of you have a car? I need a lift to the airport.'

'You're leaving now? Oh. Well, Ersan does.'

'How much will he charge?'

'Twenty dollars.' His voice is heavy, like the girl's. I kiss Cansen on both cheeks. The man heaves himself out of his chair. 'Now?' he says.

'Right now.' I nod back at the bag. 'And for twenty you can carry that too.'

In the first year of the seventeer
founded in England. It called its
of Merchants of London Trading
ple called it other things. The Eas
Company, or just the Company,
land's Army of Acquisition. For c
countries, the eyes out of Peacock
trading them for gunpowder or
transported the balas rubies of th

But now I am losing track. I'm getting ahead of myself. The lives of stones are so long that the characters of their owners become progressively more insignificant. It is so easy to move back, to try to see the whole picture of the jewel, and then to find that humanity has become blurred against the passage of time.

Three years into the new century, Elizabeth the Virgin Queen died. She had brought England from bankruptcy to being the most powerful state in Europe. Her dynasty died with her all the same. The throne went to her cousins and enemies, the Stuarts, and in 1605, the accountants made a list of valuables received by their new king, James the First. I find the records in London, quarter-bound in goatskin. The hundred and ninth item is all that I'm looking for:

A Fayre Flower Wth three greate ballaces in the myddest a greate pointed dyamonde, and three greate perles fixed, Wth a fayre grate ple pendente, called the Brethren.

In one portrait James wears it as a hat-ornament. The cords of the shoulder-knot have been lost, but the basic structure is unchanged. A triangle of stones illuminated by its single diamond eye. James had the stones reset in the same form for his son Charles to woo the Infanta in Spain – although the alliance of sea powers never came about, and Charles eventually married Henrietta of France. Their jeweller declared the Brethren's diamond to be 'The most complete stone that ever he sawe'.

It was seen, then, as one of the greatest of the English Crown Jewels. It is almost the only piece of that hoard which survives. Four decades later, the great jewelled artefacts of England were destroyed. The Crown Jewels – the Regalia most of all – were

, stone by stone. Only a handful of items sur-
or Clock Salt, with its panels of rock crystal. The
cup of the Kings of England and France. The Spoon of
lia. The Three Brethren.

their portraits, the early Stuart kings are as similar as sib-
gs. Their generations are cool, poised, smooth as jewels in oil.
The paintings are propaganda images; the charisma is there, the
incompetence almost hidden. There is always a veneer of smarm.
By 1625, Charles the First's secretary of state was already record-
ing that he had 'sent towards Harwich all the jewels within his
range', including the Three Brethren. The King had ordered his
supporters the Duke of Buckingham and the Earl of Holland to
the Netherlands with ten major jewels for pawn, and the message: *The saide Jewells and Plate are of greate value, and many of them
have longe contynued as itt were in a continuall Discent for many
Years together with the Crowne of England.*

The money raised lasted Charles twenty years. The Brethren
was redeemed. In 1640 it was even reset with a range of new
pearls and an additional table-cut diamond. But in 1645, with
revolution looming and without finances to meet it, Queen Henrietta Maria fled to Holland with the great Tudor jewels. In her
baggage were the diamonds known as the Sancy and the Mirror
of Portugal, the 'second best ruby collar' of Henry the Eighth
with its chain-of-office links, and the Brethren.

Selling the great jewels was as difficult for the Stuarts as it had
been for the Magistrates of Basel and Berne. No one was rich
enough to buy them. The less fabulous gems were eventually
pledged to the Duke of Eperon, and when the pledges were not
redeemed he sold them to Cardinal Mazarin, who was said to
have loved jewels even more than his God. The Brethren was not
among the works sold. Henrietta sent back to her husband huge
quantities of gunpowder and carbines and coin. None of it was
enough to win him the war.

On 9 August 1649, Sir Henry Mildmay signed the Commonwealth order for the destruction of the English Crown. Keeper of
the Jewels, Mildmay became known as the Knave of Diamonds.
The regalia were melted down, the gems sold off or smashed
with hammers.

'Now Edward's Staffe is broken,' wrote the antiquarian Thomas

Fuller. 'His Chair overturned, Cloaths rent, and Crown melted; our present Age esteeming them the Reliques of Superstition.' The inventory of that time is a catalogue of loss. A list of how fragile jewels can be. There is the comb of old stained bone, an artefact used in the ceremony of anointment since the time of Alfred; and the 'Rock Ruby' – the Black Prince's ruby – wrapped in paper and sold for £15.

> King Alfreds Crowne of gould wyerworke sett with slight stones,
>   and 2 little bells.
> One robe of crimson taffety sarcenett, valued at 5s.
> One livor cullrd silk robe. Very old.
> One old combe, worth nothing.

The crown jewels were broken up. But the Three Brethren was no longer with them. Still whole, it passed onwards through the hands of bankers and merchants and royal consorts. Saved by the profligacy of the Stuarts.

⚒

My name is Katharine Sterne. These are notes for me to follow, notes for my head and feet. Footnotes. I am looking for a triangle of stones, connected by crude spurs and bones of gold.

I read my pages over, in transit, in the similar rooms of different hotels. I find a story in them, although it isn't mine. The account begins where it belongs, six hundred years ago, in the duchy of Burgundy. The beginning should be that of the stones, not of me, and that is what I have written. And that is how it should be. My life is part of the story of the Three Brethren, not the other way round. It is a question of perspective.

It is very old, the jewel. Half a millennium. I see history only through the life of the Three Brethren, and it is like peering through the wrong end of a telescope. The dukes of Burgundy and the magistrates of Berne. Fuggers, Tudors and Stuarts. Twenty generations of humanity reduced to ants.

I think that after a certain age jewels cease to be possessions. At that point they become the possessors. The Three Brethren is like a crown, or the third sarcophagus of Tutankhamun, the innermost, which is entirely made of beaten gold. These things are

45

past ownership. The Brethren has been the turning point of many lives, and mine is only one. I am the footnote.

For six centuries there have been people like me. We have all wanted the same thing. It connects us, a thick, deep rope of desire. Our lives repeat. There may be others now, although I don't know who they are and I think that, if I'm lucky, I will never find out. But in five years I have become good at what I do. I have confidence in myself. I've even acquired a trade. I can buy jewels, sell them, transport them across borders. Sometimes it helps to be a woman, and sometimes not. The jewels themselves are always movable, despite any restrictions. They are carried from Ilakaka to Damascus to Baghdad to Geneva, London, Tokyo; by motorboat, aeroplane, taxi, hidden under the tails of sheep, in the guts of travellers. A great mercurial trade, always in motion.

I look for what is precious and tangible, and my life becomes these things. There are worse ways to be. There is a substance to what I do. I have held jewels it is a privilege to touch. A girasol ruby with its phantasmal star. A cicada carved from mutton-fat jade, taken from the mouth of a buried emperor. Trojan gold, worn on my wedding finger from Ankara to Los Angeles. And one day I will find the Three Brethren. I know what I want from my life. It is not the physical value of the jewel. Objects can be precious in other ways.

Ismet the merchant is thirty hours behind me. I think of the gun at the young man's belt, the false diamond in its box. I wish I could believe we have nothing in common; but what the merchant said was true. He looked at me and recognised something in himself. The search, or the jewel trade, has changed me. I'm not sure which. It is a respectable business, mine, but an inhumane one. For the people who make lives from them, stones are more than ornaments or currency. They are a kind of drug, a crystallised heroin. A fetish. They attract violence.

In sub-Saharan Africa, in diamond country, there are death squads trained to clear villages from alluvia-bearing land. The squads consist of children, some of them young as ten. They are cheap, a diamond expert once told me, and easy to train. Sometimes they hold their guns like toys. And sometimes not.

In Muzo, Colombia there are *guaqueros* who sell emeralds scavenged from the government mines. The stones are laid out and talked up, the worst soaked in oil of cedars. And every dealer has a gun. Guns in handbags or strapped to ankles, to crotches. 'My old woman is happy,' says a man with an earring made of cemetery gold. 'She has a TV and a chihuahua. It's progress!' There are two murders a day in the mines. Just as a precaution, you understand.

There are trace elements of gold in human hair, in seawater, and in trees. They are inextricable, these lodes. There are people who would mine them if they could. Ismet would wring them out and leave the waste behind. I saw it in his eyes. I am not so like him yet.

I was on a night train through Russia. A man came into my sleeping compartment. He had a knife, and he asked for jewels. I don't know how he knew me, I didn't recognise him, but then he looked easy to miss. His features and physique were somehow anonymous, a big, grey, benign-featured man. It may be that he had been following me for some time.

I gave him what I had, which wasn't much: a bulse of poor diamonds from the open-cast mines of eastern Siberia. It is the only time I have had jewels stolen from me, although in the trade it is, of course, something of an occupational hazard. I gave him the packet of stones and he put it carefully inside his jacket, zipping the pocket shut, and then he tried to kill me.

At the time it seemed natural, the escalation from want to extreme violence. I was scared – almost too scared to move – but not, at gut-level, surprised. Now I wonder why he bothered. Possibly he meant to rape me, although I had no sense of that. Possibly he was scared I would go for help, although he didn't look scared; and he had time in which to be gone, miles of forest in which to hide. I wonder, sometimes, if he only wanted to kill me in the same way as he wanted the stones. He was shorter than me but heavy and it was hard to fight back in the small compartment. He didn't bother to use the knife.

Up close, his eyes smiled. They were blue under epicanthal folds. He was all baby fat. I couldn't hurt him through its rolls and layers. He kept his face away from my teeth and his hands around my neck. His skin smelt of diesel.

I wanted to hurt him back. It was important to me that he felt what he was doing. I turned under him and shoved my elbow as hard as I could, up into the side of his head. It struck the temple, and I think I felt the bone give. There was no blood, but he made a coughing noise and pulled off me, then fell back down. I felt a wet heat across my crotch as his bladder went.

I believed he was already dead, but for some time I didn't think about it. My first thought was for myself. I undressed and washed my clothes and skin with bottled water and soap, scrubbing the hurt off me. The body became a blind spot in the dark motion of the carriage. Forest and snow passed by outside. When the cleaning began to hurt I stopped and dressed again. Then I was surprised to see him.

There was still no blood on his skin. I took the stones from his pocket. I carried him out into the gangway and left him, stained with his own piss, like a drunk. I locked my door and didn't open it again that night. In the morning, when I got off, he was already gone. I think he lived, although he was a grey, ordinary man, not one to notice, and in Russia drunks die all the time. Sometimes I feel the weight of him when I am asleep or alone. I am often alone.

I was in a hotel in Montreal. There were two sellers with an old French necklace. It was a delicate work, a fan of gold filigree set with riverine pearls and small sapphires, dark as caviare. My job was to wear the necklace out of the country on a flight to Marseilles. For a day we stayed in the hotel room, settling the price, seeing no one.

The sellers were a Californian and a Sri Lankan called Check. Check did all the work. He wore bright shirts and had round cheeks. On the telephone he spoke to the clients in Fanugalo, the complex pidgin of African jewel miners. The other man sweated badly. While Check got me clothes, a hired car, and a flight, the Californian took cocaine. He seemed to have an endless supply of white paper packets, like bulses of stones. He didn't like the smallness of the room and he said so, often. He hated the French, the smell of our sweat, the way room service knocked, the way the light beat off the river outside and winked and twinkled through the faded orange curtains.

Late in the afternoon I took the hired car to the airport. I was thinking of my father, somewhere in the country around me with his new life and, perhaps, new family. At the third traffic light someone opened my passenger door and got in. It was the Californian. He was sweating feverishly and he had a gun. He told me to drive out of town and I did what I was told. There were spots of blood on his shirt. I don't know what happened to Check, if he was killed or if he got away somehow. I liked him. We drove until there were no houses or towns as far as you could see.

The Californian didn't bother to take the jewels off me. He sat turned towards me, with the gun cradled in his lap. I knew he was going to kill me. My head went empty waiting for a shot. Then after a few hours the tension became boring and I stopped thinking about it. I turned on the radio but he clicked it off and told me to keep driving.

Outside the light was bright and low, I had to narrow my eyes against it. The air-conditioning was broken, and it was hot inside the car. I looked over and the Californian had begun to fall asleep. My hands were sweating, and sometimes they slipped a little on the wheel and he would wake up. Each time it happened he woke up less. His eyes looked red even when they were closed, the light illuminating the damaged skin.

When there were no houses left I reached over and took the gun out of the man's hands. He didn't wake up until I stopped the car under a stand of pines. They were bent over, hunchbacked. It was almost dark. I pointed the gun at him and listened to him swear while I got out of the car.

I began to walk southwards. My heart was slowing, the adrenaline burning away. I wondered if fear could leave any mark inside my cells, some permanent damage. I kept walking all night. At one point I left the gun and the car keys in the hollow trunk of a tree, pushing them down into the soft peat mud. Later I threw away the necklace too, in a shallow pool under the pines, green with cat's-tails. I sometimes wonder if anyone ever found it. I imagine it's still there. Like all jewels, it was a beautiful thing.

※

I fly east, over the crumpled earth of the Taurus Mountains. The lapidary is closed on my knees. I am going to Diyarbak'r, and the woman who buys old pearls.

A flight attendant leans against her drinks trolley. Her eyes are washed out with air miles and dry humidity. The man in the next

49

seat passes me over a coffee. He has too-white teeth, a creased suit, tanned skin. He smiles at the lapidary. 'What are you reading?'

'Work.'

'Work, shmurk. Professional traveller, right? You like it? Same shit, different place, right? You want to borrow this?' He flashes his novel, *A Passage to India*. 'My wife gave it to me. I'm not getting it. We can swap.'

I shake my head. 'I don't like fiction. Thanks anyway.'

I look out of the porthole at lightless dark. I think, Jewels have a way of returning to their past. Perhaps the Brethren has been in Diyarbak'r before. But then the Brethren has been everywhere. I could follow it for a human lifetime and never search a tenth of the places it has been.

The plane roars around me, the sound distant through its metal skin. I open the lapidary. My same shit. The endpapers are heavily marbled, like an image seen out of tune. The text is badly composed, a treatise on the Asian origins of the Tudor Crown Jewels. Details of a 1530s inventory, a folding altar from Ely, sold on the black market of the time: *The Thinner part thereof plated with gold, and garnished with saphures, balaces, small sparckes of emeraldes, and course perles.*

There is a Bombay library register folded inside the cover. It is an antiquity itself, the few names on it already strange after a century – Ody, Shukla, Swaddling. Another name in thin handwriting, almost illegible, like someone trying to imitate a signature without understanding the letters themselves. To my tired mind it looks like 'Mr Three Diamonds'. I put the book away and sleep.

I dream of white hair. It is growing down through my head, into the muscle of my heart. I can feel it, cool and hard and thin. The way it grows inside me is crystalline. It is slow but it has momentum. The white hair is inside me, like a shaft of tourmaline underground. Now I have dreamed of it, it will always be there.

The dream fades, strengthens. I am on the seafront near home. There are stones in my hand. Flints from the beach, two grey, one black. The sea crashes into the sunlight.

The sound is deafening. I turn away from it and there is a woman coming, distant, down the steep avenue towards me. The trees hide her face, and as she walks closer the face remains hidden, the walker becoming taller, until at a certain point the trick of vanishing-points is overcome and I see it is myself and I stand, only realising I have been holding my breath as I cry out.

I wake. It is almost light outside. The plane is coming in over canyonscapes and rocky flatlands towards Diyarbak'r. I can pick out a line of electricity pylons stretched out across the alluvial plains, every one collapsed like a shadow. The plane's own shadow grows bigger, flitting across fields of watermelons, pocked tower blocks. In the distance a huge river creeps southwards, glistening like something cut open. Nothing else moves for miles.

At the municipal airport the emergency power is on, casting ruddy light. I carry only hand luggage, and I leave quickly. Out of the runway bus windows I can see only two planes, one the Turkish Airlines Airbus 310 we arrived in, the other an unmarked 737-400, dull silver.

Outside there are taxis waiting, the drivers smoking in the early light. I show my envelope to the first I come to. He screws up his face, then waves at the other drivers. They go into conference together, stabbing at the faint postcode. When the driver is satisfied, he waves me into the back of his cab, holding the door open.

We drive out into the flat land. I sit back. Mountains rise in the distance, and ahead of us, looming up, I can see the office blocks and black basalt walls of Diyarbak'r. I close my eyes. My hands rest in my lap. I am searching for the Three Brethren. I listen to the windscreen wipers moving through constellations of dust:

Hush
   Hush
      Hush.

2
Brothers

Hush was the sound of the river rising. Years later, when he came back to Iraq, Daniel found that this was what had stayed with him. It was the flood tide of the Tigris at night he remembered, the sound of it gathering.

He returned in the spring. It was April, the month of floods. In Mosul he bought new clothes for Salman and himself, black robes, slippers and socks, small turbans dyed with indigo. The drab clothing of Jews in an Ottoman country. Daniel traded them for four links of his gold watch chain. He helped Salman dress, pulling sleeves over his knotted hands. On himself, the chafe of linen felt alien. His body had forgotten it. The brothers were both thin from the year of travelling, and the robes flapped around their arms and ribs.

It was a slow journey south to Baghdad. The Tigris was too high to navigate. Even with fresh coach horses at Tikrit, it took four days on the sodden roads. While Salman muttered in his sleep, Daniel looked out at the country where they had been born.

Iraq. It was an Arab name, descended from the Persian. Its meanings overlapped like old tidemarks: Two Veins, after the rivers; the Country of Roots; the Country of Fighting. Daniel knew other words for the place now. European constructions, precise as land claims. Mesopotamia, the Land Between Rivers. There was rain over the eastern mountains, he saw, skeins of it drifting. He looked out away, west towards the Euphrates.

He was twenty-eight years old. For the first time, he saw clearly how the two great rivers defined the land. Among the rice fields and liquorice trees there were levees, faded meanders and marshes, canal systems from prehistory. The mounds of the old civilisations, nothing left but names and spars of stone. Babylon, Nineveh, Nimrud, Ur. The Tigris and the Euphrates shifted in their sleep, leaving cities beached in the dunes. The landscape was haunted by the two rivers. And between them lay Baghdad, he saw. Like a heart.

They drove into the walled city through the Gate of the Talisman. It was evening. There were no gaslights in the streets, only lamps, the wink of tallow dips. The Kurdish coachman swore at the jam of horses and asses. Daniel thought, *I am home, we are home*, and he reached out for Salman's hand, pressing it against the seamed, cracked seats.

And then as the days passed, he found that they were not home. They had been gone too long. Even the course of the Tigris had been displaced, flexing through the desert. The rich Jewish families had gone east to Bombay, China or Japan. The poor had gone, fewer remembered where. In the house on Island Road, Daniel found three families of Druze. In their twisted Arabic, they told Daniel what he needed to know but did not want to hear. That the old Jewess had died. Three years ago now; had he known her? The synagogue had paid for her burial. No family to say prayers over her grave.

Judah, the old rabbi, remembered him. They went early. It was hard to find the place. Daniel recited the familial prayer for the dead. The rabbi helped him when he faltered. He wept only later, alone, not letting himself frighten Salman. The sound clanging off the walls around him.

They took rooms in Judah's house. The granddaughter cooked for them. A quiet woman, her food, like Rachel's, flavoured with vinegar and tamarind. Sour and familiar. At supper Salman talked in his wheedling voice, stories of jewels and crowns. Daniel didn't let himself be ashamed of him.

Over lime cordial, the rabbi explained how new people had come to the old town, Druze and Sabians. No one had known Rachel. She had stopped going out. Once an Arab family had broken into the house, insisting that it was empty. Rachel had chased them away, laughing, bare-headed, with a knife. She had died in her sleep, Judah said, on the flat roof in her summer clothes. So the Druze had found her, at least. They had been attracted by the birds.

In the days he walked. He tried to find the city and his place in it. Daniel went through the muddy roads of the Jewish quarter, the squat domes of half-abandoned synagogues giving way to the minarets of mosques around the Khadimain market. On across the river into the walled city.

It was late, the evening muezzin had already sung. He climbed through the Maidan quarter to the Citadel. Even the walk seemed harder. He found that he missed the ease of macadam. It felt to Daniel as if time had run backwards here, decades stripped away. On the public heights he had to stop and catch his breath before looking out. From here, he could see everything.

And everything was changed. It was like something from a story. The sailor waking from a night in the city under the sea, to find that a century has passed in his absence. Time falling away into some inconceivable vault. Daniel looked out over Baghdad and recognised nothing. The elephantine columns of the great synagogue, the oil palms in private courtyards, the noise of the evening markets and the children settling to sleep on roof terraces and balconies – he remembered none of it as it was.

The warm wind tugged at his eastern clothes. Daniel pulled the robe looser across his chest. As he did so, he felt the watch hanging there on its shortened chain. He brought it out. It was a repeater, the out-case of rayed gold. A legend chased small around the winding stub: *Tempus metitur omnia sed metior ipsum.* 'Time measures all things, but I measure it.' An Englishman had shown him what that meant, in the waiting room of a palace.

He opened the out-case. The works had run down. On the white face the maker's name was illegible in the gloom. It didn't matter. Daniel knew it by heart. Its litany of English words divided by black numerals.

Rundell **XII** & Bridge's,
of Ludgate **XII** Hill, London.

He closed it and listened. Over the murmur of traffic came the sound of the river tides. If he closed his eyes, nothing had changed. It could be 1820 again. He could be nine years old. Lying awake on the roof, listening to the river. Dreaming of diamonds.

Nothing here is different, he thought. *Except myself.*

He looked down at the Tigris. Lights glistened in the current. On the far bank, the shanties by the water's edge were dark. The tides were gathering around the bridge, piling up white against the brickwork piers.

Hush.

And as he listened, Daniel began to remember. He saw what it was he had gone searching for, love for his brother subsumed into his brother's love of things. He stepped back, unsure of his footing, giddy with memory. As if he had fallen away inside himself. He saw what he had left behind and lost.

The house with two doors. The flight paths of bees. Salman made whole. Rachel made living. He closed his eyes on all of it and heard the sound of the Tigris rising in the night.

There had been no 1820: Daniel remembered knowing the year by other measures. 1820 had been 1198 by the Muslim count. The Jewish cycles no longer mattered to him, and instead of these he remembered himself. Nine years old. Alone in synagogue. Calculating the centuries since the Era of Creation. Outside Salman was calling for him. A child yelling the name of a river.

For as long as Daniel knew, there had been the river names. The brothers had been called after the Two Veins even before the state had given them a surname, ben Levy, a Jewish family recorded in Arabic in the Turkish viceroy's offices. The words had felt part of them in the order they came, Daniel thought. First names first. River names second. Surname last and least.

1820. 1198. Even the names of the years changing. *'Phrates, are you there? Where are you, 'Phrates?* A boy's voice by an open window.

They had little family. Hagah and Leah Levy had died of cholera a year after Salman's birth. Daniel remembered nothing of his parents he could be sure of. Rachel and Judit had become his family. They were more than enough.

It was Rachel who gave them the river names, although it was no longer her who used them. The surviving ben Levys had picked up on the habit, then the families they had once been tied to, the old in-laws. Finally it was the cast-net fishermen at the docks, the Bedu children drinking like goats at the street fountain, the Turkish city guard on its noon patrol.

Salman was Tigris. Daniel was 'Phrates. They were good names. The brothers liked them because they made them liked. Salman was six and Daniel was nine. There was no other reason why a name could be good.

They were good names because they were fortunate. The rivers were one more thing to believe in, and Old Baghdad was full of beliefs. There were the Sabians, with their love of water and stars. Grandmother Judit, with her dark hints of Jewish cabbalism. Yusuf the honey seller and Yusuf the official beggar, with their Bedu superstitions. When the brothers were young, before they knew better, flood season had its consolations. There were offerings in the form of treats, as if Tigris and 'Phrates were charms against drowning.

They were good names because they fitted. Nicknames are never accidental. Salman couldn't have been the Euphrates, and Daniel was no Tigris. And then again the names were good because they were a concealment.

By the river, or killing time at synagogue, the brothers would hear the rivers called for, and in answering they felt themselves hidden. It was like dipping under shallow water. They were no longer Daniel ben Levy, Salman ben Levy. With the river names they could submerge themselves, raceless, out of the order of things. It was a kind of charm. A small magic. When he was older Daniel wondered if Rachel had meant it that way.

She looked like their father. Judit said so. She was strong, like Hagah had been. Rachel had contracted plagues three times. Her left eye was blind, pinked with blood where the fevers had burst the vessels. Her cheekbones were massive and angular. Behind her back, as she hollowed perfect dumplings in their kitchens, the wives of the rich Jews called her the Nag's Head.

In the right light, making sweet lime cordial in the early morning, the slant of her face was beautiful. Daniel thought so. She had never married. When Daniel was nine she was still young; she only looked old. But then everyone did. The desert heat seamed their skins. Hunger drew it tight.

The Nag's Head. There were other names for Rachel, too. She wore no hair cloth in the streets. She kept a kosher kitchen, kept the sabbath, but no more. She wore gold earrings outside her house. Stubborn, the rich wives called her. Mulish and disrespectful. Barely a Jew, they said. As if race could be lost with ritual. As if the laws didn't make everyone something.

She did what she liked. She wore earrings when she wanted to. Two rings, thick heirlooms in Rachel's thick and heavy ears – that was a clear blasphemy. Even the Karaites, who were unsure if they believed in God, were sure they were offended by

Rachel's earrings. She was left to her own ways only because she was unmarried. The zero of a childless woman in the house of Hagah Levy. A great family reduced to two odd boys and a pair of spinsters.

She worked every day. Even, in secret, on the night of the sabbath. Rachel's religion was her own affair. She believed what she saw with her own eyes. She was sure she had never seen God. She had seen people die of plagues – slowly, sadly, in their own muck and blood. The mass graves and pits. And she watched those who had survived. Her brother's mother-in-law, her brother's children. They were hers now. She thought of them often as she worked.

While they slept she would sit up at the long kitchen tables, the one for meat, the other for milk. She would take off the earrings and put them with her other heirlooms. It was a miser's habit, done without miserliness. It was selfish only because it was important to Rachel herself. She didn't love the gems as gems. Objects are precious in other ways.

The earrings were Persian, white gold. They had belonged to Rachel's grandmother. They reminded her of her childhood, four generations quarrelling under one roof. Beside the earrings there was a half-yard of cloth of murex, frail with age, traded by Hagah's great-grandfather. Its purple dye was iridescent and precious: it was centuries since the last murexes were trawled up and boiled in the dyers' vats. With the cloth was her mother's ankle chain of Indian gold and topaz. She held the heirlooms in her hands. They took her back. They connected her to the dead by their crude spurs and bones of gold.

Under the cloth were the brothers' circumcision gowns. To Rachel they seemed eerie. Waistcoats for babies. They had been worn by the brothers and by their father, and by Rachel's own father: brothers and brothers and brothers. Their buttons were coral and turquoise, to ward off the devil's eye. Rachel repaired their mothworn sleeves and folded them away neatly in a box of terebinth wood that lent everything it held the smell of turpentine.

The earrings were her resistance to the order of things. In Baghdad the confusion of life was deceptive. For Rachel and her nephews there were rules to be followed. The laws of the Jews

60

and the laws of the Turks. What Rachel thought of laws was her own business. In her house people came and went, the Kurdish fishermen, Sabians and Muslims. On cold nights Yusuf the official beggar would sleep in her spare rooms, grinning his sumac-stained grin. A Muslim sleeping in a Jewish house. But the order was there all the same. Rachel couldn't change it. It was fixed as the strata in desert limestone.

They were aliens in an Arab country. For as long as there had been Jews in the world they had lived in the land of two rivers. But here and now, Daniel, Salman and Rachel were *dhimmi* – tolerated peoples. Not infidels in the domain of war, not Muslims in the domain of peace. They were like the Christians and the Sabians, who believed in God but refused the final prophecy of Mohammed. Pitied, picked on, but not hated.

Above them were the strata of the rich Jews, who had moved out of Old Baghdad into the walled city. Sassoon the Prince in his courtyarded palace. The Exilarch in his great columned synagogue. The merchants who bought opium from China and shirts from Manchester, and whose wives conducted arms races of gold, but always behind closed doors. Higher than them were the Arabs themselves, and above them all were the Turkish ruling class. Their men wore gold fob watches, silk socks, green fezzes. They looked down at the provincial Iraqis in their *charawiwa* turbans, the northerners in their patterned headscarves, the potato-faced country people in *kufik* robes and headdresses grown hard with a sweat that smelled of animals.

It was as if you could only have so much disorder in one city. Under the flooded sewers and jammed streets, there was the rock stratum of order. Rachel got away with her resistance because she didn't matter. And her nephews got away with theirs because no one recognised that resistance could lie in river names. Least of all themselves.

At night, in spring, she would tell them stories.

'Not a children's story, Auntie.'

'Not a children's story. Lie back.'

Not the histories of the Jews, which they learned at synagogue. Rachel told the brothers the old tales of their country. The curse of the sirrusch, the dragon-dog with eagle feet, that hunted the grave-robbers of Babylon. The gods of the old cities, Sin with the blue beard and Ishtar the lover. A mass of deities swarming like flies above their sacrifices. Human gods, cowering on their walls like dogs as the great flood rose towards them.

'I wandered the banks of the river, and as I watched it disappear into the cavern I struck upon a plan. "By Allah," I thought, "this river must have both a beginning and an end. If it enters the mountain on this side it must surely emerge into daylight again; and if I can but follow its course in some vessel, the current may at last bring me to some inhabited land."'

Her voice was low. Softer than a man's. Changeable. Rachel the dumpling maker becoming Sindbad the Sailor. An old man telling tall tales. Daniel could feel her next to him, Salman further away, the sound of the river beyond them. It was March. The water was high.

'Emboldened by these thoughts, I collected some large branches of Chinese and Comarin aloes and, laying these on some planks from the wrecked vessels, bound them with strong cables onto a raft. This I loaded with sacks of rubies, pearls and other precious stones, as well as bales of the finest ambergris.'

All through the warm months they slept outside. On the roof, where the slightest breeze might reach them. The space was crowded with Rachel's sun-drying trays, their wood stained with the residues of date syrup and tomato paste. Next to the trays, the water jar perspired in the dark. In the morning it would be silhouetted, fat and dark and cool. Vultures high above it. Some nights the brothers heard owls and always there were the croaks of night herons on the river, the bloody smell of tomato from the wooden trays.

'Then, commending myself to Allah, I launched the raft upon the water.'

She stopped, listening. The younger boy dozed with his mouth open. Rachel resisted the desire to lean over and close it. Daniel lay curled in on himself. A mosquito landed on the pale wing of his shoulder and Rachel brushed it away without touching the skin. She began the story again. Quieter, coasting between passages. Reinventing them.

'The current carried me swiftly along, and soon I found myself in the house of ben Levy. I rejoiced to meet my nephews, Salman and Daniel, and my beautiful aunt, Rachel. I gave them gold, and distributed alms among the poor of the city. Such is the story of my sixth voyage. Tomorrow, my friends, I shall recount to you the tale of my seventh and last voyage.'

Her joints cracked as she stood. She stepped away to the stairs and went down into the house before allowing herself to stretch. She took off her earrings and placed them on the meat table. Above her, a desert breeze moved across the brothers, warm as skin. It was like sleeping without sleeping.

Hush.

'Salman. Do you hear the river?'

'Yes.'

'It's high. Aren't you scared?'

'No.'

The moon caught in their eyes. Sometimes, when the floods came, they whispered themselves awake until morning. On other nights they were only talking in their sleep and neither would realise. Or one brother would only know it when the other stopped making sense.

'No.' Daniel's voice croaked. His mouth was dry. He let his head drop to face the water jar. 'We could swim away.'

'We've got the names.'

'And anyway, we could swim. All the way to Basra. Everything would be under the river. Yusuf's beehives. The sand like the bottom of the sea.'

Salman wondered if bees could swim. He could imagine them underwater. A shoal of them, like small fish.

'Basra is too far. I want to stay here.'

'Yes. We swim up to the roof. We look down and there's the synagogue.' Daniel giggled in the dark, soft and whispery. 'Wet as a shithole. The *bimah* floating away like a boat.'

'Then we live up here. Me and Rachel. You and Judit. Yusuf's bees.'

'And Yusuf. And Yusuf's family.'

'Maybe.' The moon moved across Salman's face. He raised his hand and watched it scrutinise his fingers.

From across the rooftop came street sounds. One voice talking in Arabic. A late drover encouraging his flock. The ring and clonk of goat bells. Beyond that, the sound of the river.

In the morning Rachel would be there, sleeping next to them.

63

Daniel remembered Elazar, too. He had been their last male relative, a great-uncle. On his visits to Baghdad he had slept by the water jar. He was a merchant from Basra, trading guns and medicine, steel and skins, silver and precious stones. He had three colours in his beard. White, black, rust. An Arabic dialect the brothers could barely understand. A tendency to sleepwalk. The last time he came, Daniel had found footprints in the residue of the syrup trays. The whorls of Elazar's big toes had been impressed firmly into the brown lacquer. The footprints had gone towards the edge of the flat roof and stopped dead.

He never came back. He died at sea. Daniel and Salman didn't miss him. He was distant as their family name.

'Daniel?'

'Yes.'

'How would you change the world?'

They smiled together. It was one of their games. There were always rules. Salman made them. Daniel broke them.

'If I could change the world, I would make Rachel rich as the viceroy. All the Jews would have money. All the Arabs. Not the Turks. We would ride bay horses. We would have green turbans. You would have coral buttons. We would be rich as the merchants of Bombay. We would buy new slippers for Rachel. And tomorrow, mango pickle and rice for breakfast.'

The words ran out into the night air. He went quiet. He had forgotten the sound of the river while he talked. Now it came to him again, and along with it the one voice talking, and the night herons.

'Salman?'

Above him were the stars. No cloud. A stretch of black without people. The sound of the Tigris, emptying into quiet. A loneliness crept into Daniel and he turned towards his little brother. Half-curled, a question mark in the dark. 'Salman?'

'You did ten things. You can only have one thing.'

He lay back. Muscles and heart easing out. 'One thing?'

'Yes.'

'It's not enough.'

'It is.'

'Then what would you do?'

'If I could change the world, I would make it into diamond.'

The light caught in Salman's eyes. When he turned his hand, the moon was extinguished. Snuffed out in his fingers, like a candle.

He was with Rachel, shopping for rice by the Four-Footed Mosque. The crowd was slow and Salman bored. When he began to whine Rachel sent him back along the Island Road to the house, knocking at the western door.

No one answered. Grandmother Judit was sleeping off walnuts in the kitchen. Daniel was away downriver, looking for lion tracks under the tamarisks. Salman walked round to the desert door. When no one answered there he began to feel scared.

It was an old fear, and always the same. Salman would imagine that his family had died. Most of it had. What was left was what he clung to with such ferocity. Now, along with the fear, came a wildness. If everyone were dead, he knew other places he could go and live. And so he went.

He walked to Khadimain. In the bazaar he had never felt alone. There were more people, he thought, than were ever likely to die. On the outskirts were cordial hawkers and a chickpea man with Indian monkeys on chains. He kept going. Past the stalls of fruit, gunbelts, samovars, cagebirds and Korans. The compact crowds of housewives, the licensed circumcisor, the confectioner stirring vats of *halqûn*, the duck man with marsh birds tied living at his waist.

His feet were full of anger. They walked by themselves. Salman kept going until he came to the heart of the bazaar, where the costermongers ate kebaps sprinkled with sour-sweet purple sumac, and drank tea under a market roof of spread awnings. He stood until a Levantine woman sat him on a café stool and gave him a paper cone of *zahtar*. When the food was gone and she was no longer watching, he got up and kept going.

At the far side of the bazaar, where the ground began to slope towards the river, he came to the stall of Mehmet the lapidary. His legs weren't walking by themselves any more. He wasn't crying, although he felt thirsty. There was a bulbul in a wicker cage. Under its voice, Mehmet was polishing a moonstone. The wheel rocked as he pedalled. His stool was padded with old carpet. The light settled in the stone like milk in a cup.

Rachel found them there together, an hour later. Not talking. Watching together until the jewel was done. As if the work had been shared between them. By then Salman had seen all he thought he would ever want.

Mehmet was an old Marsh Arab, his face riddled with smile lines. He cut whatever stones the jewellers brought him, cheap or precious. Moonstones ground down to cabochon domes. Balases faceted in the European style. Grains of diamond and olive oil hissing on leather. After he had found the place Salman went back often. It suited Rachel. If Daniel was out, she would never know where he had gone, but Salman was almost always with Mehmet. His needs were more predictable.

Once the old man let him stand beside the wheel. When Salman was ready to go, Mehmet pinched a grain of polishing grit off the leather-lined wheel. He held it out to the boy, the light catching in it, a brilliant point of diamond.

Salman carried it home between his thumbs and presented it to Rachel. Standing beside her, craning to see. Edgy with the possessiveness of a first-time giver, until she wrapped the grain in the cloth of murex and stored it away. A week later, when she looked through the heirlooms again, the diamond chip had disappeared. For days she looked for it while Salman raged at her, the veins standing out in his forehead. A little old man, tottering with righteous anger. When she became angry herself he brought her another present. A green locust's wing, beautiful as faience. Rachel was careful not to lose it.

He was unlike his older brother. Salman did what Daniel had never done and fought the boys from the mosques when they called him *dhimmi*, coming home bright-eyed and bleeding. Salman liked Baghdad with its smells and noise. The deafening silence of the desert scared him, and the sirrusch crept into his dreams on its ruined eagle feet.

Some days Daniel would go and help Yusuf with the beehives. It was the only time Salman would go into the desert. He enjoyed the sound of the bees. Sometimes there were words in it, he thought. If he closed his eyes it became a kind of muezzin. When he looked again there would be the flight paths of insects passing around him. Daniel holding slats of comb for the honey man.

66

Yusuf spoke only an unintelligible desert Arabic. He had the fine-boned, long head of a Beduin, and at nineteen he was married with five children. Daniel liked his quietness. For hours there would be no sound but the murmur of the hives in the sun. In the end Salman wouldn't be able to stand it and he would walk back home alone, leaving the others to carry the slats of honeycomb, heavy as looms.

Their house was at the edge of the old city. It was grand, made for a greater family than they had become. Sand wore at the eaves.

There were two doors. When he was small it had seemed to Daniel as if they led to different homes. The house could alter physically, depending on how you approached it. Everything was changed, from the felt shape of rooms to the patterns in the floor tiles. The valency of the air, the quality of light.

From the city it felt crowded, filled up with the smells and sounds of people. The doorstep was worn down in a soft curve, like a shape in flesh. Through the window grilles you could hear the street and Khadimain, three blocks away.

But from the west, the house felt deserted. It was built on a slope, and the rear entrance was a full storey higher, making the building feel smaller. Through the doors light starred the floor tiles in hot constellations. This was Grandmother Judit's bedroom, where she slept all day. It smelled of bedding and old skin. The windows were blocked with the leaves and veins of vines and sweet pea. If there were voices, they seemed distant. If Daniel closed his eyes to listen, there would be the sound of bees from Yusuf's hives. Beyond that, the desert.

Judit was ninety-five years old. She was their mother's mother, an in-law with nowhere to go, proud to live in the old ben Levy house. When she was awake, she would tell the brothers implausible facts about their own ancestors. Before the plagues came the Levys used to live for hundreds of years, she said. Like Abraham and Noah. Rachel's mother's mother Sarah had drunk nothing except rainwater and lived to a hundred and nine (Judit said). On the first day of every month (Judit said) Sarah and her long-suffering husband Hezkel would haul out wooden rain-butts, and on the last day they would heave them in. She had died one morning in 1783, her heart stopping as she was pulling her butt in through the western door.

In spring the brothers would sit with Judit in the kitchen with its bars of sunlight, stunned with food and fabrications. Sometimes, in flood season, she would describe their rivers to them, the Tigris and Euphrates. The stories of their courses. Making them magnificent, as if their gods might be listening.

Salman and the Tigris were dark, fast, and dangerous. They always looked old. Salman's river was that of Baghdad; whereas Daniel's was that of the desert. It absorbed life. Lost in his thoughts, Daniel was jostled but unharmed. Bullied, sometimes, but still trusting. And the Euphrates was wide, meandering. A continent-sized river, its sandbars shifting like great eels, making shipping impossible. Longer-lived than the Tigris, and where the two rivers met to the south, the Euphrates was the more abundantly green, with white kingfishers ghosting over the water.

River names. Rachel invented them, but she didn't use them. In private, she had become disturbed by them. The city was full of beliefs and old, vindictive gods. Rachel herself believed the names had become ominous.

She watched Daniel from the western door. He was with his brother and Yusuf, carrying home the honeycomb. Even walking he was slow. But there was nothing weak about him. The passivity, Rachel thought, hid or generated some kind of strength, something that might one day even become magnificent itself. Beside it, Salman's quickness seemed frail.

She looked away. Once, teasing them with the names she had invented, the words had stopped in her mouth. In the back of her mind, the belief had welled up that Daniel would outlive his younger brother. She never used the river names again.

The house with two doors. The flight paths of bees. Salman made young. Rachel made living. If Daniel had been told that one day he would remember none of it, he would have laughed out loud with fear.

At the edge of the desert, two boys were walking. One was taller than the other. One was broader than the other. It is like a riddle. One was holding a slat of honeycomb. One was holding nothing. They were so alike, they could have been brothers. The desert air shimmered around them.

There is a point in time when the story of the Brethren becomes three stories. Another point when the three stories reconverge. Physically, it makes it difficult for me to follow. I wish I had three heads and three pairs of eyes to find the jewel. Three spare sisters.

There are so many places to look. I have a whole world to search. Some nights, when I am alone, I dream that I have failed already because what I am trying to do is impossible: the Brethren is lost for ever. And then I imagine abandoning these notebooks, with all their work. Someone would discover them. The love of the jewel would take them and, who knows, they might find it. I don't think I could bear that. It would be as if someone had stolen my life.

Three Brothers, Three Sisters. A year after the Crown Jewels of England were destroyed, the shoulder-knot of Duke John the Fearless changed its name. For six years it was known as *Les Trois Soeurs*. Simple, muscular and masculine, the Brethren underwent a sex change.

No one knows why it happened. My theory is that the transformation came about because the jewel itself had been altered. For years, the Stuart kings had replaced old stones or added new ones – table-cut diamonds, hanging stirrups of pearls. The Brethren became a more glittering prize. The structure must have seemed more delicate under the weight of stones. But Charles and Henrietta had also disturbed the simplicity of the jewel. The balanced geometry was gone. The gold spurs were loaded down with glitter. The restored work had the gorgeousness of a Lalique brooch or a Fabergé egg, priceless kitsch. For two decades, the Three Brethren was a jewel in drag.

It was also the last crown jewel of England. But by circumstances it was exiled from the Commonwealth along with its owner, Queen Henrietta Maria. For years the King's consort went on trying to sell it. Desperate for guns she hawked it around Europe, a travelling saleswoman in powder and paste. In that time the new wealth on the continent was banked in Holland, and it was in Rotterdam that Henrietta finally managed to rid herself of the knot. She sold it for a fraction of its value, one hundred and four thousand Dutch livres, to a Monsieur Cletstex of the Bank of Lombardy.

Holland, like England, was a country enriched by the sea. And like Basel and Berne, the Low Cities were centres of capitalist power. Jacob Fugger would have taken personal pride in the rise of Rotterdam, the fortunes made and lost in tulips and spices. Holland was a country, finally, that could afford the Brethren, and inside twelve months the jewel was sold twice, first to William of Amsterdam and then to Andries of Zoutkamp, the Prince of Herrings. Both men were merchants at the height of their powers. Their purchase of the great jewel demonstrated to the whole of Europe, crowned and otherwise, that even a merchant could dress in the diamonds of a king.

In the painting by Van Dyck, Andries of Zoutkamp has the physique of a self-made man: a worker's muscle running to fat. He looks pale under well-tailored clothes. His skin has a quality of wetness. Andries had money in fishing and in the Dutch East India Company, but he was also said to have amassed a fortune years earlier, as a privateer. He got where he was by himself, and he never married. Andries was a man who made enemies easily, in the way that others might make friends. Finally, in November 1655 he grew tired of the machinations of city life. He retired to his last great acquisition, a *borg* manor estate betwen Zoutkamp and Uithuizen in the far north.

What remains of the house feels desolate. The walls are surrounded by pollarded trees, avenues of black stumps, Moore sculptures facing across the empty fields and EU greenhouses. The fortified buildings themselves are just gutted ruins. Where brickwork survives it is black, like stone in an industrial city.

It is the place where Andries's enemies caught up with him. During his first winter in the north, the merchant's manor was burnt to the ground. Councillors and militia were sent from Uithuizen and Groningen to determine the cause of the fire, but they were held back for a day by heavy snow. By then, there was nothing left for them to find. The cindered bones of Andries, a woman and child had been recovered by three surviving servants. If there had been scavengers in the ash and snow the investigators never saw them, and the survivors said nothing.

It is the human loss that matters. A man, woman and child, not the stones; although the diamond could also have burned. I think this despite myself. In a heat of such intensity, the gem can have survived only if it were protected by some other form of carbon. It would have to be contained. In a box, in a pocket, or a hand. Skin and bone would do.

There is a surviving report of the deaths, written for the Bailiff of Groningen in 1656. The pages are tanned dark as eelskin. They mention the woman and child, who were never identified. They give precise official explanations: *The fire at the Zoutkamp borg appears to have been brought about by nothing more than human oversight. Agreement is made that in likelihood, the flames arose by mishap, such as an unattended hearth, bed warmer, or pipe.*

For the records, the Prince of Herrings died smoking in bed. There were other theories. Zoutkamp had been the wrong place for Andries to attempt retirement. The far north of Holland was a place characterised by blunt, physical enmities. For decades, the city of Groningen had tried and failed to dominate the rural borgs around it, and the two sides fought a continual, sullen war across the fenlands and polders. In contemporary accounts of the death, Andries is portrayed as an outsider, meddling in a sectarianism he barely understands. An old man, out of his depth in the backwaters. In Groningen, there were people happy to see Andries gone.

He had been a wealthy man. Items known to be in his possession included the Van Dyck portrait, of which only studies survive. Seven-tenths of an Ashanti gold mask, cut into sections as pirate booty, 'Two score potts of thea', and the Three Brethren – the Three Sisters. According to the investigators, none of his treasures survived the fire.

I see the scavengers, moving slow and bent. Snow falls into their eyes and hair. Through the thatch tied to their feet, the hot ground burns their soles. Somewhere ahead of them, under the char, a knot of jewels waits to be found. And all around them is the landscape of ruins, the dykes and the mudflats, the dunes of the Rottumeroog sand island which is neither land nor ocean but a world in between, and the icy Wadden Sea.

One story, three stories. From this point, the history of the Three Brethren is fragmented. Some time after the fire, the burnt shape of the shoulder-knot was discovered. In the hands of scavengers

71

and merchants, the triangle of gems was split up like pirate booty. What had been famous was made anonymous. The gold spurs and bones lose their identity, but the stones themselves have survived. And so there are three trails: of the diamond, the rubies, and the pearls.

I am beginning with the trail of the pearls. It leads back on itself, as the histories of jewels often do. It returns to England, where the Commonwealth of the New Model Army had lasted barely more than a decade. When he took England from the Cromwells, Charles the Second claimed a Crown which no longer possessed a crown. It was an embarrassment he couldn't afford in any sense. In 1661 he awarded the dubious honour of Crown Goldsmith to the jeweller Robert Vyner, and opened his account with an entire set of regalia. Vyner was never fully paid for his work, and his appointment ended in his bankruptcy. There is a massive deficit in the accounts, a shortfall of £15,000.

Still, the crown was remade. As it turned out, the heart of it had never been lost. Old stones were set in the new collets and arches: Saint Edward's sapphire. The Stuart sapphire. For a decade, the Royalists had been gathering their king's jewels through the black markets of Europe. Like prosthetic hands, the sockets of the new crown were shaped to the old gems.

And along with them came the pearls. There were four of them, large and baroque, with a grey lustre. The Brethren pearls were not beautiful, like the rubies or the diamond. They lacked the perfection of stone. They were organic jewels, with the lovely ugliness of living things: the taste of oysters, the smell of sex, the colouring of skin. They had been harvested long before the invention of cultured pearls, which are barely pearls at all but only beads coated with nacre. In terms of rarity and price, they existed in a time closer to that of the Roman general Vitellius, who paid for an entire campaign by selling just one of his wife's pearl earrings. Three were drilled lengthways and the fourth breadthways. They were not called the pearls of the Three Brethren. Instead they were known as Queen Elizabeth's Earrings.

The Elizabeth in the pearls' name was not the Tudor, with her jewelled skeleton and ermine eyes. This Queen was a Stuart. Elizabeth of Bohemia was the sister of Charles the First. In a painting of 1642 that now rests in the third warehouse of the

British National Portrait Gallery (warehouses that are not marked on public maps) she is pictured wearing four large baroque pearls as earrings. Charles had given them to his sister in 1640, when his great knot was reset, its old pearls removed and new stones installed.

After the end of the Commonwealth, when Oliver Cromwell's body had been dug up and hung in chains, its head cut from its torso and buried in a secret place, Elizabeth returned to England. She was old and sick, and soon after her nephew Charles took the throne she died. She was buried in London in 1661. The Black Death and the Great Fire passed over her head like flood tides.

The three oval pearls were set in the English crown with a fourth jewel to match them, and they stayed there for two hundred years. The last Brethren jewel, '*a very big and fine pearl shaped like a pear*', was placed in an envelope with the old settings of Elizabeth's earrings. The envelope was locked away in the treasury of the Tower of London. It remained there for centuries, gathering dust with the frames of empty crowns, the bills of Robert Vyner, and the Knave of Diamond's list of beautiful things.

The trail of the rubies is longer and more broken. In an archive in Paris, I copy down the nineteenth item on a list of jewels, auctioned in Constantinople in 1663: *Lot nineteen shall be a very fine Balascus, lasque cut in the old fashion, of seventy qirats.*

No seller's name appears by the stone. But it was bought by a Frenchman. His name was Jean-Baptiste Tavernier. At fifty-eight, he was the greatest European jewel merchant of the century.

Tavernier was a big man, barrel-chested, barrel-hipped. Heavy, as if desire could show in flesh. His eyes were attentive under tired lids. After years of travelling, Jean had finally married in Paris, and in Constantinople he was undertaking his sixth and last great journey to the East. He was travelling to settle his affairs, most of all with the Mogul Emperor Aurungzeb, before retirement and the quieter life of a family man.

His journals don't show whether he recognised the Brethren jewel for what it was, not yet. I believe he did. No one knew more about jewels than Jean-Baptiste. No one loved them more. Waiting for passage in Constantinople, passing hours at a minor auction house, I believe the merchant recognised the ruby as one of those from the lost Three Brethren. Buying it changed him. Tavernier spent the rest of his life trying to reassemble the jewel.

Instead of returning home to his new wife, Jean-Baptiste travelled onwards for five years, crossing from Turkey to India and continuing to Afghanistan. There was no trace of the other balases in Asia, however, and it was only when he returned to Paris that Tavernier found the information he was looking for. In his private diary of 1686 there is a single sentence underlined. The quill stutters in the black ink: *'Les Trois Balases! They are known to the merchants from Muscovy.'*

He was as an old man by then. Still, the next year he left Paris and his family again. Part Odysseus, part Sindbad, Jean-Baptiste undertook a seventh journey, travelling north for the first time in his life. In 1689 he died in Moscow. His grave is there. When I visited it there were frost patterns on the stone. Perfect crystalline symmetries.

I think that he died content. His possessions were returned to his widow in Paris. Among them were three matched balas stones.

Two years after his death, Tavernier's unsold stock of jewels was auctioned by his family. The three balases were bought by a representative of the Mogul court in India. In fact, once Tavernier had possessed them, rumours of the Three Brethren rubies had begun to spread. What Jean-Baptiste valued, the world learnt to value, and there were fourteen separate bidders for the rubies at the Tavernier auction. Their buyer was Aurungzeb, last great Mogul Emperor of India, eleventh descendant of Timur the Lame.

Aurungzeb had dealt more closely with Tavernier than with any other Western merchant. On the trader's last visit to the East, the emperor had allowed him to see and hold the imperial jewels; in his journals Tavernier has beautiful line drawings of the most remarkable stones. They included the colossal balas known as the Timur Ruby, *Khiraj-i-alam*, Tribute of the World, and the Great Mogul diamond, the eye in Aurungzeb's Peacock Throne, of which the Koh-i-Nur survives as a fragment.

Still, like Tavernier, Aurungzeb was an old man. In late pictures his face looks both withered and overgrown, the eyebrows heavy, the eyes lost in folds of skin. He lasted for another sixteen years, crouched in his jewelled throne. In 1707 he died, and with him the great Mogul dynasty of India came to an end.

It had survived for a century, and six generations of rulers. In its wake, the whole subcontinent began to come apart. Half the forces of India and Europe strained to regain it: princelings, tribes, the manoeuvrings of the French, the bribery and violence of the East India Company of England. In their acquisitive hands, the Mogul treasures were scattered across continents. And with them went the Brethren rubies. Their trail turned back on itself. As the histories of great stones often do.

༘

Until the day he left Iraq, Salman believed that the world was flat. He was young then. He trusted what he saw with his own eyes.

Much later, when his mind had gone, the idea returned to him in a more insinuating form. He began to insist that the world was not only flat but becoming thinner. The depth of the earth was finite, beyond it was abysmal space, and the exertions of humanity were wearing it away. In the cities, where the ground had been worn thin as a crust of sand, the wrong footstep could send one crashing into darkness. In that time of his life Salman sat unmoving, his eyes fixed ahead. His world became the fleshy curve in the step of a half-forgotten door. The flat earth was one more part of his paranoia, another hook on which to hang his fear.

But that came later. When he was young, Salman only believed his eyes. He saw the slightest impurity in a bad ruby, the fleck of false gold in lapis lazuli. He saw how Rachel seemed younger as he and Daniel grew older, and that this was a deception. Their aunt was more than fifty years old, in a time and place when most people would die in their first three decades. As the brothers began to work, Salman saw how Rachel wore her heirloom earrings less, as if she meant not to harm her nephews' business. But he also saw how the lobes of Rachel's ears had grown stretched under the weight of gold. As if the earrings were still there, under her skin.

His eyes were brown. It was a hard colour, thick as old blood. He saw that his brother's eyes were mutable, altering from brown to green when light fell on them. He watched Daniel at a distance. His sinewed height and hooked face. Their father's profile, Judit said. A long shadow trailing street children, stooping home along the Khadimain Road.

He watched the city around him. The Jews were beginning to leave. They had been there for five millennia and they departed only gradually, over a number of years. Every spring a few more would go. They took ship at Basra for Bombay, Calcutta or Rangoon. East, always east.

Salman sat on the step of the eastern door, mending a bartered gun, and watched sand blow in from the desert. It settled in doorways where no one lived to sweep it back. Beyond the end of Island Road, Yusuf's beehives were engulfed by dunes, miniatures of Nineveh and Ur.

Even at night and in the early mornings, the air in the streets smelt of bad meat. The odour settled everywhere, sweet and acrid. Without ever having travelled Salman knew it as the smell of dying cities, where things that have been drawn together begin to come apart.

Salman watched it all with his eyes, trusted them, and thought of how he might alter things. He wasn't a child any more. He didn't want to change the whole world, only the lives of those he loved. At nights he lay awake on the flat roof next to his aunt and brother, planning their escape. But when he slept, he dreamed of the sirrusch. Ruined eagle footprints under the tamarisks. The desert passing over the city like a flood tide.

He still had the determination of the child in the Khadimain bazaar. There was always something bitter in Salman, a store of violence. A sump of poisonous water waiting to rise. At nights he watched his aunt sorting the weevils from cheap rice, his brother carving a nine-holed flute from a mulberry branch for the street children. He saw their contentedness in small actions, and the frustration boiled inside him. He wanted to shout at them, to shake them by the necks until they were scared enough to listen. Salman wanted them to believe that there were better lives than this. He wanted to take them there. He had the fierce generosity of someone who needs love as much as they love others.

The brothers became traders. For the Jewish men of Iraq, it was practically a racial profession. When they began to work together, Salman bought his brother a watch and chain. He did it on impulse, because he wanted to give Daniel something. Anything would have done. The watch's casing was thick gold. Under the out-case its face was white. Salman bought it in secret from Ibrahim the Marsh Arab. Its glass was cracked and the hands were rusted together at a quarter past three, and Ibrahim traded it for the weight of its gold rather than its mechanism. He didn't say where he had got it and Salman didn't ask. He traded it for five gallons of paraffin, a dozen pairs of scissors and a meerschaum pipe carved with a map of the Levant.

It took Salman five months to repair. He bought new glass for the face and polished it on Mehmet the lapidary's wheel. He took out each cog and hairspring of the works, teasing the dirt from the blue steel, aligning the jewels. He liked the way each part served its purpose. There was nothing workless inside the watch. It was neat as the organs and bones of a fish.

Once he had put it back together, Salman wound the watch and lay with his head beside it, listening to it run. It gained five minutes every hour, to the second. He was immensely proud of its reliable raciness.

When he was given it, Daniel held the watch in both hands, cradling its weight. He didn't know what to say, so he said nothing. On the watch's winding stub was a single spiralled line of unintelligible script, and on the white face two more lines of an alien language divided by black numerals. They were the first words of English that he learned to read. They said:

Rundell & Bridge's,
of Ludgate Hill, London.

Daniel kept them by him every day for the rest of his life. They became traders naturally. It wasn't the life either of them would have chosen. It had begun with Mehmet the lapidary.

As soon as Rachel would let him, Salman had apprenticed himself to the Marsh Arab. Mehmet did a regular trade in the cheaper jewellers' stones. If there was sometimes not enough work for two men, Mehmet invented it. He lived alone in a shack on the outskirts of town. He had always been a quiet man. Age had made him gentle, and Salman had never known him as anything else.

He was proud to work with a boy raised in the city. An educated young man, who could calculate the city tithes and write

Hebrew and Arabic. He taught Salman to work stone in the simple ways he had taught himself. The step and table cuts, which reflect light but cannot catch it. The cabochon, which is less a cut than a polishing. Mehmet had even invented his own version of the brilliant by studying European jewels, and copying the order of their sixteen facets, although he never managed to balance them. The geometry of Mehmet's brilliants was never true. They spilled light too quickly, like a step cut. They couldn't hold illumination, the stone made into a vessel, a lobster-pot for the light. Mehmet the lapidary had learned his trade accidentally, by necessity, and beyond his four cuts there were methods he never knew of. The ancient Mogul. The double brilliant, with its thirty-two facets. The Star.

Sometimes the goldsmiths brought beautiful stones. Seed rubies from India, or cloudy Egyptian emeralds from the old cities. Most days they came with the cheapest gems. Green turquoise faded by desert heat, grey-blue *khesbet*, runnels of chalcedony. Salman loved them all. Their colours capturing the light. The ring of their names. The smell of their dust.

It was months before he knew anything was wrong. It was June. Under the market awnings, struts of light lodged themselves into the crowd. Salman was watching Aziz the Kurdish fishmonger across the aisle, combing his knife through the grain of a salmon.

He looked back at his own business. He and Mehmet were working together at the polishing wheel, a stone to each side, when the marshlander's hands began to shudder. He shook his head and said something – a curse, Salman thought, although it was incomprehensible. He stopped the wheel, thinking the lapidary had grazed himself, before he saw that he was crying.

He was bow-legged, thin, with the slightly swollen belly of habitual malnourishment. Salman watched him as they ate, later, in the quiet of his shack. He looked no different from most other old men. There was nothing to show he was sick, although this was what he said, again and again. Salman, trusting his eyes, found that curious.

'You are well enough to cut stone.'

'There is such a thing as homesickness,' Mehmet said. 'There are so few of my people here, in the city. I remember, before you were born, they attacked Baghdad. I was already here then, you see? Fighting against my own people. There is such a thing as loneliness,' he said. When he looked up at Salman again his eyes were wet with pleading.

They left a week later. Salman had never travelled so far from Baghdad. It was six days' hard ride to Mehmet's country. No Jew was allowed to ride a horse, and Salman's mule was slow and reluctant in the waterlands.

As they rode, Mehmet began to tell him why he had come to Baghdad. His voice was old and cracked. He said he had wanted a son, and when his wife had given birth to girls he had killed them. Three children in three years. He had buried them alive in the wet ground, each as it came. When the tribal council found out what he had done, he had been banished for life. He didn't know, now, if they would let him back. Or if he could let himself return.

He told Salman he was sorry for what he had done. His old head nodded on its weak neck. The lines of his face made it look as if he was smiling.

The waterlands smelt of mud and shit. After Mehmet had told him about the children, Salman found he couldn't talk to him. His mouth tasted of bile. Once a red boar started up in the reeds. It was as big as the mules and they skittered sideways, almost falling. Salman and Mehmet stopped often, while the old man searched for the invisible roads along safe ground.

Before noon on the sixth day they came to an expanse of water dotted with cat's-tails. In the middle of the lake was an island, and on the island was Mehmet's settlement.

It was bigger than Salman had expected, five long wickerwork halls surrounded by huts and outbuildings. Tarada canoes, sleek and well kept, were pulled up by the far shore. They reined in by the water's edge. For some time Mehmet only watched. Mosquitoes hung around them. Across the water, two children were playing with the carcass of a green lizard. A woman came out of the nearest hall and carried them both inside. When she had gone, Mehmet dismounted. He took Salman's arm tight in his hand, thanked him, and waded out to the island and was gone.

Salman watched until he was sure the old man wasn't coming back. Then he reached down for the reins of Mehmet's mule, and turned both animals to go.

There were four riders behind him. Quiet men, waiting until he had finished waiting. Three of them had rifles, Salman had no weapon, and for a moment he thought they would kill him. Instead they led him to the edge of the marshes, then accompanied him home. By the end of six days Salman knew the name of one of them, Ibrahim, and that they were all Mehmet's blood relations. Beyond that, they said nothing.

Still, a month later they were back at the Gate of Darkness. Four horsemen in *kufik* robes, asking for the Jews with the river names. Ibrahim brought goods to trade, and he sold them cheap. It became a routine, and then a livelihood. Mehmet's tribesmen would come each month, and Salman would buy what they had found or stolen on the desert roads.

The Marsh Arabs needed bandages and bullets, kettles and paraffin. In return, they brought bitumened cowries and copper ingots from the mounds of Ur. Scraps of Babylonian gold, small as linseeds. Cylinder seals of carnelian on bronze axles. An English sovereign and an American fortepiano with eight keys missing, like teeth. A locket containing Christ and the Bleeding Heart. A broken watch with a white face.

Daniel never believed the world was flat. Not even when he was a child, and the only globe in Baghdad was part of a Rowley orrery, a relic locked in the palace of Mahmud the Second. He knew the earth was round because he felt it. What Daniel thought and felt was his own business.

He pictured the planet in his mind. Because everything in the sky moved, he imagined it in motion. He theorised that all movement caused erosion, and the earth would be polished into a sphere by space itself. He decided that the natural tendency of all things veered towards curves, not lines. Since the earth was a natural solid, its simplest form would be a sphere.

He became a trader because Salman wanted him to. He didn't mind it. If the choice had been his alone he would have done manual work, cast-fishing or harvesting. Anything with a rhythm of movements, a repetition in which he could lose himself. Trading never came to him naturally. The life left him no time to think.

April, 1831. There was news of flooding to the south, where

the limestone desert gave way to softer ground. It reached back to Baghdad overnight, the river's *hush* deepening to a roar. It sounded as if the city was arguing with itself. Yusuf the official beggar came to the house legless with hashish, insisting that he could hear the voice of Noah in the tide.

'We need animals,' he breathed at Daniel, hanging from his shoulder. 'Animals. Doves and elephants. A ship for the elephants. Boy, where's your hammer?' He slept on the roof for a month, his restlessness keeping them awake. Muttering in his sleep. Old names from the stories of great floods, like curses: *Noah. Shem. Nimrod.*

The marshlanders brought news. South, where the rivers met, the water had never been so high. There was no proof of anything worse. No death. Rachel waited for it, watching the poor digging bulwarks below the shanties. Listening to the mewl of buzzards. She slept as little as her body would let her. When she dreamed it was of the plague. The sound, from her childhood, of carts at night, piled with their soft dark lumber. She locked the grillework of the windows, closed the doors. Her brother's sons helped the militia sandbag the lower streets, wading through water that was already ankle-deep.

It was a fortnight before the Tigris began to ebb. The city stopped, the markets quiet, half-empty. On the eighteenth night of flooding a child of the Kurdish fishermen fell sick. By the time news of her death got out to the Jewish quarter her father was already dead himself. Plague had set into the low-lying districts like a rank wet rot. It was cholera, the disease which lives in bad water, which kills by defecation. As if the most basic acts, breathing or loving, could be contorted into something poisonous.

Two days later Judit complained of a headache. She was in the kitchen, getting in Rachel's way. The old woman's face was flushed when she spoke. As if, she laughed, I have anything to blush about. They carried her to bed in her room by the western door. She died before morning, almost before the disease could show itself, a bowl of red *halqûn* left on the table beside her.

She was the first death on the Island Road. When her body was done with Rachel nailed up the doors herself. Two of the Sabians fell ill that night, after baptising themselves in river water. Yusuf the honey seller's children in the small hours. The youngest first, then one after the next, so quickly there was no time to mourn while Yusuf and his wife cleaned the sweat and faeces. The day the oldest's body was burned, Yusuf himself fell on his way to work, and found he couldn't stand. His fever lasted six days. His wife built his pyre by herself. When it was done she went back alone to her desert people.

They buried Judit in the Jewish cemetery, halfway between the desert and the river. After she was gone Rachel became withdrawn, and accusing. 'I have no one to talk to,' she said once, as if she was not talking to Daniel as she said it. The house felt different. Four people had occupied it in a way that three could not. Three, Daniel thought, was a less human number. He found that he missed Judit's presence in the house more than he missed the old woman herself. It surprised him. He wasn't ashamed of it.

There was no food which could be trusted. Olives from the highlands sold for the price of meat. In the old town Daniel would sell artefacts to Hüseyin, Imam of the Muslim Kurds. More often he would walk through the walled city to the Alien Quarter, making any money he could from the Europeans. Few had stayed through the plague. Those that did bought little. There was the French Consul Monsieur Lavoisier, who spent his days hunting lion in the thickets of mesquite. The Bavarian merchant Herr Lindenberg, who drank laudanum at a thousand drops a day, and spoke for all the German peoples. Most regularly there was Cornelius Rich, Surveyer of both His Majesty's Government of Great Britain and the East India Company of England.

He was a big Mancunian, muscled like a manual worker. His accent was unsoftened by years spent abroad. His laugh was surprisingly high-pitched, feminine, like that of an old woman. When the summer heat settled over Baghdad and the knowledge of his backwater posting became unbearable, Cornelius would go to the viceroy's office. He and Mahmud would drink raki flavoured with apricots and argue violently all night over the ethics of the Battle of Navarino, when a British fleet had broken a truce, opened fire, and destroyed half the navy of the Ottoman Empire.

Cornelius taught Daniel to read the maker's name on his bartered watch. He called Britain 'the Empire on which the Rain never Stops', and drank to overcome his homesickness. In the courtyard of his great house his servants maintained a small cricket pitch bordered by liquorice trees. No one ever played on it. The grass was scorched to nothing.

He traded with Daniel because the Jew learnt more English in six months than Cornelius had learnt of Arabic in ten years. He bought faience beads from Babylon or Ur, packing them up with letters to his fiancée in England. In return Daniel would listen to him. A thickset man, talking of England, as if he could bring it back with him.

London was four months away by sea. The East Indiamen went southwards around the Cape, turning back up the coast of Africa. Cornelius talked of how his fiancée would unpack Daniel's beads in her parents' house in Edgbaston. Her name was Dora. She had artist's fingers. Daniel learned all this. Cornelius showed him a lock of her hair, coiled back on itself behind glass. To Daniel its blondeness looked like something cut from the scalp of an old woman.

They sat together in the courtyard. Cicadas chirred in the liquorice trees. The moon lit up the dry grass. Cornelius Rich and Daniel Levy talked about the dangers of the Suez land crossing, the whiteness of blackthorn in spring, the ways to trap coney in winter.

'I'll tell you what I miss, sir. White skin. There's no shame in a dark complexion, none, only I like white skin on a woman.'

Daniel drank his tea. The servants had mixed it with milk. Over the months he had stopped noticing the taste in his mouth.

'That and the nights in a big city.'

'Manchester.' He said the name only, having only Cornelius's words for it. His stories.

'Aye, that. And London also.' Cornelius leant forward, his chair creaking under him. 'Now, you should see London. Acknowledged centre of the world. All men should see it before they die. There are more Scots on the Thames than in Aberdeen, more Irishmen than in Dublin. More Papists than in Rome, I shouldn't wonder. The grand capital of the grandest empire the world has ever known – you don't get more acknowledged than that. If we were there now – if we were there, we should be entirely lit up with gaslights! That is something to see, sir, let me tell you. London Piccadilly by gaslight. Imagine that.'

Daniel tried to imagine it. The smoke of the mosquito coils

drifted towards him and he turned his face away. 'I have never travelled.'

'There's better places to be at the end of it.'

'My family is here.'

'Take them along with you. Aye, and there's no denying families.' Cornelius paused, shifting, uncomfortable. Thinking of Dora, of her skin, which was so pale it was not really white, but blue. And beside him in the cane chairs Daniel thought of Rachel, pressing limes. The house with two doors around her, solid as an heirloom. He tried to imagine her leaving, knowing she never would. It was too precious to her. Her body had grown too used to it. Stretched by the weight of wood and stone.

The man beside him took out his pipe, lit it from the coils. He waved one hand, punctuating the air. 'You're an intelligent man, Mister Daniel. Think on it. Baghdad is a plague pit. Foul, if you don't mind me saying. There are Jews in London, and doing very well thank you. Only last month I read in *The Times* that there are Semites at the Bar. And a good thing. Now then, how would you describe your own business, sir? Jewels in the main, would it be?'

'Jewels?' He had never thought of anything as his business.

'Well, so then London is your place. The jewellers' Mecca. All the best goldsmiths, like your Rundell and Bridge's. All the best stones and customers. I recall a sale a year or two ago – I've probably the article somewhere, but be that as it may – the buyer was an English banker, Thomas Hope. And the jewel was a blue diamond. Blue, mark you. The story went that it was part of an even greater stone. There was a fellow called Tavern, you see, who sold it to the king of France – I forget what came next. Suffice to say that this gem bought by Hope is a chip off the block of the old diamond. A chip, you understand. Now, sir. Hazard a guess to what it weighed.'

He shook his head.

'Forty-four and a half. Carats. I tell you it's true, and *The Times* carried it. Imagine such a diamond. That, my friend, is London.'

Daniel imagined it. He sat in the dark under the liquorice trees and pictured the jewel and the city. Their cold lines and planes. Rachel, pressing limes. The natural curvature of her arms and face.

Summer. The brothers stood by the Gate of Darkness. The sun

was hot and rising. The sweat itched in their beards. All morning they had been waiting for Ibrahim. And as they waited, they talked. They argued about the time that day and night began, the colour of the face of God, clockworks and women, bullets and singing, the ways of sowing emmer wheat, the facts of cosmography. One was taller than the other. One was broader than the other. The gate traffic milled around them.

'So you still believe that the earth is a plane.'

'Yes.'

'With oceans falling off its edges.'

'Edges, ends. Yes.'

'And fish? Salman?'

'A number of fish must fall.'

'What number?'

'I don't know.'

'So. And meanwhile, we are circled by the sun.'

'Circled by the sun, and the moon. And beyond them, the stars. And beyond them, our God.'

Salman looked away. Olive trees glittered on the high ground. Green-silver, green-silver. The road edged under them, and the river. Two lines running south between alluvial fields.

He waited for Daniel to start arguing again. His own voice sounded blunt in his ears. He didn't mind that. He felt blunt. He often felt blunt. And he always felt it was better to be honest.

'Our God, of course,' said Daniel. 'Does he circle us too?'

'Brother, what are you doing here? Why can't you go home and let me work?'

'Because today I feel like talking. I will stop when Ibrahim arrives. Really, I am interested in this circling God. He is making me dizzy. Tell me, because I would like to see it, what time does He rise and set tomorrow?'

Salman turned on his brother. 'Listen to yourself! Use a little common sense. There is a difference between discussion and blasphemy.'

Daniel shrugged. He was thinner than Salman, with a tall man's clumsiness. At any rate, it had been years since they had fought physically. At twenty-two his beard was already streaked with grey. 'I don't mean to insult anyone. I am only saying that the world that has been made is a sphere.'

'I know what you say.'

There was a cloud of dust far off down the road now. Salman couldn't see if it was Ibrahim. He hawked and spat in the roadside dirt.

'A sphere! And your English friend tells you it circles the sun and moon.'

'No. Only the sun.'

'Only the sun, of course. And the moon?'

'The moon orbits the earth.'

'How clever. Everything circles everything else. It sounds like a kind of children's dance. What circles the moon? The stars?'

'No. Each sphere also rotates on its own. The earth, the moon and sun. They spin through space. The older Muslims will tell you the same. It is not unlike a dance.'

Salman began to laugh. There was a crowd of men at the Gate of Darkness, drovers and farmers. A few of them looked round at the sound. Daniel watched their faces. The big, wide features of the Sumer, the epicanthal folds of Mongols, the lantern jaws of the Beduin. All of them curious or suspicious, none of them smiling. He glanced back at his brother.

'What I am saying is clearly true.'

'Clear as a fart in a copper bazaar. The earth is spinning?'

Daniel nodded, and Salman leant towards his brother. 'Then jump, and surely it will go on without you. If you can leap up here and come down arse-deep in river mud, I'll believe the whole universe is round. Until then, you can keep your foreign bull-shit to yourself.'

'Tigris! 'Phrates! *Salaam aleicum.* You look like you are about to kill one another.'

They stepped apart like children caught fighting. Daniel shaded his eyes. Ibrahim was leading his horse towards them. His face was lined, smiling. He could have been Mehmet's son, cousin, brother. Beyond him were the shapes of other men and horses, merged together in the dust.

Salman clapped his brother on the shoulder and walked away from him. 'Ibrahim! *Wa aleicum es.* You are a few hours late.'

'I apologise. There are sandstorms to the south.' The marshlander's Arabic was accented, lilting. He called over his shoulder to the other riders. They came closer to the city walls. Circling the crowd at the gate, not getting too near. Salman saw the way Ibrahim watched them. Pained, critical.

'How is Mehmet?'

'Weary.' Ibrahim turned his smiling mask again. 'I will always be grateful that you brought him to us. I have something special for you today.'

'Not another musical keyboard, I hope.'

Ibrahim shook his head, unbuckling his saddlebag, bringing out a bundle wrapped in muslin. It fitted neatly in his arms. He passed it to Salman, not letting it go until he was sure the other man had it. It was heavier than Salman had expected. Under the muslin, the bundle was cold. He smiled. Rocked it. 'What is this? A child from Babylon?'

'Not a child.' Ibrahim glanced round at the other tribesmen again. They were not only staying away from the city gate, Salman saw, but from him. Or from the bundle.

He looked back at his brother. Daniel was by the gates, in the private company of his own thoughts. Salman resisted the impulse to call out to him. He didn't need help. He set the bundle down on the ground and unwrapped the layers of muslin.

Inside was an earthenware jar. The mouth was sealed with bitumen. The pottery itself was engraved with characters. Salman recognised them as Arabic. The shapes were subtly unfamiliar. He nudged the jar with one hand. There was a scuttle and a rustling. Something hard. Something soft.

He glanced up at Ibrahim sharply, curious to see his face. The sun was behind him, darkening the expression. The Marsh Arab was staring at the jar with a mesmerised fascination. Like a cat watching shadows.

For no reason, Salman thought of Mehmet's children. The three girls buried alive. Bundles of muslin in the wet ground. 'Ibrahim.' He shook his head, thinking what he meant to say. 'I'm not sure this is something I want.'

'Oh no. You do.'

'Are you sure?'

'Yes.'

He stood up. Clapped his hands free of the jar's touch. 'Then put me out of my misery. Tell me what it is.'

A wind picked up dust devils on the road. It caught the length of muslin at their feet. Ibrahim bent down and began to roll it around his hand, neat as a turban. A careful man of an economical race, wasting nothing. 'There is a place not far from Basra, an old town that has been left to the desert. The sandstorms uncovered it a fortnight ago. We found this container there. The inscription is hard to read but our old people know it. They say that this jar contains the medicines of a prince.'

'Medicines? You surprise me. From the way your friends are acting, I thought it must be a plague.'

They watched the marshlanders together. The hardness of Ibrahim's face relaxed. 'My cousins are uneducated and superstitious. They say that this kind of medicine is not a part of Islam. Therefore it is an unholy power. A black magic. They say it has sent them bad dreams. They believe Allah will curse us if we keep it. Since I wish to live with them, I cannot possess the contents of this jar. And for all I know they may be right.'

Salman touched the jar with the tip of his sandal. 'For all I know they may be right too. Their Allah is my Jehovah. Ibrahim, what do I want with old medicines?'

'Medicines is the old name for them. Now we would think of them more as amulets.'

'Magic.'

'Good luck stones. Fetishes. East of Persia, they have things like this. They call them *nauratan*. They are fetishes set with nine jewels. And here, this writing says these are the amulets of a prince. Do you understand?'

'You are suggesting this –' he looked down at the vessel again. It wasn't really a jar. There was no lip or handle. The clay was thick and rough. An ugly object, built for a long containment '– this thing contains jewels.'

It lay between them. They looked down at its squat weight. It was nearer Salman than Ibrahim now. Without having to ask, he knew that if he picked it up now, the vessel would be his. All he had to do was claim it.

He shrugged. 'Well, this is certainly interesting. But if you are right about it, I cannot afford to buy it from you. What would it be worth?'

'Whatever someone would give for it.'

'Some price that would pull my tongue out, I'm sure. And if

you are wrong, I don't want it. I deal in trinkets and paraffin, not–'

Ibrahim raised his hand, claiming the air. His teeth were the colour of old ivory, Salman thought. Relics and antiquities. 'Salman ben Levy bar Israel, I have never bartered with you for profit. You must have wondered why I travel so far north. Do you think we have any need to come to the Turkish cities we hate, just for paraffin and pipes?'

He stopped talking. Salman could think of nothing to say. The marshlander leaned towards him. His breath smelt of goat meat. 'Friend, you brought someone back who had been dead to me. Something that is worth any price. I have always come here to repay that debt.' He stepped away. 'The jar is for you and yours.'

Behind them, a small man began to argue about his gate toll with the Turkish guards. Salman listened to his shrill, harsh voice. He could smell fish in the man's cart. Rank carp baking in the sun. He looked back. Daniel was watching him and Ibrahim. The two men, and the jar between them. He began to walk towards Salman, tall and stooping, and as he did so Salman felt a jolt of emotion. A possessive anger, as if Daniel might take Ibrahim's gift from him.

He bent and picked up the dull earthenware vessel. He held it in both hands while Ibrahim replaced the muslin in his saddle-bag, climbed onto his horse, turned it south.

Daniel arrived beside him. He had walked fast, and his breath came quickly. 'You have finished already? What have the marsh-landers found for us?'

'Amulets.'

The sky was brighter now. The wind seemed to intensify the light. As the Marsh Arabs started off Salman felt an intimation of loss and he called out. 'Ibrahim! We will see you again. Next month, yes?'

The horses and the wind were picking up storms of dust. The shapes of the riders merged together. One of them raised a hand, but Salman couldn't see if it was Ibrahim or another man. He watched as they rode away southwards. He knew he would never see them again.

'Amulets?'

He looked at Daniel. Behind him the dust was already settling, and Salman could make out the olive trees on the high ground. They winked like spearheads. Green-silver, green-silver.

'What kind of amulets?'

The house was empty. Rachel was still out at work. In the kitchen Salman set the jar down. Faintly Daniel could smell yesterday's fire. Cold rice. Terebinth wood.

He put his hand out and touched the jar. Its earthenware was pitted. The old script had been carved while the clay was still wet. He could make out only fragments. A word that might once have meant *medicine*. He peered at the seal, nicked it, talking quietly, mostly to himself, speaking his thoughts.

'There is metal under the bitumen. It looks rusted shut. Bronze or copper, I think. This is an odd thing.' He rocked the vessel on its base and heard the scurry of objects inside. Something soft, something hard. There was a repulsiveness about the sounds, and he stepped away and spoke up. 'These inscriptions – there are scholars in al-Karkh who could read them for us. Hüseyin the Imam . . .'

He looked up. Salman was beside him. In his hands was Rachel's meat cleaver, a heavy wedge of iron. Daniel laughed gently. A quiet man. Not speaking, keeping his thoughts to himself.

'I want to open it.'

'Now?' Daniel watched his brother's eyes. They had become hard. Eager in a way he hadn't seen for years. It reminded him of the way Salman had looked the day he had given Rachel the diamond dust.

'Why not? It is only a jar.'

'We would be better to wait.'

'For what?'

And Daniel said nothing, only shrugged and stepped back. Not stopping his brother, then or later. Not asking himself, yet, if he could. He watched Salman set the cleaver flat against the vessel. There was an excitement in his eyes, and also something darker, prefigured. Daniel could see it faintly, like the shadows of cataracts.

Avidity. It was that he stepped back from. Not Salman, who righted the vessel, steadied it, and split it open.

I picture the Brethren. Not the shoulder-knot of Burgundy, but the stones which gave the jewel its name. Spinels from Persian Badakshân, on the banks of the Shignân. Three stones as big as wishes.

In some paintings they are almost black, or it may be that the pigment of the paint itself has darkened over centuries. In others they are thick red, like a bottle-depth of Burgundy. They stand out as flat blocks of colour. Their numerical arrangement holds the eye. It is unusual in jewellery to have three equal stones with none predominant. Three is an uneasy number. It suggests cabals, talismans, trinities.

I can see them with my eyes shut. Their plaques are held by hooks and wishbones of gold. They reflect the light without catching it. They stain it red and violet.

The table cut is a simple way of working precious stone. I think of it as more primitive than the cabochon, because it echoes the natural facets of a crystal in a way that a dome does not. It is effective because it has a minimum of artifice. It is all the Brethren rubies need, because they are beautiful in themselves. There are people who say the beauty of jewels arises from their rarity, as if the sky or the sea becomes ugly or mundane with familiarity. Some things are intrinsically beautiful. When the balases lay on the lapidary's bench like raw meat waiting to be cut, they were already desirable. Go further. When they were still underground, the aluminium oxide reacting with the rogue atom of magnesium, they were already precious. It took five hundred, a thousand years for them to grow. I imagine them underfoot. The soulless lives of stones. It takes a long time to make the perfect jewel.

I follow the trail of the balas rubies. They changed hands quickly, in a way the complete knot rarely did. I have traced the possessors as well as I can, because sometimes great stones return to the places they have been. From this distance of time, the desire involved in the transactions is lost. There is an illusion of loathing in the way the stones are passed so rapidly from hand to hand, as if they were somehow dangerous; though no part of the Three Brethren has been cursed, not at any time I am aware of. Among old jewels it is unusual in its curselessness.

After the death of the last great Mogul emperor, the balases are invisible for more than half a century. It is 1762 before I find their owner again, and then only as he is in the act of giving them away. His name is Mohammed Ali Khan. His title is Nawab of Arcot, Nabob of the East India Company of England, Sovereign of the Carnatic.

He wraps the Brethren stones in grey silk. He is sending them to England as a gift. A small gift, a gesture from one king to another. He sits in a long room, verandahs facing east and west, but without servants. The palace is quiet, and he is arranging the jewels himself. They are more than he can afford to give. More than he has ever been able to afford.

There is a line of sweat where his turban presses against his forehead. It is dark by the time he has finished his chore. Mohammed Ali Khan unwinds his headcloth. For the first time he notices that his hair is going white. There are thick strands among the darker curls, tough as the hair of a dead man.

He stops, hands raised to his head, listening. There are people speaking English outside the door, creditors from the Company, and he turns away, closing his eyes. From beyond the verandahs comes the wordless sound of the sea. He listens to it until the voices are all gone.

Mohammed reminds me of Charles the Bold of Burgundy. As human beings they are not alike, but there are similarities in the way they dealt with power. I look at images of the last Valois duke, and know that if I reached out to touch him he would flinch away from my hand. Whereas Mohammed would take it. He would press my fingers against his protuberant, sensual lips. He is a man who lived for the sensation of touch. His skin has been polished smooth by lovers.

He is a warm man, and Charles was cold. But they were alike because they had the same weakness. They were both men obsessed with the appearance of strength, even at the expense of the strength itself. Mohammed loved the physical weight of power, the weapons and the Mogul jewels. In paintings, his hands are always full. He wears bracers of pearls around his biceps and daggers in his sash. A diamond medallion around his neck and a scimitar in each fist. In one painting by Willison his sword hand rests on a long footman's sabre. A steel spike curves up from the inversed hilt. Mohammed's fingers curve gently around it.

Charles wore jewelled hats and steel. The Nawab of Arcot dressed in feathers and silk. There is the portrait of Mohammed in white, an apparition on a blood-red carpet. Mohammed in cream, a pearly king in curly slippers. The one and only truly original Mohammed, up to his neck in rich thick pink.

He wrapped himself in silks as if he was the jewel. He saw himself as part of India's new royalty. Not a puppet ruler, but an ally and equal of the kings of England. The East India Company thought of him differently. In the letters of the Army of Acquisition, Mohammed is discussed as a client or an employee. An expendable commodity. A temp.

It was the Company that put Mohammed where he was, and the Company that finished him. In 1751 the succession of Arcot had been divided. The French had backed the more legitimate candidate, and so the English – by choice as well as necessity – had supported the more energetic usurper. Mohammed gained his throne with the help of East India Company bayonets, and from that beginning he was up to his neck in more than pink silk. The Company men were all around him, stifling him with their suggestions and propositions, their ends and means.

The last Valois duke had ruled a state with the riches to support him. Mohammed did not. Arcot was a coastal province, a long stretch of land south of the Krishna river. It had been torn by centuries of fighting between the Muslims and Marâthâs, the French and the English, the French and the Muslims, and it could not afford its new Nawab. When Arcot couldn't buy Mohammed what he needed, he turned to the Company.

They gave him what he wanted. They lent him silver and soldiers, as the occasion demanded. Their interest rates began at a competitive thirty-six per cent, moving down to twenty per cent as their client's resources ran thin.

Half a century before the Europeans really got their hooks into Asia, Mohammed was a victim of foreign debt. As the interest on his loans remained unpaid, the sums involved became fantastically great. They dominated the correspondences of the East India Company for years. Faced with bankruptcy, Mohammed tried to bribe the Council of Madras with Arcot silver rupees. When that didn't work, he sent outspoken complaints to George the Third. The young king sent back small gifts and cordial assurances. High hopes but no help. The two men never met. They were worlds apart.

The letters Mohammed sent to George are in the Oriental Rooms of the British Library. They are still contained in the Nawab's mailbag. It is made of pink silk. It is tied shut with gold tinsel.

In the paintings – and there are many – he always looks amused, tolerant. He is almost smiling, almost not smiling. It is the expression of a boxer posing at a photo call. Whatever his sensualities or weaknesses, Mohammed was not a gentle man. In politics and war he was as vicious as the English who supported him. If he had not been capable of violence, he would not have survived. Mohammed once had an enemy decapitated, his head tied to war camels, dragged four times around his city walls, placed in a box and sent to the Imperial court for the Emperor's pleasure. In the studios of his painters he is a Prince Naseem. The truly original Mohammed Ali. Swords out, gloves up.

He died old and powerless, but in the clothes of a king. He had everything he wanted. By then he had already sent the Brethren stones away. A small gift between equals, from one king to another. A box of jewels sent with four ambassadors on the Company ship *Valentine*.

Mohammed's presents were so superb that when they reached Buckingham Palace, the King of the first British Empire was almost offended by their opulence. Queen Charlotte liked them better, and she wore them for the rest of her life. The jewels lit up her fine, broad features, echoes of her mulatto ancestry. She gained more from Mohammed's hopeless gesture than the Nawab ever did. His packages of silk contained diamonds the size of apricot stones, ropes of riverine pearls, and three old balases: *A trio of the most spectacular flat almandine rubies, matched one for the next in the superiority of their weight and water.*

The Brethren stones had returned to the rulers of Europe. When Charlotte died, Mohammed's gifts passed to her daughter, Mary Louise Victoria of Saxe-Coburg-Gotha. A generation later, Mary Louise left them to her own daughter. She was born in 1819, and her name was Victoria Alexandrina Guelph. Her mother called her Drina. She was never amused by the nickname. Even as a child, she signed herself Victoria.

Queen Victoria was less than five feet tall. Her eyes were fish-like, protuberant, china-blue. There was a stoniness in the way they settled on the world. When she was lost in thought Victoria had a habit of gaping, like a carp.

Her upper lip was slightly deformed. Her voice was startlingly beautiful, bell-sweet. Her character was hard and clear. She always got what she wanted.

There is a miniature of her, aged eight, by Plant, in which she herself is a miniature. A porcelain doll, with a brooch portrait on her satin dress. A hall-of-mirrors of smallnesses. She did not grow up certain of any power. There were many claims to the throne of England. It was years before people began to see Victoria as queen-in-waiting.

She spent her childhood locked away in the crumbling gilt rooms and stale safety of Kensington Palace. It was like being trapped inside a wedding cake. Victoria Guelph grew up to be meticulously honest: but she was also possessive. Avid as only the once poor and suddenly rich can be.

She lived at the heart of the biggest empire the world has known. It was a place of incomparable wealth. It was a time whose poverty was distinguished from that of the Middle Ages only by its veneer of coal dust. The life-expectancy of the working class was twenty-two. People remember Victoria Guelph as a popular queen, but she was as hated as any ruler. By the time of Albert's death and her retirement from public life in 1861, Victoria had survived three assassination attempts. The third was by John Bean, a hunchbacked boy, who raised a gun to the royal carriage in the Mall. His escape was followed by the arrest and rounding up of every hunchback in London. Victoria's England was a place and time of extreme richness and brutality.

The East India Company and its imitators brought her jewels like the heads of the vanquished. From India, the Army of Acquisition brought Victoria the Koh-i-Nur and the Timur Ruby – the jewels that Aurungzeb had once shown to the merchant Jean-Baptiste Tavernier. From Ceylon, she received the three-hundred-and-thirteen-carat cat's-eye of Kandy, which remains the largest stone of its kind on the surface of the earth. Victoria was sent the Great Cross of the South from Australia – a monstrous, naturally fused mass of nine pearls; and black opals from Oceania, which she distributed to her family and friends, like sweeties.

She loved stones, and rubies above all else. She always got what she loved. Albert's wedding present to her was a suite of opals and diamonds to his own design. By 1855 she was wearing so many rings on every fat finger she could hardly hold a knife and fork. Over her life, she spent £158,887 on gems at Garrard's alone.

She was a little woman, with cold eyes and a sweet voice. A cold, sweet woman. I am not interested in her personally. What draws me to her is that she remade the Three Brethren. I would like to know how she did that. Three hundred years after Bloody Mary and Elizabeth wore the knot on their breasts, Victoria did the same. She inherited the rubies. The pearls she came to possess along with the throne, and those set in the crown today bear no relation to the original Queen Elizabeth's Earrings in either colouration or quality. These trails had come together again. Which leaves only one stone to follow, and that is the diamond.

There is almost no trail. I have nearly no story to tell. The diamond lost by the Prince of Herrings was found by the Queen of England, but the way it travelled is invisible, like a brilliant dropped into water. For a long time, when I began to look for the Brethren, I believed the old diamond had been burned in the far north of Holland, or broken and cut into anonymous stones. I have spent five years finding its one reference, buried in the fading copperplate scrawl of a goldsmith's assistant.

The question I ask myself now is not whether the diamond survived. It isn't where Victoria acquired the stone, although that would be interesting and, perhaps, useful to know. I wonder sometimes whether the East India Company brought it to her, like a head on a plate, or whether it was another heirloom, like her grandmother's Indian rubies.

I have followed the jewel through four hundred and forty years and across two continents. It isn't enough. It means nothing, because Victoria Guelph is the last owner of the Brethren I can trace. After her, the jewel is never seen again. The question I ask myself is not who brought the Brethren to Queen Victoria, but who stole it from her.

In 1842 an autobiography was published by George Fox. It

was an account of Fox's career as a jeweller and shopman. George had spent his life working for the Crown Goldsmiths, Rundell and Bridge's. Rundell's was the most successful jewellers of its time, but in the decade Victoria assumed the throne that time had already passed. Under the shadow of St Paul's, the shop on Ludgate Hill became quieter every season. It closed down the year Fox wrote his exposé.

Fox's account is a piece of Victorian street literature, eccentrically written, mildly scandalous, veering between painstaking factual precision with regard to stones and a degree of poetic licence in its dealings with people. The original is bound in leather the colour of verdigris with marbled endpapers. It smells of tar.

The company's founder was Philip Rundell. 'He was a first-rate judge of the quality of diamonds and jewels of every kind,' Fox wrote.

No man nor lady ever felt more strongly that love of stones that led Mr Rundell to make such a noise in the world and to amass such riches. It might well be said no plain man nor lady, since of all our customers it was only Her Most Gentle Majesty the young Queen which showed a hunger for good stones like that of Mr Rundell. Indeed, this coming together of like minds might be seen in Her Majesty's commissions to Rundell's successors, which were for the most private and precious jewels, and which continued to arrive until the last days of the company. It was Rundell's that set the plain stone picked from a Scotch beach by Prince Albert, to be worn at the fair and ample bosom of his Queen, and Rundell's that made the brooches of sapphire and diamond to Her Majesty's own design for the Royal Wedding. And moreover, it was Rundell's who worked the finest and most romantic ornament worn in private by Her Majesty, and since wickedly stolen. This was a triangle of simple gold set with great espinela rubies and pearls good in parts. And at the centre of this work was a most superb and ancient jewel, cut to a point, in the style of what is known in the Trade as a Writing Diamond.

※

The jar split open. It broke with the *crock* of an animal skull in the

97

butcher's souk. It lay between the brothers like an accident.

Salman had brought the cleaver down so heavily that it had struck through the pottery into the kitchen table, the square front tip of the blade adding its scar to the wood. Now he tugged it loose, set it flat beside him, and leant forwards.

The earthenware had broken inwards, thick halves filling with their own fragments. Before he noticed anything else, Salman saw that there were two fingerprints in the fired clay. They were thin, smudged where the potter had reached the wet mouth upwards from its own interior.

He bent to look at the paired impressions. The air was furred with the reek of animal rot. He stepped back from its poisonous intensity and dry-retched, once, twice. He wiped his mouth with his hand and cursed in Arabic. 'That dog Ibrahim. This is no gift. It smells like shit from a plague pit.'

'Stale air.' Daniel picked up the cleaver. 'Nothing more.' With its dark edge, he nudged apart the jar's broken halves.

'We should burn it.'

His voice was soft, the breathing shallow. 'If you wanted to be so cautious, you shouldn't have tried to chop the table in half.'

'Shut up.'

'You should have read the inscription. *A plague on all fat Jewish brothers*, it might say. Too late for you.'

'I told you to shut up.' The water jar stood under the kitchen window. Salman went over to it and splashed his hands and mouth, rubbing moisture into the back of his neck. He felt edgy, and he wondered if there was a desert storm coming. Sunlight fell through the shutters and patterned his skin.

'You know what I think? I think Mehmet was never allowed back. The marshlanders killed him as soon as I was gone. And now the curs are trying to kill us. This is their idea of revenge.' There were aloes in tall pots beside him, old and overgrown. Rachel kept them indoors for their sap, smoothing it on her cooking burns. In return she fed the succulents leftover water, blood, fish and bone. There was little to spare but they didn't need much. The plants poked at Salman's legs and he slapped them away angrily, like dogs.

Daniel ignored him. Between the mouth and the base of the jar lay a rubble of pottery and decayed wrappings. Silk, muslin, fur.

The layers of cloth and skins disintegrated as he touched them. A handful of stones had rolled together at their centre, like eggs in a nest.

There were half a dozen, all smooth with facets or curves. To Daniel they looked worked. He knew very little about stones. He saw that one had been shattered, by Salman's knife or the tumbling of the pebbles themselves. The chips and grains of it winked. They were green as the cells in the flesh of a lime.

'Look at this, Salman.'

'You look at it. I hope your eyes fall out.'

The light settled inside them, red as *halqûn*, blue as meat. There was writing on the curves and facets. The elaborate knotworks of old Arabic calligraphy. Daniel put the cleaver down and picked out the largest stone. It was big as the palm-muscle of his thumb, from the knuckle to the veins and tendons of the wrist. Its surface was spotted with silk dust and Daniel wiped it clean.

It was purple, with the transparency and pitted polish of old ice. One side was flatter than the other, and on the levelled face was a line of writing. He turned the inscribed stone to the shuttered afternoon light. The script was ornate. Illegible as a cipher.

'Salman.'

'What?' He had began to scrub the skin of his palms with an old pumice. When Daniel didn't answer he looked up, gave a snarling smile and put the washstone down. He walked up to the table, shaking his hands dry. The stench of rot was gone. Now there was only a staleness, and the clean smell of minerals. Daniel held the large stone up to the light. 'There are more of these in the jar. What do you call this?'

Salman took the stone and weighed it in his hand. His hard smile faded with surprise. 'Amethyst.'

'Is it worth anything?'

'I need more light.'

Daniel went to the window and opened the wickerwork shutters. From outside came the sound of one goat bell, one cicada. The summer of a dry, hot country. He breathed in the smell of the desert and felt the afternoon sun on his face.

He opened his eyes. From the lowering light, he knew that Rachel would be back before long. He wondered what she would think of this, their gift. A jar of stones. He turned back and came round the table and stood beside Salman. The two brothers together, peering upwards.

'It looks like an amulet.'

'Maybe.'

'Ibrahim didn't lie.'

'Maybe not.'

'You should look at the others.'

Salman went on turning the amethyst. He gauged the depth of its colour. The absence of fractures. When he was finished he put it down, quickly and carefully. Without speaking, he picked out the other stones. Three of them, four. Finally, five. He stood back.

'So?' Daniel watched his brother.

Salman shrugged. He dug his finger into the green grains of the broken stone. 'This was an emerald. I should be shot for it, but I think I broke it. It's still worth a little now. Good clarity, see? Not Egyptian.'

'Where else could it be from?'

'Maybe India . . . and this looks like a sapphire. I can't be certain.' He picked up one of the amulets. An inch of clear slate-blue. The light slithered along it.

'You don't know?'

Salman turned on him. 'How would I know a sapphire like this?' He put the jewel down with both hands. 'I worked with the cheap stones. Nothing like these.'

His picked up another amulet. It was a clear crystal, wide and deep as a human molar. Daniel saw that his brother was beginning to smile again. His face was still damp, but not with water. A thick oil of sweat covered him from neck to turban.

'What is that one?'

Salman's hand jerked. His fingers curved gently around the jewel. 'These? These are our way out of here.'

'Out of where?'

Salman looked at his brother, his stooping, owlish stupidity, and he laughed. 'Here. This house, this town. Where else? The streets that flood with shit and piss every time it rains. The rotten rice and the weeks without meat. The floods, Daniel, the rivers. We don't have to die of cholera, like everyone around us. We can be gone. We can be anywhere.'

It was a big grin, infectious. Daniel found himself beginning to smile too. He imagined the jar cracked open, releasing a plague of grins over Old Baghdad. He shook his head. 'Salman, I don't want to go anywhere. I am happy here.'

'No! No, you're not happy. You don't see. Look.' Salman picked up another amulet. It was an oval red stone, flattened and translucent, like a cod's eye. He pressed it into Daniel's hand. 'This, I know, is a ruby. With it, we can buy a new home anywhere. Calcutta or Bombay. Not a house with two doors. A house with twenty doors.'

Daniel held the ruby. He could feel Salman's sweat on it. He shook his head. 'Are you sure of this?'

'There is a foul in it, very small, but it is a ruby's discolouration. It is as good as a goldsmith's mark.' Salman was talking quickly now, bent over the table, picking out stones. 'A balas ruby of ten or twelve carats. This we can sell wherever we go. A fine amethyst – this is our passage. This is a milk opal, not so good. This a sapphire, I am almost sure of it. And this–' He picked up the clear jewel again, gripping it. His hand shook. He said nothing.

'We are rich then.'

Daniel was surprised by the sound of his own voice, the unhappiness in it. He didn't feel unhappy. Only cautious, as if there might still be a danger here. Not a plague from a jar but something more subtle. He tried to catch his own thoughts, but Salman was taking his hands. Pressing the clear stone into his palm.

'Rich. Do you remember the game of changing the world?'

Daniel remembered it. Despite himself, he smiled again.

'The game of changing the world. You always tried to have too many wishes. Well, now you can have anything. We can leave here. We can buy Rachel a house with twenty doors. In India we can ride horses, Daniel. Twenty horses. Horses with green turbans. Or we can go to London, if you like. You choose. I don't mind where. 'Phrates? You choose for both of us. Say yes.'

He shook his head. Not meaning to answer Salman, although it was the answer he meant to give. With the clear stone in his hand, there was no room in his head. Not even for Salman, his brother, who was half his family. The voice next to him was a buzzing incoherence. He looked down at the jewel.

It was heavier than it looked. Dense, like a bullet. It was shaped like a pyramid. Daniel felt that it was old in a way Ibrahim's jar was not, although the vessel had been dull with age, and the jewel looked as if it had been cut yesterday.

In the afternoon sun, the five facets did something extraordinary. They caught the light inside their matrix, and released it brighter than it had been before. They swallowed the sun and threw out rainbows. In those first few moments, as he held it, Daniel thought the Heart of Three Brothers was the most beautiful thing he had ever seen.

He turned it over. There was an inscription on the pyramid's base. The writing was simpler here than on the other amulets, as if the lapidary had found it difficult to carve. Daniel could almost read it. He frowned, making himself work harder.

'Daniel? You choose a place. Please, for us both.'

The words resolved themselves. He repeated them softly, only to himself. 'To keep one from ghosts.'

'Where?'

'It says it is to keep one from ghosts.'

He looked up at Salman. His wide face and dark skin. He was paler now. His hands were curled into fists. The sweat was thick on his cheeks.

'You have to come.'

He put the jewel down. He listened to the words his brother didn't say. *I cannot go alone.* Through the crystal, he could see the table. Old wood, new scars. The jewel lit them up. It made them more beautiful. Daniel spoke quietly, the way he would in a synagogue, so as to disturb nothing.

'Salman, this is our house. Our father was here, and our grandfather, and his grandfather.'

'It is rotting around us. A rotten house in a dying city.'

He spoke up. 'It is the house of our family. Because of that, Rachel will never leave it. Think of her and you'll know it's true. And I will never leave Rachel alone.'

They stood together in the long kitchen. The broken jar between them. From the Island Road came the sound of street children laughing. The broken note of a nine-holed shepherd's flute. Distantly, Daniel wondered if it was the one he had made for them. He would have to teach them to play it.

The door opened beside him and he only half-turned, knowing it would be Rachel. No one else came to the house with two doors. Not Judit or Yusuf the honey-slat seller, Yusuf the official beggar or Mehmet the lapidary. She was out of breath from the weight of her load. There was sand in the folds of her clothes, and the hem of her dress was dark with river mud. She still had the laundry basket balanced on her head, one arm raised to balance it. Now she hoisted it down to the ground. Distantly, Salman saw that she wasn't wearing her earrings.

'Boys. I see neither of you thought to bring in my drying trays. There's a storm coming.'

'You are home late.' Daniel's voice was breathless. He waited for Rachel to look up at his face, to read the tension there. Instead she walked past him to the table. She picked up a fragment of pottery. Laughed.

'So this was what all the shouting was about. The marshlander traded you this, did he? He can sell a Jew a broken pot. I'm impressed.'

'We were not shouting.' Even as he said it, Salman felt how quiet his voice was now in the darkening room. Rachel pulled a stool from under the table. Sat. The potsherd still in her hand.

'Ah. Just a little. I could hear you from some distance across the Tigris. Is this what is going to buy me a house with twenty doors?'

Daniel spoke without moving. Keeping back. 'Not that, Aunt. The stones.'

'Ah yes.' She picked through them. The milk opal, the sapphire. 'Yes. They're pretty things, aren't they? Are you sure, Salman, they're worth what you think they are?'

'No.'

'Ah.'

'Aunt – Rachel –' he bent his head, trying to get the right words out '– the stones are our chance, I'm sure of it. Perhaps God meant them for us–'

'God? Tch. Now you sound like a rich Jew. Only the wealthy love God so much.'

'But we can be rich, all of us. Old Baghdad is dying. And we are young, Daniel and I. There are other places, and better lives–'

'Yes, there are, and yes, it is. You are quite right. You are practical, Salman. You have grown into a good, practical man.' Rachel said it without smiling. Her slippers were wet and she took them off, then the socks. Underneath, her feet were curled up on themselves, the nails uncut, like the claws of dead birds. She laughed, her face in shadow. 'Look at me. I am monstrous today.' She blinked up at Salman. 'I am turning into a sirrusch.'

'Aunt–'

'I can't leave, Salman. I'm too old, too set. Your brother understands. I know you don't.' She tidied her shoes beside the stool, picked up the wet socks, hobbled to the empty hearth. Clicked her tongue. 'Daniel, where is the flint and steel?'

He moved, stooping to find the tinderbox, not speaking. Behind him Salman shook his head, his voice loosening inside him. 'We must leave!'

Rachel put down the tinderbox. 'Yes, you must. Of course. But I'm not coming with you. It is time you were both going.'

'No.' Daniel stood back, caught off guard. 'Rachel? We will not go.' The words almost a question. At the hearth Rachel bent to bank up the old ash.

'Yes you will, my love. If I say so, you will. You won't stay in this house if I do not wish it.'

He took another step back, as if he had been struck. The breath wheezed out of Rachel when she stood.

'Salman? Wrap up the stones. There is cloth in my basket. Daniel, I want you to take them to Hüseyin the Imam. I trust him better than the jewellers. He knows old Arabic, and he likes jewels. More than a man of God should. Ask him about them.'

She stood, and Daniel saw she was smiling at him. A cold, sweet woman. 'And come back soon. I don't want you gone yet.'

He went. The jewels under his arm, wrapped in hessian. It was an hour until dusk, but the bats were already hunting. He could hear them around him as he walked. Their flutter, like leather gloves shaken out.

There were words running through his head. Salman shouting, Rachel quiet. Daniel didn't want to hear them. Instead, he listened to the city around him.

Beyond the bats were the ordinary sounds of voices, calling voices home. From the lowland fields, the grieving of an ass. Far away. Beyond the city, clear air and silence. He listened to that and thought of nothing.

Hüseyin's house was quiet and unlit. Daniel knocked and waited for the servant. Next door, a goat had been tethered to the minaret pillars of the Four-Footed Mosque. Daniel watched it idly. He imagined what would happen if the goat strained so hard that a pillar came loose. The minaret toppling like a hashish smoker. Its marble feet pulled from under it.

He knocked again. No one came. The servants Daniel remembered were old Turkish women, a cook and a housekeeper, both unpleasant and half-deaf. Either characteristic might prevent them from answering the door. Between the Kurd's house and the mosque there was a dusty alley, and Daniel went down it. Along the back of the property the garden wall had fallen across a patch of waste ground. Daniel hitched up his robes and stepped over the rubble, under two overgrown pomegranate trees, up to Hüseyin's verandah.

He could see the old man now, sitting in a wicker chair, reading and smoking. The stained vase of a hookah stood beside him. Before he got too near and the Imam heard him he called out, raising a hand.

'Sir! *Salaam aleicum!*'

The old man looked up. Daniel saw he was wearing spectacles. They were too big for his face, the wire loops poking out behind his turban like the antennae of a cricket. He put down the book and waited for Daniel to climb the verandah's rotten steps.

'What are you doing in my garden? Trying to steal my pomegranates? You are a little old for that.' His voice was precise, wiry, like his body. Daniel could think of nothing to say before he was waving him in. 'Sit down, sit down. You want tea? Nurten! Tea!'

Beside the wicker chair was a small stool. Daniel sat down. From inside the house came a clattering of pots.

'One of the Levy boys, isn't it? Which one are you?'

'Daniel, Imam. I came to sell you three old seals, from the mounds of the Palace of Nineveh. It was some months ago.'

'So you did. I had forgotten.'

'I am sorry to bother you.'

'Well, you do. And my book is interesting.' The old Kurd picked up the volume. Daniel saw that the title was in English. It was nothing he could understand. 'I would like to read until Nurten comes. Then we can talk. Sit quietly.'

'Yes, Imam.'

He sat. Beside and above him, Hüseyin sipped smoke from the hookah. The smell of it hung low over the two men. Daniel looked around at the verandah, the unkempt garden beyond it. He had never been inside the Imam's house for long as a trader, but he remembered it from the time Salman had left home, years ago. He had come here then with Rachel, as they looked for the lost child. The atmosphere had not changed. It was a ramshackle, open house, the sense of indoors and outdoors blurred by the quantities of balconies and terraces, courtyards, roof gardens. He saw now that the house reflected the character of the Imam. It took confidence to live in such an open space. A trust in God, or a carelessness.

The bundle of stones rested on his knees. Nurten came out with tea. Her face and hands were stained like the vase of the hookah. The Imam sighed, put down his book again, took off his spectacles, and looked straight at Daniel. Waiting.

He unwrapped the stones. It was not necessary for him to talk. When they were all revealed Hüseyin put his spectacles back on. Clumsily, not taking his eyes off the jewels. He reached across for them and Daniel lifted the cloth into the Imam's lap. He waited. The tea cooled beside him.

'May I ask where you got these?'

His voice was softer now. The form of address more polite. He was turning the amethyst in his hands. The light turning with it.

'We were given them. My brother was given them.'

'A gift?' He peered at Daniel. The spectacles had slid sideways. He prodded them back straight.

'Yes.'

Slowly, the Kurd looked away. 'Well. You have generous friends.'

In the quiet he could hear someone crying, streets away. A woman or child. When it stopped, he spoke to break the silence. 'We deal with the marshlanders.'

'Do you. But your brother is apprenticed as a lapidary, I seem to recall. You don't need my help with stones.'

'We can't read the Arabic.' He picked up the tea in its small glass. Already it was cold. He put it down. 'And my brother worked only with cheap stones. He says these–

'These are not cheap stones. I see. Well, this one is amethyst. And it was not written by the Marsh Arabs.' The Imam held the writing aslant to the faint light. *To keep the fields from locusts. A talisman of some kind. I think the script is Indian. Not ancient. More old-fashioned.'* He put the amethyst down. 'Who did the marshlanders steal these from?'

Daniel shook his head. Already the old man was picking up the other stones. Reading their hard, cold scripts. *'Against toothache. This is an opal. And this, I do believe, is a sapphire. For the poison of scorpions. And this a ruby of some description, from its size I would guess a balas. To make men good. And this–'*

He picked up the clear jewel. Daniel repeated the passage as Hüseyin squinted at it. He whispered it. 'To keep one from ghosts.'

'You can read this?'

Daniel nodded. The Imam was looking at him again, long and hard, his face still snarled up from squinting. The jewel was still in his hands.

'Yes. You always were an intelligent boy. You should be in the priesthood, with a head like yours. Not hawking and trading.'

The jewel pinched between his fingers. The knuckles white. Daniel kept his eyes on it.

'What is that one made of?'

'This? Spinel, maybe. Or *yâqut*, zircon. What did you think?'

He shrugged. 'It is very beautiful. I thought it might be a diamond.'

'Diamond?' Hüseyin jerked forward in his wicker chair. His arms on its arms, elbows stuck out. Like a cricket, thought Daniel again. 'Diamond! Ha! ha! My God, boy. If this were diamond, it would buy you the whole of Baghdad, old and new. For what that would be worth.'

Daniel watched as he put the clear jewel down. It seemed to him that the Imam's fingers lingered on it. Only for a moment.

'Still, as it is you are rich men. I am glad for you. Where will you go, eh? Bombay? Sassoon ben Salih is doing good business there, I hear. You could do worse. India is best, eh?'

'No.' Daniel stood up. 'Thank you, Imam. You have been most kind. I must go now. My family will be waiting for me.'

The stones were still on the old man's lap. Unwrapped. The

107

last light gleamed in them and was gone. 'Wait, boy. You want something to eat? Stay with me. Talk. No?'

Hüseyin wrapped the stones with slow reluctance. When he was finished Daniel took them from him and left the way he had come. At the front of the house he began to walk north on the Island Road, towards home. But at the junction with Khadimain Road he turned east. Walking for the sake of it, down into the Old City.

The bundle of hessian felt warm under his arm. He kept his muscle tight against it. Around him lamps were starting to be lit in the wooden houses. In the Souk Hannoun the butchers were closing up their cages of chickens, the shohet slaughterers cleaning their knives at the old street fountain. Daniel walked past them, down the muddy roads to the city docks.

The Tigris was quiet. He stood by the fishing boats and river ships and listened to it, the faint hush of its tides. Overhead, across the water, the Citadel loomed. The battlements still red where the sunset reached them.

He thought of the stones. He thought of nothing. The city around him, which he knew was dying. He tried to keep it in his mind. So that when he was gone from here, he would forget nothing of it.

He turned back. It was uphill to the house with two doors. The low roads were mired and he trudged, bent over his bundle, the tiredness settling into him. The house was dark and he went in without lighting the hallway lamp. He tried to picture it all around him. The mezuzah in the eastern door. The pattern of the hall tiles, that could change according to the direction from which you came. The atmosphere of the rooms. The valency of light.

He walked through to Judit's room. There was bedding here, ready for the winter. Daniel laid it out by the western door, where the vines shouldered their ways through the shutters. He undressed in the darkness. The air was warm against his naked skin. He unwrapped the stones, lay down and slept with them beside him.

He was alone in sleep. On the flat roof his brother lay awake, the mosquitoes chiming in the air above him. The breeze moved across him, warm as his skin. Salman dreamed of London with his eyes open. An empire on which the sun never set. New lives.

In the kitchen Rachel sat at the scarred table. She had made rice for Daniel. It sat in the bowl, cooling, unnecessary. The terebinth box was open in front of her. She took out the circumcision gowns and smoothed them in her hands. Waistcoats for babies. Brothers and brothers.

The buttons of coral and turquoise were cold against her fingers. She held them, trying to make them warm. She folded the gowns gently and cried to herself. Not gently, but silently. Her face monstrous with sorrow.

And in Judit's room, Daniel slept in the humid air. The storm was still hours off, and unbroken. The bundle of jewels lay open beside him. The opal, the sapphire. The Heart of Three Brothers.

It phosphoresced. Daniel was not awake to see it. In the dark of the room, the diamond began to spill light. It bubbled out of the five facets without sound. The jewel glittered for no one but itself. As if it had been woken by sunlight.

茶

I am following the traces of a broken jewel. It has been the turning point of many lives. Mine is only one.

I think of the Writing Diamond. I try to imagine it.

There is no other stone like diamond. It has particular qualities of purity, self-possession, and weakness. On the Moh scale of hardness the diamond is ten, the maximum from which all the rest are measured; but this is deceptive. For one thing, diamond is the only gem which will combust, burning with a clear, quick white flame. It leaves no ash. It is as if the crystal were somehow organic, like coral or amber, skin or bone. And diamond is brittle as bone. Drop a brilliant and it will shatter like glass along any internal flaw. There is hardness but no flexibility, and brittleness is an unforgiving quality.

It is a beautiful stone. A cut brilliant is spectacular. Its internal faces reflect light totally whenever it strikes them at any angle greater than 24°13′. Sometimes it can seem as if the crystal is more light than solid. There are even some diamonds which phosphoresce after exposure to the sun. They boil over, glimmering to themselves in the dark.

Still, the beauty of a brilliant is only half in the stone. The secret is in the cut – the balance of facets, the deep precision of geometry. And the brilliant wasn't finally perfected until 1917, when Marcel Talkowsky arranged the sixteen facets (each of which has its own name – skew, skill, bezel, quoin). In the history of diamonds, the brilliance of light is a recent phenomenon.

It is an elemental jewel – pure cubic carbon. Diamonds are like a mathematical solution to what a gem should be. No other jewel has that simplicity. But again, the purity is deceptive. It is only terrestrial diamonds which always have a cubic structure. Sometimes diamonds are found in meteors, and their form is hexagonal. There are even diamonds which aren't made of carbon at all, but boron, and these stones are blue as ice shadows. And there is the diamond's skin.

Hold a diamond and you touch hydrogen. The *nyf* of the stone, its rind, is overlaid with a surface of elemental explosiveness. The arrangement of atoms in the crystal is acquisitive, reaching outwards like so many hands. The hands catch what they can, taking hydrogen from the oil of your fingers or throat, or from the air. In this way the diamond makes itself a second skin.

This is the first irony of diamonds. However much people try to be near them – and people waste their lives in this way – diamonds are never touched. People kill for them, pay fortunes, lose years. In return, the stones give them coolness, light, and a surface of violence one atom deep.

This is the second irony of diamonds: the crystal is a lie. The truth is in the hydrogen. Diamonds draw violence to them like magnets. They inspire a deadliness in humanity, a morality which values stone above life. They wear death invisibly, weightlessly, as if the lives of their owners were as transient and insubstantial as air.

3

The Function of Pain

The driver wears a cheap quartz watch. Its strap catches the hairs of his wrist in its metal backbone. Each time it bites he shakes his hand and the cab swerves towards the gutter. There are street children there, searching for something to play with. Stones and dust and broken fruit.

A glass eye swings over the dashboard. Above it is the rear-view mirror. In the mirror I can see the driver's own eyes. I think he looks gentle. I know appearances are deceptive. He has long cheekbones and long eyelashes, dark and delicate, like those of a cow.

We don't talk on the way from the airport. The radio is turned up loud, fading between local stations. Turkish pop, US Airforce FM. The driver sings along in a small, absent voice. We don't talk. I'm tired from the night's transit, I can smell it on me. And I have had enough of taxi drivers.

The music shifts from Turkish to English, East to West. The driver offers me a cigarette and I take it. The smoke wakes me up. I lean against the window and look out at Asia while the Kinks play in the trapped air.

I was born, lucky me, in a land that I love. Though I'm poor, I am free.

I am looking for the woman who loves pearls. It is not yet six o'clock by the driver's watch. The window glass is already warm against my cheek. I see a mule cart between two crumbling high-rise blocks. The sound of the dawn muezzin begins. Beyond it, through it, comes the thunder of a Turkish fighter plane. I crane back to see.

When I'm grown, I shall fight. For this land I shall die, where the sun never sets.

We come to a junction crowded with trucks and ranked taxis. On the wide pavement is an empty fountain. Above the dry cascades stands a statue of Atatürk surrounded by stone children in Western clothes. And over them all loom the buttressed walls of Diyarbak'r.

I didn't think they would be so big. The ancient works are thick as houses. A London terrace with arrowslits. Black as grime in an industrial city.

From the East to the West, from the rich to the poor, Victoria fucked them all.

The driver clicks off his radio and pulls up. I feel in my pocket for money. Glött's envelope is still there, and the remaining stone of my three Sri Lankan rubies. I pinch it, feeling its hardness. It is my last little wish, the means to my ends. It only took one stone to bring me here, and another changed into pearl. I am already one step closer to the Three Brethren. If I didn't believe that, I would be nowhere at all.

The taxi driver has no change. I overpay him an amount which means nothing to me. He gets out of the yellow cab as I do, smiling the hurt smile of a shy man, waving a piece of paper.

'Please. Lady. Yes.'

It is a simple map of the city. I can make out the wall and the airport. A big *You Are Here* arrow by the taxi rank, as if a foreigner could be nowhere else. I take out the postcode envelope and the driver nods and nods. He grabs the map back and points at it, his finger crumpling the district inside the city walls. The old centre of Diyarbak'r.

I thank him. We shake hands. The watchstrap nips his skin and he flinches away. He drives back west between high-rises, towards the air terminus.

I sit under the statue of Atatürk and look at the map. Above me, the stone children offer up their stone flowers. The area inside the city walls isn't large; I could cover it in two days. But there are only two main roads, and between their cross, the warrens of backstreets are only sketched in. If Glött lives there, it won't be so easy to find her.

The sun is getting stronger. Writing shows through the lit paper. I turn it over and on the other side is a Message of Welcome from the Diyarbak'r Office of Tourism: A NEW FLAVOUR IS COMING TO DIYARBAK'R. DIYARBAK'R, RENOWNED FOR ITS BIGGEST WATERMELONS, IS ALSO THE CULTURAL AND COMMERCIAL CAPITAL OF THE REGION. DISCOVER THE ATTRACTIVENESS – IN DIYARBAK'R!

I look around. In front of me a man is trying to sell a glut harvest of withered aubergines. Women in black pick at their purple organs and scrotums. Under the city walls are costermongers grilling entrail kebaps. I see no tourists, no foreigners. I wonder if the Office of Tourism would help me find a German woman in the old city. They must have time to spare.

The sun creeps up across my chest. It is hotter than Istanbul here, and I am already travel-soiled. Every time I move I catch the muggy smell of my own sweat. It would be lovely to be out of the heat for a while. Not for too long, just a few hours' rest. The jewel can wait until I am clean.

I go and look for somewhere to wash and sleep. It takes some time. Three blocks behind the taxi rank I find a tourist district of two hotels. The larger building is called the Pansiyon Dijleh, and the smaller the Formula 1 Hotel with the 't' missing. A cart full of vulcanised shoes has overturned in the middle of the road, and I pick my way through them to the smaller building.

In the lobby a woman is vacuuming in long strokes, leaning into it. The carpet is too old to ever be clean again. She turns her Hoover off reluctantly, takes my money, gives me a key on a chequered keyring. She tells me that breakfast is extra lira and that I am allowed no visitors. Her English is better than my Turkish. She closes the room door behind me.

The bed is overhung by an air-conditioner the shape and size of a washing machine. When I turn it on the air tumbles and clatters inside it. I put down my bag and go into the shower room, switch on the light. It catches me, frozen in the washbasin mirror. I look surprised to find myself here. The skin of my face is tanned, and the faint smell of aeroplanes is on my clothes, an aftertaste of air freshener and vomit. I shuck off the shirt and chinos, throwing them out onto the bedroom floor.

When I am naked I stand in front of the mirror again. Transit is catching up with me, I look like shit. I also smell like shit and feel like shit. These are the days when I try to draw no conclusions about myself. I turn the shower on and step into its clean white noise.

The water is hot and good. I close my eyes and let the grime steam off me. I think of nothing. Not the Brethren or myself, not the woman who loves pearls. My head is cleaned out. When I'm finished I go out into the bedroom, close the blinds, and lie down on the cigarette-burned sheets. The moisture dries on my flushed skin and I sleep.

The smell of breakfast wakes me just after eight. Someone is burning sausages. I'm hungry enough for it to make me salivate. I get dressed in clean youth-regulation jeans, a Reebok towel T-shirt and sandals, walking clothes. The rest of my bag is packed, never unpacked. I check I have my notebooks, the last ruby, the conch pearl. Then I go downstairs.

The woman is still vacuuming in the same place, turning between the stairs and the entrance hall. It is a slow, lonely kind of dance. A single formula for life, a Formula 1. I go up and smile and give her the room key.

'You come back tonight?'

'Maybe.'

She looks down at the chequered keyring. 'It is a good room.'

'It was perfect. Thank you. Actually, I have to meet someone now. An old German woman, Deutsch – maybe you know her. Von Glött. Have you heard the name?'

She studies me, up and down, and turns away. Under her, the carpet has been worn to the consistency of old money or skin, and I leave her to it. Outside it's cooler and I'm glad of it. There are clouds over the city walls, long herringbones of cirrus that filter the sun. I walk towards them, into old Diyarbak'r.

It is crowded here, and the crowd is unsmiling, occupied with existence in a hard place. I am not directing myself anywhere yet, not searching for Glött with any kind of method. First I want to see the city in which she has chosen to live. I am feeling my way towards her.

I watch the people. Their clothes, hands, faces. The old women with blue tattoos on their foreheads. The mobile phone man outside the Diyarbak'r Bank, with perfume to match his Armani jacket. I watch them watching me, and the last thing I do is listen to the words and voices. The street children working themselves into a giggling hysteria of *whereareyoufrom?* and *whatisyourname?* The women warding off my evil blue eyes with a kiss and a shake of the fingers. The sleek, bored young men at corners whispering after me: *Hey fucky fucky, cheaper than tomorrow. Where are you going, pretty girl?*

I don't answer them. Not because they are dangerous, although some of them will be dangerous. Because I have no interest in them. I know where I am going, and why. It is more than most people can say for themselves.

No one lives on the main roads. The two big streets run between compass points, crossing at the centre of the old city. They are lined with banks and sixties shopping arcades, their concrete and marble already old with grime. Above the shops are windows full of dusty professional signs: *Doktor, Avukat, Profesör*.

The gutters are crowded with food stalls. I buy a paper cone of boiled chickpeas. A girl in shorts with go-faster stripes tugs at my sleeve and says something in Turkish or Kurdish, so fast I can't tell which. I give her the cone and she eats quickly, while she has the chance.

The life of the city increases towards its heart. By the time I arrive at the crossroads the mucky streets have been swallowed up in a bazaar of technicolour plastic buckets, clotted cream, slats of honey. Crates of grapes, sacks of sumac. A fishmonger waits behind plates of Tigris carp, a smith mends an adze in shafts of blowtorched sunlight. Without even realising I have done it, I step off the main road, into the backstreets.

The sound changes first, then the light. A jet passes overhead and its sonic boom echoes down distantly, muffled by rooftops. I look up from a cart of burgundy armchairs and find I don't know where the sun is. My sense of direction leaves me. It only takes a second. I don't even have a name for the space I am standing in. Not a backstreet, only the space left by buildings.

The buyers and sellers mill around me. By necessity, people are closer here. I feel a hand caress the skin of my arm, from elbow to armpit, but when I turn there is no one to face. The hubbub of the crowd rises and falls, peaks and troughs. When I feel ready, I start to move again.

This is a different kind of Diyarbak'r. The old quarters feel permanent in a way the main roads and high-rise blocks do not. There is a sense of travelling backwards through time. I wonder if there is a conversion rate. One year back for every ten miles east. But it is not that simple: it is more real than that. I am not in a previous century here. Only a different one.

I stop by a meat market and buy bony shish kebap from a

butcher's wife. There are low stools and I sit and eat with my overnight bag tucked between my feet. Beside me, the sun comes through a side of goat. The meat stained with light. The kebap woman brings me a metal bowl of drinking yogurt with ice. I wash away the taste of salt and fat, get up, and keep going.

Now I am off the main roads, the street children follow me more openly. One of them has a plastic cone trumpet and he blows it, the note split with his effort. Each time I smile at him he skitters sideways, but he doesn't give up. I don't mind him. The men watch me more obviously here too. The children keep them back.

I feel my way. If she lives anywhere in Diyarbak'r I guess Glött will be here, in the old city. Often the snickets open into plain squares, washing strung out to dry over scrubbed concrete. Twice, though, I come to the locked gates of bigger houses. Through the bars I can hear doves and water. There are courtyards in there, striped colonnades of black and white stone, introspective windows. Wealth turned in on itself.

I take my time, looking at Diyarbak'r. I do it because Glött will have done the same. Jewels are the epitome of every physical thing – book, watch, city, face – that anyone ever covets. And those who love jewels tend to be covetous people. I look for what the German might desire. It is the only thing I know about her.

It is not a pure thing, the love of stones. I have never thought of it like that. Whatever else jewels mean – the memories and wishes they are bound up in – they always become tainted with something else. It is the irrevocable power of what is precious. I walk through the City of the Black Walls and think of the Three Brethren, its hooks and spurs. But then I always do.

The alleys open into a gold market, a warren of shops all selling the same charm bracelets and medallion-woman necklaces. I have no time or inclination to buy here, but at the end of the arcade is a lapidary's workshop with a window full of unset gems. Inside, two men with fine white beards offer me a Roman signet. It is a good seal, worked from carnelian, to which wax won't stick; but the carving isn't older than the lapidaries themselves.

I give them back the signet and buy an old Persian talisman instead, a pale turquoise inscribed with Cufic script. It is tenth or eleventh century, maybe twelfth, no later. The lapidaries ask for five dollars and I give them fifteen. It is worth many times that.

Their living is more or less honest, and so is mine.

Outside I catch a glimpse of the sun. It is past noon now. I walk against the crowd, moving east, and then the crowds give way to sudden desertion. I begin to turn the wrong corners. They lead to dead ends, crannies, rookeries. A man slumped on a rotten sofa with his hand on his scabbed penis. A rubbish heap full of new-born kittens and the smell of warm meat. The street children tug at my trousers, trying to lead me away. I go on without them for five minutes, ten. The alleyways are deserted. The sound of the plastic trumpet horn fades away.

I round one last corner and the city wall is in front of me, black and broken. The fortifications have crumbled away down a sheer cliff. I walk to the edge. The ground breaks up at my feet and I put a hand out to the basalt blocks to stop myself from falling.

Half a mile away the Tigris crawls. It is low in the heat, and the landscape is flat and dull around it. In the far distance there are mesas where the river basin rises to the mountains. I have walked across the old city, from west to east. I turn around, looking back the way I have come.

This is a quiet quarter. Somewhere there is a cage of birds, the nasal *me-me* of small finches. Nearby there is a woman's voice singing to the rhythm of her work. In the narrow streets I can hear the creak of a rusty bicycle being pushed along, foot by foot.

It echoes against the high walls, coming closer. An old man limps out of the alley to my left. He is wearing a blue cardigan and a red baseball cap. He has no bicycle. The noise is coming from his false right leg.

Halfway across the clearing the man stops and leans back. The woman is no longer singing, and the cagebirds have gone quiet. Everything waits on the sound of the old man's prosthesis. He turns his head and looks at me. Square on, unsmiling. Then he leans down with a grunt, hauls the limb around ninety degrees, and starts walking west. He leaves behind the faint whiff of alcohol. It hangs on the air until he is out of sight, and the finches begin to cheep again.

I watch him as he goes. He isn't exactly an advertisement for the benefits of alcohol. Still, the first thing he makes me think of is good, cold beer. The second thing I think is that an ex-pat would be useful here, anyone who I can share a language with. I think how a bar might be the place to find them. I have seen no drinking bars in Muslim Diyarbak'r.

The smell of alcohol is still on the air, an invisible, human vapour trail. I follow it. It is not something I am good at or take pride in, following old men down alleyways. Still, I have done more difficult things. I walk a corner behind him, back to the main street, listening for his rusty leg. After a couple of false starts he turns right and goes into a restaurant. I wait for a few minutes, then go up to the shopfront. There is a Pepsi-Cola sign over the door. A name, *Sinan Lokatasu*. A second notice has been hung in the window. In small letters someone has written:

Welcome to the best pleace in down town,

and below it, in big blunt script:

BEER SERVED HERE.

I open the door. It is light inside, the sun falling down a broad shaft of stairs. There is a Formica bar, four tables, a microphone on a chipboard platform, two waiters lying asleep on rows of chairs. Towards the back, a couple of men in blue overalls are playing a game of backgammon. The one-legged man is standing beside them, talking in an asthmatic monotone. He doesn't look up when I come in, nor does anyone else.

I sit down at an empty table and wait for the waiters. A heavy-set man in a white apron walks in from the back, looks at me and away. I watch him trying to evade my presence. There is nothing else to do in here but look at people sleeping or playing backgammon. Eventually he wanders over, nods his head back, and waits.

I smile. 'Hello. Do you have a beer?'

'No beer.'

He sniffs. Part of me, the weak part, wonders if I still smell of sweat. I don't lower my face to find out. I nod towards the shopfront, and the sign in the window.

'"Beer served here" – no?'

He looks at me sullenly. He has full pouting lips, thick eyebrows, a beauty spot high on the right cheek. Pantomime features. With a wig on he would make an excellent ugly sister.

I raise my voice. Only a little. 'I would like one beer. Please. *Lütfen.*'

'No beer–' As he says it one of the waiters starts to talk. He does it without sitting up or opening his eyes. His voice is mild but not quiet. The pantomime man listens, asks a question back, then looks at his watch and shrugs. He wipes his hands on his apron and points at the stairs. 'Go up. Please.'

I go up. At the top of the staircase is a terrace. Vines break up the sun into a manageable heat. I walk down between paper-clothed tables to a chair overlooking the main street. There is no one else on the terrace and I sit, enjoying the sense of space. The tablecloth in front of me is smudged with old food and wind-blown grime. The whole place feels like an evening venue, its staff resting before night. I try to decide how long I can make myself wait here, for ex-pats who may never come, and people who may know nothing.

I weigh up my patience. In the window of the building opposite is a sign for a *Doktor Gürsel, Operator*. A line has been crudely drawn through the final word. Shadows move behind the blinds. On the Doktor's roof sits a silhouetted crow. Black as a weather-vane.

'Your beer.'

I look up. It is the sleeping waiter. I don't recognise his face, only the mildness of his voice.

'Thanks. I was beginning to think it would come in a paper bag.'

'No.' He smiles at me. I realise that even when they are civil or kind, few people smile in Diyarbak'r. 'Not in a restaurant. Are you here for long?'

'In Diyarbak'r? No.'

'No. For business?'

'Yes. Your English is very good.'

He smiles again. 'No, no.' He stops talking as if he meant to say something else. I watch his face. His eyes are dark and bright as the tan of his skin. Like his voice, they are easy things to covet. Easy to desire. I feel a flush of lust. I know it doesn't show. I wait for him to say something else.

He holds out his hand. We shake and he sits down. 'My name is Aslan.'

'I'm Katharine. I know an Aslan in Istanbul.'

'Yes. It is a common name. Joe Public. It means Lion. I am also from Istanbul.'

'Really?'

'Yes. This is my grandfather's restaurant. He needed help. Most people here, they are trying to get to Istanbul or Ankara, always west. But I came – the other way.'

'East.'

'Yes. East.' The noise of the street rises. I look away, over the tubs of vines. On the pavement below, a man in an *îma* headcloth is shouting at someone else, out of sight. Two more men hold him back. His voice breaks, as if he is on the verge of crying. Behind me, Aslan talks in his quiet voice.

'It is not a good place to live.'

'The old city is beautiful.'

'Yes, but most of the people in Diyarbak'r are Kurds. They don't want us here. For them it is a war.'

I turn back. The beer is open on the table and I take a sip from the bottle. Aslan starts to bow and move away and I wave him back.

'Wait – will you sit with me? I need someone to talk to.'

'Of course.' He sits down again. The wind flutters at the tablecloths. He is younger than me by a year or two, maybe more. I watch him trying to think of something to say.

'Where are you from, Katharine?'

'England.'

'England. London?'

'Near London.'

'London! I would very much like it.'

'Maybe. Go in summer.' I put down the beer. Lean forward. 'Aslan, there is someone I am looking for here. I've come a long way to find her.'

He shrugs. 'If you tell me her name . . .'

'Glött.'

'The German?'

I sit back. Smile the easy smile of relief. 'You know her.'

He shrugs again. 'Everyone knows her.'

'Everyone? I've just spent all morning trying to find likely people.'

'Oh well, maybe not everyone. Also, not everyone likes her. Katharine, forgive me, my grandfather doesn't like me to, but – may I have some of your beer?'

'Sure.' He pours a mouthful of lager into the unused glass. I watch him drink. It feels like an intimate gesture, this sharing of alcohol, in a city where I know no one. 'Why don't people like her?'

He stops drinking, smacks his lips, smiles. 'Ahh. Why? Actually, most people like her very much. It is only the old Turks, the Atatürks, you know? The German woman has land in her own country, farms, factories. Every year she flies labourers north from here. She has her own aeroplane – a very rich woman, you know? Ver-r-ry rich. But most of Diyarbak'r is Kurdish, so most of her workers are Kurdish. They come back from Germany with their own money. They set up their own Kurdish businesses. The old Turks don't like that. You see? But everybody else loves her.'

'Where does she live, Aslan?'

She is in the old quarters, where I knew she would be. Aslan draws me a map. He does it carefully, taking his time. He asks me to come back before I leave. I tell him I will. I don't know if it is true.

When he has finished the map I kiss him goodbye. The skin of his cheeks is soft with unshaven down. From the back of the restaurant the one-legged man watches me go, head back, drinking.

It is late afternoon before I find the house. I duck under a striped stone archway. Sunlight falls acutely across one side of a broad courtyard.

It is a beautiful place. There are trees in the yard, old cedars. The ground under them is paved with broad black flags. Female basalt, which is more porous than the male. Which will remain cool under the feet of its owners, even at noon on a hot day. The walls are built from male stone. Closer-grained, black and white, hung with jasmine. There is a pool with lilies and slow earth-coloured carp, umber, ochre, loam. Beyond them, an open atrium with a small fountain and stone benches. Between the seats are two doors.

The second-floor windows are empty, dull with grime. Still, there are spyholes in the doors. A camera above them. From somewhere in the house comes the sound of a wooden flute, a repetitive phrase. The longer I stand listening, the less sure I am whether it is a flute or a bird.

I walk across the courtyard and knock at the middle door. The birdsong stops in mid-phrase. There is no other sound from inside the house, no voices or footsteps. When the door opens I am half-looking away, back at the courtyard with its water and light.

In the doorway is a giant. Even without his turban he must be more than a foot taller than me, and I am not a small woman. His face is dark, aquiline, Semitic. I find myself focusing on the size of his hands and the features of his face, as one would with a baby. His bulk and silence catch me off guard. He waits for me to collect myself.

'I'm sorry. I'm looking for a woman called von Glött. Is this the right place? Do you speak English?'

He makes a movement which is half a nod, half a bow.

'My name is Katharine Sterne.'

He waits, one hand on the door. I see that he is holding something in his other hand. It is smooth as the barrel of a gun.

'I am in the jewel trade. Pearls.'

Nothing in his face acknowledges me, but he takes his hand off the door. The object in his other hand is not a weapon but some kind of woodwind instrument. There are holes drilled through the red grain.

He ushers me in. The hallway is whitewashed stone. The arched ceiling is low and badly lit. There is a smell of mothballs. From somewhere far away comes an American accent. The sound of shooting.

'Please.'

I look round. The giant is hunched over, waiting. In the passageway his strength becomes ludicrous, turned back on itself. I follow him down the corridor. On each side there are statues, Persian and Babylonian, cryselephantine and alabaster. Ottoman skeleton clocks, ticking at one another from long shelves. There is a sense of accumulated wealth, the residual beauty of old empires.

The giant walks fast. His feet are bare and soundless. From somewhere comes the sound of Americans again, and the end of the hall comes into sight. There is a curtain of black beads, light clicking through them. The giant parts the strings and I step through.

Inside, an old woman is watching television. She sits with her back straight in a room full of kilims and sofas. Her hair is a steely chemical blonde. She is wearing an oyster cashmere dress and big fleece-lined slippers. The television is massive. On it, Arnold Schwarzenegger is the Terminator. A landlord in a string vest knocks at his door. Arnold looks up from a stolen book.

Behind him, Diyarbak'r sunlight burns through a fretwork screen. A gin and tonic ticks on a brass side table.

I glance round and the giant is gone. When I look back the old woman is already watching me. She is fine-boned, like old china. Her skin is almost translucent.

'Who are you? Are you tax?'

Her German is upper-class eastern. Nothing urban, not Frankfurt or Berlin. In London they would call her a sharp old bird, but there is something intrinsically Germanic about her. It is partly the dark elegance of her clothes and make-up, the Gothic blackness of her one rope of pearls. And it is partly a strength. She looks resilient and brittle as diamond. Contradictions which are true all the same.

Her eyes are shrewd and bored. It would take very little to make her throw me out, and all I have to offer is one conch pearl. Now I am here, it doesn't seem like much. I need to get her attention quickly, and to keep it. I choose my words and stick to English.

'I like your house.' When she says nothing I try again. 'I always thought that people who admired stones surrounded themselves with beautiful things.'

'Stones?' She barks at me, as if I might be deaf or inattentive. 'I can't stand stones.' In English, her accent is stronger than Schwarzenegger's. On the screen, the Terminator is walking through a haze of crossfire.

'Jewels.' I take two steps into the room. Three.

'Jewels, yes. And I do. Everything I have is beautiful. My taste is immaculate.'

'Really. What went wrong with your carpet slippers?'

There is a pause, long enough for me to wonder if I have misjudged her. She pulls herself up on the sofa, as if she is preparing to spit. Instead she takes a small, precise drink of her drink and smiles, slightly. 'Since you ask, I am waiting for new slippers. From Paris.'

She puts the drink down heavily. I can't tell if it is anger or drunkenness or simply bad coordination. Her head wobbles as she watches me. She is very old. 'Evidently you are not tax. They usually come from Germany and they always know how to dress. And they are never so rude. You are extremely fortunate, my dear, that I have a sense of humour. What is your name?'

'Katharine Sterne.'

'What are you doing on my property?'

I walk over to the table, and put the conch pearl next to her gin. The light glows against its raw pink flush. The old woman picks it up with extreme care, as if she could break it between finger and thumb, like the egg of a tiny bird. Although it is not a brittle jewel, the pearl. Delicate, but with an organic strength. The roundness of the nacre is more resilient than the planar growth of a crystal. I start to describe the jewel, its weight and source, and Glött silences me with a hand.

Gunfire and background music boom from the television. When the old woman has seen all she wants to of the pearl she closes her hand around it. Looks up at me again. Pats the sofa beside her.

'Come. Sit. Am I to understand that this is a gift? Or I will pay you five hundred dollars. No more.'

'I didn't come here for money.'

She opens her hand again. The pearl glows against the grey of her skin. Her head leans to one side and she smiles again. 'This is charming. Charming.'

'I came here to talk to you.'

'And you get what you want.' Her hand closes. 'I think so, Katharine Sterne.'

'Sometimes.'

'Sometimes. We will drink first, talk later.' She scrabbles around in the sofa cushions until she finds a remote control. She bangs it three times against the side table, calls out, mutes the television – all at once: 'Hassan! Tea. Food. Milk.'

There is a whisper of sound from beyond the bead curtain; nothing else to see or hear. I imagine the giant, moving through the mansion on his great bare feet. But the old woman is talking to me again and I turn back. 'My name is Eva von Glött. While you are here you will call me Glött or ma'am. You want milk with your tea. You are English?'

'Thanks.'

She is rolling the pearl between her fingers and palm, like the last nub of a bar of soap. On the wall behind her is a picture of a man in forties monotone. He is faded by exposure and Eastern heat. A handsome face, clean-shaven, smiling clear out of the past. A German army uniform. 'Such beautiful things, pearls. Do you like diamonds, Katharine?'

'Like is probably the wrong word.'

'I knew it. Diamonds!' Her laugh is unattractive, a high beauty-parlour giggle. 'Diamonds are merely glorified coal. In heaven the angels will throw diamonds on the fire. And coloured jewels are all vulgar. Baubles. They are all stones, and why would I want to wear stones? Do I look like I need to be weighed down? Am I going to float away? When I die, I will have enough stones on my chest, thank you. But pearls–'

Hassan the giant comes in with tea, a bowl of olives, a bowl of persimmons. I watch him put the tray down on the side table, pour two cups. He doesn't look at either of us. All his movements are quiet, like his walking. The tray he leaves behind is old lacquer, inlaid with leaves of gold. Beside me, Eva von Glött is still talking, on and on.

'Pearls, yes. They have such a subtle beauty, so elegant. They grow. Little lives. They are a function of pain.'

She picks up an olive. Eats. Extracts the stone from her teeth. She is happy talking, and I wonder who she has to talk with, in her courtyarded mansion. I try to keep her going.

'Pain.'

'Pain? Yes, pain. The oyster has delicate flesh. Easily hurt. When grit becomes lodged there, it wraps up the pain in pearl. It smooths away the hurt. The pearl is a function of pain. But that must be part of its beauty, don't you think?'

'I hadn't thought about it.'

'I think so, and I have thought about it a great deal.' She drinks her tea. It smokes in the half-curtained light. 'They have the charm of beautiful girls. They come in all the colours of human skin. You have good skin. If you looked after yourself, you could be quite pretty.'

'If you say so.'

She begins to watch the television again. We sit together on the sofa, not talking. The woman who loves pearls and the woman who loves stones. Old friends, insulting one another.

The sound is turned off. A man and woman are having sex. Light and shadows fall across their flesh, their faces. All the colours of skin. Eva von Glött watches them with her mouth open, but only a little. When I can wait no longer I begin to talk, quietly.

'I am looking for something. I heard you might be able to help. It's a jewel. A great jewel. I've been looking for it for . . . I'd do anything to . . .'

I look down at my hands. The red knuckles, like conch pearls. I trace a shape on the skin. A triangle. A diamond.

'It is a triangle of gold. A medieval design, from Burgundy. A knot as big as the palm of my hand. Gold set with eight stones. One diamond, three rubies, four pearls. The old name for it is the Three Brethren, *les Trois Frères*. It is–'

'I know what it is,' says the old woman. She doesn't look away from the screen. Her voice is soft again. Thoughtful. 'You are very clever, to find me here. Or very lucky. To bring me this nice gift. It is a gift?'

'If you like.'

'My father once held the Brethren.'

'What?'

There is silence in the television light. I turn and stare at Glött, I can't help myself. Her face in profile is softer, but the eyes remain sharp. The remote control is still in her hand.

'Your father owned the Brethren?'

'You don't listen,' says Glött. 'My father collected fine jewellery, but he had no talent for money. This jewel you want. He was offered it in London. At the turn of the century. I think so. Unfortunately it was too expensive for my father. It was quite ridiculously expensive, and he was no longer quite ridiculously rich. It slipped through his hands. He regretted that for the rest of his life. He used to talk about it when he was drunk. It made him cry.' She pauses the film. Turns to me. 'I could never stand to see men cry.'

'Who bought it?'

She shrugs. Pouts.

'Who was the seller?'

'How should I know?'

I sit quite still, watching her. What she says could be true. I know the Brethren was in England in the nineteenth century. The facts fit the fact, and the old woman looks as if she is telling the truth. Still, appearances are deceptive. I weigh her up. She begins to fidget under my gaze.

'You don't believe me?'

'I don't know.'

Glött sets her lips. She doesn't look embarrassed now, only proud. I have made a mistake. Sooner or later, I find, I always make a mistake. 'I've heard stories of the Brethren before. People who have it. People who know people who have it. Always just stories . . .'

'You don't believe me.' She picks up the control. Turns on the film again. The sound of gunfire fills the room.

'Do you have any proof?'

'Not for you.' She whispers it. Her face is stony now, her eyes settling on the screen. Lips and cheekbones precise as waxwork.

I sit beside her. My eyes are on the film but I see nothing. I try to gauge the situation. Dispassionately, because I would never claim to be a good person, only good at what I do. If I leave now I will have to come back, tonight or tomorrow night. However large he is, I have only seen one guard, and one camera. But theft is no solution here. I don't know what I want in this house, or what is thievable. All I have seen is an old woman with a head full of words. I would steal them, if I could.

The despair begins to rise up inside me. I try to force it away. Every day, for five years, it has become harder to ignore, and today is not a good day. Beside me the old woman cackles. When I look up she is watching me with bright eyes.

'You're in trouble now. Aren't you? It shows. If I won't help you, what will you do? If I don't give you something. Where will you go? Eh?'

I don't know. To myself I can say it. Not to her.

'How long have you been looking?' Her voice is gentler now. I shake my head and stand. The conch pearl is on the side table and I take it. The price of a flight to wherever I am going.

'Wait. I said wait.' Glött is pulling herself out of the sofa. Her legs are thin, stiff as sticks. They shake as she stands. 'You will wait when I tell you to. I asked you how long you have been looking. Because I wonder how much you know about jewels.'

'Everything I need to.' I take a Turkish million-lira note from my pocket and wrap the pearl in it, like a bulse.

'Yes, I'm sure you do,' says the old woman. She takes an unsteady step towards me. Raises her voice, as if I am already gone. 'I need someone. A servant.'

'I'm not a servant.'

'A worker. Someone who knows what they are looking at. My father liked stones. I have more than you have ever seen. Also many more than I will ever want.' She takes another step. She is steadier now, tall for an old woman. 'I have a proposition. Since you are here. I want you to catalogue my father's stones.'

'Why should I?'

'To get what you want. My father's diaries will be here. Business records. Work for me. We will see if we can find them.'

The exit is beside me. Sunlight inches through the curtain.

'I am taking pity on you, Katharine Sterne. Make sure you accept it while it is still offered.'

I turn round and put down my case. The pearl is still in my hand and I hold it out. Glött waves it away. 'Pff – keep it.'

'No, it's for you.' I walk over to her. 'I've never liked them.'

'No?' She raises a pencilled eyebrow. Takes the jewel. 'Then I will teach you why you do. We have time.'

An aeroplane thunders overhead, a weight of metal balanced in the hot sky. Glött smiles up at me. Her teeth are blue-white, pink-white, yellow. All the colours of pearls. She extends her hand and I reach out and take it.

⽊

The lives of stones are the lives of the dead, which always lead back, never ahead.

My notebook looks old. I am burning the pages at both ends, charring them black with ink. I write methodically, covering all the steps I have taken. It is not like President Araf's diary, with its precise little secrets. I do not write this so that it is never read. Here, there is an address from a soft-porn calendar. Here, a telephone number in northern Switzerland. In between, footnotes. The pages look old and so do I.

It is late as I write. Outside my window is a courtyard of black stone. The walls of this building are male basalt, and if I went outside and put my hand against them, I would feel their retained heat. The female stone would be cool underfoot. There are bats, I can hear them. They are fishing with their voices. Casting out little weights of sound. Reeling them in.

I am in Diyarbak'r, in the house of Eva von Glött. I am writing the history of the Three Brethren, which is the story of myself. All its owners are dead, and the jewel is lost.

The leather flutter of bats. The house around me, heat fading from its stone roofs and corridors. For someone who loathes it, Glött has chosen herself a stony place to live. Possibly a house of pearl is still beyond her means. I imagine she'll upgrade in a few years' time.

Sleep nags at me. My pen is wandering. I am writing nothing tonight. I am not drawing the treasure map, the Brethren at the end of it, three steps east and one step back. This is only for myself. Soon the notebook will run out and then I will regret the pages I have wasted.

On the table beside me is a turquoise inscribed with Cufic script. The strokes of the characters are linear, primitive as axe-cuts. They are seven, eight, nine hundred years old. They will still be legible when the bleach in the pages of my notes begins to fail, the paper turning back to the colour of wood, the ink degrading. When the records written in my lifetime have been delaminated, the photographs faded to red skies and purple silhouettes, the inscriptions on jewels will be unchanged. Nothing is more permanent than stones. They are the Rosetta, the Avenue of Avebury, the Record of Darius.

All day I have been looking for an old woman. Tonight, I find myself thinking of my mother. She died when I was seven. Her name was Edith and she was old when I was born. I have a stone of hers somewhere, a garnet from a broken rope.

Edith. She smelt of the darkroom: old photographs and dried-out swimming pools. The darkroom smelt of her. Nothing in the house was as important as the blacked-out pantry beside the kitchen. It was the only room we could never know, an unexplored chemical darkness where Edith could disappear for minutes or hours, unreachable, the door not to be opened.

In bad dreams I imagined her dissolving into the dark as the door swung ajar, blackening like silver salt. A Eurydice of a mother. Only sometimes were we allowed inside, one at a time or fighting for the stool by the trays of hypo and developing fluid. In the airless space Edith would lean over us. Her yellowed fingers would pull pictures from the dark. Her voice: *There, and there. Abracadabra.* Particles of black silver growing into smiling faces. The smell of it was like nothing else. The scent of dangerous and precious things.

I find it hard to write about her. It pulls me away from my life. When I think of her I'm always looking back over my shoulder.

But this is the quality of the dead: they lead you back. Jewels do the same. The Three Brethren has lured me through five hundred years of history, and in the history of jewellery five hundred years is only the beginning. The earliest jewels are a hundred times older than the Brethren. Ostrich-shell beads, from the east of Africa. Along with worked stones, they are the oldest evidence of modern human intelligence. That in itself interests me: that jewels and weapons are the ways we recognise ourselves. The impulse to make these two things is our common ground, unchanged over fifty thousand years. We identify the function of the jewel as instinctively as that of the axe-head, and we infer intelligence from them both. The weapon is made from a need to kill. The jewel is made out of a love of things. Love and death are how we recognise ourselves in our ancestors. It is only to be expected.

They lead you back. I'm out. It is night. This is years ago. The club is in Hoxton and it is winter outside, but here, where people are dancing, it's warmer. I am looking for someone. The crowd moves around me as I move through it.

The club walls are painted black. Music beats against them. The bass shudders inside me, under my breastbone. No one talks here, and not many of the people are dancing, nothing that purposeful. But they move, and they watch. There is pleasure in movement here, a low-grade adrenaline. A slow, furred static of sex.

I am looking for the man I came with. I left him talking to the DJ, but when I go back to the record tables he is gone, no one knows where. His name is Tricky, like the singer. His girlfriend is called Tricia. Tricky and Tricia. I am not his girlfriend. Nevertheless, I am with him, and I want him to take me home tonight.

I move through the crowd. Behind the sound system is a matt black door. I try the handle and step through.

Inside the room are piles of gigantic speakers, scarred, black and monolithic. Between the speakers is a cot bed. On the bed is a boy. He is wearing a pair of combat trousers, no shoes, a cut-down string vest. He looks Japanese, both in himself and in his choice of clothes, and he is smiling. Not necessarily at me. There is a blue pill in his belly button.

I smile at him, or smile back. Even in here the music is loud. I have to shout a little. 'Have you seen Tricky?'

Now he is certainly grinning at me. He points at the pill, snug in its cavity of flesh. I shake my head.

'No – Tricky. You know Tricky?'

He shrugs. His shoulders are thin. The skin is tanned a colour between ochre and ash. It occurs to me that he is beautiful. Not handsome but really beautiful, like a girl. When he talks his English is good. It has a slight accent, American or Canadian. 'No, but I wish I was him. Are you sure you won't join me?'

He takes a pantomime breath, holds it in, and puffs out his belly. His face is staring and surprised. With the pill in its orifice he looks like some strange parody of a belly dancer, and I have to laugh. The music is muted now and I realise the door has swung shut. I don't look round. I nod at the pill.

'What is it?'

He picks it out. Holds it up between finger and thumb, next to his grin. He turns it, like a key. His eyebrows go up, dark and thin. 'Trip or treat?'

'Trip or trap.'

'No!' He sits up and looks wounded. More pantomime. 'Come on. This cost me about forty bucks. That's how much I like you already.'

'I never take sweets from strangers.'

He holds out his hand. 'Yohei.'

'Katharine.' We shake hands. I sit down on the camp bed.

'There. Now we're not so strange.' He holds out the pill. It is bright blue, the colour of a fine turquoise. Yohei lies back, wrestles with his trouser pocket, and pulls out another pill. It looks the same as mine. He holds it up.

'Katharine, I would like to make a toast. Okay?'

'Okay.'

'To sweets from strangers.'

'Sweets from strangers.' We click the pills, like little dice. They last all night. The next day, after the sun comes up, we make love.

I remember kissing him. There were tiny hairs on his forehead and cheeks, a down that caught the light like dust. He was a gentle lover. I only knew him for six months before he went back to Canada. In the way such things happen in real life, I suspect I'll never see him again. We talked about that once. There was a term in Japanese, he said. *Eng*. It was both a concept and a word of advice. It meant that anyone you meet may be the most imporant person in your life. Therefore, that every stranger should be treated as a friend. Loved before it is too late. You never know (he said) in which night your ship is passing.

He loved Britain. He was obsessed with the Royal Family. It was his Japanese blood, he said, and if it hadn't been the royals it would have been some other British icon. There were worse things than Diana, he said, in a society capable of sock suspenders and hotels that sold food like aeroplane meals.

When we went to the Tower of London it was Yohei's third time. I had never been before. He gave me a guided tour. We were both hung over, juicy with sex. It was a white-skied day. England in the spring.

'Don't feed them.'

'Why?'

'It says. Look.'

He looks. A yard out across the lawn are two signs. One says: KEEP OFF THE GRASS. The other says: DON'T FEED THE RAVENS. Two of them step up towards Yohei. Coy, sidestepping birds. Muscled as pitbulls. Their beaks are like something from the Royal Armoury.

'Listen, if ice-cream cones could kill these fuckers, they'd have been dead centuries ago.' He throws them half a cigarette. The nearest bird snaps it up, *clack*. A man walks past backwards, murmuring into his camcorder.

Yohei stands up. 'Okay. Jewel House.' I sag.

'Jesus, Yohei, what did you have for breakfast?'

'You. Come on. I thought you liked stones.'

'I do.' We are walking already. There is a queue outside the Jewel House door. An old woman asks me if I can direct her to the little girls' room. Yohei directs her. The smell of traffic drifts down from Tower Bridge.

Inch by inch, we advance inside. Pressed in with the crowd, we pass Rundell & Bridge's Offering Sword with its swirls of brilliants and emeralds. Between two travelators is a long showcase full of crowns. Yohei points them out as we trundle past. The Queen Mother's. Saint Edward's. Last of all, the Imperial State Crown.

It is covered with diamonds like bright encrustations of salt. The brilliance makes it hard to see and we go back again for another pass. I take the back travelator, Yohei the front. He waves his hands through the glass, pointing out jewels for me. The Stuart sapphire is big as a plum but thin, a sliver of blue the colour of eyes. On top of the crown's four arches are pearls called Queen Elizabeth's Earrings. To me they look like ugly things. Four greyish veiny epiglottises hung over the throaty folds of the velvet cap.

'Here. Swap.' Yohei grabs my hips and pushes me back. Now I am on the front travelator, and he is on the rear. He tells me to look out for the Black Prince's ruby. I'm more interested in him. I'm watching his eyes through the glass when I see it.

We are face to face, the stone and I. It is a malformed ovoid of blackish red. There is a hole drilled through it that has nothing to do with the crown. The hole is clear because it is plugged with a smaller ruby. The stop is paler. A small droplet of blood on the thick clot of the stone.

The ground catches up with me. I stumble and almost fall. Yohei is there to catch me, and one of the guards. They laugh, and then Yohei stops laughing. 'Katharine? Do you feel all right?'

I say something. Nothing important. I don't remember. He looks into my face. 'You're white. Even for an English person. And you feel cold. We should get some air.'

'No. It's warmer in here. Just give me a minute.' I stand with my back to the crowns. Someone comes off the moving belts and bumps against me. I don't look round. Part of me wants to. I don't let it.

'Jesus. You look like you've seen a ghost.'

I look up at Yohei. I make myself smile. 'I've come to the right place for that, haven't I?'

He laughs. We laugh. We go. I don't look back at the ghost inside the glass. It is three days before I return, alone. I go round and round the constructions of jewels, and look at only the one gem. It is the first stone I really love, although it won't be the last. My first balas ruby. I want to reach out and touch it. I feel a movement inside me. A shifting in the blood.

It is addictive, the way stones lead you. Once you start, it's hard to stop. Even if you don't like the places you are led. Sometimes all it takes is one stone. The face of the Timur Ruby, for example, is carved with the names of its owners, all the way back to the vanishing-point when there are no more people to own it. First Akbar Shah, then all the others, step by step: *Jehangir Shah; Salil Oiran Shah; Alamgir Shah; Badshah Ghazu Mahamad Farukh Siyar; Ahmed Shar Duri-i-Duran. This is the ruby among the 25,000 jewels of the King of Kings.*

Or there is the Black Prince's ruby, that malformed bolus. You can trace its uneven outline back through the frames of empty crowns, all the way to the English Reformation. And further: the jewel itself is transpierced and stopped, from the times and places before it was set in a Western crown. Further. The chemical structure is spinel. A balas ruby: aluminium, oxygen, magnesium. Furnace heat. A thousand years of darkness. In the end it is always the same. There is nothing left but stones.

I wake alone, in the night, and wonder if that is what I'm looking for.

☆

I open my eyes. The stone house is silent around me. I have no memory of what has woken me, only an awareness of sound. I wait for it to come again and it does, a short cry.

It could almost be the voice of an animal, fox or hare. Something trapped. It has that need and wildness, although I know it is human. Beyond it is a rhythm of movement. Faint through the stone walls.

I wake up fast. There is a sense of danger in overhearing love-making. I feel my eyes and ears working at the dark before I am even thinking properly. My heart beating the blood awake. The cry comes again, and I know for certain it is a woman. It doesn't disgust me, not yet. There is an attraction. Somewhere close to me, something crucial is happening, and I am no part of it. I am stopped, unlistened-to, listening.

I sit up. Even my sense of smell is heightened. Glött's house reeks of limestone, like a church crypt. Beyond that is a suggestion of preservatives. Salt, camphor, turpentine. Underneath it all, the sour odour of age and loss.

In a cheap hotel they would mean nothing, the sounds of sex. I would almost expect them. But in the reclusive silence of Glött's house, they are out of place. For a moment I picture the old woman and Hassan the giant involved in some complex position of intercourse, and I push the image away. A smile tugs at the corner of my mouth. The longer the sex goes on, the more comical it becomes.

And then even the joke is old. What I hear becomes a simple rhythm of body parts, breath pushed out of lungs, muscle working against muscle. It is monotonous as a coughing fit. I pull back my one sheet and stand naked in the cool dark, listening. It is hard to tell which direction the sound is coming from. Around me are the dim shapes of the bed, a desk, a chair. A clothes chest of sweet-smelling cedar.

I pick up the chair, invert it, and prod its legs against the ceiling. I do it hard. Only three times. The sounds go quiet. If I could apologise I might, but I can't. Communication by chair stretches only so far.

I put it down, sit at the desk. Turn on the light. My watch is there, and my notebook. It is a Tollit & Harvey Major Pad, black, foxed, ringbound. Fat with use, as if the words inside are exerting their own pressure. In my bag there are nine more books, all the same, parcelled together. One is still empty. They show me where I have come from, these last five years. They tell me where I am going. It is three in the morning, and I am as alone as I have ever been. I get a pen from my bag and begin to write, and when I am too tired to do any more I put my head on the desk and I sleep.

The sun wakes me, hot on my hair and the crook of my arms. I open my eyes and see the notebook under me, its hard black cushion smeared with drool. I wipe it clean, push the chair back. Push back my hair, knead the ache out of my shoulders.

Light from the courtyard blankets the room. I feel tucked up in heat, sleepy and irritable as a girl. To wake myself up I take out what I will need to work. I don't unpack because I don't plan to be here long enough for that.

My loupe, which is a jeweller's magnifying glass. My last ruby. My dollars which, along with the ruby and the seal, are the only valuables I have left. My pen and notebook are on the desk and I take them too. My head is where it should be and beginning to work. My watch. It is late, I have overslept, but I am not here for employment, after all. Only for information. *My father once held the Brethren.*

Yesterday's clothes are on the floor and I put them on, a Daks shirt and good jeans, the colour still deeper than indigo. Hassan is playing his wooden flute, I can see him in the courtyard as I dress. I rub a clean circle on the dusty glass. He is leant against the wall ten feet away with his back to me. His head is cocked to one side. I see how the hair is cut back behind his ear, the skin exposed over the skull's raised bone. I imagine what it would be like to kiss him there. He is a beautiful man, a statue of a man, but I am not looking for men.

Inside the lid of the clothes chest is a mirror. I look down at the reflection of my throat, the hollow under which a chain would hang. I don't have jewellery of my own any more. It has been a long time since I wore jewels for pleasure. As if nothing will do except the Brethren. All the same, I feel underdressed in my travelling clothes. In transit people only meet knowing they will never meet again. And that is the way I like it. All things kept simple, no time for friends or enemies. I go back to my bag. There is a comb inside, toiletries, a minimum of make-up. I work at my hair until it shines before I leave.

The hallway smells of coffee. There are dusty alcoves in the east wall, and someone has left flowers there. Two tiny water-lilies in a blue-lipped dish. It is done so carefully and the care is so unexpected that I feel ashamed. It's a long time since I did as much for anyone, although I dislike cut flowers, their deadness. I turn left down the corridor towards Glött's room.

At the end of the corridor is a staircase to a lower floor. It shouldn't be here. I have gone the wrong way, and it surprises me. My sense of direction is not poor, but in Glött's house I am lost. There is something about the low white halls, the rareness of windows, the absence of light. It is like being underground. I follow the stairs down.

Before I reach the bottom the air begins to change. There is a damp warmth, and a faint smell of resin sweetened by steam. It is an odour I associate with both Chinese food and Turkish baths, and with Glött I sense that either thing is possible. The first two doors I come to are locked and no light shows under them. The third is larger, and wide open.

Wet footprints zigzag across the tiled hall. I turn on the light and look in at the German's private sauna and pool. The room is empty, but the water is still disturbed, rocking against green-glazed tiles. From down the hall comes the sound of a woman's laughter, young and at ease with itself. I turn towards it. At the end of the hall are double doors and I walk through.

It is a kitchen, long, high, and comfortable. A place to consume food as well as prepare it. Between the roof beams, grimy windows let in big blocks of sunlight. There is a lot of wood, expensive and oiled. Wheelbacked chairs and four heavy, scored tables.

A young couple are eating breakfast at the nearest table. They are blonde, tanned, sleek as the Armani perfume man. Similar in their beauty. They could be lovers or siblings. Both are dressed in swimming costumes. Water still beads the girl's shoulders. The boy looks up at me and smiles. Fox teeth.

'Good morning! You must be the stone girl.'

'Stone girl?' His accent is clear, precisely Germanic. The words confuse me only because his stress is wrong, he has emphasised 'girl' instead of 'stone'. The mistake is more elementary than his English itself. I don't quite have time to wonder why before he is talking again.

'I am sorry. I didn't mean to offend you. Maybe you would prefer me to call you the stone lady.'

'No. I–'

'But you are Katharine Sterne, yes?'

'Yes.'

'Of course you are. And Eva has you here to work on the stones.' His mouth is closed now. He is still smiling. There is something distracting about his eyes, I find myself looking away from them. From the far side of the kitchen, two washing machines look back. Round black eyes in a square white face. 'You must be hungry. Join us.'

'We have eggs and coffee and ham.'

The girl's voice has an undertone of laughter, as if she has said something funny. She is pale and perfect, a corn-fed German blonde. I feel a stab of envy, hard and sexual. She pushes her plate towards me.

'Here. Have mine, I'm full.'

'Perhaps she doesn't eat ham,' says the boy. The girl looks up at me.

'You do, don't you?'

I shrug. 'Anything. Ham's fine.'

The boy pours me a Pyrex glass of coffee. The girl watches me sit and eat. They don't introduce themselves. Beside the boy's plate are a packet of tobacco, cigarette papers, and a Ronson lighter. He makes himself a cigarette with quick efficiency, lights it, sits back. I catch a whiff of paraffin on his fingers. Brass and nicotine. Evening smells. I wonder how it is that I feel excluded from something I have just been invited to.

'So. Have you seen the stones?'

My mouth is full. I swallow, meaning to speak, but the boy is already talking again. 'Oh, you will have a treat. They are quite something, the Glött stones. Some of them have been in the family since the first Fuggers.'

The muezzin begins outside, somewhere close. I speak up against it. 'The Fuggers? Joseph Fugger?'

'I always thought it sounded like a Jewish name. Still, there is nothing so wrong with that, these days. But they are the same family, yes, Fuggers and von Glötts. You didn't know?'

'No.' I think of the old woman's father, crying over the Brethren. Glött herself. *You are very clever, to find me here. Or very lucky.* 'No, I didn't. And you are related to Eva?'

His eyes crinkle as he pulls on the cigarette. It makes him look older. 'Yes. But you must be careful, Katharine, not to call her that. She doesn't like it, not from anyone. Excuse me.' The girl is trying to meet his eyes. He turns away from me with stiff politeness. An old-school restaurateur, or a host.

'It's late, Martin. We have to go.'

'Of course.' They stand up together. Martin smiles down. 'I am sorry. Please enjoy your breakfast.'

'Thanks. I think I will.' I watch them out of the door, the sound of their footsteps echoing back. When they are quite gone I push the food away and sit drinking coffee and thinking of Joseph Fugger and Eva von Glött. A little piece of evolution, from the prototype capitalist to the miserly recluse. And on the heels of their images comes another thought: great jewels have a way of returning to their pasts. It is like the whisper of an old record left to play too long, the hiss of the phrase repeating and repeating.

Across from me are Martin's cigarettes and Ronson lighter. I wonder if he left them on purpose. I don't take them for him because, I suspect, the less I have to do with Martin the better. It isn't that I don't find him attractive; it is partly the attractiveness that repels me. I have known other men like Martin, other women like the girl. And I distrust beauty in people. When the coffee is finished I go and find Eva.

I pass my bedroom, the alcove, the flowers. Three wide steps lead down to ground level. There is an inner window and I stop to look out. Outside is a tiny courtyard, no more than a well of space in the rambling body of the mansion. I can see up three floors to blue sky, and down to cobbles. A single tree grows in their centre. It is something exotic, I don't recognise the species. It reaches upwards towards the light, cramming leaves against walls and windows.

There is music somewhere, a cello and piano. The acoustics of the hallway make it sound as if it is coming from behind me, but I keep walking. A larger hall opens out on the left. At the far end of it hangs a jet bead curtain. A stone door in a stone house. When I get there the music is still playing.

The curtain whispers and clicks as I part it. Glött doesn't hear. She sits with her eyes closed, a cigar in her hand. On the sofa beside her is a plate of figs. A mouse is eating the figs, which are bigger than itself. It senses me before the old woman does, vanishing down the back of the sofa.

The music swells. A sound system looms in the corner behind the television, a black pillar inlaid with red lights. The old woman's eyes are still closed. I take her in while I have the chance. She looks strained, as if the music makes it hard to breathe. She is wearing black slacks and a man's shirt, grey with white herringbones. On someone so old the effect is androgynous, and I wonder if it is intentional.

She feels me watching, looks up sharply and turns the music off in mid-crescendo. The quiet it leaves behind is punctuated with the sounds of Diyarbak'r traffic. Car horns, distant, slight as the voices of finches. Glött reaches for her glass. She drinks without looking at me. Her hand is shaking. Only a little.

I go and sit down beside her. 'Good morning.'

She snaps her face up again. As if she didn't frown enough the first time. 'What?'

'I said good morning. Do you remember me? My name is Katharine–'

'Of course I remember you.' She mutters something in German, an angry old woman with shaky hands. I don't move, not yet.

'What was that music?'

'Eh?'

'I said what are you listening to?'

She looks away. 'Messiaen.' The light catches in her blue eyes. 'Camp music.'

'Camp?'

She makes a sound of irritation, *Tch.* 'Camp, camp. Messiaen composed at a stalag in Silesia. In my time Silesia was Germany. Now they tell me it is Poland. Messiaen was captured by the Germans, very early in the war. There were musicians in the camp. The great composer wrote for them. There was a cellist. His instrument had one string missing. These things make the music what it is. My first husband met him several times.'

I watch her glance up towards the picture on the wall. Absently, checking his presence. 'Is that him?' I say, and she nods, not looking at me.

'Yes. They shared an interest in music. And rainbows.' She smiles tightly.

'He's handsome.' We look at the photograph together. The

142

dead man's dark hair, his soft eyes. 'Is he German?'

'Yes. He was also Jewish. For many years he was a distinguished officer in the army. His family were acquainted with Hindenburg. We left Germany after Hitler came to power. That in itself was hard for him. His family had lived there for almost as long as my own.'

'Did you love him?'

'He was a remarkable man.' The way she says it, it sounds like a weakness. Her hands have begun to shake again. I watch her remembering. Below her wattled neck hangs a long rope of riverine pearls. They are misshapen. Beautiful as old skin.

The quiet begins to reassert itself. I let it only because it is useful. In normal circumstances, people will say a great deal to avoid silence, but then these are not normal circumstances. The house of Eva von Glött is full of quiet. It occurs to me that she is entirely at home with silence, that it may even be part of the reason she is here.

She speaks as I am about to give up, words falling out of her. 'He died when he was still very young. I believe he thought he would live for ever, but then the young often do. Do you think you will live for ever?'

'No.'

'No, I can see you don't. I distrust music because no one burns it, Katharine. Even the Nazi can love Schubert. Writing, on the other hand, is unequivocal. Do you believe one can be stunted by love?'

'Of course not.'

'Even if it is unfulfilled? It can be unfulfilled in such a great number of ways.'

Her voice is lucid with alcohol. The words I don't understand. She turns her head away, dismissing me. All the same I see that she is crying. Her clothes are fine under the jewels. The shirt well made, Turnbull & Asser or van Laack. It almost fits her. I wonder if it was his.

'I'm sorry,' I say, as if there is anything I should apologise for. 'I didn't mean to disturb you. I wondered if you remember anything this morning.'

'About what?'

'The Brethren. The Three Brethren.'

Her wet eyes register nothing. She has forgotten. The despair

143

shifts inside me, half-awake to its own strength, and then the old woman is cackling with bright hilarity. 'The Brethren!' Her head swivels. 'We have an agreement, Katharine Sterne. First you will work for me. Then I will remember. Yes?'

'You have an unusual memory.'

'I have a perfect memory. The main thing for you, my dear, will be my father's papers. Somewhere there are details of the jewel's price, dates, places. Transaction papers. I will remember in time.' She subsides back into the sofa. A sharp old bird, brooding on her own thoughts.

'They have stories about you, in Diyarbak'r.'

'What stories? Who?'

'Someone I met. He said you employ many workers. That you have your own aeroplane. What kind of business are you in?'

'Business? I am in the business of money, like everyone else. What business are you in, Katharine Sterne?'

'Jewels.'

'No! You are in the business of money. Jewels are just the flavour of it. Jewel-flavoured money, political-flavoured money, pickle-flavoured money – it is all the same. All business, mine and yours. Jewels most of all.'

I know she is wrong. About me, she is wrong. I don't say it. 'You didn't answer my question.'

'If I wanted to talk about myself, I would live in Paris. I don't want to talk about me.' Glött stubs out her cigar in a dish of rice-patterned porcelain. When she looks up her eyes are blackened, ashy. 'I want to talk about you.'

I shrug. 'There is nothing to tell.'

'Of course there is.'

I sit back. The sofa gives off a sour animal must.

'Eh? You think you are ordinary people, the things that you do?'

'More or less.'

'More or less!' She stops and drinks. Over the lip of the glass, her eyes stay on me. 'More less than more. Are you married, Katharine Sterne?'

'No. Ask me another.'

'Never?' She is genuinely surprised, staring. It makes me laugh as I shake my head. 'You have family?'

'A sister.'

'You are close?' She is gauging me. A lie detector in pearls. I shake my head, no. 'So you are alone. Why do you want the Three Brethren?'

It catches me off guard. Not the change of direction, but the astuteness of the question. It is what I would ask myself, if I could.

'Because–' I am thinking of my own head. Opening it up, like the back of a watch, the shell of a crab. My whole life clear, a mechanism in flesh. But it isn't like that. It is never so easy. 'I just do. Because it is perfect. The perfect jewel.'

'Ah? Perhaps you are right.' Glött is no longer looking at me. From the back of the sofa she digs out a cigar case of dented silver. She extracts a fresh panatella and matches, lights up, smokes. 'Tell me, have you heard of the Crown of the Andes?'

'No.'

'No?' She puts on her surprised face again, a pantomime expression. It reminds me of Yohei. Sweets from strangers. 'I understood that you were an expert in stones.'

'Stones, not crowns. Ring the Queen Mother.'

She looks away from me as if I have failed her. 'I hoped to find that you knew a little more than this. The Crown of the Andes was made by the conquistadores of Spain. It was an artefact of their conquest of the Andes, or that is what they intended it to be. They put into it the finest of everything they took. It was carved whole from a single piece of gold, a hundred pounds of Incan ore. This was four centuries ago. They set their crown with four hundred and fifty-three emeralds–'

'You think emeralds are vulgar.'

'They are, of course. But if you pursue vulgarity with great enthusiasm it comes to have a certain rank style. Four hundred and fifty-three emeralds, of which the largest was forty-five carats. That stone having been taken from the Incan King Atahuallpa himself.'

Smoke gathers around her as she talks. From outside comes the sound of a truck changing gears, years away.

'For centuries most jewellers in Europe thought the Crown of the Andes was a myth. It was considered to be a Holy Grail of stones. But it was legendary, not mythical. It still exists.'

'Really.'

'You don't believe me? It even has its own secret army to

protect it. The Confraternity of the Immaculate Conception.' She puts the cigar down in the porcelain dish, taking care not to break the lit ash. Sighs out smoke. 'The Crown of the Andes. I don't know if it is the perfect jewel. But there are many objects, many artefacts, that could make that claim. Don't you agree?'

'Maybe.'

'Maybe certainly. Then I will ask you again. Why do you want the Three Brethren?'

It is so easy to underestimate the old. I open my mouth to answer and find I have nothing to say. I sit there, blinking in the light and smoke. She begins to cough, and it is only when I look at her that I see it is laughter.

'There. That's better. What is the time? Where is my watch?'

I find it for her. It is an International. Old gold, old leather. There is a smudge of mouse-shit across the buckle. Glött peers at the small face. 'My God, what time does it read?'

'Almost two,' I say, but she knows, is not listening. She doesn't need my help. Already she is tottering up out of the sofa. Her anger boils up again out of nothing.

'What do you think we are doing, sitting here talking when you should be working? Why didn't you tell me? You are here to catalogue stones, not to listen to music. Are you prepared?'

I shrug. She peers down at me, as if I were another watch-face to be distrusted. 'You don't look prepared.'

'I'm as ready as you are. Shall we go?'

And we go. She walks fast but stiffly, as if her legs refuse to bend. If she finds the stairs difficult she doesn't say. I go up three flights behind her, watching her work against her age, as if I could catch her. As if I care so much or intend to be here, one day, when she falls.

There are more windows on the upper floors. As we walk I catch glimpses of a flat roof garden in a landscape of eaves. Beyond Glött's house, the old town and the new. Buntings of peppers drying in the sun, orange and red and old-blood black.

'I will expect a preliminary report from you this evening. You will eat with us at eight o'clock.' Below I see the central courtyard. Doves with splay-feathered feet shuffle round the pool like inmates. Hassan is under the trees, hosing down the basalt paving.

'Us?'

'I have a relation staying. Martin.' Her voice warms to his name. She doesn't mention the girl. 'Supper is served in the kitchen. Hassan will come for you. You have something to wear? Jewellery?'

'No.' We reach the end of the hall. There is only one door. Eva takes out a ring of keys and fusses through them. 'I can find my own way.'

'I find it odd you carry nothing with you. A lady should always have jewellery. For those times she misses the feel of gold. If you wish to borrow something of mine, you may do so. Anything you see.'

'Thank you,' I make myself say, although the generosity jars a little. It feels too easy, like bait. 'You don't come up here often?'

The door unlocks. She gives me a quick stare. I follow her inside.

It is quiet as a library – quieter, that is, than somewhere simply left empty. It feels as if it has been locked for many years longer than I have been alive. There are skylights through which faint columns of sun fall. Under each light stands an urn and plinth. The nearest pair are Blue John crystal. They catch the sun and turn it purple.

It is not what I expected to find in Diyarbak'r, this place. Glött's room of stones is like all the gemmological archives I have known. There is always this hush. Always the drawers, cut stones at the top, uncut by the floor. There is always a smell of preservatives, although jewels need no preservatives. I feel at home here. More than that, I sense a commonality. The impulse in this room reflects something in me. A kind of love that no longer requires people.

By the drawers rests a set of librarian's steps. It is skewed backwards, a staircase to nowhere. In the centre of the room is a single leather-topped desk. I walk over to its fossilised clutter. A chair tucked in neat as a shirt. Two green glass lamps. A manual typewriter. A parcel with a Berlin address, mummified in wrappings and dust. A German newspaper yellowed as old ivory, dated Christmas 1903. The headline: AMERICAN FLYING MEN.

An empty bottle of claret, the glass beside it quarter-filled with dust. I pick up the glass. It smells not of wine but of calvados. Eighty-five years old, the essence of apples.

'My father cared a great deal about stones.'

'I can see that.' The wooden strata loom above me. Altogether it is a massive collection. A lifetime's achievement.

'I never liked them.'

'You said.' I put down the glass. On the floor by the chair, tracks in the dust. 'Someone has been up here.'

'Here? Not for a very long time. Now, to business. I mean to sell all of this, as soon as I know what price I can get for it. You will see that my father catalogued everything as he went along. He liked people to think he was a consistent man.'

I leave the desk. Each drawer has an identification plaque of yellowed plastic. They are all in German, Gothic script. The terms I know in a number of languages. Beryl and chrysoberyl, quartz and cryptocrystalline quartz. *Pyroxene 3-22. Amphibole 99-129.*

'Which, unfortunately, he was not. Do you have any German, Miss Sterne?'

'Some.'

'Your knowledge of stones will make up for your inability. You are free to work in English.'

'Fraülein–'

'Glött. Please.'

'Glött. I'm afraid I don't see what you need me for. Everything here appears to be in good order.'

'Appears.' She coughs or laughs, again it is hard to tell. 'You think I brought you up here to admire the view? How can it appear, when you have not looked at the stones? Eh? Look.' She yanks open a drawer, the stones rattling in their cavities. Picks them out clumsily, a child playing havoc with a box of chocolates. Drops them into my hands.

The light is better beside the urns. I turn the gems in my palms. I can see what they are already, all the usual suspects. 'Your father had a good eye.'

'They are valuable?' I hear her moving in.

'Depends. Probably not in the terms you mean. They're jewel-quality. These are onyx, this is bloodstone, with some kind of signet carving. Ah. More agate, more jasper. Moonstone.' I look back at the identification plaque. 'But this is wrong. The moonstone isn't a quartz. It shouldn't be here.'

'A prize for effort. Nothing for observation.'

The old woman leans on the urn beside me. I could tell her that the stone lip is delicate, that Blue John is fragile, but she wouldn't care. Her hands are white on the purple crystal.

'Pick any drawer here, you will find the same thing.'

'Why?' I look around. The urn rocks on its plinth and I put a hand out to stop it falling. 'I mean, how did this happen?'

'Because my father was a useless man.' When she talks loudly I can smell her breath. Tobacco and oil. I try not to flinch away. 'I have spent much of my life putting his life right.'

'And what do you think I can do here? Recatalogue the whole collection?'

'That is what we agreed. My help for yours.' She watches me, waiting. I look up at the shelves again. In the disorder they hide, they become mythic. They are the pile of wheat and barley. The field to be cut, husked and baked into bread by morning. The stable heaped with shit. I don't try to stop myself as I begin to smile.

'What is it you find so funny?'

'The idea that anything in here could be found.' I try and take in the room with a one-handed gesture. It isn't enough, which is the point. 'Fraülein, this isn't possible. It would take a team of professionals many months to do this. Alone, it would take me years.'

'And you don't have time?'

'No, I don't.'

'We had an agreement.'

'No. We didn't.' I watch her eyes. They catch the light, shining. 'You want it, don't you?'

For a second I don't know what she means. She leans towards me. Tobacco and oil. 'You want the Three Brethren?'

A claustrophobia rises up in me. Glött walks back towards the door. Her voice echoes against the room's hard surfaces. 'It is up to you, of course. But it seems a pity. To come all this way. My father's papers are all here, all the accounts, the records, the details you are looking for, the Brethren transaction: it will be here somewhere. Everything is.'

'I can see that.'

I stand quite still. She gives me time. I am trying to decide, not whether I will stay, but why I veer back from doing so. It is not the collection so much as the feeling that I am being forced into something. In the doorway the old woman waits.

'What if I find the transaction tomorrow?'

149

'Then you must go and get your jewel. Of course.' Overhead, a pigeon walks across the roof tiles. The tickertape of its footsteps starts and stops. Stops. Starts.

'And if I don't?'

She smiles. Blue-white teeth, brown-white, ivory. I think of them after she is gone. The colours of pearls and skin.

It takes a considerable amount of time to find nothing. Time has never been my problem before, but these things can change. Glött's collection reminds me of something from a folk tale, as if I could walk out tomorrow and find that a century has passed.

Nothing is where it should be. By evening I have redistributed a rubble of minor gems, butter and honey ambers and ruin agates. But the drawers are full of the unexpected. They are Cornell boxes, exhibits in an exhibition. In one I find a carving knife, its blade sharpened almost to nothing, a lick of steel. In another, a chess case full of mothballs, boxes inside boxes. In *Diamonds 6* I come across a sealed jar. It contains what the alchemists used to call a Tree of Diana: a crystal of silver, its tiny struts and spars suspended in liquid like a laboratory foetus. And on the desk papers, repeated again and again, is a faded sepia signature, *R. F. von Glött*. The man who cried over the Brethren.

I was wrong about him. He had no eye for stones, only the money to buy what he liked. And he liked everything. Loved without discrimination. His character is all around me, preserved in his stones. If any of them has value, it is only because money goes to money. It is hours before I discover there are real jewels hidden here.

In a wall of drawers marked *Miscellany* I find a piece of violet coral the length of a child's fingerbone. A balla, which is a spherical diamond, the crystals intergrown into unworkable hardness. In the desk's middle drawer, next to an American revolver, are ten Islamic manuscripts illuminated with ochre and welts of gold. I record their presence along with everything else, hammering on the typewriter. I take nothing, although the balla alone could fund my search for some years. Today I am the honest lapidary bent over her loupe. I don't want money from Glött, just information. I only ever take what I need. This is what I tell myself.

At four o'clock there is a bang at the door. I turn round and the old woman is leaning there, a cocktail glass slopping in each hand.

'What have you found?' She is already drunk. I put down my loupe, walk over, and take the drinks out of her sticky fingers.

'Thank you. Nothing.' I sip the glass. She is watching me, rouged and expectant.

'It is a frozen margarita.'

'I know what it is.' I stop myself. The reality of the work has made me sullen. 'It's delicious, Fraülein.'

'There are more in the kitchen. I made a mixer . . .'

'Fraülein – Glött–'

'Eva.'

'Eva. I have to work.'

'Of course, of course, you are looking for your lost brothers.'

'Brethren.'

'Brethren!' She laughs, head back, not far from hilarity. 'Aha. You make me feel young, Katharine Sterne. I must thank you. You are remarkably old.'

I shake my head, not understanding. She talks through me. 'Now! I will make you another deal. Drink this drink with me, and I will make a toast.'

I give her back a glass. She holds it as if she is drying her nails. Glött in party mode is a different creature from the recluse, brooding over old music and the philosophy of pearls. We toast.

'To your Three Brethren. That they fall in your way.'

'That they fall in my way.'

'*Cam cam'a dêil, can can'a.*'

I try to copy her words, and fail. We both laugh. 'What does that mean?'

She frowns and knocks her glass against mine like a hammer. It doesn't break. 'Not glass to glass but soul to soul.' Then she smiles up at me. 'I will see you at supper.'

'Maybe.'

'Maybe certainly!' She goes. I listen to her on the stairs. She doesn't fall. I would be no help to her if she did. I get back to my own work.

When the daylight is gone I stop. There is more I could do, it is only the stones which require natural light, and I haven't written anything that might remotely be called a report. Still, Glött isn't going to sack me. Whatever position she is in, wherever that places me, we are not employer and employed.

At the door I look back at the fossilised room. The lamps lean forward in the gloom like animals sleeping. The house is quiet around me as I walk back through its corridors. Somewhere there is a window open, I can hear Diyarbak'r. When I reach it I stop. Lean out.

Cities seem more alike at night, and also more beautiful. They can also seem less dangerous, although this is deceptive. The air is sweeter. What smells, smells less. The night light is kinder, more human. In the dark, Diyarbak'r is sixties blocks, neon lights, yellow cabs. The people in their evening clothes, the women in their evening gold. I see men, walking arm in arm. Brothers in arms. It feels like a long time, days, since I have seen people so alive in themselves. It could be Rio de Janeiro out there or Bangkok, Tokyo or Istanbul. It could be anywhere.

It is a long way back to my room. Twice I take wrong turnings. There is a complexity to Glött's house which makes me think of drawings by Escher. Aqueducts along which water runs backwards. Staircases that end at their beginnings, all their laws broken.

It is past seven. The flowers outside my room are gone. Incense burns in their place. I lock my door and lie down on the bed. Close my eyes. Behind them I see the miniature courtyard. It comes to me before I am wholly asleep. Not a dream, but something more urgent. I can see the tree in the night air, the trunk in its dark lift-shaft of space. The leaves pressed against stone.

It is weaker than a dream. I try and push it away and immediately it is gone. For a space of seconds I am left with nothing. Not awake, not asleep, but trapped in between. Against the pillow, inside my skull, the sound of blood comes beating upwards from my heart.

茶

It is humid today. The heel of my hand dampens the page as I write. I can hear the muezzin before dawn, after dawn, at noon.

It is still an odd sound to me. Natural but out of place, like the moon in daylight.

There is the sound of children in a school nearby. Today they are being wolves, the playground is full of small lupine voices. Yesterday they were sirens. Police cars and fire engines. I can see them from the windows outside the stone room. They are six, maybe seven. It is an age I remember well in myself. Adrenaline gives memory great precision. What I remember of that time, I recall exactly.

The stone room clock ticks above me. It is an Ottoman skeleton timepiece, the works housed in a glass dome, as if time could be kept out with the dust; or kept in. It reminds me of the house itself, with its bare stone; and beyond that, of the life of the old woman. The transparency of her desire. I have been here two days and found nothing.

I am writing the story of myself, which is also the story of the Three Brethren. It is a question of perspective. The jewel has been the turning point of many lives, and mine is only one.

Have I written this before? But I am part of it, that is what I mean to say. The history of the Three Brethren does not begin with John the Fearless or end a hundred and fifty years ago in London. It still exists and I am still writing it. I am pulling the pieces together. One of them is me.

My mother was always clean. It was important to her, so it was important to us. She washed her hands before she ate and so did we. She never put off work and I still don't. She kept silver milk tops in a jar, rinsed the bottles, recycled them. I remember sunlight inside the glass, webs of bubbles.

Edith. She was old when I was born. She still exhibited every year, and worked for *Visual Art* and the *Sunday Times* which was, she said, politically questionable, but the lens justified the beans. I remember not understanding her and liking it, laughing instinctively because it meant she was joking. She hated journalism, the lies and generalisations passing through her hands. But she was a good photographer, serious, with a dislike of light work – which meant social snapshot diaries, the tabloids were beyond her. Edith couldn't credit a world that read page three and wrapped chips in the rest.

She wore prescription sunglasses. She believed in astrology but not in God. Her hair was magnificently white. She still had better legs than anyone else's mother. Edith always meant to have a family once she had made a success of her career, and that was exactly what she did. Having a husband was not part of the plan. Edith liked things simple.

I remember very little of my father. His name was Patrick and he was Canadian. He was ten years older than my mother, who was old herself. Anne tells me he is retired now, living in Florida with a new American wife and grown children. I have little interest in him. He is not what I'm looking for.

He was an underwater geologist, and although I was too young when he left to have understood this myself, I remember associating him with the sea. I remember his clothes. He wore tweeds, cords, plaid, fabrics made in the colours of a northern country.

They smelled of damp. I imagined him walking underwater from Canada. He stepped out of the sea, clambered out on Southend Pier and walked the twenty miles to our house, the wind drying him as he came.

My mother lived without fuss, and when she died she left no mess. The washing was done. Her book was finished. She was reading – so I am told – Marquez's *One Hundred Years of Solitude*. I never went to the funeral, May wouldn't allow it. But I saw her dead. There was no blood on her, not a speck on her. No proof of a life cut off in mid-step, of something unfinished.

Except in us. In me. I am unfinished business.

Afterwards we lived with May, my mother's mother. She liked poetry and German cars. She hated the Prudential and Buckingham Palace. She'd worked as ground support in the war. Back then she could strip a car and reassemble it in fifteen minutes. There hadn't been much else to do in Southend until the Blitz, so she'd stripped cars all day, timing herself. She was eighty-one when we moved in. Her arms were like the sailor's on her cigarette packets.

Her house was a mile away from home, on the Southend road. It always smelt of cabbages, even though we never ate anything much except fish fingers. We made good school drawings: one grandmother, two daughters, three dogs. A pyramidal family was more interesting than the two-up, two-down units in picture books. There was a tennis court in the garden where we played goal-to-goal football. It only needs two of you, and there were only two of us.

My sister is called Anne. She is five years older than me. I used to love her like a film star. She used to understand everything, even Edith's jokes, when I understood nothing. I remember her first boyfriend, Stewart. He was popular at school because he could fart like a seal barking. I was jealous of him, jealous of her for having him, proud to have them both.

These days she runs an international charity. She travels a lot. Her fiancé is called Rolf and he makes me laugh. Presumably he farts but not, I think, like a seal barking, not in public. I am public. It is years, now, since I have seen either of them. My sister has a life that works in all the ways a life should work, and I'm happy for that. I don't want to get in its way. I try and keep away from Anne, not because I have stopped loving her but because she doesn't understand what I'm doing and I wouldn't want her to.

She left over a thousand photographs. Anne kept a great many of them, I think; I didn't want so many myself. Now I have only three of the ones that fell, the photos that were there when I found her. I can take them out as I write, peeling them from their places, pressed between the pages of my notebook.

(1) 35mm, taken with the Leica. Handheld, shot from Edith's height. Anne stopped in mid-step, catching herself in a photo-booth mirror. She is eleven, dressed in her new school uniform. Already she is more beautiful than I will ever be. In the mirror she looks curious, still surprised by herself. It is the summer before her mother dies. Behind her, in the mirror, the tide is out. Southend Pier diminishes towards its vanishing-point.

(2) Monotone. A tripod shot. Mud at a farm gate. The soil is red, ferrous; Herefordshire, possibly, where Edith had friends. The shot is all texture, a Cufic of hoofprints and dog tracks. Boot-marks. The churned tread of a tractor. Mud slumps back into the ruts and cavities.

(3) Myself. An older photograph, a polaroid kept with the others for no perceptible reason. I am sitting at the kitchen table,

barely tall enough to see over it. On the table is a birthday cake with chocolate icing and a pond of green jelly. I am wearing a floral dress and a small cone hat. My eyes wait for the cake. Head back, the hat-elastic white under my chin. Behind me, the dark is locked up behind the darkroom door.

I don't keep it for myself. There is a blur on the image. Rare and precious, my mother's finger, exposed in the foreground.

I'm moving in now. The events spiral towards their point. I'm getting to it one facet at a time. Skew to skill, bezel to quoin.

I am in my sister's house. This must be five years ago. It is midwinter in London and the bookies are still taking bets on a white Christmas. It is my sister's birthday. From downstairs comes the hubbub of party voices, laughter. I am taking off my great coat, throwing it on the bed, when I see Anne's computer.

She was talking about it downstairs. I wasn't really listening. It is a present from Rolf, her new German boyfriend. The desk is surrounded by empty oversized boxes, patterned with big black and white splotches. Like square cows, I think, but then I have been drinking already, was drinking before I arrived here. It is a week since I gave up my degree in linguistics at the School of Oriental and African Studies. I have other things to do with my life, although Anne doesn't agree. I have begun to look for something.

Rising between the colossal boxes is an equally colossal computer. There are speakers, towers, the plateaus of a keyboard and scanner. It reminds me of a doll's house, although Anne never had a doll's house, was never a doll's house kind of girl. The monitor is on, a screen saver spiralling through colourful abstracts. Pyramids, triangles, surfaces, planes.

I sit at the desk. The computer still smells of packing. It is brand new, like Rolf. I touch the keyboard and the patterns disappear. In their place is an Internet menu. Lazy sister, I think. Wasteful, to leave your computer on. Still, I am curious. I don't have a real computer myself, only a second-hand college Amstrad that sheds a foul green light from its stained monitor. The Internet is new to me, and potentially useful.

It is thirteen years since my mother died. Two years since I saw the Black Prince's ruby. I have been haunted by it ever since.

It is five months since, while researching balas rubies, I first came across the story of the Three Brethren. I wanted it at first sight. I can't say why.

I touch the keys of my sister's computer, *ta ta ta*. The menu is a list of sites. The names rise as I move through them, a slow progression past www.anchor.ouija.co and www.big.bazongs.co.uk. If there are quicker ways to do this I don't know them. I am an outsider here. A surfer; a traveller of surfaces.

I sit drinking, one finger on the down button. The wine stains my mouth, I can taste its residue on my lips. When I look at the screen again I have reached www.jewsforjesus, and I reverse and stop. There are almost forty sites that define themselves by the word 'jewels'. I choose one at random. An hourglass symbol appears. When the sand runs out, the site opens.

It is a chat room, or at least a chat-room company. Along the screen's edge is a menu of meeting places, space for hire, *TV Soaps, Armchair Football, Lonely Hearts*. Alongside them a username waits patiently in its box: STERNE7. I wonder why Anne comes here, who she talks to, and where. The cursor blinks on *Jewels and Antiques (The Net's Only Collectibles Chatroom!)*. I double-click and the room appears. Abracadabra. Boxes within boxes.

There are several people inside. Their texts scroll across the screen, one after the other, like waves. Two of them are discussing animal motifs in the Oxus Treasure. A third wants to talk about his revolutionary new method for boiling Thai rice. I leave a message anyway. My typing is fast but inaccurate. I always make mistakes. It isn't just the drink.

STERNE7 JOINING, HELO. I'M LOOKING FOR A JEW CALLED THE THREE BRETHREN. ANY HELP? K.SNERTE.

'Christ, I can't even spell my own name,' I say. And then before I can correct myself my sister is calling for me. There is a question in her voice. I have been gone too long, absent from her celebration. I leave the screen and go down into the crowd.

At five in the morning I finish helping Anne clear up. My eyes sting with smoke and tiredness. Look, she says, leaning over the kitchen sink, snow! I go upstairs to get my coat. I am looking forward to being outside. The feel of first light. The fat flakes waking me as they fall.

The coat buttons are a complex manoeuvre. I am working at them when a movement catches my eye. The computer is still on. The screen saver tumbles through its blueprints of snowflakes and crystals. I go over, touch the keys. The chat room is still there. My message has been erased by subsequent small talk. Somewhere it is day, I think, and people are seeing this in natural light; and as I watch a new line spells itself out: 71192X. TO STERNE7 – WE REPEAT AGAIN: JEWEL. NOT JEW. WHO ARE YOU?

I feel myself come awake. Without intending it, my bad typing has produced a codeword. And someone has broken it. How interesting. I think how naive I've been, not to use the Internet before today. I type: STERNE7. TO 71192X – MY NAME IS KATHARINE STERNE. WHO ARE YOU?

The answer comes back immediately. As if the typist has been poised, waiting: 71192X. A WORKER.

STERNE7. FOR WHAT COMPANY?

The screen stays empty. I look at my watch and wonder how long I can stay. How long Anne and Rolf will want me around. Outside the dark is fading to a cold morning light. When I look back again, a new message is already surfacing on the blue-lit screen:

71192X. WE ARE RESEARCHERS. WE WOULD LIKE TO MEET YOU. WE WOULD LIKE TO KNOW WHAT YOU KNOW.

I reach for the wine again, clumsily, so that it almost falls. I drain the glass as I type. Inattentive, already thinking of sleep. STERNE7. WHERE?

71192X. WHERE YOU ARE.

My mind blinks. The sensation is reptilian. A slow nictitation during which I think of nothing. Then the fear begins.

STERNE7. WHO DO YOU WORK FOR?

71192X.

I stab at the switch. The screen winks out with a small, painful grunt. I think of Anne, of Rolf. Should I tell them? But it could be nothing. I try and think if I could be found through the Net, but I don't know. It is a world I have no experience in. I back away into my sister's room.

It leaves too many fingerprints, the Internet. I don't trust it. Inside the computer you never know when you are being watched, or where from. The next country, the next room. If there are other people looking for the Brethren, then the Internet is the worst way to make the search, the most dangerous. There are better ways to find a jewel.

I am not the only one looking. I don't know who the others are. Even so, I take a certain comfort from them. As if their threat proves me right.

My first stone was a birthday present from May. I was eleven. It was an amethyst the size of an egg. The purple was so faint you had to concentrate. You had to hold it just right to catch the shade of wisteria flowers.

I think of my mother's voice in my ear. Her cheek next to mine in the bathroom mirror: *There. You're so lovely, I could eat you up!* The stone egg was like that. I wanted to consume it. To get it inside me. I slept with it in my bed, the way other children still kept their old toys. I walked to school with it in my mouth. Anne tried to stop me. She was afraid I'd swallow it the way, years before, I'd once swallowed a pencil stub. The amethyst clicked against my teeth like a Glacier mint. It stopped me getting hungry. I was filled up with stone.

I began to collect gems. At weekends when we went to Margate I beachcombed for carnelian and agate. I divided my stones on scientific principles. I didn't love them yet. I liked their differences and their repetition. They were alike but not alike. Rhymes sung in different voices. There was something safe in that. Something to be sure of.

This isn't the reason I'm looking for the Brethren. None of this. I am sure of it. I'm not looking for a means to escape the past. The past is there in everything I do. The need for something was there already, long before Edith died. I remember it, always. The feel of obsession: like a reservoir of love gone sour. Inside me there was a love waiting to happen, and eventually, the jewel is what it happened to.

Doctor Angel was not our doctor, Doctor Sargent was. The hospital was the same but the corridors were different. In this building the walls were green from the floor to the middle and brown from the middle to the top. In Doctor Sargent's building the walls were yellow with a band of red down the middle. When I was smaller

Anne told me it was a go-faster stripe. It made people get well quicker, she said. I didn't believe that by the time Edith died. I missed the stripe, though.

'Doctor Angel isn't our doctor,' I say. 'Doctor Sargent is. Why can't we see Doctor Sargent?'

'Because Sargent's a GP. This one's a blood doctor,' says Anne. We are walking down the two-tone corridor with a nurse. She has an old plaster on her left knee under cheap stockings. Knees are more important when you're a child. At three you can recognise your parents' knees at thirty paces. I read it in a magazine. At seven the effect is probably residual, but even so, the nurse's knees are closer than her face. From her knees I know she doesn't look after herself properly, and so, at first, I'm glad I'm staying with Doctor Angel. His knees are behind the desk. His head is red. He says hello, then goes on writing. I sit waiting to be noticed.

The room smells of disinfectant and unwashed clothes. The sign on the desk says: Dr Angel. *Haematology*. The third word is years beyond me. The doctor keeps coughing. It makes him sound like a small, aggressive dog. *Ghrr-ghrrm*. When he coughs I want to hit him. I think he's rude, not to talk to me. People have been talking to me for days.

'*Ghrrm*.'

I look around. There are no nice pictures on the walls, just a poster showing eight types of blood clot. Each clot has a name, Chicken Fat, Currant Jelly. Like flavours, I think. Chicken fat crisps. Chicken fat pasties. Currant jelly ice cream. Currant jelly jelly. I know what a blood clot is.

'*Ghrr-Ghrrm*.'

'You should make it better.'

'Mm?'

He looks up. His eyes find me but he doesn't see me, not properly. He has no feeling for children, no like or dislike: we are invisible to him. I don't know this as I sit in the examination room. I see it now, watching him from my stone room in Diyarbak'r, listening to the tickertape of pigeons' feet overhead.

'You should make your cough better. You're the doctor.'

He smiles as if I've made a joke he doesn't understand, and goes back to his writing. I am already bored, have been bored for some time. From outside the window comes the sound of water.

I imagine it. There is a blue fountain with red fish. I feed the fish. I have a packet of chicken fat crisps. I scatter them over the water.

I sit and watch Doctor Angel's head. The bald skin is red. I wonder what he drinks. My mother drinks Dutch gin, neat. There are still two bottles left. I wonder if we can give Doctor Angel the leftover Dutch gin. It would make his skin redder. He feels me watching. He stops reading and looks up.

'It's Kate, isn't it? How old are you, Kate?'

'Eight,' I lie. I want to see if he is clever enough to find the truth. It is a test. He winks and smiles. Already I am failing him.

'Eight. You know, I have a patient who is eighty-eight. Eighty-eight, two fat ladies.'

I say nothing. I have nothing to say to him. 'Kate, do you understand how your mother died?'

'Don't say that.'

'I'm sorry? I–'

'I don't want you to say that word.' But I shrug, as if it doesn't matter. The window is open, but the room is still humid, overheated. My dress is stuck against my legs. I imagine being outside, running in the cold December air. The fountain, the fish. Blue and red.

'I see. Well, your – she had a pain in her legs. That was a thrombus, a blood clot that forms in the deep veins. It's important to understand.'

'I know what a clot is,' I say. I think, Thrombus After Eight Mints. It isn't much of a name. Even for a clot.

'You're a clever girl, aren't you? Now then, sometimes a clot happens when people are inactive – when they don't move enough. Then the blood doesn't move either. Or sometimes, the clot happens because there's something in the family. Like blue eyes. That's why you're here. For a test.'

'We have them in school.' I wonder how Anne is doing in her test. If blue eyes help. I wish she would come back. There is a feeling in the room, nothing I really understand. It feels as if the air is clumsy. As if something might hurt itself here.

It is five years before claims of malpractice against Doctor Angel reach the local newspapers. A year more before he leaves Southend Hospital, a health authority committee driving him first to the private sector, then to a clinic in Malaga. I followed his progress for some time. I had an interest.

The blood doctor smiles. His teeth are splayed out in the middle, as if he has put too many in his mouth at once. Greedy teeth. 'Clever girl. Do you like tests, Kate? How about sports, or games?'

'My name's Katharine,' I say, and he stops smiling. The air lurches between us. He clears his throat again, looks down, and goes on talking.

'Well now, then, you see, the thrombus broke up into two bits. One of them, an embolus, went up into your – into her head. That's what affected her. Doctors call it a cerebral embolism. You may not want to know all this now. I'm trying to help you understand later, Kate. Katharine.'

I say nothing. I am too busy thinking of Thrombus cough sweets. Green with a red stripe down the middle.

'A cerebral embolism. Hers was quite exceptional. Highly unusual integrity.'

I imagine the blood in my mother's legs. It is motionless. Thickening, like mud at the seaside, mud squeezed underfoot. Doctor Angel is still talking, his voice curving up into a question. I look into his wet eyes.

'What?'

'I asked if you'd like to see it? The embolus. The clot. You're a clever girl, and you know what a clot is. I think it might help, don't you? To get things out in the open. To have things clear.'

I say nothing.

He says, 'To see it.'

'Okay.'

He smiles again and stands up. In the corner of the room is a trolley with two cluttered trays. Doctor Angel gets a jar from the bottom tray. When he brings it round I catch sight of something red, and it is only then I understand what he is doing.

I don't want to see what he is holding. I think about shutting my eyes, but I don't. I say nothing. I wish Anne was back. I'm not scared. I think, Ford Thrombus. I wish I was far away. My mother driving.

'Here. Do you want to hold it?'

'No.' He doesn't hear me. My fists are white against my sides. Doctor Angel brings the jar down to my face. I can't look at it too hard. It hurts my eyes, like the lights at the dentist's.

The jar reminds me of fishbowls. In the clear liquid hangs a jewel. It is a deep red rose, big as a baby's fist. A drop of paler blood clings to its side.

'There now. You don't see that very often, do you?'

'No.'

'No.' I look up at Doctor Angel. He is smiling through me, not at me. I can peer back eighteen years now, into his damp eyes, and see that he is trying to help in some way. To get things out in the open. He doesn't understand that he is doing anything wrong. There is a confusion there that I can't comprehend, then or now. Perhaps he never did either.

I don't get angry until he turns away with the jar. Then I stand up and begin to scream. I am breathless with rage. Anne comes with the nurses and we leave. I never get to take the test. At the hospital gates May's car goes faster, faster, the railing blurred into one long stripe.

不不

On the ninth night I dream of Istanbul. In the dream I am buying fresh pistachios. I have eaten nothing else all day.

Something is following me through the crowded streets. I catch only glimpses. It is a dog, but scaled, monstrous. Its muzzle is almost level with the heads around it. No one registers its presence. I reach the Sindbad Tourist Hotel, but when I go up to my room the door is ajar, the lock broken.

Everything is gone. The rubies, the notebooks, the case with its exterior of veined leather. It feels as if someone has stolen my soul. And as I stand there, lost, there is a noise in the stairwell behind me. A click of claws on the chipstone steps.

I wake before first light. Usually I am sharp at this time of day but not this morning. My head feels like an accident waiting to happen. I go down to the kitchen, brew some coffee and burn some toast. After carving off the residual carbon, I take my breakfast up to the roof garden.

Glött is there before me. She is reading an out-of-date issue of the *Frankfurter Allgemeine Zeitung*. On the ironwork table beside her is a glass of sour cherry juice and a bottle of vodka. She looks up at me, nods, looks away.

I sit and eat my burnt toast while the sun comes up. The stone tiles begin to warm under my feet. It is going to be a beautiful day.

'Stop staring at me.'

I look up at her. 'I wasn't.'

'You always stare, Katharine. You are like a cat. I have cancer, you know.' She snaps the newspaper flat. Folds it. 'You can't see it. I am very old. It only kills me very slowly. Some people blame it on plastics.'

'What do you blame it on?'

'The communists.'

'Communists?'

'Do you like Martin?' She catches me off guard, not for the first time. Glött has a butterfly mind, but the butterfly always gets where it wants to go. Sometimes she seems mad; but then the rich are eccentric, never mad. Being rich and eccentric only means that society accepts you because it can't afford not to. People play by the rules of your games. The richer you are, the crueller they can be. Human chess or self-styled kingship. I wonder what rules Eva plays by, and if I am following them.

'Martin? I don't really know him.'

'Of course you do.'

'I don't know. I don't know if I like him.'

'You could do worse.'

'What does that mean?'

'Martin will inherit this place. You don't like it here?'

'I never said that.'

'Think of all those north European houses. The heads of foxes. It gives me the crawls.'

'Creeps. Eva, I'm not–'

She talks through me. 'Animals coming out of the walls. It is beastly. The Arab nations are older and more civilised.'

I think of Martin. His smell of tobacco and brass, which suits him. His girlfriend, Helene, who suits him too. I still don't know what he is doing in Glött's house, or what he does when he is not here. I can imagine him smoking months away in Thailand or Goa more easily than I can accept him in eastern Turkey. The only thing that doesn't suit Martin is Diyarbak'r.

'My mother always used to say that men marry down, women marry up.' She nods encouragingly.

'Is that supposed to be a compliment?'

She pouts. 'Martin is a handsome young man.'

'My mother used to say that beautiful people are like beautiful cars. Expensive to keep and bad for the environment. I never used to understand what she meant.'

'What utter nonsense.'

We sit together. More together than apart, although the table is between us. Eva von Glött drinks her cherry juice, thinned with vodka. I drink my cold coffee. The brightening blue of the sky hurts my eyes.

'You look tired,' says the recluse. She is wearing a panama hat and Armani sunglasses. The sunglasses are too big for her. They make her look like an insect in lipstick, although no one is about to tell her that, least of all me. Possibly that's the point of being a recluse in the first place.

'I was dreaming. It kept me up.' An aeroplane goes over, east towards India. I talk softly, watching it go. 'Something about a dog with scales.'

'What? What kind of dog?' She says it as if it would be her property. It irritates me and I don't answer. 'A dog with scales, was it?'

'Mind your own business. What did you dream of?'

'Sex. I usually do.'

She is leering at the thought. I have come to like Glött more than the place she lives in. Beyond the landscape of rooftops I can see the city, lowlands stretching to mountains in the east, plains to the south. Strata of distance, still grey with river mist. I prefer bigger cities than Diyarbak'r, and smaller horizons. The east of Turkey is too empty for me. This is a place I sense I could lose myself.

'There is a dog with scales in local myth. The sirrusch of Mesopotamia. You are dreaming of this place's past.'

'It wouldn't surprise me, I've been here long enough.' I sip my coffee. Cool and bitter in the hot light.

'What were its feet like?'

'I don't remember, Eva. I didn't look. Maybe it was wearing heels, would that help?'

'Don't be ridiculous. I am asking what kind of feet did it have? Were they claws, like a bird?'

'I don't know. It doesn't matter. And this was Turkey the last time I looked. Mesopotamia must be –' I look south '– not here.'

She picks up the bottle of Stolichnaya. Thins the cherry juice one more time. The bottle looks heavy in her frail hand. 'I like young people. I find them charming, when they are not talking. They are ignorant almost by definition.' She takes off her sunglasses. Stabs at the landscape. 'All this, up to the mountains, is Mesopotamia. The Land Between Rivers. Here is the Tigris, which the Arabs and Turks call Dijleh. A hundred kilometres behind us is the Euphrates. You see? The rivers say we are in Mesopotamia. Not even Atatürk can change that.'

She goes quiet. We sit watching the Tigris. Around it are acres of watermelon pits and flat irrigated fields. There are already people working around the melons, small with distance, reduced to the repetitions of their actions. It is what the history of the jewel does to its generations of owners. I follow the valley with my eyes, down towards Syria and Iraq. I can probably see them from here, although it is impossible to be sure. The Land of Two Veins, Mesopotamia.

When I look back the old woman is watching me. 'You probably think this is the end of the world. Eh?'

'It's not that bad.'

Her mouth thins as she squints into the sun. 'Diyarbak'r is five thousand years old. You can't imagine it. It is a privilege to be here. A privilege, Katharine. The Romans were here, and Alexander, Timur the Lame. Alexander had a great shoulder-knot, did you know? A great clasp, like the Three Brethren.'

'What happened to it?'

'It's lost, of course.'

I lean toward her. 'Eva, I'm glad you like it here, but it's not what I'm looking for. No offence. I'm just trying to find the Brethren. Have you remembered anything yet?' She ignores me. I speak up. 'About the Brethren.'

'Oh! That reminds me.' She leers at me again. 'I had a telephone call from an associate of mine. His name is Araf. He is President of Golden Horn Shipping and Air. But then you know that, don't you?'

She watches me go still. I think she enjoys it. 'You didn't tell me.'

'Why should I? He didn't call you. Besides, it was days ago.'

'What did he say?'

'That you are a thief.' Glött cackles as if she has made a dirty joke. 'That I should telephone him if I saw you. And that you are on a wild ghost chase. Ghost, he said, eh? Such a foolish man.'

'And what did you tell him?'

'Nothing. He sent me a calendar once.' She puts her sunglasses back on. 'New money. Grotesque taste.'

'Thank you.'

'No, it was my pleasure.'

Her head wobbles as she smiles. She looks drunk now. It's not yet noon. She's hours ahead of schedule. I stand up and stack the cup, the plate, her empty bottle and glass.

'I should go and work.'

'Of course you should. I will see you at supper?'

'Maybe.' I say it as I'm walking away. Her voice comes back distantly, like an echo.

'Maybe certainly.'

The stone room waits as I left it. When Glött first brought me here her father's collection was hidden behind a façade of order. All I have managed to do is break down the façade. It has taken me ten days.

I put down the breakfast things and consider the stones. They are held back in the archives like a landslide waiting to happen. The furniture has ended up arranged in attitudes suggesting furtive escape. Urns retreated against the walls. Archive drawers crowded over the librarian's steps and the tiled floor, as if I have caught them in the act of surging towards the exit.

At the far end are the *Miscellany* shelves. In principle, if the details of the Brethren transaction exist, this is where I should find them. But then nothing in the stone room is where it should be; if anything, that seems to be its underlying principle.

It's two days since I broke the Glött system, and it hasn't helped. Alongside the gemmological divisions of minerals are geographical subdivisions for objects that contain more than one type of stone. Jewellery in these sections is classified according to its dominant jewel. A gold bookmark set with Mikimoto cultured pearls, for example, is in one of three drawers marked

Miscellany: Japan. A Louis François Cartier sketch for a necklace of chalcedony and Egyptian emeralds is filed in the twenty-seventh drawer of *North Africa*.

It is the system of an unsystematic man. So many raw jewels come from Africa or Asia that there are nearly a hundred drawers for India alone. And the system is no use for the Brethren, since the shoulder-knot has no primary stone. Either that or all its jewels are dominant, the pearls according to number, the rubies by virtue of carats, the diamond by reputation. And if Glött's father had settled on one of these, which country would he assign it to? How much did he know about the Brethren, and where do the stones begin?

I get to work. For two days I have been looking through the countries that might represent the shoulder-knot, the five drawers of France, the twelve that are Persia. Yesterday I gave up halfway through India, and now I start where I left off. In the first drawer is a golden locket containing a Koran no larger than a human molar. In the second, a set of twelve agate plaques. They are carved with pictures of Buddhist demons and women in a variety of sexual positions. Most of them are rape scenes. I put them down like soiled tissues.

It is not a beautiful collection. The more I see of the old Glött's acquisitiveness, the less I like it. What he desired in jewels had less to do with beauty than with completeness. If he hadn't been wealthy he would have collected something else, beermats or butterflies or budgerigars: the impulse would have been the same. It feels as if he was trying to reassemble the world in one room. I have nothing in common with him, only stones.

By noon I have gone through fourteen drawers. The dust stains my hands and face. Twice I come to archives I've worked on before, and the jewels are not where I left them. I try not to think about what it means, because I know it means that I am fallible. In the stone room I need to be infallible.

Oddities turn up which have nowhere to go, and I pile them on the desk. There is a smiling Buddha, two inches high. It is carved from ebony and iris quartz, which has iridescent inclusions of water. The Buddha's eyes twinkle over his bellies and love handles. There is a tray of natural baroque pearls divided by form – Odds, Butterflies and Twins, grotesque functions of pain.

A lapidary's scales complete with thirty seeds from the locust tree *Ceratonia siliqua*, from which the carat measurement was derived. I experiment with them. Any four seeds will measure one carat. Every seed looks like every other. Thirty trees in thirty seeds, coiled like fists.

When the sun goes off the skylights I stop, stand back, and begin to sneeze. The impulse has been suspended by concentration, but now I can feel the mineral dust in my throat and nose. Even my sweat smells of its sweet dry talc. I wonder if I am becoming allergic to jewels and the thought makes me laugh, my echoes intrusive in the silent room.

It is past five o'clock and I need a break and a bath. The breakfast things are still on the desk, surrounded by Lost Oddities, and I take them down through the mansion, its floors and stairwells and courtyards.

The corridors are half-dark. Against my feet the stone is not warm, not cold. In the house I follow Hassan's example and walk barefoot. I know my way now and I don't get lost, although this is relative. In Glött's mansion I've found ways to lose myself inside a single room.

The bathroom is empty. Lights ripple off the surface of the pool. I shower quickly, half-watching my own body. In the clouded mirrors it looks graceful, the belly stretched flat between the curves of breasts and thighs. I don't mind it. I don't feel attached to it. My body has grown into itself these past few years. It is more graceful now than I ever feel myself.

I close myself inside the sauna, the smell of stones fading as my skin dries and moistens with fresh sweat. Even in warm countries I like the feel of saunas. The hot, resinous consistency of the air. The confined space, which is half-lifepod, half-coffin. When I'm done, cleaned out, I sit back in the pool. Lying still, all I can see is the mineral plane of the water and at the farthest extents of myself, the islands of my knees and nose. Distantly, I can hear someone playing a piano I didn't know existed. I wonder who it is. Which one of us. The house echoes with faint traces of its occupants and refugees.

De-stoned, cleaner than my clothes, I wring out my hair and tie it back. The house feels still around me. Glött is watching another film, I can hear it from far away. The voices turned up too loud, the sound of a car moving through rain. I pass her room and go on upstairs. The lights of Diyarbak'r are coming on outside the high windows. It makes me think of London. Not the city I have lived in so much as the one in which the jewel has been, which Elizabeth saw with her ermine eyes, Victoria with her stone-cold gaze.

Someone is in the room of boxes. I hear them before I am close enough to see anything, a muttered voice carrying through the quiet house. I have time to think it doesn't sound like Glött before I turn into the last corridor. At the end is the stone room door. It is open as I left it, and inside is Martin.

He is bent over the desk. From this angle I can't see his face or hands, but there is something unpleasant about the language of his body: a hunched eagerness that makes him look old. Miserly. The desk-light greens his hair. As far as I can see he is alone. He is talking to himself, a whisper of concentration.

In his hands are a jeweller's loupe and a baroque pearl. A Lost Oddity. He squints down at it, face clenched. There is a small, harsh sound that makes me think of stone workshops, and after a moment I realise that Martin is grinding his teeth.

The lamp is so close to his hair that he must be able to feel it, but only his hands move, and his jaw. The tray of pearls is still on the desk. And there is more to observe in what I cannot see: the iris quartz Buddha is not where I left it. I think of the chair, its tracks in the dust, and this morning's missing jewels. It would be interesting to know how much Martin has taken. I could move in on my bare feet and be by his shoulder before he knew I was there. Just to see his face.

I stop myself. Not because I am afraid of Martin. But at best I am a thief watching a thief. A kind of voyeur, watching a man steal from someone who loves him. I've never been in the position of needing to do the same. I don't know – I don't know how I can be sure – that I have not done worse things than this. I hold myself back, feeling my wet hair cool in the dark. Its braids and leashes.

He puts down the loupe and rubs his eyes with the heel of one hand. With the other he holds on to the pearl. He looks at his watch, puts the pearl in his shirt pocket almost absent-mindedly, and stands to go.

I start to walk again before he has time to look up. I make sure he hears me. He has plenty of time to turn round, smiling with his fox-teeth. 'The stone girl! How are you? Are you still on duty?'

'Yes.'

'You do work hard, don't you? So what do you think?'

'About what?'

'The stones, of course. The collection. Eh?'

'It's unique. I didn't know you came up here.'

He shrugs. 'Sometimes.'

Now I'm beside the desk. The Lost Oddities rest by my right hand. Some of them are more lost than others. 'Where's Helene?'

'Beautifying herself. I don't want to talk about her.'

From below us comes the sound of Hassan's flute. A simple phrase, repeated, developed. I don't look away. 'Fine. What do you want to talk about?'

'You. I see you are making yourself at home, Katharine.'

For a moment I think he is talking about the state of the stone room. But he is looking at me, not at the archives. His eyes settle on my feet and hair. My breasts. Like flies, I think.

'But we both are, aren't we?'

It offends him more than I intended. For a second he looks genuinely angry, I can see it moving through the muscles of his face, like a spasm. Then the smile creeps back. He looks at his watch again, for my benefit. 'As you say. Will I have your company for dinner?'

'I need to eat.'

'Good. I'll look forward to it,' he says, although his face disagrees.

I watch him leave. When I'm sure he's gone I sit down and count the baroque pearls. There are two missing, along with the smiling Buddha. Everything else is as it was. The drawers littered across the floor. The locust seeds balanced in their scales.

I look up at the archives. Their faces stretch away, out of the lamp's light. Somewhere in them is evidence of the Three Brethren. It is like a game. Pick the right drawer and find a reason for going on. Pick wrong and you discover everything you were never looking for. A drunk with a prosthetic leg. A rape scene carved in agate. A boy stealing pearls from an old woman who loves him. Ugly things. I'm still there when the stone room clock strikes seven.

171

I'm late to eat, and underdressed. Martin has put on an evening suit and a heavy blue gold watch, and both Helene and Eva are wearing pearls. A single cultured string on the girl, a thick, dark rope on the woman. For my own part, I've managed to put on a pair of shoes. It is like this every night in the stone house. I sit at the low-lit table and watch them, the old woman, the young couple, dressed for a party that no one is celebrating. Hassan serves the food.

'So,' says Martin, not looking up from his portion, 'Katharine, you are enjoying our family jewels?'

'Stones.'

'Jewels.' Nodding as he contradicts me. 'A word from the Latin *jocus*, a jest. Meaning, in your language, a joke, a jeering merriment, a ridicule. An idle tale.' He cuts his meat. 'What idle tales can you tell us, Katharine?'

Glött butts in. 'Katharine! You are the only one not wearing pearls.'

Wait your turn, I want to say, and don't. She isn't drinking yet. Her eyes are sullen in the dimmed light. Helene looks up as if the entertainment has arrived.

'I hadn't noticed,' I say.

'Well it's true.'

'Really. I don't see Martin wearing his.'

'Martin,' says Eva, pulling herself up, 'is a man. He has no pearls.'

'You'd be surprised. So he gets a Rolex, but we have to wear the excretions of shellfish. In this heat.' There is wine opened. I pour for myself. 'I don't think it's quite fair on us. Is it, Helene?'

She fingers her necklace and says nothing. The conversation lapses, as it always does. Hassan brings egg and lemon soup, stuffed vegetables, kebaps sprinkled with fresh sumac. Good things, well made. Nothing expensive or imported except the wine. Opposite me, Martin and Helene eat with the appetites of lovers. Glött consumes little herself. After the first course is cleared away Hassan serves her a glass of hot milk. She drinks it slowly, without apparent pleasure or displeasure.

Helene pushes away her plate. Her hair has gone lank in the evening heat. She smokes while Martin finishes. She is smiling, but her eyes are bored; the smile is just for show. I wonder how much she knows, or cares. When Martin is finished he sighs so loudly that it sounds like a kind of belch.

'*Danke, Eva!*' His face is florid from wine. Dressed up, he has the sharp, useless look of a stockbroker or a lawyer. His German is lax, but his voice smiles for him. 'That was remarkably delicious.'

'It was the same as always.'

'On the contrary. You are too modest, as usual.' He talks across me, over me. I do nothing to show I understand. 'What do you have planned for this evening, Eva? We could play cards, the three of us. It's still early. And you could show us your pearls.'

'Tomorrow. There is a good satellite film tonight.'

'We could watch it together.'

'No.' Glött is stirring her milk. She doesn't look up, and so she doesn't see Martin's face. The hardening of anger in the muscles as he stands.

'Tomorrow then.'

He waits for Helene to put out her cigarette before saying good-night in English, in German. After they have gone Hassan takes away the crystal and porcelain. When it is cleared he doesn't come back. I am alone with the recluse. There is no sound in the kitchen but the warm hum and rhythm of dishwashers. Distant traffic through the open windows.

'You are extremely rude.' Her voice is loud in the quiet. I look up and she is watching me with bright, unhealthy eyes.

'About what?'

'About–' She makes a grab for her necklace. Shakes it. 'I will have you know that these are pearls from the *Margaritafera* fresh-water mussel. They are extremely rare. The mussel can live for a century. A hundred years to make one good pearl. That you should respect.'

'I'm sorry, Eva. I can't help it if I don't like pearls.' She says nothing. I watch her, shut up hard and grey. An oyster in her last life or the next. '"I will have you know"?'

She sulks for a minute more. When she smiles I'm glad of it. 'One day you will realise you are not always right.' She holds up her drink. 'Hassan makes this for me. Do you know what it is?'

'Pearls crushed in vinegar.'

'Don't be ridiculous.'

'Boiled milk. We have cows in England too.'

'You see? Ha! You are wrong already. It is milk with pow-dered orchid root. You should try it. It would put some colour in your cheeks.'

'I don't want colour in my cheeks.'

'You could do with it. How are my stones?'

'Not good.'

'What can be not good about stones? Do they need more colour in their cheeks? I am prepared to be surprised.'

I could choose not to tell her. I could leave tomorrow and go back to Istanbul and start again. It is a kind of failure I am used to, and Glött wouldn't know what was happening until the day she went into the stone room and found the drawers empty, and Martin gone. It would be easier, at least, for me.

Even so.

'Martin is stealing the jewels.'

'You are being stupid,' she says. She is untangling the ropes of her pearls. Combing them out.

'No. He's stealing them and he's doing it fast. You asked me to work on the collection and this is all I have found. At this rate, I don't think I'll have time to catalogue it all before it becomes un-collected again. I'm sorry, Eva.'

'Why? You think I don't know?' Her voice is tired, singsong. Her hands work at the pearls. 'You are being stupid.'

'What are you talking about?'

She talks fast, whispering. 'For God's sake. I don't care what he does. I would rather have him here. He is precious to me.'

'More precious than your father's jewels?'

'Of course!' She laughs. 'Of course. You think I can't afford to lose a few stones?' Glött glances up from her pearls. She isn't a sharp old bird any more, but a sadder, blunter kind of animal. 'I am sorry but I find I pity you, Katharine Sterne.'

'Really? Well, that's very kind of you.' The anger pushes me upright. 'I'll remember that tomorrow, while I waste my fucking time on your vanishing collection.'

'No one is keeping you here. Don't blame me for what you choose.'

Then I choose to leave. I almost say it. The words are in my mouth, on my lips. I don't say them because there is something here I need, if I can just find it. If I just knew where. Just knew how. My life circles itself in these questions. But I already know I'm not going anywhere tonight, and so does she.

'Goodnight, Eva.' I say it as quietly as I can. She watches me all the way to the door. The corridors are unlit. I think of her as I walk. Her tall form bent at the empty table. When I come to my room I keep going, all the way to the main door. I step out into the courtyard.

There are no lights. My eyes adjust. I take three steps past the fountain and stop, the night air stops me. I can hear it, the sounds it carries. Water in the fountain. The tiny call of a gecko on the wall above me, *to-kay, tokay*. The background noise of cities.

On the far side of the courtyard I make out a bench, white stone under the trees. One hand up to ward off branches, I cross the yard, sit down, close my eyes. Somewhere in the old city streets a dog is whining. Soft, a ghost in the darkness. It reminds me of things there is no value in remembering. The male basalt of the walls is warm against my back.

I don't know if I sleep. When I open my eyes, my hands are cool and the stone around me is damp, as if a light dew has fallen. Hassan is standing beside me. He is bent forward under the trees just as he stands in the hallway, as if even the outside world is too small for him.

'You made me jump,' I say, although it isn't true. I'm not surprised to see him. It may even be that I was looking for him here, halfway between the house and the city. I don't know my own mind. Not tonight, perhaps not ever.

'Did Eva tell you to find me?'

'No.'

'Good. Will you talk with me?' I move up the bench. When he sits down my head reaches to his shoulder. Up this close, I can see he is old. The flesh of his hands is already receding between the bones.

He makes no sound. It makes him easy to talk to. 'This is a beautiful space. I wish I'd come out here more often.'

'You are leaving?' His English is stilted and studied. His voice is deep but there is a lilt to it. A grace. He is a graceful man.

'I wish I was. Have you ever noticed the air inside the house? It feels of nothing. It has no sound. Why is that?'

'I don't know.'

'Nor do I. Some types of stone have that effect, of course. But it feels like a trap. I feel like I've fallen into a trap here, but I can't remember how.' I stop myself whispering. 'Where are you from, Hassan?'

'The mountains.'

I turn towards him, watching his profile. 'Are you Kurdish?'

'Yes.'

'Are you happy, working for Eva?'

He sighs inwards. Smelling the air. Jasmine and cedars. 'I was young when I began. It was many years ago.'

'You must know her better than anyone. And she must know you.'

He doesn't answer. I stop talking. We sit listening again. A yardbird *jucks* somewhere nearby.

'I wanted to thank you. For the flowers.'

'They were nothing.'

'And the incense. Those were kind things.'

He shifts against me. I feel the warmth of the muscles in his thighs. 'You are a guest. And I am glad to have met you.'

I can't see if he is smiling. 'Hassan, have you heard of the sirr-usch?'

'Yes.'

'What does it mean?'

'It means nothing. It is a monster. The head of a dragon, the feet of an eagle, the body of a dog.'

I press my hands against the stone bench. 'Did Glött ever tell you what I'm doing here?'

'You are looking for something. She says it is a beautiful thing.'

'It is.'

'Things are beautiful for a reason.'

'No. Jewels have no reasons.'

He shrugs. 'There are different purposes. Some flowers are beautiful to spread themselves. Some to trap.'

I laugh. 'Trust me, I'm not trapped by what I'm looking for.'

'There is a story my mother told. Sindbad's eighth journey.'

'There isn't one.'

'All the same, she told it. Sindbad is old. His house is full of young merchants feasting. One of them tells Sindbad of a land to the far east. In the land is an emperor. In the emperor's palace is a harem. In the harem is only one concubine. She is the most beautiful woman in the world. The most beautiful thing on earth. Since her birth no man but the emperor has seen her. Not even her own father.'

A gecko creeps across the wall beyond him. Its skin is pale, exposed against the dark basalt.

'Sindbad sails to the land with many jewels and a single faithful retainer. The emperor is twice as old as Sindbad and ten times as fat. He is pleased with the jewels Sindbad gives him. Because of the gift he makes Sindbad an adviser in his palace. One night, Sindbad orders his retainer to find a way into the harem. The retainer ties a rope round his master, lowering him to the tower window. Sindbad sees the concubine oiling her hair, and having seen her he goes away content.

'But now the world becomes ugly to him. The concubine is the most beautiful thing on earth. Even though he is an old man, Sindbad wants only to see her again. Everything else fades from his sight. In this way, in a year, he goes blind.'

I watch his face. The gecko above him. It hunts in small movements, an inch up, an inch right. Monstrous in its vertical world.

'Sindbad asks the retainer to take him back to the harem. The retainer refuses. Now Sindbad begs him. So again the retainer ties the rope around him. He lowers the blind Sindbad to the window. When the concubine appears, Sindbad finds he can see her. It is midnight. As he watches, she takes off her robes to sleep. Nothing Sindbad has ever seen has been so beautiful. He opens the window, unties the rope, climbs inside. The concubine has never seen anyone with such love in their eyes. She sleeps with Sindbad all that night. In the morning the guards find him there. He is imprisoned and sentenced to a bad death.

'Through bribery the faithful retainer releases him. By ship they return home to Basra. Sindbad is no longer blind, but he is changed. He finds no pleasure in his own city. His feasts and the stories of his friends mean nothing to him. He is weary of the world, because he knows he will never see anything as beautiful as the concubine again. And so, in the end, he dies.'

'What happens to the woman?'

He stops, catching his breath. 'Nothing happens to her. She lives as she has lived.'

'I liked it better when Sindbad lived happily ever after.'

'As you say. It is just a story.'

'Like the sirrusch.'

He says nothing. A plane goes over, invisible in its dark distance.

'I'm looking for a jewel called the Three Brethren. There are some papers here. Finding them would mean a great deal to me.'

I watch him nod. He doesn't look at me.

'Do you know where they are? Hassan?'

He stands up, brushes down his robes, and nods again. It is all one quick movement. As soon as I say goodnight he is gone.

I sit alone in the warm dark, thinking of the Brethren. I can turn it in my mind like a riddle, or the pattern of a screen saver: *A triangle four inches square. Two hundred and ninety carats in eight jewels. Four pearls, three balas rubies, two of nothing. One diamond in a half diamond.*

I think of Eva. So scared of loss that she will let a man steal from her. Just to have him near. I pity her; but then she pities me. When it comes to pity we are evens. The gecko turns back on itself, a white glyph on the black stone wall. It stops quite still, readies itself, and strikes.

※

There are people who say that stones have souls, but they are wrong. There are also people who believe that stones are alive, at least in the way that trees, say, are alive. For the most part, these people are also wrong.

Cut stones are dead. For the most part. You just have to touch them to know it. They are mined from their source rocks and sheared up into pieces with steel cleavers. The hard *nyf*, the skin, is cut off them like the scales from a fish. Of course they are not alive.

But they are dead. It is a particular quality. Nothing is entirely dead without living first. Underground, there are living stones. They are growing, and they are changing all the time, the quartz into amethyst, the opal into chalcedony. Growth and transformation. All of them are, in the simplest sense, alive.

Cut stones are dead as wooden chairs. But I think that stones are like trees, and that they die in the same grindingly slow way that they live. They are like fallen trunks, which for years put out new leaves. Cut stones are like that, mindless and centennial. It is not what you would call life. It is more like a kind of forgetfulness.

We had three dogs. They were presents from May on Anne's eleventh birthday, Edith would never have bought them. Their names were Pudding, Chocolate Pudding and Pudding Now. Anne chose their names. They were spaniels from the same litter. Edith never liked them; there was nothing clean or ordered about them, not even in their names, which Anne refused to explain or change. After a few months no one could remember which was which anyway, and the names stopped mattering. They were all the Pudding, Puddings plural. They smelt of wet fur and warm dog-shit and love.

I'm walking back from primary school. It's winter and already dark. Children echo under the wet drip of plane trees. English trees, which I miss when I am away from them: massive in the narrow streets, fountains frozen in their functions. Anne doesn't walk with me any more, hasn't done so since she began at the comprehensive. Now it's her boyfriends who take her home. I keep my eyes on the damp, black pavement. Home is six hundred and eighty-two steps away and closing fast.

When I get there I have to knock because I don't have a key. Anne has a key but I don't. Anne says I might put it in my mouth and swallow it. I did that once with a pencil stub. Edith swears it went in blunt and came out sharp. I don't know why she doesn't give me a key.

I knock again. Inside I can hear a Pudding whining, and already something is wrong because it doesn't come closer. I can see nothing except the hallway's darkness, mottled through the textured glass of the door. The world through a cube of ice.

I sit down in the porch and wait for Anne. The step is damp and it seeps through my dress. It takes less than a minute for me to blame my sister, to hate her for having a key and not being here to use it. There is a spare by the kitchen door. It's strictly for emergencies.

I try and imagine where Edith has gone. Working; shopping; swimming; drowning. I rank them in order of probability.

Working gets nine, drowning one. It is one-in-ten likely to be an emergency. I go round to the kitchen door and let myself in.

One Pudding lies by the darkroom door, stretched out like a dog-shaped draught excluder. It whines, and when I come in another starts. They remind me of *A Christmas Carol*, which is due on BBC1 any week now. The ghosts of Christmas Present, Past and Future. Whooo, says the draught-excluding Pudding.

The darkroom door is shut. No light shows under it. On the kitchen table a book lies closed. On the sideboard are our clean clothes, one woman's, two girls'. Bras and vests in separate piles.

I put the emergency key back, close the door, walk in. I am trying to make no sound and failing. I don't try because I want to surprise Edith, but because I don't want her to know I used the emergency key. If I can get upstairs, my entrance will be finessed. The ordinary transformed into the perfectly elegant. I walk round by the washing machine and stop.

The door to the darkroom is not closed shut. An ordinary, out-of-the-ordinary thing: Edith never leaves the door unlocked. Sometimes, if she is working, the door is left open for air, but there is no sound from inside. I go up to the door and press my face to the crack. There is nothing to see. Only the smell of swimming pools, hospitals, Edith's hands. Precious and dangerous.

The Pudding gets up. The door swings back. Edith is sitting in the darkroom chair. Her head is leant forward, she is asleep. Her hands hang at her sides. They have finished all the things they have been doing.

Laughter bubbles up inside me and I gulp it down. It is four steps to my stool from the door. My heart goes fast. I am playing a game. It is to do with fear and perfection. I take one step. Another.

Sometimes I think about death. Not often. My head is not a glass dome with my past inside, time kept out. But I think about how the dead survive in people's minds.

It reminds me of the way in which stones live. Slow, forgetful, refusing to be gone. I carry the traces of Edith's death. Not the memories of her alive, which are something to be cherished. I am talking about the death. Glött says the pearl is a function of pain, and there is something in that. I wonder if I am making myself a pearl. Taking a death and turning it into a jewel. Since pearls grow, like small lives.

Mostly, though, it is not the death that occupies me. Most of the time I think of the Three Brethren. The more I know about the jewel, the clearer its character becomes. The weight of it in the hand, like a second hand. The thin bones of its gold. The warmth of the rubies, the more human beauty of the pearls, and the coldness of the diamond. The occult stare of that one eye. Old stones, mindless, centennial. I want them. It feels as if I always have.

There are diamond experts who are as precise as wine-tasters. They can recognise which country and mine a crystal is from just from its colour and shape. By the standards of these people I am an amateur, and their standards are not wrong. I know only so much, and only what I have taught myself.

But then I am a specialist. My field is not all diamonds, but one diamond. Not all rubies, but three rubies. In the company of lapidaries, there are people who recognise this. They taste me on the air, the sour love of my obsession, and they leave me to myself.

And that is the way it should be. It is a private thing I am doing. It involves only two of us. No one else. There is me, and there is the Brethren. *Cam cam'a dêil, can can'a*:

Not glass to glass but soul to soul.

※

In the morning it is raining and Hassan is playing his flute again. I watch him in the courtyard, sheltering under the thick green eaves of the cedars. Overhead the sky is still that of an arid country – painfully blue – and the rain itself stutters, unsure of its own intentions.

By the time I go to work it has already stopped. I can still hear the flute, though. It carries clear through the basalt walls of the house, up through the Escher stairwells and yards. It's as if the stone has become porous overnight, and I think of what I said to Hassan. The air feeling of nothing. Now it seems alive. Hassan, the granter of wishes. I work with the door open.

It is noon before I come to the last drawer of India. I open it up and pile it on the floor with all the others. Inside is a patch of saffron-yellow cloth sewn with seed garnets, a spent mousetrap, a small pile of paper and a smaller pile of bones. Nothing much for Martin to steal. I find this comforting.

I rattle the bones in their makeshift coffin. There are mouse teeth and mouse toes, clean and neat as watchworks. The back-bone is broken under the trap's killing bar. I take the papers out and wipe them on my skirt. There are three pages, and the mouse never got to any of them. The top one isn't paper at all but thick card. It has threads along one edge, old bindings. The other pages are pressed against it. As if the words themselves once exerted their own pressure. To me it looks like a notebook, or the remains of one. I am looking at what my own records will become.

There is a pattern on the card. I turn it to the light and jerk back. It is as if I have opened a door and found a face pressed against the space beyond, waiting for me.

The image is faint, a sketch executed in lead pencil. There is a triangle the size of a human heart. A rectangle inside each face, a circle at each point. At the centre is a diamond. From the body hangs a tear.

The flute music stops. The two pages are stuck to the cover and to one another. I sit down on the cold tiled floor and work them apart, carefully, all fingers and nails. When the back sheet comes away it is delicate as a crust of sand. I balance it on my palms and the tips of my fingers, lean forward and read.

There are only four lines, of English and German. The writing is Glött's father's. Not the precise, Gothic script of his public cor-respondence but a more private hand. Disarranged as the room of stones.

> *– Die drei Brüder. Mr Pyke.*
> *35 Slipper St, Whitechapel – the lower door –*
> *Mount, Fallowes, Three Diamonds.*
> *– Der Preis muss noch vereinbart werden.*

'The price to be decided.' Under my breath I repeat the last line, the rhythm of the German. Already, though, I'm thinking of Glött. She told the truth the day I arrived. The knot was sold in London, a century ago. However it was stolen from Victoria, whoever stole it, the jewel still existed sixty years later. And if it was whole then, it can be whole now. I always knew it would be.

I picture Whitechapel, the East End beyond it, docklands.

These are places I know. Even if the street number was written a century ago, it is somewhere to start from. And then there are the names, Pyke and Mount. Buyers or sellers, people or companies.

My mind creeps over them, and catches. I get up, gather the transaction papers and everything that is mine, and go down through the stone house to my bedroom. My overnight bag is in the same place it has been for a week. I open it up and get out the auctioned lapidary.

For a small book it is heavy. If I'd been in transit I would have thrown it away days ago. The title page calls it *A Definitive Essay on the Indian Origins of the Crown Jewels of Tudor England*, by V. J. Joshi, published by Macmillan & Co, 1893. Folded inside the cover is a register for the Bombay & Districts Public Library. The fourth name is written in a thin, oddly characterless script. As if someone were writing without understanding.

Mr Three Diamonds.

I go back to the transaction notes. The last sheet is unlike the rest. There is no trace of binding. At the head of the page is a shape, symmetrical, decayed. If I narrow my eyes it could be an address. A crest, even. The paper is badly eaten up by old damp. There is very little writing. I might not have perceived it at all if someone had not already pencilled in the lines.

> *– The Mr Levys.*
> *Wate for me doun at Blackfryers Sures.*
> *I will hav yr. 3 bretheren.*

It isn't the handwriting of Glött's father. The retracing might be his, though it is impossible to be sure. Certainly the style of the original seems older than the turn of the century. The script is clumsy as its wording. There is a signature, but again it is unclear, a child's imitation. The pen stutters in its ink. The details mean nothing to me. They are, at least, something more than a faded postcode, or the address on a soft-porn calendar.

I pack quickly. It never takes long. I don't leave the lapidary behind. When I'm finished I go and look for Eva. The main door is open, and as I pass I see that the courtyard is full of sparrows. There are clouds of them, settling and unsettling in the cedar trees. There is no sign of Hassan. As if he was never there at all, and it is only the birds I've heard all morning.

She is in her day room, trying on pearls. The jet bead curtain clicks itself still behind me. Glött is staring herself down in a full-length mirror, a box of jewels on the sofa beside her. On her two-piece is a brooch of gold wasps encircling a yellow pearl. She has her back to the door, although I can see her face. She doesn't turn round to look at me because she doesn't need to. 'Come! I need your opinion.'

I walk up beside her. She fingers the brooch. The bag is still in my hand. I don't put it down. 'It's beautiful.'

'Of course. You can borrow it, if you wish. But does it suit me?' We stand side by side. Her face is taken up with the worries of dressing. The *angenehme Sorgen*, the pleasant dilemmas. I watch myself smile.

'You're asking if a brooch of wasps suits you? Don't tempt me.'

She laughs, high and girlish. Behind us the bead curtain is still moving slightly. I can hear its click, like stone fingers. I unzip the bag and take out the papers. 'What have you there?'

'What I came for.' I say it softly, but it pulls her away from the mirror's viewpoint. She grabs at the papers with her thin hands. Like bird feet, I think. Bird claws. When she is done she stares at me.

'Where did you find them?'

'In the stone room.' I think of the mouse bones. The old paper, uneaten. Hassan's gifts. 'Where did you think they would be?'

Her head wobbles on its thin neck, once, twice. I don't know what else I expected. I put my hand out for the transaction papers and she gives them back. When she speaks again her voice is almost timid. 'Where will you go?'

'London.'

'And if that isn't the end of it? You made a promise to me.'

I look back at her. She stands straight-backed. In the mirror's tilted surface we are giants, like Hassan. Monsters, like the sirrusch. 'What promise?'

'To catalogue the von Glött collection. You have not finished.'

'That wasn't it, Eva, and you know it.' I say it quietly. She shakes her head.

'My God. You always get what you want, I knew it. Selfish girl.'

'Not always.'

'You have the ethics of a stock market!' She spits it. All the

184

hardness comes back into her eyes, like blood risen into skin.

'Because it's my business, Eva. The jewel is my business.'

She picks up the brooch and throws it hard at me. It misses and hits the remote control, heavy gold, toppling it off. A film starts up on the television. Harrison Ford is shooting at a beautiful woman. She runs through shop windows. Glass and music crash around her.

'You are wasting your life. Martin likes you. We like you, Katharine.' At her sides, without her realising, Glött's hands open and close. Mechanical with desire. Beyond her, in his photograph, the first husband watches with his fixed smile.

I reach out and hug her. It catches her off guard, otherwise I don't think I would have managed it. The breath goes out of her. This close, I can feel how thin she is under the well-cut clothes. She holds on to me for a moment, reflexively, her hands gripping my shoulders before I let her down. She calls out as I reach the jet curtain. The beads tut behind me. I hear her again as I walk down the corridor to the courtyard, her voice becoming stronger.

'Katharine. Katharine Sterne!'

The door is locked. I unlock it and walk out of the verandah, past the fountain. Beside the pool Eva's voice reaches me again. I can hear the tears starting up in it. A pattern, repetitive as birdsong.

'Katharine. Katharine! Katharine!'

It catches something inside me and tears it open. The shock of it makes me stumble, the bag coming off my shoulder. Inside me it feels as if a door unlocks itself on a cold night. For a second it is blown wide. Then the force swings back. The door is shut.

I hoist the bag up and look back. Hassan is there. I see his silhouette at a high window. I knew he would be waiting here, or hoped it. The gratitude fills me up, blossoms inside me, and I raise a hand and watch him reflect it, waving back.

He stops when I stop. At the archway pigeons clatter around me. They are pure black except for clean white breasts. It is as if the stone of Glött's house has seeped into their nests, their eggs, the veins of their feathers. I start to walk west. I don't look back again.

茶

I consider the properties of stones.

They are dead. It is a quality which gives them a certain relia-
bility. I know more about the minerals of the Three Brethren than
I will ever know about myself, my agglomeration of living and
dead tissue, solid and liquid, human flux. In twenty-five years
every cell in my body barring the substance of my bones has
lived and died and been replaced. I'm not the person I was.
Whereas the stones of the jewel are unchanged. The ruby ruby,
the diamond diamond. I know it like the back of my own hand.
Or better. I know, at least, what I am looking for.

They are desirable. It is to do with beauty: it is to do with money.
The two things twist into each other and become inseparable. It
means that the love of stones is never a pure thing. It is mutable,
good and evil, because jewels themselves possess the property of
mutability. We give them that. They are the small wishes of acquisitive people, flights and sex, mansions and palaces. It is the power
that money has, the slightest of powers, entirely human. I think of
the Brethren and wonder what I am bartering it for.

They lead you back. This is the last thing, the property I repeat
to myself, riddle, mantra, penitence. I remember it now as the
plane turns west towards Ankara and London, its thin hull of
metal and insulation loud around me. The great jewels are thousands of years old. They pass through the hands of people and
often the hands leave no trace, but they are there all the same.
They leave impressions, invisible, like atoms of hydrogen drawn
to a surface of diamond.

They lead you back. I watch ice crystallise on the porthole glass
and wonder how far I can go.

4
Three

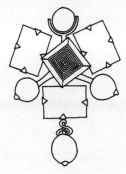

In the late summer of his twenty-second year, Daniel Levy and his brother Salman left Iraq with jewels sewn into their clothes.

It was 1833 by the Christian calendar. The ninth of September, although there are other ways to calculate time. Hüseyin the Imam would have called it Jumadah II. To Rachel and Daniel, waiting at the docks, it was six days before the Feast of Tabernacles. The eighth year of the two hundred and ninety-fifth lunar cycle, the twenty-third year of the two hundredth solar cycle since the Era of Creation; although what Rachel and Daniel believed of Creation was their own business.

Salman arranged their passage to Basra. Daniel and Rachel waited for him on the steps of All Angels', the church doors locked since the last plague, the portmanteau at their feet heavy as a step itself. They held hands and talked little. Keeping their thoughts to themselves. Faces in the cast shadows of their heads. They looked similar, cut from the same stone: tall, quiet, aquiline. Variations on a theme of strength.

'We will write.'

'You must do as you please.'

'Then perhaps Salman will write for the both of us.'

A boatman hallooed from the river. Traffic navigating the islands in midstream.

'Your eye hurts today.'

'No more than always.'

'In England there may be medicine we can send.'

'No doubt.'

On the islands two young men were mooring an old tarada canoe, carrying their women over the shallows. Daniel watched them unpack blankets for a picnic. They had done the same, he and Salman and Rachel. Years ago, so long he could no longer remember for sure who had done the carrying. He went on talking, surprising himself by it. Making conversation. The watch in his pocket gaining time. 'I wandered the banks of the river. And as I

189

watched it disappear into the cavern I struck upon a plan. "By Allah," I thought, "this river must have both a beginning and an end—"'

'You recite it badly.'

'I have not inherited your talent for that.'

'You're too old for stories.'

'Sindbad. He always came home richer and happier. We could come back too.' He said it quietly, knowing she wouldn't answer him, not expecting her to. 'Rachel.'

'Too old.' A fisherman passed them, forearms dotted with scales and gutting blood, half-fish himself. 'Sometimes I think you should be more like your brother. Practical.'

'That is what you call it?'

'I do. And busy.'

'As a fly in shit.'

'This morning he says you'll be goldsmiths.'

'Then this morning things are simpler. Last week it was steamboat proprietors. We have stones and gold, he can work them, I can sell them.'

He thought of the jewels without desire. Rachel had shared them unequally, accepting only the opal and the broken emerald for herself. Daniel had offered to sell them and she had refused that also. He wondered, now, if she meant to keep them. The last gifts of her last family. Something by which to remember something. *I have nothing of yours*, he thought of saying; but it was not true, and already she was talking again.

'So, now. Don't hold yourself so carefully. People will notice you're carrying something.'

'I feel like King Midas in disguise.'

'And tell Salman the same. The fool looks like he's trying to hide a pregnancy.'

'He has the belly for it.'

'He has nothing of the kind. You'll do all right, whatever you do. But you'll need broad shoulders. Where you're going, you'll be outsiders.'

We are already outsiders, he wanted to say, and did not. 'Salman has the shoulders of a vulture. Enough for both of us.'

'Salman is a boy in the body of a man and he always will be. You look after him.'

He nodded. 'And who will look after you?'

'There are only three of us. If we leave one another, one of us will be alone. And I can look after myself.'

She was wearing her earrings, Daniel saw. He reached out to touch them, to make her smile, and as he did so his knuckles grazed the long bones of her cheeks. The Nag's Head bones. He thought of Midas again. The hand reaching out to make something precious. In the distance he could hear Salman calling and he lowered his hand and stood up to go.

The river journey came cheap. It was not that Salman bargained hard. The boatswain was a Levantine, two decades on the river, but the young Jew he found distracting. He watched everything, charmless and uncharmed. It was the unblinking way a child looked at the world, or a seabird. There was a hunger in it which the riverman disliked. Only after the deal was struck did he wonder about the evil eye. For the sake of business he kept his thoughts to himself.

He was still young, Salman. Nineteen, trusting his eyes. Watching Rachel as they left her behind on the river quays of Baghdad, he saw how the crowd jostled her and that her loneliness there, among unfamiliar people, was what they took away from one another – that and the jewels from the jar. Salman saw how they could come to share alienation like a familial trait. Basic as stubbornness or the lines of cheekbones.

He didn't like the sea. It was something he felt at first sight, quick as an instinct. In Basra harbour old Turkish three-deckers waited at anchor, their hulls slick with rot. Beyond them the Gulf moved. It wrinkled and shifted like the *Sirab*, the water mirage of the desert. To Salman it seemed that the two things weren't much different. The sea was more real but no more solid. He didn't trust it. It gleamed, Salman thought, like something cut open.

They waited two days for an East India Company ship. There were other ways to travel. North overland, or west by Suez, London was barely two months away. Cornelius Rich had allowed none of that.

'Sea roads are the engine oil of the Empire,' he had told them as he wrote them a letter of introduction on Company paper. 'Salt water keeps the wheels of commerce grinding, Mister

Salman. Would you doubt the British Empire? No. And mark you, the land passage is infested with bandits and all kinds of vagabonds.' Despite the decade he had lived abroad, Cornelius felt and believed what the English still felt and believed: that passage by sea was better than that by land. Not necessarily quicker or even safer, just intrinsically nicer. Foreign vagabonds were so much more complicated than death by water.

The *Scaleby Castle* arrived loaded with cargo from Bombay. It sat so low against the Company wharves that the brothers had to climb down to it by ladder. Without Cornelius's letter and the amethyst they wouldn't have been let on at all. As it was, McInnes the purser found them mess space on the orlop deck, their hammocks cramped in with crates of capons that themselves found no room in the hold below.

No one else joined the London ship. There were Jews on the docks waiting for passage eastwards to Rangoon. In their drab black robes they looked like mourners, not people setting out for new lives. Salman wondered if he looked the same. Above him, the wind began to muscle its way into the sails.

He listened to it as the vessel began to move. Behind him was Basra, its yellowed brick buildings, the mouth of the Tigris opening through it. Salman kept his eyes on them, the city and the river, as they diminished. He looked back until the land sank under the waves, Iraq taken away from him by the silent rotation of the earth.

For the three months of transit Daniel lived with the constant sensation of loss. Rachel was not at the heart of it. It felt as if something was always about to be stolen from him. Not the jewels: only twice in his life did Daniel feel any real love of stones. What he missed was a water jar, a pattern of light on a tiled floor, the bloody smell of tomatoes drying in wooden trays.

In the hammocked dark of the ship he would wake and discover himself searching his pockets or the portmanteau, as if his home could be there. The possessiveness felt alien to him. Not the homesickness, but the need for physical things. Not even Rachel so much as Rachel's tomatoes. He wondered if the jewels had anything to do with that, and if he were changing.

He could feel them, the sea moving their weights against him.

Around his thighs were cotton bags of gold scrap, traded for guns from the marshlanders. In the loose cloth under his arms he carried a hundred carats of spinel and amethyst. Inside the brothers' shirts Rachel had stitched the buttons from their circumcision gowns, a tiny, stony currency of coral and turquoise. Daniel had watched her do it, folding away the gowns when she was finished. Smoothing them flat. The stones swung against him like ballast weights.

The *Scaleby* was a three-master, green copper flaking from its teak bottom. Near the bow it stank of shit. The rest smelt of tar. Besides the brothers there were few passengers. No one talked to Daniel and Salman except McInnes and a Marist from Lyons, who tried to convert them. They were the foreigners who slept down by cargo. They were practically cargo themselves.

They talked to each other. Softly, as if their language was something that could be stolen. They argued about the greatness of Babylon and London, and whether letters had been made before numbers. Or Salman would leave his brother, climbing upwards through the ship. He liked the machinery of masts and pulleys, the forces of wind and human muscle. The sailors singing the work into rhythms.

The parson had a daughter who was sweet as sugar candy.
I said to her, 'Us sailors do make lovers neat and handy.'

She says to me, 'You sailors is a bunch of bloody liars,
And all of ye is bound to Hell, to feed the flaming fires.
And all of ye is bound to Hell–'

Their chorus a mess of accents, West Country, Liverpool, Scots, Irish. The Indian Ocean hissing around them. Salman kept his eyes on the thin green coast of Africa.

The fire down below, me lads, is very hot an' jolly,
But the fire there's not half so hot–

'Stay out of the crew's way,' McInnes told him, 'and we'll all get on nicely. Specially in bad weather. This is advice I'm giving you. The big waves are animals, they'll knock you down if they can get at you. The men also.'

They slept between looming crates of mail and spices, vats of saltpetre and indigo. A foot from their heads, the ocean whispered and ticked in its separate darkness. Daniel lay with his own thoughts. Of his grand uncle, Elazar, drowned at sea. The imprinted patterns of his sticky toes. Of Rachel, alone. Of Midas, the king cursed with dreams come true. Desire manifested in an epidemic of gold.

He remembered the things Salman had said they would find, now they had jewels. Horses and houses, happiness and new lives. Nine days out to sea Daniel watched rain smatter against the porthole glass and wondered how far they would have to go to find so much.

There is a quality to long transit which is not unlike dream. The days and nights have a sameness, turning back on themselves. It felt to Daniel as if time had come loose and the order of things were repeating, and when this ended it seemed as if he was waking twice. Out of sleep and out of himself. He opened his eyes and heard, beyond the creak of hammocks, the creak of ice. It was the last hours of night. Salman still slept beside him. Daniel went up alone into the white air of London.

Mist hung around him. Daniel's face ached with the cold of it. He breathed tentatively. The air was no longer exactly light or dark, only pale. The *Scaleby* moved through it under low sail. From the bow came the dull beat of the fog drums.

His eyes adjusted. Now Daniel could see shapes. A mass of masts and chimneys, the bulks of stone warehouses and outbuildings. Ship lights. The smog stank of sewage and vinegar. The sweet, rank smell of an industrial city.

'Good morning, there. One of the Mesopotamians, is it not?'

McInnes had come up beside him, sure-footed in the gloom. Daniel could make out other people beyond him. The Marist raised a hand, bulked out in an old astrakhan coat. Ready for the cold. Daniel shivered. 'Daniel Levy, sir.'

'So it is, the tall one. Well. Doubtless this is quite a sight for you, the East India Docks. Quite a sight. The greatest city in the world. Are you not already glad you came?'

Glad. Daniel attempted to feel it. 'I cannot see the sky.'

'Sky? This isn't Paradise, Mister Levy. The sky is not the point.' The purser grinned, without warmth. 'I was asking, sir, what you make of my city.'

'It is beautiful.'

'It is.' He clasped his hands over the rail. 'I'm right glad you think so. Smells like the shit of old fishwives, but glorious still. This end there's not much but marshes. Slums. You'll take the Commercial Road west, if you want the city. Leastways there'll be cabs waiting for you.' McInnes leant beside him. His hands, Daniel saw, were raw with saltwater gurry sores. 'By the by, Mister Levy. I meant to raise the question of your fare.'

'We have paid in full–'

'Beg pardon, no. My interest was in the method. The stone. The amethyst is good, so my mates tell me. Would there be more where that came from?'

'I–' There was a shout from the boatswain and McInnes excused himself before Daniel could reply. His breath condensed into silence.

Sounds came to him, distorted by smog. The rattle of chains loosened on a quayside crane. The concatenation of casks rolled along wharves. The shout of one voice, the bleat of one goat. He turned and, seeing Salman through a break in the air, called out, made room for him at the rail.

'Tigris. We have made it.'

'This is London?'

'McInnes says so.'

'And you believed him.' Salman peered over the side. From below came the exclamations of ice, shelving away into the deepwater basin. 'He could put us off anywhere. Keep the profit.'

'What did you expect to come to? Jewelled gates? Houris on horseback making eyes at every arrival? You are too suspicious.' Daniel watched his brother begin to smile and was glad of it.

'New lives, 'Phrates. I can hardly believe it.'

He didn't answer. They stood together, looking out at the import docks. Something loomed up beyond the rail, a cliff of stone moving past them. Involuntarily, both men stepped back. It was a moment before Daniel recognised the shape as a quayside. The loaded ship still sat far down in the water.

New lives. Under his breath, Salman repeated it to himself as he climbed the ladder to the North Quay. He could feel the stones on him. The jewels from the jar, which were his, given to him in repayment. Around his neck hung the clear stone. Still cool, distinct against his own blood heat.

195

And Daniel climbed after him. The water below him smelled of human faeces. He had never expected that of London. He tried to recall the city as Cornelius had described it. Piccadilly by gaslight, and a city bright and cold as a diamond.

He pictured it in his mind. The jewels chafed against his skin. Somewhere in the white distance, church bells.

It was 2 December 1833. The first Monday after Advent. A cold year for the brothers to arrive in, and a cold time. In their first weeks the Thames froze over and the docklands sat empty, cut off from the sea. The roads to the north were impassable, and London waited for thaw under its accretions of ice.

They stayed at the Sabloniere Hotel on Leicester Square. The room was narrow with white mouldings. The gas lamp hissed and murmured in human voices. On the first night Daniel woke in the dark, Salman snoring fitfully beside him. He got up and went to the window, dazed but sleepless with transit. Outside, the Square lay empty. The moon, in its first quarter, hung faint over the rooftops.

London. It didn't seem beautiful to Daniel, only permanent. The smog washed over it and only darkened its brick and ashlar stone. He thought of the old cities of Iraq. Babylon under its tors of sand, deserted by the rivers. London didn't feel like it would ever be left behind.

He made himself comfortable on the window seat and waited for morning. There were already cabs parked opposite, post-boys dozing above the warmth of their horses. Sunrise came slowly, imperceptible as the motion of a clock face, the fog lifting to meet it.

The clatter of goods carts echoed upwards. A landau passed, southwards towards the river. At its window, a flash of bright colour. A young woman's clothes, Daniel thought. They were as rare on the streets of London, he saw, as they were in Baghdad. He began to watch for them more intently, in a phaeton, in a rookery doorway. Silks and jewels and skin.

At ten o'clock he fell asleep, his forehead pressing gently against the glass. No one looked up to see him. Beside the Gun Repository the old women went on selling hot wine until noon, their hands and forearms stained with lees. And across from

Daniel's window, light fell across the lowered blinds of rented rooms, a sign of sickness or prostitution. But then in London Daniel knew no signs. He had left that understanding behind with everything else, except the jewels.

December 6. The morning before sabbath. The hotelier, a man with hands smooth as calfskin gloves, gave them directions to Bevis Marks. Their hair and clothes were impregnated with the smells of tar and cardamum, the black linen still stiff with salt. Salman unpicked the stone pockets himself before he would allow the robes to be laundered, stitched them back when the washing was done.

The synagogue was empty when they arrived. They waited for it to fill. Two turbaned foreigners in the shadow of the balconies. The Sephardim with their foreign clothes and service, their muttered Spanish and whiff of imported cigars, the galleries of lantern-jawed women looking down at the outsiders – they had nothing to do with the brothers. Daniel and Salman never attended again. It was as if they themselves were not Jews at all, but something less particular, Semites only in the broadest sense. Blood without religion.

They walked back together. Not talking of the Sephardim. For days London would make them speechless. It was like a different century. Not a future or a better one, Salman didn't see it that way. Only an alternative. It was different from the landscape Cornelius had described to Daniel and Daniel to Salman: more human, less perfect. Cobbles turning to asphalt turning to waste ground. The pace of it dazzled Salman, the hectic sprawl of commerce, from the prostitutes calling after them to the great hoardings for Potter's Wonderful Worm Lozenges and Dubbins's Curry Pastes, and the streets of ostrich feather importers, incorrodible teeth inventors, oyster dealers, muffin bakers, ever-pointed pencil makers, ginger beer manufacturers, scum boilers, and the silver and goldsmiths, the brokers of diamonds and pearls.

He discovered Clerkenwell alone, two days later. A dark figure, built like a wrestler, loitering in the streets of goldsmiths and Jewish dairies, the missions where foreigners would be paid a halfpenny to hear a Christian minister, the houses of Western Jews. Salman observed them from a distance, talking to no one.

Keeping the crowds around him, a moving human camouflage.

He measured himself against what he saw. The men, their jewels, and the lives they had made. The windows were full of rabbits' feet and monkey paws, Irish bog-oak carved into shamrocks. Gimcracks, Salman thought. Tricks made with skill at best but little talent. The men were dressed in English clothes and hats, or else they leaned in doorways with their heads bare, smoking pipes. The wives with baskets of prayer wine and kosher meat. Nothing else Jewish in them but the cut of their features.

'Wonderful Worm Lozenges.' He murmured it, enunciating each word. Above him the lamp sighed like a woman turning in her sleep. He could hear Daniel breathing. They lay on their beds with their shoes off. Talking sometimes, then quiet for hours.

'I thought you were in love with stones.'

'Everything is for sale here. Worms and jewels. There are nightmen who make livings from human excrement. There is something wonderful in that.'

'I'd prefer stones, if it's all the same to you.' The sound of an argument filtered down from the room above. A man shouting, a woman's voice rising to meet it. 'What shall we do with the jewels?'

'Hire them to the King.'

'Ha. Nevertheless, we can't carry them for ever. Walking down Piccadilly every day like a pair of chandeliers.'

'I have already talked to the hotel owner. He knows a shop to rent. Good, small, cheap.'

'Where?'

Salman didn't answer. Under his breath he began to sing a muezzin's cry. In the London room it sounded out of place, comically lost. His voice faded away and he lay staring at the stained ceiling as if amazed to find it there, or himself under it.

'Tigris? Where is it?'

'Commercial Road. Good for the dock trade and the city. I said I'd see it tomorrow. Will you come? I could use your English.'

Daniel nodded. 'If you like. You know what you are looking for?'

'Aye. A fortune.'

'We already have that.' Daniel watched his brother turn away. Above them the shouting stopped abruptly. In the silence Salman could hear snow outside, wind funnelling it against the glass.

'Only one.'

'One is enough.' Daniel lay back and closed his eyes. He fell asleep quickly, the light twitching across his face. And Salman said nothing, not out loud. Above him, the lamp hissed and choked on its own gas. He reached up into its glare and turned it out.

They left early. Sheep were still milling in the Strand. A cart had overturned by Fleet Street, and the brothers picked their ways between hoof-smashed cabbages and upside-down crates of hysterical poultry.

It was a handsome road, the Commercial, a little self-important for its public of sailors and dockers and its smell of river mud. The buildings were new, shops and houses intermixed. Near the mid-point of each terrace was a plaque with the name of its developer or the name he had chosen over his own: Honduras, Union, Colet. Street children followed them, laughing or begging, keeping their distance.

There were eighteen buildings in Hardwick Place and the vacant shop was the last. Its curved display window was boarded up. Above the shop were two more storeys, the servants' floor narrower and less decorated than those below it, as if its builders had run out of room in the grey London sky.

'Wait here.' Salman trudged round to the back of the house. Daniel watched him go, London beyond him. Even here he felt lost in it, as if its influence spread out over the intervening piggeries and frozen marshland. Little rose above the warrens of houses except the stabbing primacy of steeples. In the distance loomed the dome of St Paul's.

When he looked back there was a girl beside him, her feet wrapped in rabbit skins. Her face was anxious, as if she had something to say and there was no time to say it. The street children had not peeled away as the brothers left the city. The Stepney slums were not far eastwards. Across the road two older boys leaned under a shop sign for Lawrence's Sea Water Baths.

He smiled, and the girl's face went slack with fear. Daniel watched her decide whether to run. An omnibus went past behind her and she stepped forwards into the gutter and its piles of shit-encrusted snow. She was whispering almost inaudibly;

without seeing her face he wouldn't have realised she was making any sound at all. Her voice was reed-thin, accented in a way Daniel would take years to recognise. All he could make out was the intonation of a question. He bent towards her.

'Are you Joseph and Mary?'

Across the road the boys wriggled with laughter. The girl's head dropped. She didn't cry. Daniel saw that one of her feet was bleeding. From somewhere came a woman's hard voice.

'Martha? Get here!' The boys twisted with laughter again. One of them began to shout as the girl stumbled away.

'Where's your donkey? Where's your donkey? Ahaha!'

The voices carried to Salman as he walked. Beside the house was a rise of waste ground scattered with oystershells, a horse trough, sycamore trees. At the back were fenced dirt yards and allotments stretching down to the river. The gate of the last house hung on a tarred rope. Salman opened it and crossed to the back-door steps.

He had almost reached them when he heard the noise behind him. It sounded like a small bell being shaken. He turned round and stopped moving.

There was a dog in the far corner of the yard. Its yellow head was raised, watching, and now it stood up, not barking. Salman didn't recognise the breed, only the attitude of a fighting animal, the readiness to attack without warning. It was the size of a goat, thin-legged, all its muscle concentrated in the neck and jaws. As it moved forward its chain went belling through the ring until it fell in the dust by its feet.

There was the sound of a tongue clicked against teeth. They both looked up, him and the dog. In the open gateway stood a woman. Her hair was bare and black. Her eyes were the colour of her hair, but soft. In one hand she held a packet of meat. On one cheek was a dab of blood.

'That's enough, Fellow.' The dog turned quietly away to its corner. Only when the woman looked back at Salman and smiled did he realise that she was beautiful. He wanted her immediately, without depth, from the blood on her face to the small, neat swell of her lips.

'You must be here about the shop.' Her voice was kind and uncomplicated. Salman nodded. The woman smiled again, wiped her hand on her skirts and held it out. 'I'm Mrs Limpus.'

'Salman. Levy. I am pleased to meet you.'

'Which comes first? Which name?'

'Salman.' Her fingers felt damp with water from the street pump. She pulled them out of his. Nodded towards the house.

'There's two rooms, the shop at the front and another at the back. It's twenty-two pounds a year for them both, eight shillings and fourpence-halfpenny a week. There's sea coal in the cellar, you can help yourself to a fire of an evening. Any more is extra. You won't find cheaper.' She waited, as if expecting him to disagree. When he didn't she went over to the dog. Unwrapped the offal from its stained brown paper. 'You'll want to look inside.'

'I'll take it.'

She looked up. Appraising him. 'Leastways you'll want to look.'

'All right.' He nodded. His brother waiting, already forgotten. Together they watched the dog begin to eat, delicately pulling its lips back from the yellow teeth. Before it was done Jane Limpus came back to him, took the keys from her skirts, and led him inside.

Epiphany, 1834. The sign was yellow on black. It cost Salman three shillings, the first twenty letters free, from a painter in Limehouse.

LEVY BROS, JEWELLERS,
GOLDSMITHS & DIAMOND WORKERS, EST 1834.
Prop. Salman & Daniel Levy

Goldsmiths. For the Jews of London it was practically a racial profession. They moved into the house on Commercial Road as if they were coming home. At an auction in Whitechapel, Salman bought the repossessed stock of a bankrupt lapidary. A crucible, tripod, oil burner, and the work table blackened with their char. A wheel with its leather gone. Congealed in the cold, a tin of olive oil and diamond dust. A dish of jeweller's rouge and a polishing cloth worn through with it. Two bottles of medicinal wine. A child's sampler in a broken frame. A lost-wax mould of the King's head that revealed – when Daniel opened it – a pair of hibernating wasps, snug in the aural cavities.

The jewels from the jar Salman hid in a roll of turban under the floor by the side of the hearth. With the last of the Babylonian gold he entered his business in the London Trade Directory of

1834: S. Levy, Jeweller. Only his own name. The jewels, after all, were his. For the first time in four months he slept as if sleep belonged to him.

Daniel lay awake beside him. The streets kept him sharp. The Commercial Road was never wholly quiet. Birds sang all night in the fields, exhausting themselves in the wait for spring. Their songs were new to Daniel, unintelligible as the accents of street children. The voices of city drunks faded west, the dockers eastwards.

> *Here's to the maiden of bashful fifteen;*
> *Now to the widow of fifty;*
> *Here's to the flaunting ex-tra-va-gant quean,*
> *And here's to the housewife that's thrifty.*
> *Let the toast pass. Drink to the lass,*
> *I'll warrant she'll prove an excuse for a glass.*

When he did sleep it was a shallow state, without nourishment. He dreamed badly, of Rachel and betrayal. Wakeful, he thought of Jane Limpus. The composure of her voice, its amusement and intelligence, and under all of these things a vacancy. A mind that spoke without pleasure, only for business.

> *Here's to the charmer whose dimples we prize,*
> *Now to the damsel with none, Sir;*
> *Here's to the girl with a pair of blue eyes,*
> *And now to the nymph with but one, Sir.*
> *Let the toast pass. Drink to the lass . . .*

He lay still, his brother warm beside him. Not realising he had fallen asleep for good until the sound of church bells woke him at dawn, a ring of three from Stepney, twelve from St Paul's, and in hearing them Daniel felt the absence of the muezzin for the first time. Like a deafness.

Lent, St Swithin's, Hallowmass Eve. They purchased graniteware from Edinburgh, cut steel brooches from Manchester. Bought low and sold high. Salman worked his own jewellery at nights, the air sour with dust and acid, and in the days Daniel sold or hired whatever his brother made. His silence out of place behind the shop counter. They didn't make great jewels, not yet, only what they could sell. For three years, they took the work that came. The wives of new convicts would stand in the narrow shop while Salman carved them Newgate Tokens, prison poetry etched on silver sixpences: *Once these hearts in love was joined. Now one is free, the other confined.*

But now the story is moving ahead of itself. Its time works in complex ways. It folds back on itself and repeats, or years contract to a scale that seems barely human. Less animal than mineral. As if it were the stones that were important, and the lives of their carriers insignificant. Not the other way round. As if the brothers never lived.

They lived at 18 Hardwick Place, in the house of Jane Limpus. She was sweet-natured with them. The sweetness was there to hide a bitter heart, but the Levys were not to know that yet. They had chosen London for their jewels, and London was the place their lives were settled. It was the stink of oystershells. Rain and light. Halls of smog.

A mass of pigeons. Hoardings over waste ground. The steam of raw macadam.

Women in whalebone. Wind in the lime trees. Train dust, rolling like ebonised pollen across the shop displays.

And the sound of the river. The bellow-rush of wind through trees. An alienation carried with them, always, familial as the lines of cheekbones.

✗✗

In Camden Town the street vendors are selling matching his 'n' hers magnetic tongue studs. It's not what I'd call jewellery, but then I have old-fashioned tastes. The Tube exit is congested with stalls, a picket-line of pizza slices and fried onions. I walk in the gutter to avoid the crowds. Three blocks north of here is my old apartment. I have belongings there. Mail sometimes. It's a year since I was here to pick it up. As far as it goes, this constitutes my home.

Children run past, monstas in parkas. By Inverness Street I stop and put on my cotton jacket. September in London feels cold after Diyarbak'r, although the pollution here catches the light. Even now, at seven in the evening, there is a bright haze over the railway bridges and terraces.

There is a sense of dual atmospheres for me here. If I look at the crowded streets in a certain way, at a certain angle, they shift around me. It feels physical, in the way memories can seem physical. Even the quality of light seems to change. The present becomes occluded. I am two people here, separated by years. One of them is lost, the junctions leading off to nowhere she knows. The other one is me. My life is better than it has been. If I blink right, the years between us disappear.

On Castlehaven Road I stop by a row of shops. Above the first display window is an illuminated sign for FishWorld Aquaria & Vivaria. On the window itself is a photograph of the owner, Mr Yogalingam, looking unpleasantly surprised to find himself smiling. Behind him is a long tank of creatures that look like Christmas tree lights. Superimposed on the glass is a diagram:

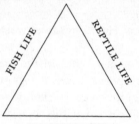

I go inside. The aquarium shop is a long rectangle walled with tanks. Their cubes of illumination compensate for the dim flutter of striplights. At the front there are goldfish on sale at fifty pence a pair. Further back the occupants become more exotic. Ghost koi and lionfish, geckos walking across glass ceilings. I always felt there was something vaguely illicit about these animals' presence here, in London. As if they should have been confiscated at customs, like drugs or knives or leopardskin shoes.

At the back, by the snakes, sits a boy in a scuffed office chair. He swivels, nodding into a mobile phone. Watching me as he talks.

'Yeah.' He is Asian, handsome. Hard in a way that marks him as born English. 'Yeah, like maggots. They're Chinese, ain't they. 'Cos they look like fucking rice.' His box-fresh trainers are up on the counter. He wears a Mao-collared leather jacket. I can smell it over the odour of reptiles.

He leans away from me. 'Japanese then. They're both tight anyway, acting like their pussy's white as cherry blossom. Listen, we got to talk about this later. I'll ring you. I'll ring you. Later.' He switches off the phone and talks to me without looking up. 'Can I help you?'

'I'm looking for Mister Yogalingam.'

'He's away.'

'He's been storing some things of mine.'

'What kind of things?'

'Clothes. Mail.'

'No. There's nothing like that here.' The boy's attention drifts towards the vivaria. I put my bag down on the counter beside his trophy shoes. His eyes swivel back to me with a slow, adolescent hostility. As if he's done everything he could possibly have done for me. He can hardly believe I'm still here, taking up his airtime.

'I used to rent the room upstairs. My things are in the garage. They've been there for five years.'

'That stuff. That's yours?' I nod. Wearily, he kicks his feet off the counter. 'Prove it.'

I don't smile. He doesn't smile back, although he's flirting now. Sleek, slick. 'My name's on the mail. Katharine Sterne.'

He sorts out the keys, watching me, and goes to look for himself. It's some time before he comes back. I wonder if he's going through my belongings and if I care. My neck aches from the long haul across Europe. I knead the pain as I wait. Behind me, something knocks against its glass like a visitor. I keep my eyes on the sign above the counter:

48 HOUR GOLDFISH GUARANTEE.
FOR REPLACEMENT THE FOLLOWING ARE NECESSARY
1. RECEIPT, 2. WATER SAMPLE, 3. DEAD FISH.

The boy comes back in, sits down, dangles the keys onto the counter. 'I brought the bags into the backroom. For your convenience.'

'Thanks. You didn't need to do that.'

'Don't flatter yourself.' As I go past him he is already turning back to the vivaria. He watches them with the aimless fascination of a TV addict surfing channels.

The backroom is decorated in flock wallpaper. Dark spaces

mark the tenancies of old furniture. Now there is nothing but an imitation mahogany wardrobe and my possessions in a pile beside it. The wardrobe door leans open. My own ghost hanging in its mirror.

I go through it all methodically, taking what I need, exchanging what I don't. Adjusting to climates. A leather coat and a black cashmere roll-neck, coal wool trousers and a Harvie & Hudson fitted shirt the colour of absinthe. Clothes from a time when I had money but nothing else. No Brethren in my life; no life, almost. In a tube bag is a pair of black ankle boots, new but scuffed at the toes. They look to me like the shoes of someone who doesn't watch where they're going. I can tell myself that I have changed.

From upstairs comes the slow beat of a trip-hop bass-line. I sit down to my mail. The envelopes are seamed with age and damp, as if they have been steamed open. There is less to read than the last time I was here. Even the junk offers have begun to diminish. My life has become like those rare days when no one knows where you are, or when they think you are somewhere you are not. My whole life is like that. There are worse choices to make for oneself.

In an envelope with last year's postmark there is a letter from Anne. I fold it into my pocket to read later and open the bin-bags of books. The texts are almost all academic, from the time when I still did something: when people could ask me what I did and I could give them an answer that made sense to them. In with the linguistic theses is a slew of CDs and two photograph albums. I don't open them. I know what I have here. This is not what I am looking for.

I pull out a London *A to Z* with the covers missing. On the title page is my mother's clear signature. I run my finger along its old indentations. I still know her street atlas better than London itself. It is marked with old pencillings, routes and searches in another time and place. Cheam fell out years ago, but I've never been there and I don't intend to start now. The index is intact. I look up Slipper Street. There is only one, ten minutes' walk towards Whitechapel from Aldgate East Underground.

What I don't need I pack away. When I'm finished I put on the leather coat. It has a faint aroma of petrol. The street atlas fits its pocket. I go back out to the shop. The boy is bent over his mobile again, punctuating a silent monologue with grunts of acknowledgement. He stops grunting when I come in. 'Got what you want?'

'Thanks. I'll see you.'

'May you live in interesting times.'

'You too. Say hello to your dad from me.'

He calls out as I get to the door. 'He's not my dad.' I look back and he leers, as if dadness was the last impediment to immediate sexual relations. 'I heard about you, by the way.'

'Good things, I hope.'

'All kinds of things. That you like jewels.'

I turn in the doorway. 'Where did you hear that?'

'From Anil. Mister Yogalingam to you.'

The goldfish watch me from behind their sunken castles. I close the door and step back between them. 'And where did he hear it?'

He pats his chest with exaggerated delicacy. 'I just work here. Yeah? I don't know who comes here always.'

'Someone came here?' I walk back up to the counter. The boy scratches the stubble on his throat. His eyes drift down to the cash register on the counter and back up to me, slow and bright as fish.

I take out my last dollars and put thirty on the counter. Now I'm in England they look out of place, too small and uniformly green. 'I don't have a lot of sterling.'

The boy shrugs. 'Money's money.' He leaves the dollars where I put them. He talks at his own pace. 'Anil's in here a few weeks ago, he starts telling me about you. He's chuffed because someone came in and offered him money. You're quite a cash cow really, ain't you? Everybody creams a little off you. They told Anil about you and something about jewels. I don't remember.'

A wave of dizziness passes over me. I sit down on the desk. There have always been others looking for the jewel, of course, Tavernier and Victoria, centuries of them. I have followed their traces, trusting their footsteps. But they have never been this close. It feels as if a fault in time has opened. As if Mr Three Diamonds has appeared at my shoulder. I remember the lines of words, surfacing on a blue screen. Years ago now, less threatening with distance: WE WOULD LIKE TO KNOW WHAT YOU KNOW.

'They?' My voice sounds sick.

'They. He said they.'

'Men or women?'

He stops to think, twisting his lips. 'Men.'

'What did they pay him for?'

He shrugs lazily. 'Most probably to tell them when you came back.'

'Did he let them go through my things?'

'No.' His smile fades. I know he's lying. It reaches him in some way, this detail. Without touching it, I can feel Anne's envelope in my pocket. Seamed with age.

'They went through my things.'

'Listen.' He sits forward, frowning as he thinks. 'I'm not going to tell Anil you was here. All right? I'll put your gear back in the garage, he won't know the difference. And when you want to pick it up ring first and ask for me, I'll sort it out. Here.'

He writes his name and mobile number on the back of a Fish-World card. All the gesture has gone out of him now. He looks angry, with himself or Yogalingam or with me. I take the card because he wants to give it. I don't read it as I put it away. I already know I won't come back here again.

Outside I make myself stop. My body wants to get away fast and I don't let it. There is no one to run from here. Across the road three girls head for Camden, laughing, bindis and glitter on their pale skins. A Daewoo goes past with music on, the driver a black black boy with corn-row hair. I find them reassuring, these faces. Seeing them makes me feel as if I've come home, though home is the last place I should want to be.

WE WOULD LIKE TO KNOW WHAT YOU KNOW. I have been naive, I think. I have worked as if avidity for jewels was a historical phenomenon, not a human one: as if no one else is capable of doing what I do. Every lost treasure has its own believers. I knew there were others, should have known, should have been more careful. I try to picture the men who are looking for me. Looking for the jewel. Evidently they haven't found either of us yet.

'Look clever, love.'

A pensioner in a flat cap shepherds an old woman along the pavement. Her hair is pink as candyfloss. As they pass he nods back at me. Cracks a smile. 'For a minute there you looked older than us. Only for a minute.'

When he's gone I check the time. It's past eight. Slipper Street can wait until tomorrow. For now I need somewhere to rest; to get my head together, as the FishWorld boy would say. Camden no longer feels like the place for it.

Chalk Farm is two minutes' walk. When I get there the Tube lift is out of order, water running down its cagework. The stairs are lit by hooklights. Passing the station axonometric I remember I've left the photo albums behind, but that at least doesn't matter to me. I'm in no danger of forgetting the people I love, even without photographs.

At King's Cross the passages are full of music. A saxophonist in a catsuit competes with a sour cellist in tails. The last of the rush-hour crowd edges around them. By the BEWARE OF PICKPOCKETS sign they reach for bags and jackets, instinctively, while the pickpockets themselves loiter unseen, waiting for victims to do just that. I cross the road away from them. There are bed and breakfasts here, anonymous places above takeaways. Rooms for arrivals, departures, prostitutions, and nothing more intimate. A hundred yards up the Gray's Inn Road is a glass-fronted hotel lobby and a sign: Ashlee House Budget Accommodation. I press the security buzzer and go inside.

The receptionist watches the door lock behind me. There is a scar by her hairline. It would be easy for her to hide it. Instead she wears her black hair pulled back from the forehead, braided tight.

'It's thirteen pounds for the sixteen-bed dorms, fifteen for the ten.'

'I need a single room.'

She looks me over, as if I might have the wrong reasons for keeping myself to myself. Something that would break hostel regulations. When she nods I pay her for two nights and she takes me up, her wooden heels slow-clapping on the stone stairs.

The room is clean and grey as a welfare office. I turn off the light and undress in the dark. Neon winks against the blinds, the colours and words blurred into a mish-mash of light. From the dormitories down the hall comes the sound of arguments in Russian, in English.

The bed is cool. I curl into myself, face against breasts, hands between thighs. My heat spreads into the trapped London air. I close my eyes and think of Glött. Of myself, growing into her, or something like her. Eva, a continent away, wrapped up in herself like the pain contained inside a pearl.

꓿

Mrs Wasp, Essa Wicks, Mrs Etcher. Wives, women with a taste for stone and the money for it. The widow, Mrs Tell, who bought only cut steel. The beggars, Martha and her brothers, only the oldest of five in work, a skivvy at Buckingham Palace. The shopkeepers, Etcher the publican, Scrymgeour the binnacle maker. Sarah Theed the baker, who had carried sixteen children and raised ten. Tobias Carey the scavenger and nightman, who lived next door to the Eastern Jews and never spoke to them, only grinned their way with a hardness that had nothing to do with humour, that was not so different from the smile of an animal. Jane Limpus.

There were more people on Hardwick Place, Daniel thought, than had lived in the whole of the Island Road. In the quiet of his thoughts, he felt out of place among them. They left him with a sense, not of knowing, but of people falling away, never to be met again. Martha and her brothers a line of eyes at the window, gone by the time he opened the door. It felt as if he himself was falling, not at home in Limpus's rooms but still, somehow, in transit.

'Mrs Limpus, Mister Levy, has worked for her living,' said Sarah Theed to Salman, 'just as I have done. A lacewoman. But not a businesswoman. As you see, you being in the shop now. "Mrs" means a wife.'

She spoke with helpful loudness, although Salman had known both her and English for a year. 'Or a widow. Jack Limpus has been gone these ten years. Handsome Jack the tar.' Between them, the sweet warmth of house loaves. Sarah wrapping them in paper. 'That means a sailor, Mister Levy. Childless, she is.' Under her breath, 'Better for her were she a widow.'

'How so?'

She looked up, startled, flour on the moon of her face. 'Lord, Mister Levy, your English is improved! It is the learning of the Jews. Any better and you shall read my thoughts before I can speak them. The loaves will be tuppence.' And he had paid with the thick discs of English coins, smiling, and walked the yards home.

Jane Limpus. Salman watched her bartering with Etcher or Carey, cabbages and river fish for scavenged goods or bottled ale. She kept no servant. Had nothing to speak of, Theed said, except the house itself and Fellow. Fell, splayed claws big as a child's hands, eating his waste meat in the yard. Salman felt that she was liked, though she kept to herself and Hardwick Place left her to it. For days she would be gone, the rooms above silent. Then she would reappear without warning, waiting in the morning crowd at the pump. Hauling nightsoil down to the river.

To Salman, watching her, it seemed that she was removed from the scheme of things. That she had removed herself. She never stopped in for Theed's oven-hot gossip, or drank at Etcher's Royal Duke. He wondered why, and what she lived instead of that life, and with whom. Some days he lay for hours on the trundle bed, listening. His eyes following her movements across the floorboards. Walking and eating. Dressing and undressing.

He looked like a thug in Western clothes. A Brunel, roughhouse, soiled overcoat emphasising his thickset body. In the shop he kept to the workroom. Away from the customers. At nights he would work silver repoussé by the light of the crucible while his brother drowsed, the hiss of the wheel insinuating itself into Daniel's dreams. In the mornings Salman scoured the table for every spore of stone lost from the dop the night before.

There was a pattern to his days. In the afternoons he would wash and walk into Whitechapel or the West End to look at the jewellers' showrooms. Just to look, never to buy. He watched them from a distance, Robert Garrard on Panton Street, Rundell's the Crown Goldsmiths in the cold shadow of St Paul's. The hothouse creatures of Hanoverian high society, moving behind gaslit glass. It wasn't ambition that made him go, or jealousy, but something more like longing. In the displays of gilt and jewels he saw a reflection of the life he had promised himself and those that were close to him.

He never went in. The salesmen wouldn't have let him if he'd tried. In the evenings he would eat with Daniel, or go alone to the King Lud at the foot of Ludgate Hill, where the apprentices came after the workshops closed. He would listen to their talk of cleaving and bruting, their boasts of balancing the fifty-six facets of a triple brilliant. Their rumours that the King was sickening, and that when he died the new crown would be the making of them all.

Salman sat and learned the politics of jewels. When the workers came in from Rundell's, he heard about the men who presided over them. Edmund Rundell and John Gawler Bridge, who the workers called the Young Vinegar and the Young Oil. The acidic jeweller and the unctuous salesman. Salman heard how the Crown Goldsmiths had made their fortune from French diamonds bought cheap from refugees in the war, and how those diamonds had run out when Philip Rundell retired. In the King Lud they said that Philip's last wish had been to die under his diamond-table, and that Edmund loved jewels more than his uncle ever had. They toasted him, *To the Young Vinegar!* Baring their teeth as if they hurt.

He saw Edmund Rundell himself only once. It was autumn. He had been loitering on Ludgate Hill at sundown. A man had come out of the jeweller's, walking to where a black and gold barouche waited. Two passers-by had whispered his name. Salman had caught only a glimpse of him, the impression of great wealth. Before the coach moved off, a long white hand at the window, hooking the blind.

The work was hard and he slept well. The dreams he remembered opened onto the desert: lions' footprints under the tamarisks. Light hurting the eyes. He would wake with a hunger to feel it again and look out southwards onto Shadwell and the Thames, the dreams translated into a vista of marshland and black curlews.

He was a strong man but brittle, and brittleness is an unforgiving quality. The foreign clothes hung on him as if his shoulders were hunched against them. Once, embracing Daniel after a good sale, Salman found that his brother had begun to smell like an Englishman. Sour with the infantile odours of meat fat, milk and eggs. It surprised him because his own sweat never changed, however much he consumed. It kept its bitterness.

For twelve months he wrote letters to Rachel, posting them from Charing Cross on the first of each month for one shilling and eleven pence. Parcels and gold every quarter. A reply never came. After a year he sent only the money, turning back into himself and his work. Daniel found him harder to talk to, harder even to argue with, as if they were growing apart.

Sometimes he would take the jewels from their hiding place. They were still whole. Perfect things. At night, as Daniel slept, Salman would unwrap the turban cloth and hold the precious objects in his hands. He remembered how it had felt to break the jar open, like opening up a skull, and the way the old jewels had caught the light. He pressed them between his fingers. The bolus of the ruby, the slab of the sapphire, the lucid pyramid of the clear jewel.

June, 1835. He woke after closing time and dressed by the window. Increments of light and shadow crossed the floor from the casement, the oil-lit shop, the darkened room. The days were long now. Outside there was still the remains of daylight. He could see Fellow laid out in the heat. From the shop came the sound of paper. Salman could picture his brother, stooped, hawk-faced. Reading the *Illustrated* or the *Sun*. Accounting for the takings, if there were takings to be accounted for.

He went out into the yard and heard the click of the dog's claws as it came to him. Over time he had come to like the animal more than he would have expected. He rested his hand on the warmth of its head, feeling the smooth skin over the massive skull, then walked to the pump. Leaning his face under the water. The cold shocking him awake.

When he shook free Jane was there. She was close, only a step away. It occurred to him that she was always closer than he thought. Against her hip she balanced the weight of a metal basin. Her eyes, watching him, were unreadable.

'Good evening, Mrs Limpus. A fine day.'

'Mister Levy.'

He stepped back, blinking water from his own eyes, looking for the right words in a foreign tongue. Nodded towards the basin. 'I shall help you.'

'With this? It needs washing yet. I can manage myself.' She swung the basin away from her hip and under the spout in one habitual, graceful movement. Swilled out its muck, grinned up at him waiting.

From the river came the sound of the late shift bell at the Imperial Gas Light factory. When Jane was done with the basin she passed it to Salman and washed her hands, slipping the water up

213

her arms. Her skin was too white, he thought. As if she was blood-less under it.

They walked back together. Salman carried the basin. When he looked at Jane her eyes were already on him. She gestured up-wards. 'Look at the moon. In England we say there is a man liv-ing in it. You see his face?'

He followed her hand with his eyes. His sight was good. He saw no face. 'Where I come from, Sin is the name of the god in the moon.'

'Sin is a poor name.'

'No, he is – he is good. His beard is blue.' He spoke up into her laughter, encouraged. 'The thin moon is his sword and the round moon is his crown.'

'Is that something the Jews believe?'

'That is different.'

'I'm sorry. It's no part of my business–'

'No. We are Jews, my brother and I, but Sin is a god of my country. It is an old religion. I believe in him not like a god, more as if – as if he were a face in the moon. Or fingers to be crossed for luck. Wood to be touched.'

'Do you believe in God?' Her eyes had come back to him. 'The Jews believe in God, do they not?'

'Yes. In God, of course, and more.' He bent and picked a length of grass from the foot of the yard fence. 'We believe there is an angel for every blade of grass.'

She took the blade. Her eyes smiled. 'Now you've killed an angel.'

'No.' *No, but I have found one,* he thought. And his eyes said it, and her eyes read it, and when they met his again they looked away.

They purchased cheap stones, the stock of a jeweller's in a poor neighbourhood. Marcasite and cairngorms, shipped to London by canal or Company ship. Daniel brought them back from Limehouse and left them on the work table while Salman slept. In August, waiting by the import docks, he saw the Marist mis-sionary who had travelled with the brothers on the *Scaleby Castle*. Vehement, malnourished from sea journeys, the Frenchman had insisted on giving Daniel his Bible, pressing it into his hands before he was called to board a ship to the Comoros.

It was their only book. A Christian Bible in the house of Jews, soft leather, supple words, the endpapers marbled the colours of the Union flag. The familiar Torah, Prophets and Writings reworked into an alien order. In the summer evenings, while the light was good, the brothers read to one another. Learning the book's new language from its old myths and voices.

'"For surely there is a mine for the silver, and a place for gold where men find it. Iron is taken out of the earth, and brass is molten out of the stone. Man setteth an end to the darkness, and searcheth out all perfection: the stones of thick darkness and of the shadow of death."'

Salman's voice, stilted with effort. The *jug jug* of choughs in the sycamore trees.

'"He breaketh open a shaft away from where men sojourn. They are forgotten of the foot that passeth by; they hang afar from men, they flit to and fro. As for the earth, out of it cometh bread; and underneath it are the places of sapphires."'

'*Safir.*'

'I know what sapphires are, brother.' The flop and tick of pages. '"Gold and crystal cannot equal it: and the exchange of it shall not be for jewels or fine gold. No mention shall be made of coral, or of pearls: for the price of wisdom is above rubies."'

'You like her,' said Daniel. He sat at the table, Salman on the yard steps. Their supper eaten, the plates uncleaned, meat eased from mullet bones. A cool evening, an east wind coming off the river.

'Who?'

Daniel went to the hearth, lit a taper from the coals, brought it to his pipe. When he didn't reply Salman turned back to the book. The smell of Virginia tobacco drifted out to him.

'You talk too much.'

'I talk very little. You like her all the same.'

'Don't you?'

Daniel sat back down, the pipe nestled in the crook of his thumb. 'In Iraq they say you should wed your opposite.'

'You slip past my questions. How could she be more my opposite? She is English, I am a Babylonian Jew.'

'Your opposite would be a gentlewoman. A lady, Tigris. Also

shy, tall, fair and intelligent. I think Jane Limpus is two of those things.'

'It has no bearing. I am not about to marry anyone.'

But I wonder what is it that you are about to do, Daniel thought. He didn't say it. He turned back towards the fire and watched the embers crack, bright as the stones hidden under them.

There was the sound of her crying out. It brought Salman awake so quickly that he barely noticed the transition. When it came again he was already moving, out of the workroom, up the stairs. He opened the door to the room above and stepped in.

He had never been upstairs before. It was all plain plaster and bare boards, as if it had never been lived in. It was some time before Salman noticed these things.

Jane Limpus sat hunched forward on the floor, the curved glass of a broken lamp scattered around her. Her right leg was outstretched, both hands reaching out to cover it. Blood ran through her fingers. Hair covered her face, and when she looked up at Salman all he could see was the whites of her eyes, teeth and skin.

'In the cupboard next door there is gin. Fetch it here.'

He had no time to look at the second room, only to sense it. It was north-facing, cooler, with more furniture but no more sense of humanity or occupation. When he came back only Jane's mouth seemed to have moved, the lips pulled further back into their rictus.

He opened the bottle and poured the alcohol over her hands. She groaned, head twisted away. Salman watched the tendons in her neck and the blood thinning between her fingers.

'Hold my foot. Hold it. Don't touch the glass!'

Her voice rose, shrill. Salman gripped her, the foot staining his lap. She pulled up her skirts and tore strips out of them. Her legs were white and muscular as her arms. Salman turned his face away. In his hands, the woman's bloody extremity felt like a distinct animal. He could feel its pulse.

'Now. Oh. Now.' She leant forward again, holding out the makeshift bandage. 'You shall have to take out the glass. I can't see it well enough myself, you must do it for me.'

He raised the foot. A smooth blade of lamp glass sat snug in the hard flesh of the heel. Its sunken arc was more than three inches from end to bloody end. Transparent swirls of alcohol still moved across its red surface.

'You won't let it break in me.'

'No.'

'You won't let it break in me. You won't . . .'

He held her gaze, waiting for her to close her eyes. With one hand he held her ankle steady. With the other he took out the glass. It came easily as a bone from cooked fish. Above him he heard Jane groan again, and then her hands were down between his, winding the bandage tight around her wound.

Sun caught in the shapes of broken glass. Salman knelt down and picked them up. They were like a puzzle, he thought. The guillotines and scimitars fitting together into something altogether different. When he had every piece he carried them outside, dumping them in a heap of oystershells beyond the sycamores.

When he came back Jane was crouched where he'd left her. Salman sat down opposite. They didn't look at one another. The September light came in around them, turning the bare room golden. From outside came the sound of Fellow. The belling of his chain.

The gin was at Jane's feet. She unstoppered the green glass and drank. Head back, the spirit trickling at the edges of her mouth. When she was done she put the empty vessel down, looked up at Salman and laughed. It was a short, hard sound. There was nothing gentle about it. Daniel would have noticed that.

She shifted along the floor towards him, keeping her wounded leg straight out. The skirts rucked up around her, her calves coming naked out of them. When she reached him she kissed him hard on the mouth, holding his head against her, hauling herself into his lap.

He put his hands back around her ankles. He felt them now as he hadn't allowed himself to before. He closed his hands and pulled the woman around him. Her skirts were already ripped. He felt the leanness of her calves, pushing his hands up the muscled smoothness of her thighs and into her cunt.

He reached inside her. As he felt the wetness there he thought of her foot again. The curved length of glass. The movement of the extremity, the way it spasmed like a hurt animal. He thought of it as he fucked her, the breath grunting out of her. When she cried

217

out again he remembered how quickly he had woken and as he came he imagined the transition had only occurred in his dreams.

Afterwards they lay together on the bare floor. The light caught in their dark eyes. They looked alike but not alike. They might have been opposites or siblings. Jane's bandages were wet, the wound had bled. Salman laid her back and changed the dressing while she slept.

'I want to show you London,' she said, and she did. After the doctor had diagnosed no sepsis, the wound washed with soap of potash and left to heal, Jane showed Salman the part of herself that he had missed. Her London was a place he had only glimpsed, as if he had walked on a frozen river at night and seen only movements in the trapped air under his feet. He slept less: it bought him time. He went where Jane took him, down into her own oil-lit nights.

Badger-baiting in the gypsy camps along the Hampstead Road. Barefisted boxing in the courts of the Holy Land, the greatest slum in London. He watched Jane haggle with the Jewish street vendors over their piles of macadam-stained clothes and whalebone. He ate oysters with the Jewish pimp David Belasco, who owned a hundred prostitutes, and in a crowded drinking booth on the Haymarket he met the Sephardi David Mendoza, seventy years old and once the boxing champion of All England.

With Jane he wandered through the ruins of Pompeii at Burford's Panorama, and made love in alleys where the old rivers ran behind the buttressed backs of buildings. The sweat of it settling in their clothes, the faint smell of each staying with the other after they were apart. And later, when their bodies were done with one another, they went back to the last house on Hardwick Place where Daniel waited. Always alone, reading or lost in thought, the Bible open in front of him. Always like a man waiting for something.

In December they went to Wombwell's Circus on Bethnal Green, where the Living Skeleton and the Saracen looked back at Salman from their own sideshow darknesses. And that night, in a basement in Duke's Place, he saw a woman gouge out a man's eyes. She did it with her thumbs. Salman turned away from it, towards Jane, and saw that she was watching with a kind of hunger. If he had known himself better, Salman would have seen in that observance a reflection of himself.

'You watched.' He said it later, in the dark of her room. Felt her shift beside him. 'And did nothing.'

'No more nor less than you.' Her voice was dry and curious. Outside the smog had come down. From the river, the sound of fog drums.

'The more I see you, the less I see.'

'Such nonsense. You are talking in your sleep, my love.'

He whispered. 'Is that what you want from me? Love?'

There was no answer. When he turned to look at her Jane was already asleep. Only later, in his own dreams, did he hear laughter.

On the second anniversary of the shop's opening they visited the Tower of London. Salman, his brother and his lover. It was a grey January day with the wind coming down from the northeast, and the attendant watched the foreigners as if he blamed them for it.

It cost a shilling each to see the British regalia. They stood in the dank cellar with a crowd of parents and children, some of them rich, none of them poor, all of them pressed up against the bars. The Crown Jewels sat on bare stone. Close enough to touch, thought Salman. They looked cheap to him, the lamps barely reflecting from the crusts of diamonds and the unset mound of an aquamarine. As if they were paste set in ormolu, costume jewellery for some half-forgotten game. Below him the children reached through the bars like monkeys in the market of Khadimain.

By the time they came out it had started to rain. The attendant kept his umbrella to himself until they reached the shelter of the White Tower, when he offered it to Jane. He peered up at Daniel. 'Mister Levy, is it? There's the ravens, Mister Levy. You see? I warrant you'd eat them, if you could.'

Salman narrowed his eyes against the drizzle, watching the birds. They were hunkered down. Built solid, as if flight was the last thing they were made for. The wind caught at Daniel's voice. 'No, sir. The flesh of ravens is not allowed to us.' He searched for more, trying to please. 'Though we may eat white doves.' Behind him Salman heard Jane's laughter, light, buoyant, like oxygen. He had heard her laugh in different ways.

It was already dark when they reached the Commercial Road. The terrace was quiet, only the Duke still open. By its light Salman recognised Tobias Carey from some way down the road. He saw that the nightman was already looking back at him, his own eyes accustomed to the dimness. Layers of clothes gave his torso an artificial bulk. Something lay beside him in the road. Only when Jane called out did Salman recognise the sound and form of the dog.

'Fellow! Heel.' Her voice was sharp. The animal came to her, its claws clicking on the limestone paving. The nightman pushed himself upright.

'Good evening, Mrs Limpus! Mister Levy, Mister Levy.' Salman blinked. From a distance, hunched forward, the night-man took on the proportions of a raven. Out of nothing he found himself recalling Rachel's stories. The old gods, swarming like flies above their sacrifices. 'Two years you've been here now, is it? Two years. And what do you say to it?'

It was the first time Salman had heard the scavenger speak. His voice was thick, with an accent Salman didn't know. He couldn't see the man's eyes, not even the shine of moonlight from them. It was hard to tell who he was speaking to.

'What do they think of what, Mister Carey?' said Jane. Salman imagined she had moved away from him, although when he looked she was quite still.

'Of what? Of this.' Tobias waved an arm at them, beyond them, towards London. 'I'm asking them what they think of the greatest city on God's earth and the *saeculum mirabile*, Jane, the most wonderful century in human history. What do they say?'

'We find we like it, sir,' said Salman. The scavenger veered towards him. Salman caught the sweet reek of rum on his breath.

'Which, Mister Levy? The city or the century? You and your brother, you're from Mesopotamia, are you not?'

'Iraq.'

'The land of Babylon. I've always thought of London as quite Babylonian, Mister Levy–'

He was aware of Jane pushing past him as she spoke. 'It's late, Mister Carey. No doubt you have work to do. Goodnight to you now.'

'Goodnight, Mrs Limpus.' The nightman watched them as

they turned the corner to the yards. His head stayed as it was, turned eastwards, until the street emptied out of everything except himself.

'I was dreaming of monsters,' she said, waking him. The smell of sex was still on him. The feeling that, with her, every part of him was used up. 'They came out of the sea. What does that mean?'

'Monsters are warnings.' He reached for her face. Cupping it. 'Of what?'

'Of whatever you are afraid of.' He watched her eyes close. Wanting to ask, not asking. A nightbird whistled over the marshes.

The more he tried, the more he understood nothing of her. It bred an anxiety in Salman which thrived on itself. He began to walk for miles, as if he could leave his thoughts behind. Instead he began to feel an impending doom, a sense of loss long before he had lost anything. As if his love of Jane were preparing him for something.

The first thing he came to hate about London was its Sundays. Later there were other things; Salman was never a man who lacked hatred: at times it even seemed as if it fuelled him, his sour, vivid energy. But Sundays were the first thing. He would walk along the river and feel the city closed down around him. The shops shut, the streets deserted, the smog cutting off emptiness from emptiness. On the Sundays it rained, London felt depopulated as a ruined city. That was what Salman hated. He walked through the dank vacancies of the greatest metropolis in the world and felt as if it was cheating him.

He began to watch Tobias Carey. They kept similar hours, the lapidary and the nightman. Passing his shopfront Salman would stop and look in, as if he had a buyer's interest in camlet and stained broadcloth. It was impossible to see if anyone sat inside, looking out.

February, 1836. He woke before noon and went out to the pump. There were carthorses at the trough and he waited until they were gone, wind running through the dead ryegrass. He let the freezing water run across his face and arms, washing the collar grime off his neck. It was only as he was walking back across the yard to the house that he realised Fellow was watching him.

The dog lay in its corner with its long head resting on its claws. Its eyes were fixed on Salman. There was a quietness to the gaze. It reminded Salman of the first time he had come to Hardwick Place. He thought of this only as he called the dog's name.

It lumbered towards him. Halfway across the yard it stopped and raised its powerful head and Salman saw that its teeth were bared. He stepped backwards, into the house, and closed the door. He didn't call its name again.

He spent less time with Jane, or Jane with him. Salman found it hard to tell where the separation began. He watched her when they were together, but more often, now, when she was away. She was often away. He never saw her go next door. The rooms sat silent above him as he worked or lay waiting to sleep.

Thaw. He walked eastwards to the docks. The cabs and carts passed him at the gates and Salman stepped back for them and then returned to his place at the roadside, as if he were waiting for passage.

I have lost nothing, he thought. Nothing, repeating it, the word twisting back on itself. As he walked home along the river he whispered the names of the old cities, places he knew only from the sound of Rachel's voice. The words becoming a talisman: *Assur and Eridu, Warka and Nimrud,*
>   *Nineveh.*
>   *Babylon.*
>   *Ur.*

爪

'Look, Charlie, budgies. Sit up straight.'

There are birds above the café counter. Their cage is stained with black and white polka dots of shit. They chirrup in time to the traffic on the Gray's Inn Road. I watch Charlie's mother drip egg down his front as he looks. 'Can you see the budgies?'

'Buggies.' He opens his eyes wide, as if this is what he's been waiting for all his life. To me the birds look like a health hazard, but then I have a different obsession. Everyone has their own white whale. For Charlie's sake I hope his isn't a budgerigar.

The café is warm with morning light and the smell of frying.

Outside London is blurred by condensation, softened, redirected. The loud red blob of a bus goes past towards King's Cross. Anne's letter is still folded in my coat and I take it out and read while I wait for my order.

'Breakfast special, love.' The waitress wears a big red name tag which calls her Dolly Lemon. They suit her, name and tag. She is wearing an apron illustrated with garden birds. *Great Tits of Britain* printed across the top.

'Thanks.'

'Ta. Shout when you want more tea.'

I prop the letter against the HP sauce. Anne's handwriting is like mine, each letter distinct from the next. She tells me her work is going well, the charity has new UNESCO funding, in a month she will be posted to China. She hopes that I've found what I'm looking for. There is other news, small talk, before she mentions that she and Rolf are having a baby in May. I sit in the café warmth and wonder whether I've been an aunt for four months.

It makes no difference to my life. I put the letter away, the seamed envelope that I may not have been the first to open, and finish my food. When I'm done I get out Edith's *A to Z* and look up Slipper Street again. I tell myself that I know where I'm going. Outside the traffic crawls around a ditch full of road-diggers, and I walk through the cars to King's Cross and take a Hammersmith and City train east as far as it will go.

Underground, I think of the child. Anne always said if she had a girl she would name it after Edith. It's something she has always wanted. Her own little white whale, red in the face with the effort of it all. I can imagine her with a baby in her arms, her fierce, smiling concentration. I hope it doesn't look like Rolf. I hope it is a lovely child.

The carriage rocks in its loud darkness. The overnight bag sits heavy on my knees. I think of stones. I have no illusions about them or myself. The Brethren is a cold thing to desire. Jewels are not lovely, although I love them. In human terms they are functional things, beautiful in the way a shark is beautiful, or the camouflage pattern of a tiger. Nature, making something for the greatest possible use, makes something of the greatest possible beauty. And nothing has more uses than a jewel.

At Aldgate East the subways emerge in a landscape of traffic islands. All the signposts are bilingual: A1202 and Leman Street, A13 and Commercial Road. The air is gritty and aromatic, as if you could set it alight and run machines off it. I cross over to the Commercial Road and keep going.

High-rises loom up ahead. In the side alleys Bengali children play out the last dog days of their summer. I pass Ki Wi Fashions – up to BIG SIZES, the shop selling saris at wholesale prices. Outside BAJWA & Co. Immigrant Lawyers, Est. 1983 I stop and check the *A to Z*. On its intricate, colourless pages Slipper Street is just around the next corner.

I look up again and find it makes no sense in the world around me. There is no corner for anything to be around. In the place Slipper Street should be there is a space between tower blocks. An empty bench. A council sign: NO DOGS NO BALLGAMES. Three magpies squat on the worn grass.

The street atlas is open in my hands. I flip it shut. On the title page, under Edith's signature, are the publication details. This is the 1973 edition. The high-rises in front of me are ugly, prematurely aged. I walk around them twice, and when I'm sure of my own idiocy I sit down on the bench where Slipper Street used to be and swear myself wretched.

Dock traffic goes past towards Limehouse. There are words carved on the bench between my legs. Street names inscribed in a hard-lined script. The graffiti have spread to a cluster of municipal bins beyond the bench. I throw the atlas in and make myself look up at the high-rises.

Every floor is like every other. Nothing is different except the colour of curtains. From here, the inhabitants are reduced to a code of nets and blinds. Between the blocks there are abandoned shops and a pub, the Royal Duke, its lone Victorian building boarded up and burnt out long ago. Across the road is its replacement, a flat-roofed construction in shit-yellow brick. A plastic banner is draped across the brickwork with an image of a playing card queen and a legend: The Royal Duchess, Karaoke every Thursday, Another Whitbread Public House. When the traffic lets me I go across and inside.

The room is done up with exposed roofbeams and an airport lounge carpet, as if floor and ceiling exist in different centuries. A fat television is suspended between the beams. On it, three horses are coming down the final straight at Leopardstown. Beyond them, the commentator's voice rises to its dry, adrenal climax.

'Very nice! Very nice.' Behind the bar is a man with red hair and freckled skin. Chewing-gum clicks as he grins, first at the horses, then at me. 'Very nice. What can I get you, madam?'

'A bottle of beer.'

'Gottle of geer? Becks or Holstein?'

'Whichever's colder.'

'One-ninety either way.' He goes to the refrigerated cabinet while I sort out the money. My pockets are still full of dollars. Their green backs and eyed pyramids stare up from the bar and I crumple them away.

The barman watches me drink, grunts an acknowledgement. 'There. Looks like you needed that. Can I get you anything else? Pork scratchings?'

'No. Thanks.' He's wearing a lilac Fred Perry shirt, the sleeves revealing thick forearms. A segmented metal watch, gold or imitation gold, a kind of medallion timepiece. A gold sovereign ring with the elder Victoria showing. East End white flash. I put the bottle down. 'You might be able to do me a favour, though.'

'Oh yeah.' He modulates the intonation. The words become half-question, half-jibe. 'And how might I do that?'

'I'm looking for a place called Slipper Street. I know–'

'Slipper Street? Heh heh. Hear that, Nev?' He shouts past me. The gum clicks and clicks. 'Nev? Lady wants to know how to find Slipper Street.'

Nev comes over. He looks like an older and more modest version of the barman. He has a bird tattoo on the back of each hand. Swallows, the inkwork dispersed with age. 'Slipper Street, love? Right then, ready? You go out of here, across the road, then' – he motions like a drowning man doing doggy paddle – 'dig down fifteen feet. First right at the water mains, you can't miss it.'

They cackle together. The barman starts cleaning glasses. 'Slipper Street's gone, love. Went in, what, seventy-nine, eighty. See all that across the road? That lot's on top of Slipper Street.'

'What about the people who lived there?'

He shrugs at Nev. The older man clears his throat. 'Well now. Most of them got rehoused. There was old folks in the streets round here what hadn't gone out of doors for years. Now they're fifteen flights up and frightening the pigeons. There's whole streets up there what used to be next-door neighbours. Now they're up-and-downers. The ones who're still alive, anyway. Why?'

'I'm looking for someone called Pyke.'

He shrugs. 'Don't know the name. But to tell you the truth, I didn't grow up round here, so I wouldn't necessarily know. If you come back tonight, though, the regulars can tell you for definite. Shame they ain't in yet.'

'Hold on, I'll tell you what . . .' On the television, the horse racing gives way to an advertisement for pantyliners. The barman picks up a remote control and mutes the volume. 'What about the caretaker, Nev?'

'What about him?'

'He'd know, wouldn't he? He was in here talking about it the other day, how they've given him a computer now. Just in case someone comes round checking things, council tax or DSS. You're not tax, are you, love?'

'No. I'm just–'

'No, you don't look it. What's his name, Nev? Henry something.'

'Henry. He's a prat. Couldn't count up to twenty-one without getting his todger out. What do you want to send her round to him for? She should stay in here. Regulars will be in soon.'

'For fuck's sake, Nev, it's only half-eleven now. They won't be in for about five hours, will they? What's she going to do till then?'

'She can come and have a drink with me.'

'Oh yeah?' He looks at Nev. His intonation is neutral again. I pick my bag off the airport lounge carpet. They both look at it.

'There, you see?' The barman grins again. The gum is pressed between his teeth, pink and baroque as a conch pearl. 'She's in a hurry. She needs to see Henry. He's all right. Tell him we sent you over from the Duchess and he'll be good as gold.'

He gives me directions. I walk back across the Commercial Road to the estate. The caretaker's office is under the tower blocks, built of the same dark brick as the high-rises above it. I press the buzzer and wait. The area around me is unlit and damp as space underground. Graffiti crawls over itself on the pillars, blue and gold, bright as the mineral scripts of illuminated manuscripts.

The intercom clicks open. A man's voice coughs through the static. I lean towards the mouthpiece. It smells of urine, as if –

with considerable viciousness and athletic precision – someone has pissed six feet up the wall into its grille. It strikes me that Nev isn't the only one with an energetic dislike of Henry. 'Hello. My name's Katharine Sterne. I'm looking for someone who might live here. Are you Henry?'

In the pause that follows I can hear music, a radio playing in the locked office before the voice blocks it out again. 'Hello?'

I put my face as near to the intercom as I can stand and shout into it. 'Nev sent me.'

'Nev? Fuck him and his mother and his mother's mother.' The intercom goes dead. I go over to the door and bang on it until it opens. The man inside is short and overweight with a blue uniform and a St Christopher's medal around his red neck. The skin of his face and neck is engorged, capillaries traced out like a street atlas. A13, A1202. I can't tell if the effect is temporary or permanent. He looks straight past me and talks before I can.

'Where is he? Tell him to clear off, the waster. Who are you?'

'My name's Katharine Sterne.'

'What are you, DSS?'

'Nothing like that. In the Duchess they said you might help me.' He hasn't closed the door yet. I shut up and wait while he looks me over. He smells of chips and vinegar, and beyond him in the clutter of the office I can see a packet of them open on the desk, a thermos waiting.

'Who said that? Nev? Fucking fat titch. He doesn't know a fucking thing.' He is hunched forward into the dark, one hand on the door both to keep me out and to support his own weight. The troll under the bridge. Billygoats gruff.

'Actually, it was the barman.'

'Mickey.' His face settles, the glare relaxing fractionally into a grimace.

'I'm here on personal business. I'm looking for a friend of my grandfather's.'

'Are you now?'

'Mickey said you have a list of residents.'

'Did he now? Quite the expert on me, isn't he? Did he also tell you I was having my tea?'

'I'm sorry. I'll pay . . .' Already the caretaker is turning back inside.

'Too bloody right you will. Close that door behind you.'

I close it. It doesn't lock. The caretaker's office smells of chips and cleaning fluids. The radio is tuned to an easy-listening station. There are half a dozen calendars on the wall, Pirelli, Playboy, Millwall Football Club. All of them are current, with the same notations and days ringed on each. Henry pulls two office chairs up to the desk, moves the thermos and turns on the computer behind it. I stay where I am. I'm taller than him, and quicker. All the same.

'The name's Pyke. With a "y".'

'Initial?'

'I don't know.'

His fingers hover over the keyboard. 'Male or female?'

'All I have is the name.'

He peers round. 'This is a family friend we're looking for, is it?'

I don't answer. He types 'PYKE' anyway. The computer only takes a second. The office chair grunts as Henry sits back. 'Pyke. George. I know him. Crusty old bastard. Sound like the kind of friend you're looking for?'

'Do you know if he lived here before the redevelopment?'

'No. But old folks round here tend to stay put. The foreigners with money, they're the ones who move out, get detached, front gardens at the end of the Tube lines. Right, 117 Pitsea. That's the west tower on the Commercial Road side of the estate. Eleventh floor. You'll be glad to hear the lift is working.' He glares back. 'The chips cost me twenty quid.'

I give him the money. He sees me to the door and points me in the right direction. The Pitsea tower is directly opposite the Duchess. In the entrance lobby is a plaque commemorating the building of the estate in 1980. There are three lifts and two of them are broken. The remaining one shudders upwards in its metal well.

At the tenth floor it stops dead and I walk the last two flights of stairs. There is nothing in the miles of corridors except the sound of people behind closed doors. The chatter of a television, the hiss of food frying.

The door to flat 117 is like all the others, institutionalised, steel plate at foot level, eyehole at head height. I only have to knock twice. It takes some time for the person on the other side to open it.

'George Pyke?'

'Yes.' He is both very old and very large. His eyes are blue and slightly protuberant in a way that doesn't make him less handsome. He is wearing a beige cardigan and cords, the clothes loose on his square frame, as if he was bigger when they were bought for him. Polished oxblood brogues. He is alone in his own home and his shoes are polished. I wonder who he keeps them ready for. I know he is alone. I recognise it in his face.

He screws up his eyes. 'I don't know you, do I?'

'No. My name's Katharine Sterne.' I put out my hand. He shakes it as if he were wringing out a dishcloth.

'Pleased to meet you. Local elections, is it?'

'No. I work in jewels—'

He starts to nod. 'And you saw the advert. You're a bit late. Most of it was gone months ago, but come on in anyway. No sense in wasting a journey. Would you like tea?'

I follow him in. Feeling my way and lost already. I have always been good at losing myself. 'No, thanks. Did you get a good response to the advert?'

'Oh, marvellous. Marvellous.' His voice drifts back. 'It was all best quality goods. I kept it all for as long as I could. Things have been a bit harder these last few years.' The hallway smells of cabbages. The wallpaper is printed with roses.

'Where were they from? The goods.'

'Oh, family. That's why I kept them so long. The way you do, with family things.'

I come out into the living room. There is a TV wrapped in baking foil, three sets of flying ducks on the walls. A smoked-glass coffee table, two worn armchairs by the gas fire. George's voice echoes back from the kitchen.

'But I can show you the last of it, if you like. Have you come far? Are you sure you don't want tea, my dear? How about something cold?' There is the sound of a fridge being opened as I sit down. 'Oh. Would you like beer or Branston pickle? I've got both.'

'Beer please.'

Above the fireplace is a row of photographs. I don't have time to look at them before George comes back in with a tray. He sets it down on the coffee table, lowers himself into the seat opposite me, and smiles. His false teeth too big for him, like the clothes. 'Collector yourself, are you?'

'More or less.'

'I see.' He nods down at the tin tray. 'There you go.'

There are two cans of beer and two glasses, a piece of jewellery and a loupe. I leave the beer. Bend forward over the lens. The jewel is pure gold, high carat. It is the size and shape of a plum and heavier, although the metal is hollow, a carved network of foliage, branches and birds. I shake it gently and something rattles inside. When I bring it closer to my face the smell of it is overpowering, and I have to pull away. George Pyke laughs like a drain.

'Pongs, dunnit?' He cracks open the beers and starts to pour, holding the glasses at an angle. There are liver spots on his hands. 'It's gold though. Old gold. Most of the stuff I had was silver.'

'It's a beautiful thing. How did it come to be in your family?'

'It was my father's.'

'He worked in jewels?'

'Not in so many words, no.' He drinks. The froth catches on his lips. He dabs it away. 'I'll tell you what. I'll give it to you for a hundred and eighty.'

'No.' I put the loupe down.

His face goes on smiling after he has stopped. 'It's worth that. I won't take less.'

'It's worth more. This is a perfume harness. It's Tudor. It was made to be worn round the neck, to keep away disease and pollution.'

'Is that right?'

'I think so. You need an auction house for this.'

'What are you, some kind of expert?'

'You'd get a better price in America or Japan.'

He sits back, the anger going out of him. 'Japan? Well now, I never could travel much. Can't stomach the food, you see. I never quite feel myself when I'm not eating right.'

I shake the harness again. 'There's something inside it, too. It could be musk, or ambergris–'

'It's a load of old cack. Pardon my French.'

'No, it should be some kind of solid perfume. It'll add to the value. It's hard to tell what it is, the scent seems to be – where did your father get this?'

'In a load of old cack. Heh. Smells of it because that's where he found it. See that photo up on the mantelpiece? Get it down here.

No, the steel frame – that's it.' I bring it down. George points, big-boned fingers smudging the steel. I can still hear him talking. The voice comes down to me from a distance. I hold the picture up to the light.

It is old, the glass plate treated with gelatin emulsion and, possibly, gallic acid. Edith would have known these things. Inside the steel frame there is only one human figure, a young man standing with arms held aloft. He is up to his ankles in low-tide mud. Behind him are the grey outlines of a bridge and the edge of a massive ashlar stone embankment. The Houses of Parliament beyond them, shadowy with smog. The man's face is all smile. A mask of teeth. Triumphant, as if he has just swum across the Thames.

'This was taken in 1909. That's my father there. George Senior. He's probably even younger there than what you are now. He was a mudlark, you see. That's what he did. What they used to do, they used to go down into the sewers. For the scavenging. Matter of fact, you could make quite a decent living out of it. Rope and scrap on your average day. Something better every blue moon. Now then. My old man was good at it. One of the best, marvellous. Oh, he used to find all kinds of things.'

It is a dark image. Hardly even black and white, since there is almost nothing lighter than slate-grey. The London sky is grimy, and the skin of the man is streaked with mud. Only his grin stands out, and the brightness of the object in his hands.

'Silver spoons. I was raised on one. You wouldn't know it, eh? He found them, see. A silver milk jug too, a quart pot. Three pounds he got for that. He said it was an art, mudlarking. A calling. You had to watch for the tides, he said. He didn't half go on. You would of thought he was still mudlarking at fifty. But people knew his name, people who knew about the business. I wouldn't be surprised if he knew the old snickets of the sewers better than anyone. All the parts the Victorians never got round to rebuilding. Bazalgette. That was the name of the man who rebuilt it. Listen to me rabbit on, I'm as bad as he was. He's been dead forty years. Forty-two. Younger than you, he is there.'

I don't say anything. Against the protective glass my breath clouds and fades almost instantly, leaving no impression. The man in the photograph holds the object up in front of him. It is small as each hand that holds it. The quality of the image is too poor for the shape to be more than an outline. A triangle blurred by the intensity of its own brightness.

'What's that in his hands?'

'That? Oh, that's a whole other story. You don't want to get me—'

'It's the Brethren.' I look up at him. 'The Three Brethren.'

George Pyke starts to say something and stops himself. His eyes look out of place when he frowns, still hesitant. 'Brothers. Three Brothers. That's what he called it. You're not here about the advert, are you?'

'No.'

'I think you better start again and tell me who you are.'

He sits straight-backed in the straight-backed chair as I unzip my bag and take out the ninth notebook. Pressed between the pages is the note from Diyarbak'r. I hold it out to George and talk while he reads the names of people and places. 'I didn't lie to you. I didn't expect you to be dealing in jewels, that's all. My name is Katharine. I'm looking for this jewel, the Brethren.'

'Slipper Street. That's a name I haven't heard in quite a while.' His hands shake as he reads it. When he's finished he looks up. 'Quite a while. It was a pretty little road. No one much wanted the towers. They went up anyway. Why was that, do you think?'

'I don't know.' I take the paper out of his hands. 'Did you live there yourself?'

'For a little while. We moved down into Poonah Street when I was still a little lad. Never went far, though. All the family lived round here.'

'And now there's just you.' I regret it as I say it. The old man blinks as if I've slapped him. 'I'm sorry. I . . .'

He smiles. It doesn't go deeper than his face. 'So you want to find the Three Brothers, do you? You'll have a job on your hands there, my girl. Put the picture back where it belongs, could you?'

I get up and stand the photograph in its place on the mantelpiece. Next to it are shots of other people, a girl with soft dimples and brushed black hair, a boy itching to escape from a three-piece suit. All the subjects are young. All the pictures are old. The frames are mock-gold and ebony. Behind me George Pyke talks with his head down. 'I'll tell you about the Brothers, if that's what you want. When my old man got it, he wouldn't talk about where it was from. That was the first thing. All he'd say was that it was from down the sewers. Now, that caused him a bit of grief. The other mudlarks thought he was holding out. That there was more where the Brothers came from. But there never was. Not that anyone found. Just the jewel in a nice gold box with a scrap of old paper.'

'What happened to those?'

'Sold. The buyers who wanted the Brothers wanted anything to do with it. Paying silly money for old tat. My old man got a bit like that later. That was the second thing.' He picks up his glass. His throat works at the beer.

'Ah. He couldn't leave the thing alone, you see. Once he had the Brothers, he couldn't stop touching it. My mother didn't stand it. Wouldn't stand for it, and I could see why, and I was only four. He touched that thing like it was a girl. He let me hold it once myself.' He peers up at me. A little proud, ashamed of it.

'What was it like?'

'Old. Heavy. Like a gun. But when he touched it, well. It was like he was feeling it up. Excuse me.' He coughs dryly. 'So there it was. In the house. Slipper Street. I remember him drawing it. I never saw him do another drawing in his life, or go into a library again neither. Even after he found out what it was, my mother had to nag him into selling it. By law it should have been treasure trove, of course, but then the mudlarks never paid too much notice to that. They had their own connections too. Business contacts, for when they needed to pass along something choice. There was quite a little auction. In the end he sold it to a Japanese gentleman. A collector. Cost him the price of a row of houses.'

'What was he called?'

He looks up at me, his blue eyes surprised. 'I thought you knew that. You've got it on that paper of yours.'

'Mister Three Diamonds?'

He nods. 'Sounds a bit obvious now, doesn't it? You would've thought George Senior or my mother would've known something was up. But they thought it was just one of them Oriental names. Little Plum, Three Blossoms. That kind of thing.'

I sit down and take a sip of the beer. 'And it wasn't?'

'They never caught up with him. As far as we was concerned Three Diamonds was the last thing he was. There was something

233

wrong with the money. Gold sovereigns, a great deal of them. It was dirty business. The old man ended up getting three years. Handling false currency. Conspiracy to pervert the course – all that. He couldn't say where he'd got it all. Wouldn't say. Or why he had so much of it. That was the trouble. Otherwise it wouldn't have been such a stretch. After he came out he got a proper job at the docks. Selling meat to the big ships, meat and fruit. But he never stopped talking about the Brothers. Not ever. It changed him. Not for the better, and all.'

He looks up at me. When he smiles, his eyes fold into their creases and lines. 'What do you want a jewel like that for, a nice girl like you? You think diamonds are for ever or something?'

'But they are.'

He leans forward and starts to sing. It catches me off guard. He does it softly, smiling, eyebrows raised. As if it were a lullaby.

Diamonds are for ever.
They are all I need to please me.
They can stimulate and tease me.
They won't leave in the night,
I've no fear that they might
Desert me . . .

We laugh together. Watching one another laugh. After a while I have to stop and wipe the tears out of my eyes and the old man goes and gets more beer and a plate of bourbon biscuits. He turns the fire on and we sit, drinking, under the watch of the photographs.

'It sounds as if he did well. Your father. The man with the Midas touch.'

'Not really. Lost the Brothers, didn't he. Schmidas, more like.'

'King Shmidas?'

'That was him. Everything he touched turned to shit. The whiff off of him when he came in. Cor. Let me tell you.'

Later he tells me he has to sleep, he's too old for this, I've worn him out. I look at my watch and find it's past midnight. He offers to let me stay, and when I say yes he goes to get me a pillow. I don't remember him coming back. In the morning I wake up tucked under a tartan rug that smells of dog breath.

There is no sound, only the warm quiet of a place where people are sleeping soundly. I wonder if this is how my home would feel. If I could get used to it. It is early, still cold, and I go into the kitchen and warm my hands over the gas stove, holding my bare arms out for inspection. There is bread in the breadbin and pickle in the fridge. I sit by the mutter of the hobs and eat four pieces of Tesco's white sliced. In the lounge I take out the inscribed turquoise and leave it on the mantelpiece. It sits vivid between the grey photographs, as if it were the stone that were alive and nothing else. Outside I walk back onto the Commercial Road and turn westwards towards the city.

水

It was a hot summer the year the King died. In winter the Thames stayed frozen for three months, the ice hard as macadam, the eight bridges redundant; but when the thaw came it set in with an unseasonable quickness. By March the river lay rotting on the tide. In the houses of the rich, windows were hung with canvas soaked in chloride of lime, and even the scavengers stayed away from the sewers. The smell of the shit of a million people rose over Limehouse, Ratcliff and Whitechapel, settling into the stitch of clothes and the pores of skin and stone.

When he was older than Judit, old as the Levys in her stories, Daniel remembered that time by how quickly it had run away from him. The pace of years in Hardwick Place, the slow grind of working days – that had been a lie, he saw. When the changes had come, they had been so fast that nothing could be done about them. Life had fallen away into itself without plot or premonition. Daniel wondered whether that was always so. It was 1920 when he thought this. His mind was boiled down to the hardness of facts. A glass of sweet tea cooled on the bedside table.

In Iraq he was not alone in thinking of the past. Along the river valleys the old cities had been excavated – Warka, Nineveh, Nippur – Europeans camped among the canebrakes. The whole world, Daniel thought, was digging for its past. Beside the tea glass lay an old-fashioned watch chain. It was not so far away that he could not have touched it, if he chose. Later he would pick it up and put it on. Not yet.

He lay turned towards the window. Tamarisks flowered in the garden outside. He recalled the ways in which his time had pivoted away from him. How his life had changed in small instances, sleights of hand, almost without his knowing it. The jar waiting to be cracked open. Fellow and his brother, dancing. The Three Brethren, placed on a table between his aged hands.

May, 1837. Hardwick Place quietened. The dock trade carriages passed with their windows shut and the curtains hooked down, as if the rank air smelt purer in darkness. It was the eleventh, a Thursday, before Daniel saw a business close for good. He was surprised it took so long.

He opened the shop blinds at dawn, and saw Matthew Lawrence the salt-bathmaker across the road. A cart was drawn up outside his showroom. Matthew and his son were loading up what they could before the creditors arrived, Martha the streetchild watching dumbly on the pavement. The bathmaker's smallest daughter was already sitting in the cart, a letter rack in one hand and a milk jug in the other.

Only once they were safely away did Daniel close the blinds again. He tried to imagine what he would take, given the chance. The gloom of cabinets and counter, waiting for daylight. The rows of jewels, silver and Vauxhall glass, waiting to be wanted. They were nothing without want. Daniel would have left them if he could.

At the end of the day he took the jewellery from its displays, piece by piece, and locked it in a metal case bought cheap at the docks. When it was done he sat at the counter with the books. Taking stock of the hours already passed. It was dusk when Jane came in. She leaned at the door, watching him, while he lit a candle and went back to work.

'Are you thirsty?'

He glanced up at her voice. Her head was relaxed back against the wall, the neck exposed. The eyes waiting for him to look. 'Because if you are I can make you up something.'

'No.' He smiled. 'Thank you all the same.'

She pushed herself upright and came over. Standing beside him as he wrote. Income and spending. Tax and gross. The smell of alcohol was warm on her skin, and with it something stronger and almost foetid. Perfume or smoked opium. 'No. You are too busy for me, Mister Levy. I can see that. Not like your brother.

You are a different kind of man. Do you enjoy this?' She tapped the accounts. Daniel raised the pen. Closed the book.

'No.'

'No. Why do you do it?'

He could feel her now, the way her skin gave off heat. My brother's woman, he thought. He sat back. The reek of her breath reached him. A tooth gone rotten. A carriage went past outside, its hoofbeats hollow in the dusk. 'My brother makes jewels. I sell them. The why of it is my own business.'

'But you have no love of it. Why do you stay with him?'

Daniel blinked. Not understanding the question, so that the woman above him smiled. 'Why? He is my brother.'

'He's a grown man. So are you.' She leaned over him, pressed against him from navel to mount. 'Are you not? What is it you want, Daniel Levy?'

He frowned. Not angry, only working to comprehend what Jane was saying. 'A family, one day, of course. Perhaps to study. There are universities in this country and in Europe. Academies–'

'But your brother wants so much more.' She was whispering now. Still smiling, her face beside his. 'He is all want, your brother Salman. You live in the shadow of his pleasures. Like me.'

He stood too quickly, so that the candle guttered and Jane had to draw back out of his way. 'Have I made you angry? Sweet Jesus.' She laughed, delighted, then went quiet again. Watching him for something. 'Then I must be right. We have more in common than you think.'

'I think not.' The candle righted its flame between them.

'Aye, but we do.' Her voice soft as the spillage of wax. 'Perhaps you and your brother might have something in common also. Goodnight, Mister Levy.'

'Goodnight.' He said it when she was already gone. Nothing left behind in the shop but the smells of her breath and her teeth and skin. He stood at the window, a tall shadow behind the glass, unnoticed by the traffic going by.

Evening. He sat on the yard step while Salman read. Nursing a pipe, looking out towards the river. Before sunset the light caught the water and turned it the chemical silver of Salman's molten metals. Later, it moved slow and green in the evening heat. Daniel narrowed his eyes against the burn of the tobacco and imagined the distance from London to Basra, the unbroken miles of water between them. That seamlessness. His brother a voice relearning old writings in the language of an alien country:

'"Oh that I were as in months past, as in the days when God preserved me. Unto me men gave their ear, and waited, and kept silence at my counsel. They waited for me as for rain; and they opened their mouth wide as for the latter rain."'

'I wonder about Rachel.'

'Why? She is well.'

'How do you know?'

'She would write if she were not. "When I looked for good, there came evil unto me; and when I waited for light, there came darkness. I am a brother to dragons, and a companion of owls. My skin is black upon me, and my bones are burned with heat."' The snap of the pages being shut. 'It is too bloody hot for this. You read.'

The Bible fell beside Daniel. He picked it up, dusted it off. Wind snapped at its endpapers. Acts, Hebrews, Revelation.

'In Baghdad the heat was cleaner.'

'No.' Daniel opened the book and smoothed its onion-skin pages. 'You forget.'

'There is cholera here as much as anywhere. Only more people to survive it. They say the King is dying.'

'They have said so for years.'

'There will be a new queen, then. Therefore, a new crown. The jewellers in town talk of nothing else. Tell me you have no interest in that. It will be the making of someone.'

'And you think it will be us?'

'Who else has jewels to match ours?'

'Aye, and the queen has only to follow the smell of the Thames to find us.'

'Then we must take ourselves to her. Levy and Levy, Goldsmiths to the Crown.'

Daniel put down the book. 'The world will not turn into diamond just for our profit.'

Salman came out from the workroom. Stepped over his brother, shirtless, wiping the sweat from his broad face. 'Such a pessimist. And you are mistaken. This is a sign.'

'The King's dying is a sign?' Daniel leaned out into the breeze, smiling. My brother is like mercury, he thought. A precious, liquid jewellery. 'Of what, pray?'

'That our luck is changing.'

'Shall I open up the shop again?' A flock of sparrows broke from the waste-ground trees. He looked away and back. 'The Chamberlain may be here this very minute.'

'God speed to him.' Salman turned. In the corner of the yard Limpus's dog lay, its yellow eyes unblinking. Salman bent towards it, spreading his arms. 'God speed to him, Fellow my lad!'

There was no sound except the quick belling of the chain. Daniel heard nothing else. He looked up, still smiling, and saw Salman stagger back. Only as the two figures turned did he see that the dog was at his brother's neck.

It happened so rapidly, so unexpectedly, that in the first long seconds Daniel found he could do nothing but try and believe his eyes. He saw that Fellow's head looked too white beside Salman's, the skin pulled far back from its eyes and teeth. Violence made it monstrous.

There was the sound of harsh breathing. Daniel couldn't tell if it came from Fellow or from his brother. In the dirt yard they danced together, the dog's foreclaws braced against the man's shoulders. In the quickened seconds he thought of the animal's cold aggression, like a mirror of its mistress.

He called out as he began to move. Down the steps, into the dirt. He shouted out again as he reached Salman. He saw that his brother had forced the dog's head back, his left hand around its neck. Daniel gripped the animal's ribcage. He pulled and the hind legs lost their footing, skittering backwards in the dirt.

When he looked up again his brother was pressing his free hand against Fellow's forehead, like a blessing. The animal pushed itself forward and Daniel heard its teeth snap together. He watched as Salman curved his thumb, turned it down and hooked it up into the creature's white left eye.

A sound came out of the dog. It was the first and last time Daniel heard it make any real noise of its own. Blood and humour ran down its cheek and Daniel took his hands away and stepped back as it shook itself, fluid flicking into the dust. Its hind legs moved again, as if it meant to run, and as it did so

Daniel realised that his brother wouldn't let it go. He called out again, his voice still not resolving itself into words.

Salman was pulling the animal now, not forcing it away. In the blind left eye his thumb turned, sunk up to its heel. Daniel put a hand out towards them both.

As if he could hold his brother back, leashed. It was what Daniel was never capable of doing. In front of him Salman twisted the hook of his extremity up into the animal's brain.

He didn't let it go until it stopped moving. Even then the body twitched where it lay. The foreclaws jerked, Daniel saw, like those of a creature dreaming of flight.

When he looked up at his brother Salman had already turned away. His right arm was dark. The blood-marks of Fellow's claws ran back over his arms.

The world began again. It was as if the violence, the suddenness of it, had left a vacuum into which the air rushed back. Southwards, Daniel could hear seagulls along the river. East, the chip-chop echo of building sites out towards Stepney. He walked over to his brother and lifted his face.

'Dead, is it?' Salman's voice was indistinct.

'Dead.'

'I am sorry for it.'

Daniel let his brother's face go and began to check the rest of his naked torso. The red chevrons of the shoulder wounds. His voice, beginning to babble.

'Why should it have attacked me? We were just talking of the King. I never trusted it, 'Phrates, not ever. The dog is dead, long live the dog. Ahaha.'

'All right, is he?'

Etcher the publican stood at the yard gate with his hat in his hands. Behind him were other people, attracted by the sound of violence, not getting too close. Etcher nodded again. 'Nasty. I've sent my boy next door for Jane. She'll be here presently.'

Daniel turned back to his brother. The wetness on Salman's right forearm was the dog's blood, not his own. It was dark and already thickening. Not arterial blood, Daniel thought, which would be brighter, fresher from the heart. This was vein blood from the eye and brain, the fluids running back up the man's sinews. There were no bite marks on Salman himself, none that he could see. Only the long, shallow wounds of the claws.

Salman laughed in his arms. 'Surely the dog was a royalist.'

'You weren't bitten?'

Salman's eyes struggled to focus past Daniel. 'I don't know, I don't – Is that Jane? Oh, Jane.'

Daniel felt her beside him. He moved back as Limpus took his brother's arm. Her voice was soft. He couldn't see her face as she passed him.

'This morning I thought you were a jeweller. Now you look like a butcher.'

'Forgive me, Jane. I killed Fell. I never meant to–'

'Damn you both.' Her head arched round, and Daniel saw the hardness of her face. In the blue-white skin, the veins standing out above her black eyes. 'I want you out by the morrow.'

'Mrs Limpus?' Etcher's weak voice called out again. 'Was the dog diseased, now?'

'I'd be pleased if you left us, Thomas Etcher.'

The crowd moved and murmured. The publican bowed his head to put his hat back on. 'I'm sorry to intrude where I'm not wanted. The worst I can say of myself is that I sent my boy for you, Mrs Limpus. Sent him next doors, where anyone should know you could be found. Would you not like him to fetch Doctor Leverton? I might know where he is also. Leastways till closing time.'

She let go of Salman abruptly. He staggered as she walked across the yard. Not towards the gate, where the crowd was already breaking away, but towards the body in the dirt. Daniel watched her stop beside it. With the toe of her boot she nudged the deadweight. When she was sure it was no longer alive she bent down, her skirts trailing in the dust, then knelt and lifted the dog's head into her lap. Daniel saw her lips move beside it. Whispering.

He looked away, ashamed of himself or of his brother. The crowd at the gate was almost gone. Now he could see other faces beyond that of Etcher. Strangers and neighbours. Sarah Theed the baker and Carey the nightman. The scavenger's face was half-frowning, half-smiling as he turned.

They took Salman inside. Fellow still lay out in the yard. When Doctor Leverton arrived Jane left the three of them alone, and when Daniel looked out again at dusk the body of the dog was gone. He never asked Jane what she did with it, not then or later; but as he watched the doctor working he imagined it. Jane digging in the allotment's soft earth. Or the nightman working for her, Limpus waiting beside him. Daniel's eyes were never as good as Salman's. He couldn't have done the fine work of a jeweller, and he never saw the way horizons disappear below one another as a ship leaves land in clear weather. All Daniel could do was to imagine. His thoughts were how he saw the world. He always kept them to himself.

Leverton was a small man with ancient stained breeches and artist's fingers. He walked stooping across the yard to the dead dog and looked at its teeth and eye, lifting the gums and lid as if he were buying a horse. He was already going through his tools as he came inside. The saw, brace and liniments.

'No disease there, Mister Daniel. Not a bit. It's miasma you need to worry about. Foul air, sir. Here of all places.'

He cleaned Salman's shoulders with water from the pump, extracted yard dirt and hairs from the wounds with a pair of iron forceps. Dressed them with lint and alcohol, muttered about the laudability of pus and suppuration, and left a roll of bandages and a bill for nine shillings and two pence.

'I always advise Brighton. Plenty of exercise and no miasmata, that's my prescription. Leave London, sir, if you can. May I ask where you and your brother hail from?'

'Baghdad.'

'Ah? That should be far enough.'

After he had gone the brothers sat together in the darkening room. Daniel by the casement, the chair pulled beside it. To the west and south-west London filled the river valley. He could see roads and illuminated squares. Jerry-boat lights moving on the Thames. For miles, the city lay spread out like cut stone on a jeweller's cloth.

Salman got up and went to the lamp. In the gloom before he lit it his bound shoulders were a spectral white. Then the wick caught and he stepped back. Daniel watched the flame play across his face. He looked calm now. From the hallway came the sound of someone coming in. Steps on the bare staircase. Daniel kept his voice quiet.

'You had no cause to kill it.'

Salman turned round. Face moving into the shadow of his skull. 'It would have killed me if it could. Cause enough.'

He thought of the crowd at the gate. The publican and the scavenger. Not too near, not too far. 'We have to leave.'

'She said that?'

'You didn't hear her?'

Salman shook his head. He turned away and sat down by the lapidary's wheel. Ready for work. 'Then we must go.'

'We take what we can from here, stock and fittings. Find somewhere else to live and trade.'

'Aye.' He sighed, rubbed his forehead with one hand. Scrubbing at the skin. 'Right. I must say something to Jane now, eh. Something at least.'

He knocked against the wheel as he got up. Daniel watched him reach out and catch it before it fell, quick in the uneven light, clumsy with shame. He sat with his head down as Salman went out to the hallway. His footsteps on the stairs. His voice calling, whispering. *Jane. Jane.*

Daniel rose and took the pipe and tobacco from the mantelpiece. He filled the pipe, lit a match from the lamp, started the pipe, and went with it out into the yard. On the steps he leaned back against the door, closing it behind him.

The smoke caught his eyes and he closed them. From Rotherhithe came the echo of construction sites, carpenters still at work under artificial illumination. From Limehouse came the rattle of dockside cranes. Nearer, the sounds of the crowd around Etcher's pub. From the house behind his back he could hear almost nothing.

The pipe went out. He took a silver matchbox from his waistcoat pocket. The sulphur flare lit his calm face. He waited for quiet, until the nothing was less than nothing. Then he finished the pipe and went inside.

He woke late, alone, with a taste in his mouth as if he had been running. The previous day only came back to him piecemeal as he was pulling on his clothes. It felt unreal, the smooth rapidity of events. Inexplicably he was reminded of the sound of ice, shelving into deep water.

He went to the window. Fellow's chain lay in its corner. There was no sign of blood. As he picked up the shop keys Daniel wondered if Jane had swept the yard during the night. Erasing the violence of the day before. Barefoot, he walked through into the showroom, leaving the connecting door wide to allow the daylight in. The blinds were down. Yawning, he went to open them.

He felt a cold impact underfoot and stepped back instinctively. On the floor was a scattering of broken glass. A piece the size and shape of a playing card had been caught flat under his heel, cracking again without breaking his skin. The blinds in front of him moved with the slight force of a breeze, and Daniel reached across and pulled them back. The shop door was ajar. Only a wedge of glass at its foot had stopped it opening wide. Two of the lights had been broken inwards, and the top and bottom bolts were drawn back. They were a long way from the broken panes, the bolts. Daniel wouldn't think of that until a little later.

He turned back into the shop. Quicker now, waking up fast, he raised the counter, stepped behind it and knelt down. The drawers and cupboard space were all unlocked. Everything had been emptied out or taken. As if the searchers had not even known what they wanted, account books or sealing wax. The metal box of jewels was gone.

He groaned and hauled himself up. As he ran back into the house, stumbling with the need not to stumble, he recalled the East Indiaman again. It came to him out of nothing, the way dreams sometimes do. The creak of hammocks. The sensation that everything was being stolen from him.

He went up the stairs without stopping, calling out his brother's name. At the landing were two doors, a narrower staircase curving upwards, the walls stained with damp and dereliction. Daniel turned the corner and went on up. At the top was a single door and he knocked, hard, then knocked again. When no one answered he opened it and stepped in.

The richness of it struck him. Light fell across an oak commode and dresser, a delftware jug and basin, an ormolu clock quietly dividing time on the mantelpiece. Faint, the smell of urine from the commode, waiting for morning. Salman still lay huddled asleep. Beside him Jane was already sitting upright, her eyes waiting on the door. She said nothing. She didn't cover herself.

She was beautiful. Her nakedness stopped Daniel. It shamed

him, as if he had come on something he had never been meant to see. His brother's woman. Her breasts were firm above the slight round of her belly. The aureoles of her nipples were dark and enlarged, as if by childbirth. He looked up again and realised that Limpus was smiling at him. Only with her eyes. Her mouth was hard and sly. He watched her eyes and remembered the bolts.

He walked across the room and shook his brother awake. 'Tigris, get up.' He spoke fast, in Judeo-Arabic. 'We have been robbed.' Salman rolled over and stared up at him. Daniel stepped back as his brother struggled out of the bedclothes. Around his shoulders the bandages were stained the colour of rust where his wounds had bled during the night. Behind his bent back, Daniel watched Jane Limpus straighten the sheets. Brush them clean.

'Robbed. Robbed, the bastard sons of English bitches. By whom, did you see them? What have they taken?'

'The stock and takings. I saw nothing.'

'But the jewels, 'Phrates. What about the jewels?'

Daniel shook his head again, not understanding. Salman leaned towards him. 'For God's sake. The jewels from the jar.'

'I was sleeping in the same room—'

'You didn't look?' Already Salman was backing out of the door, down the stairs. They reached the workroom together. Salman pushed the table away from the fireplace and crouched, still naked, prying at the loose board beside the hearth. When it came away he lay down, reaching his arm into the cavity under the floor.

He grinned humourlessly. The bundle of turban cloth came up soiled with earth and a grey silk of cobwebs. Daniel knelt down beside him as Salman untied the three jewels, the cabochon, table cut and the writing point. Against the stained cotton they were more beautiful than he remembered, the surfaces perfectly reflective. As if they had grown or changed, underground.

The light changed against them. Daniel looked over his shoulder. Jane was leant in the doorway, a thick house gown of old chenille pulled around her. Her eyes on the jewels. She was smiling again, but again the expression looked incomplete to Daniel. The shut mouth too hard and thin against the teeth.

He reached out and covered the stones. She looked up at him, surprised, and her smile twisted open. 'Am I intruding, Mister Levy? Seeing what I should not? Don't worry about your stones.

245

I've no interest in them nor their owners. I've had my fill of the pair of you.'

'We'll be gone soon enough.' Daniel picked up the bundle. He was aware of Salman rising beside him, and he remembered the attack. The violence in his brother, and him unable to hold it back.

'You will.' She tightened the cord around her waist. 'I have errands to run this morning. You'll be gone when I return.'

'The police, Jane—'

She turned on Salman. Her voice stayed mild. 'Police? The peelers don't come out here if they can help it, and the City's men not at all. There's no one round here but friends of mine. And they're no friends of yours.' Mild, milder. 'If I was you I'd go while I had the chance.'

He stood hunched. 'Is this what you wanted? I don't – No, I will not hear it. But what is it you wanted of me, Jane?'

She laughed. Salman remembered the sound from his dreams. 'I lay with you for the pleasure of it. You're a jeweller, you should know pleasure.'

'I know that your life is pleasureless. You have a cold heart, Jane. Carey.' He took a step towards her. 'The scavenger, is that it?'

Their voices had risen, choking, as if they were drowning on one another. Jane shook her head. Not to answer Salman, Daniel saw, but with a narrow-eyed, suspicious amazement. As if Salman had hurt her, reached her, belatedly, in the way she had least expected. Her voice a whisper as she stepped back. 'He'll scavenge you, should I give him the word. I'll bid you farewell now.'

Salman watched her. He stood at the window of the workroom, waiting for her to be gone. Daniel packing behind him, dismantling the wheel. Molten metal had left patterns on the table. Brands in the shape of figures, rivers, maps. It was two hours before Limpus came down, dressed and booted. She went out and walked to the next house on Hardwick Place without looking back. Salman pressed his face close to the window as she passed beyond the yards, the colours of her clothes and skin flickering between the fence pickets. His breath flared on the glass and receded.

'Now we have nothing, 'Phrates.' He whispered. Behind him, his brother's voice.

'We have one another.'

'Aye.' A broken echo. 'We have the jewels.'

It was May when they left Hardwick Place. A hot month in a hot summer, and London was never made for heat. It was a place built in the image of rain, the grey-carpeted halls and façades of ashlar stone designed for a climate of short daylight and late thaws. Now white mould grew in heavy furnishings like a temperate variant of frost.

May, 1837. Even the rain was warm. Daniel and Salman walked through it with the sweat itching in their trimmed beards and dark clothes. They still had the stones. Salman carried them. He could feel them in the pockets of his worn frock coat. For days and weeks he thought of nothing else, while Daniel worked for them both. Not Jane or her pleasure, the Crown of England or the itch of the wounds in his shoulders. Only the marshlander's jewels. It seemed to him that the more he lost the more he loved them, his three stones, precious as wishes.

冰

There are four of us on the Underground train. Opposite me sit two women in work suits and, beside them, a man with a can of Tennant's Super. The man is singing verbal graffiti. The women are pretending to be asleep. I'm looking for a man called Mr Three Diamonds.

> 'You must remember this.
> A piss is just a pish, a shite is just a shite.
> The funandmental things apply,
> As time goes by.

'Ah. Now then, fuck it. Have you any change, love? The inspector's stole my ticket.'

I give him two pounds. It stops him singing. Money itself has never interested me; or if so, only insofar as it takes me where I need to go. Still, when I feel in my pockets I find I have almost nothing left. Ten pounds sterling, forty US dollars, and the last ruby in its makeshift bulse. London bribery becomes more expensive every year. I get off the Tube at Farringdon and walk up a couple of blocks to Hatton Garden, with its shabby rows of gem wholesalers and second-hand jewellers, grilleworked windows full of stolen loveheart chains and solitaire wedding rings.

The shops are still shut, the pavements sluiced down overnight to clean away the swill from Leather Lane market. I find an open café and think of Mr Three Diamonds while my tea turns cold in its styrofoam cup.

It feels as if he's following me. I know this is an illusion. No one in my footsteps now was buying the Three Brethren eighty-nine years ago in East London. I keep meeting the name, but only because we have both been looking for the same thing, nine decades apart. Two lives turning on one point. If anything, I'm the one following Three Diamonds. He found the Brethren. The closest I've come is to have met a man who once touched it.

At nine I give the physical remains of the tea back to the boy who made it and walk up to the Holborn end of Hatton Garden. There are fewer pawnbrokers here, less of a sense that whatever you buy is someone's mother's Sunday best. In a concrete shopping mall on the far side of the street is Holt's the gem wholesalers. I ring the bell and go inside.

Little has changed in the years since I came here last. The jewel shop is unnaturally bright, as if the nylon carpet and glass displays have been worked over with static dusters and gemmologists' loupes. The room is walled with illuminated showcases, like the aquaria at FishWorld. In each lit tank are rows of stones. Backlit pipes of tourmaline, each shaft fading from pink to green. The broken pots and heads of geodes with their internal linings of crystal. From its recess above the tanks a security camera turns to follow me. Behind the glass-topped counter, the shopkeeper watches me with the same economical stare. When she speaks, her voice is raised a fraction more than it needs to be. 'Are you looking for anything in particular?'

'Actually, I'm here to sell.'

'Oh right, fine.' She has dark eyes, full lips, an expressive face toughened to articulate nothing. She wears no jewellery. Her hair a handsome mass of frizz. I give her the ruby and wait, killing time while she takes it away to the back rooms for the lapidary's evaluation. In the middle of the nylon carpet is a free-standing vivarium of lapidary exotica. I peer in at the centrepiece, a scale model of the Albert Memorial built of nothing but precious stone. A faux neo-Gothic monstrosity of malachite and porphyry and sard.

The jeweller who wears no jewellery comes back. Puts the ruby on the counter with both hands. 'Well, it's a good stone.' There is an edge of surprise to her voice, half-hidden. 'Very good. Better than we normally take without a ready buyer, in fact. Is it Burmese? With the political situation, we try not to buy–'

'Sri Lankan.' I pick up my bag. 'If you're not interested I'll take it somewhere else.'

'No, we'd pay six-forty for it. To be honest, though, if you did shop around you could probably get a touch more. Someone will have a buyer waiting for a good ruby, they always do. You probably know places.'

I take what she offers. I have no bank account any more, not in England or anywhere else, and when the jeweller checks it turns out she won't be able to raise the cash before lunchtime. I go back to the café and sit reading yesterday's *Evening Standard* while the traffic hoots and shudders on its way to Holborn and Ludgate Circus. When I've digested all the news of Tube strikes I can manage, I get the Istanbul lapidary out of my overnight bag and sit at the Formica table reading notes on the Black Prince's ruby and Elizabeth's Mogul bracelet, Henry the Eighth's lost crown and the origins of the Three Brethren. The tea boy watches me malignantly from behind the Pukka Pies hotplate. I order the Special soup and hope he doesn't spit in it.

At one o'clock I go back up to Holt's. The jeweller is eating Black Magic chocolates from the box. The wind has risen outside, and as I count out the money on the counter I can see the sky clouding up. The city looks at home under it, as if the buildings were constructed for this prematurely faded light.

By the time I come out the rain is already beginning. I cross the road to the nearest phone box and ring Directory Enquiries and the number they give me while drizzle taps impatiently at the windows.

'Japanese Embassy, Piccadilly,' says a voice made in South London.

'I'm just ringing to check if you have a library. I'm–'

The line goes dead, makes a rapid clicking noise, then abruptly switches to a muzak medley. *The Four Seasons* segues into *The Girl from Ipanema*. I hold it away from my head and wait. Outside two

men run past with tabloid papers on their heads. Half a yard behind them is a woman wearing a Budgen's bag over her hair, the
last in the field at a children's party game. Egg-and-Spoon race,
Mad Hat dash. Her heel slips on the wet pavement and she almost falls. An umbrella goes past her wearing itself inside out.

'Hello?'

The new voice is Japanese, feminine. I turn back towards the
scarred metal of the telephone. 'Is that the library?'

'Oh yes. Library and archives.'

'I need to know your opening times.'

'We are closed from noon until two every day, and all day on
all United Kingdom holidays, also all Japanese national holidays. Also for all Embassy functions.' The woman's English is almost perfect, each word carefully enunciated. She speaks like the
Talking Clock.

'But you're open now?'

'Oh yes. Tomorrow is a function. Big dinner. But today is extra
opening day. We are not closed until five o'clock.'

I thank her and hang up. Outside the downpour is raining itself out in the deserted streets. It's not the reason I'm still in here.
I squat down over the bag, take out Anne's letter, and unfold it
against the phone box wall.

She says she will be in China in a month. Already this is a year
ago. Time folding back on itself. Bracketed between her words is
a fourteen-digit telephone number. I don't know which city it
represents, or whether my last blood relative will still be living
there. Relatives: Anne may not be the last any more. I get out all
the change I have, pound coins, fifties, twenties. In the cramped
booth I can smell their soiled metal. I feed them all into the telephone's thin mouth, and ring again.

The tone sounds distant, an isolated signal piped along
seabeds or through satellites. On the fourth ring the line connects
and Anne answers. I open my mouth to speak and then stop myself. It feels as if I've been cheated.

'Sixteen twelve double three one nine. Please leave a message
or send a fax after the long beep.' Her voice repeats itself in Chinese. It sounds competent, although I wouldn't know if it wasn't.
I wait for the long beep.

'Hello, Anne. It's Katharine.' My voice sounds unfamiliar. It isn't just the echo of the long-distance line. I'm speaking too slow, too thoughtfully, as if I'm trying to remember what I mean to say. 'I got your letter. I was just ringing to see–'

'Katharine?' Her voice catches me off guard. Cheated again, I think. I picture her in her Chinese apartment, cooking or eating. At home with the answerphone on. 'Oh my God, is that you?'

'It's me.' I feel myself trying to smile. The Prodigal Daughter returns to the bosom of the family telephone. 'Happy Christmas, New Year, birthday, all that.'

'Where are you – wh–' Before I can answer her voice fades away. At a further distance I can hear her talking to a presence that might be Rolf. *Katharine. It's Katharine. I don't know –* 'Katharine? God, we didn't know where you were. It's been nearly three years. Are you all right?'

'I'm in London.'

'London? Well why the hell didn't you get in touch? Anything could have happened to you.'

I try not to say, and say anyway, 'You sound like mum.' For a moment she doesn't go on. The line hushes us. On the telephone's liquid crystal display I watch the seconds evaporate. 'How are you, Anne? Are you a mum? Am I an aunt?'

She laughs. 'Jesus. Yes you are, yes I am.'

'Boy or girl?'

'Girl.'

'Edith.'

Another pause. 'Edith? No. Why did you think that?'

'You always said.'

'Did I? I forgot. No, she's called Susannah. Sue. She's lovely, Katharine, oh, you'd love her, she's – Do you want to speak to her? Rolf–' She turns away again. *Rolf, bring her here, quick!* 'Here. Sue, this is your aunt. Katharine, this is your niece.'

I listen. At the other end of the line, something listens back. There is no sound, not even breathing. I think of three. It is an uncomfortable number. There is nothing to spare in a family of three. If the unit divides, someone will always be left alone. I whisper back. 'Hello, Sue.'

Anne comes back on. 'She heard that. She looks scared rigid. You should come and see her. Do you have time? What are you doing now?'

'You know what I'm doing. I'm looking for the Three Brethren.'

'You're joking. You're not joking.'

'No, that's what I'm ringing about.' I turn in the box, looking southwards towards the river. The phone's metal cord winds around my arm. 'It's going well. I'm getting somewhere now. Last night I met—'

'I don't want to hear about it.'

'—I met a man whose father sold it. Actually sold it, Anne. And I know who bought it from him. I might have to go to Japan to find—'

'I don't want to know. When was this sale?'

'It doesn't matter when.' A foot from my face, rain smatters against the phone box glass. 'The point is that I know where I'm going.'

'1649, was it? Medieval France? When? You don't know where you're going, you never have. How long do you have to do this to yourself?'

I press my eyes shut, stretching the tiredness out of them with my fingertips. 'The money's running out, Anne. I just rang to see how you were. How are you?'

'I'm fine. I worry about you.' In the background, Rolf's voice. Anne waits before she speaks again. 'Some things happened here.'

I open my eyes. 'What things?'

'Nothing, just odd phone calls really. Once someone tapped into our files at work. Once we got a call there and someone asked for your new address, except we didn't have one.' She hesitates again. 'Katharine?'

The telephone warbles. I turn round. There are thirty units left on the crystal display, running down fast. I swallow my anger back. It's not meant for Anne and I don't want her to hear it. 'I'm still here. The time's almost gone, listen, I just rang to see how you were. I'm glad about the baby. Sue. It's a nice name.'

'Can I call you? How do I—'

'I'll ring you again, I promise. Take care of your family, Anne. I love you.'

Only when I stop speaking do I realise the line is already dead. I put the phone down. I don't know if she heard me say goodbye and it doesn't matter anyway.

The rain has eased. I go outside and wait for a taxi. The coldness feels good against my face, clean. I think of the people who are following me. It reminds of me the dream in the stone house of Diyarbak'r. The lizard-dog, shadowing me through the crowds. The sirrusch, which means nothing – which is just a monster. By the time a taxi comes the rain has stopped. I take the ride anyway. I've had enough of the Underground for one day. For the time being I want to see where I'm going. It feels as if I'm getting somewhere, and if it isn't London then so much the better.

The Embassy is opposite Green Park, a double-fronted stone façade between overpriced carpet shops and hotels made seamy by road grime. The queue for the visa desk curves down the marble steps into the lobby. I go through the security barrier and turn right. I don't need to ask directions to the library. It is separated from the lobby only by a wall of Plexiglass.

Inside, a woman in black skirt and white blouse is rearranging books on the shelves above a low-slung communal reading table. At the table sit two Japanese businessmen in nylon suits. One of them smokes over a rumpled copy of the *Yomiuri Shimbun*. The other one is surreptitiously looking up the woman's skirt. None of this is exactly what I was hoping for. I open the glass door and wait by the counter until the librarian is finished.

'May I help you?' She smiles brightly. Pinned to her left breast is a badge identifying her as *Akiko Kurosaki, Senior Librarian*. She is younger than I imagined from her voice on the telephone, and I didn't expect the Talking Clock to be beautiful. She is sharply monotone – black hair, white skin, black eyes, white blouse – except for her make-up. Her lipstick is a deep, dense red, and her nails are painted to match. I open my bag and take out the ninth notebook, the old notes from Diyarbak'r laid flat inside the paler pages.

'I'm not sure. These are the details of a business transaction that took place here, in London, in 1909 or 1910. The buyer was Japanese. I was hoping you might have visa records from around then, but this doesn't look like the kind of place I need. Can you tell me where to go?'

'Oh yes. Maybe here is fine. This is the Embassy library and archives. In fact we have some records here that go back to the first Japanese Legation to Britain in 1884.' She cocks her head, trying to read the paper upside down. 'May I see?'

I slide it over to her. She frowns down at R. F. von Glött's haphazard writing. I point out words. 'This was the seller. Pyke. This was the buyer. Three Diamonds. If that was translated into Japanese, could it be a surname?'

She purses her red lips. 'Mitsubishi? No. Only a company name.'

I lean across the counter. '"Three Diamonds" is "Mitsubishi"?'

'Oh yes.' She smiles again, drawing with her finger on the mock-lacquer counter. Three strokes and a diamond. 'Mitsu. Bishi. Was he buying motorbikes?'

The businessman with wandering eyes looks up from the reading table and shushes us. The librarian bows and mouths apologies in Japanese. I take the paper back. Fold it away.

'Not motorbikes, no. The Mitsubishi Corporation – how long has that been around?'

The librarian shrugs. 'Maybe a long time.'

'Do you have records here of Japanese company names?'

'Oh no.' Her face falls. 'We did have them, but recently we sent them to the School of Oriental and African Studies of London University.'

'Can I go there?'

'It's more difficult.' She brightens again. Leans towards me across the mock-lacquer counter. 'But I know all the librarians. I can telephone them. You want to know any companies called Mitsubishi in 1909, yes?'

'Are you sure you don't mind?'

She winks. 'Wait here please. May I ask your name?'

'Katharine.'

'Wait here please, Katharine. It will take some time.'

As soon as Akiko is unavailable, the library voyeur begins to watch me instead. I'm not what he has in mind; after a few minutes he gets up and leaves. The plastic seat is damp where he was sitting. Another businessman comes in, sits down in the wet patch and falls asleep with his mouth open. Above him dangle three mobiles promoting Respect for the Aged Day. Cut-outs of happy wrinkly faces revolve gently in the conditioned air.

It's half an hour before the librarian comes back. When she does her arms are full of fax paper and notes in close-written, intricate characters. She lays it all out and turns on her proud red smile. 'Here. Please. I hope this will help you.'

'These are all Mitsubishis?' I turn one sheet towards me. On it

254

is a list of companies: *(12) Mitsubishi Electronics. Founded 1921. Founder Ibuse Iwazaki. (13) Mitsubishi Engineering. Founded 1916. Founder Kenzaburo Yamato.* Details of current status, profits, ten-year market value.

'All. Sometimes they are divisions of the big firm, sometimes independent. The big Mitsubishi is founded in 1870 – a shipping firm, you see? And in 1909 there are still not so many. Here, timber. This is coal. This one is also quite old.'

Where her finger stops is a single short entry. *(32) Mitsubishi-Mankin Merchant Trading Company. Founded 1894. Founder Enzo Mushanokoji. Dissolved 1910.* 'Wait. "Mankin." What does that mean?'

'"Man" is a thousand. "Kin" is gold, money, coins. This is a good name for a company. Lucky.'

Gold and diamonds, I think. I don't say it. 'Not so lucky,' I say. 'It only lasted sixteen years. This man, Enzo . . .'

'Mushanokoji.' The librarian shakes her head. 'This is a most unusual name. A rich family. Big in business.'

'What kind of business?'

'Soy sauce. Very big in Japan.' She grins. There is a smudge of lipstick on her big flat teeth. 'Very delicious.'

'This one – Enzo – if he ever came to England, would you have a visa record?'

At the end of the counter is a computer. She walks over to it as she talks. 'Sometimes the older archives are very good. Sometimes not. I can see.'

The screen winks on. She types quickly, never looking at her hands. The script unfurls across the blue screen like something growing, alive in the simplest sense. Movement in a vivarium.

'Oh look!' Akiko cries out. The businessmen frown and mutter in their plastic seats. I turn the screen towards myself. It tells me that Enzo Mushanokoji ran a company named after diamonds and gold. It records that the company traded War Office supplies and minerals. It lists the visas Enzo applied for, in France, Germany and England. Three for the last: 1893, 1904, 1909.

'This is him.' I say it only to myself. It is no one's business but mine. Akiko the librarian turns the screen on its axis again. Her anxious face bathed in blue light.

'Which was he buying, Katharine?'

'Which what?'

'War supplies or minerals?'

I put the fax papers in my bag, zip it up and hoist it onto my shoulder. 'Minerals.'

'Oh! Good.' She stands back. 'Well, it was very nice to meet you, Katharine. If you need any more assistance, please come back soon.'

I tell her I will. I know it is a lie. I leave her with her mobiles and voyeurs and stop the first taxi that tries to pass me outside. The driver has skin black as the heartwood of ebony. I direct him towards Heathrow and sit back. Anne tells me I don't know where I am going, that I have never known. She is wrong about that. I don't think of her any more. My coat creaks against the seats, leather on leather. Outside the streets still glitter with old rain and I close my eyes and picture diamonds.

፠

They took quarters in Shoreditch. For four shillings and three-pence a week they had a single room to themselves above the egg-dealing business of a Sephardi called Solomon Abendola. The smell of rot and fowl impregnated the unpainted walls and stayed with Daniel wherever he went.

He went to the peelers. He had written down everything on cheap shop paper. He had taken care with the English, allowing no flourishes, no cursive echoes of Hebrew or Arabic. He sat in a Whitehall waiting room with the papers in his hands while the officers in their blue coats walked in and out, big men, func-tional, minding their business. A desk clerk took down his name as 'Ben Levi'. His eyes were blue as gas flames. Daniel didn't cor-rect him. There were only two other chairs in the room. In one of them sat a woman with a child in her arms. For two hours she swore at the peelers in a language Daniel didn't understand. No one answered her. No one came for his paper.

The child's feet were wrapped in black lint. The woman had casts in her eyes. The other chair stayed empty. After two hours the woman got up and went out. Daniel didn't see her again. From the yard he could hear the whicker of horses and the *shee* of sabres on a whetstone. Two officers came in with a third man

256

hung between them. The third man had no face left. It dripped blood into the sawdust. Daniel left after three hours. He didn't go back again.

'We sell two and keep one.' It was evening, and the sky still light. Salman talked as he ate. On the shared plate, four potatoes stewed in mutton fat and a cut of the boiled meat. *Treyf*, the corrupt food of the Gentiles.

'We sell what we can, surely.'

'We shall keep the clear jewel.'

'It's worth nothing. Hüseyin the Imam said so. If we are to hold back a stone, perhaps it should be a good one.'

'If it's worthless then no one will want it. We need to sell what we can, you said it yourself. I say we keep it.'

Daniel watched his brother. His shoulders were still bandaged. The wounds had not healed well in the heat. In the weeks since they had left Hardwick Place Salman had found the money for medicine, Daniel didn't know where. A Soho apothecary had prescribed him tincture of opium. *To allay pain, relax spasms, and procure sleep*, Daniel had read on the blue glass bottle. He watched Salman take the dose each night. Ten drops in a tin spoon. Jane's name hung unspoken between them.

They talked softly in the leather booth. Around them, the evening crowd had left tracks in the inn's wet sawdust. Salman stared at the markings as he ate. It was a meaningless script, ugly as English. He chewed and swallowed, watching the floor. His mind full of stones.

'I say we keep it.'

June, 1837. The newspapers talked of cholera. The residents of the slum courts reported beggars whose skins had grown thickened, like the scales of fish. On the night of the nineteenth King William the Fourth died, propped upright in a leather chair to help him breathe as his heart stopped. And at nineteen years old, Victoria Guelph was declared Queen of England. The contract for her coronation was given to the most respectable of jewellers, the old king's Crown Goldsmiths, Rundell and Bridge's of 32 Ludgate Hill.

Rundell and Bridge's. Vinegar and Oil. It wasn't the most

fashionable of choices: that would have been Garrard's, a name that was never spoken in the dull gilt showrooms uphill from the King Lud. It wasn't the choice that the young Queen might have made herself, given the chance. It was a commission made by old men – Keepers and Chancellors – and given to old men – Edmund Rundell and John Gawler Bridge, still known in the trade as the Young Vinegar and the Young Oil. Their company had been Goldsmiths to the Kings of England for decades before the Queen was even born.

Black crape hung in the curved glass shop window. It cut off the showrooms from the street where Salman had once stood, watching. Mr Rundell liked it like that. After the last of the workers had gone – Mr Bridge to his wife and child, George Fox to the King Lud and his bottle – Edmund sat alone in the unlit shop. The dark allowed him space to think. He thought of the company and how long it could take to die.

The jewel displays were imperceptible around him. It didn't matter. Edmund knew their positions off by heart along with the price of every Jew's spoon and lady's watch that they contained. He thought: This is the twelfth night of Victorian England. He tasted the new word in his mouth. It clicked against his dry palate.

He was seventy-seven years old and still handsome, with the hair on his head dyed black and oiled blacker. Even the whores on Haymarket said he was a pleasure to do business with. As far as Edmund was concerned there was enough life left in him for the lot of them. In the firm they still called him the Young Vinegar behind his back, and he liked that too. He leant forward in the pitch dark, the bones of his elbows digging into the ligaments of his thighs.

He thought of Rundell's. He knew it like the back of his hand. Better, even. Outside the company his life had always felt thin and unnecessary, and he had never regretted that. He remembered George Fox, years ago at the Dean Street workshops. Talking them up to the new apprentices.

'Now, mark you! This here is what you've sold yourselves into. This is Rundell and Bridge's, the object of envy to all the Trade and the wonder of almost the whole world.'

And it had been true. Even ten years ago there had been truth in it. There had been Rundell agents on three continents when

Edmund joined the business of stones. Usher in Smyrna, Sidney in Constantinople, men whom Edmund directed and ordered and never met. Powers at his fingertips. They had delivered company jewellery to Catherine the Great and the Pasha of Egypt, and in London Mr Bridge the Elder had once served the American ambassador and Lord Nelson. For years, they had sent annual shipments of jewels via Manila to the ruler of the Celestial Empire. But there were no more orders now, and no more jewels to send.

The wonder of the world. Now it was a lie, and not even a crown commission could make it less of one. It was not demand which made a great jeweller's, but what one could supply. But there had been wonders. The company founders had once sold the Pigot Diamond. Edmund remembered holding it in his hand. Its impossible worth. A hundred and eighty-seven carats of pure watered stone, a perfect oval long and broad as the top of his thumb, with no discolouring except for one minute red foul near the girdle. Like the spot of blood in a good fresh egg. He'd thought it would be the first of many great stones. Three decades older, he knew he would never touch anything as beautiful again.

He was a jeweller by profession. Salesmanship he left to Mr Bridge. Each had learned his trade from his uncle before him, and as the older men had died each nephew had stepped into his shoes as smoothly as a shadow. They were as good as the founders, Edmund thought. Better. The decline of Rundell's was nothing to do with them. It was greed which had done it, the inability to let things go. The possessiveness of anyone who worked with stones for too long.

A horse went by outside, shoes slipping heavily on the damp cobbles. Edmund sat quite still, listening. He thought of his uncle, Philip Rundell. Old Vinegar. Out on the hunt with the lords and ladies, or down at heel at the diamond table. He had been a hard man, certainly, even violent, but hardness was admirable in business. Edmund had always thought it quite admirable. The old man had lived to eighty-one. Edmund could live longer. He felt it.

'What are you after, boy? A partnership?'

That was the first thing Edmund could recall of his uncle. The voice, thick and crass as grit on a wheel. It was the first time he had come up from Bath to London. Looking for work, certainly. He had shaken his head. The smell of too much powder and pomatum clinging to his coat and hair.

'No, sir. An apprenticeship would be more than I'd hoped for.'

'Well then.' And the old man had leant towards him. One Vinegar to another. 'That's as well. But we want no fops or gentlemen here. Eh? What we want is plain jog-trot men of business.' The stink of his breath. 'What are you, boy?'

He was a man of business. Philip's shadow, that's what he was. Not that he had ever liked the old man, only that he admired him. Edmund even admired what others had criticised. There had been his uncle's sideline as a banker for whores, although he'd always paid them near enough fair interest. And there had been the Old Vinegar's purchase of diamonds from French refugees in the Napoleonic Wars. Stones bought for nothing in a glutted market. Diamonds picked up from families with no homes or food, only cold stones. But then buying low to sell high was never a crime. If there were skeletons in Philip's cupboards then the company had been stronger for them.

It was the French diamonds which had made the company's fortune. The ones Philip had used in jewellery had made Rundell's famous, but the last of those stones had been gone a long time. The founders had taken them with them. The Old Oil had left rich, but Philip Rundell had done better than that. It was a decade since he had died, willing away one and a quarter million pounds from the company. Sucking it dry.

He looked less like his uncle every year. For a while they had been similar as siblings, Edmund and Philip. Their faces seamed and lined and hooked. Features clean as forms etched with acid. But when Philip had been old his eyes had been younger than his face. Edmund knew his own were not. Failure had done that. For Rundell's, decline had been a slow business. Alone in the dark room, Edmund wished it was done with. The firm wound down and bankrupted for good.

He had been young when he became a partner. Forty-four, in his prime, and the company with him. Now he could smell its rot in the night air. Philip's business. Edmund cleaned his tongue, rasping it against his teeth. The showroom and workshops lay motionless around him. On the shopman's desk beside him, the Commission lay waiting to be executed. Edmund didn't need to read it again.

He wished it was done with. Edmund sat in the dark and began to cough, a dry sound in the airless room. He knew it like the back of his hand. Better – much better. A jeweller's without jewels, lodged in the mausoleum shadow of St Paul's. He thought of stones, like Salman. Like Katharine, he closed his eyes and pictured diamonds.

'Mister Rundell.'

He woke instantly and kept his eyes shut, listening. It was something he did automatically, like the deafness he feigned in order to hear who spoke what of him behind his back. From outside came the sound of late-morning traffic. Nearer, the small talk of shopmen and apprentices. They kept their chat down. Edmund noted that.

It was too late to be sleeping. The shop should have been open hours ago. They are waiting for me, Edmund thought. I am an old man, dozing in his chair. He went on listening, his own informer, until the voice called for him again. 'Mister Rundell?'

It was closer than he would have liked. Smooth and insistent. Edmund had put up with it for seven years.

'Mister Bridge.' He opened his eyes, mouth curving upwards. A stranger would have thought he was smiling. John Gawler Bridge stepped back.

'My apologies, I had no intention of – you were sleeping, sir?'

'Sleeping? What did it look like I was doing?'

'As you say . . .'

Edmund watched him hesitate. John Bridge with his brown velvet coat and bloodhound eyes. He smelt of oil, Edmund thought. Of old oil and anxiety. Too many years of servility had made him rancid.

The room was unnaturally dark. Edmund pulled himself upright, sockets clicking, and fingered back the funeral drapes. Making the salesman wait, as he should. Uphill, the tall houses of Ludgate were overshadowed by the bulk of St Paul's. Its walls were stained with long stripes of grime, its cupola rising into the city's yellow upper air. The streets below were thick with people.

A coalman's horse had fallen outside St Martin's-within-Ludgate, tipping anthracite into the gutter. A crowd fought over the spillage, as if the accident had made it common property.

Edmund leaned against the curved glass frontice. 'Look at them.'

'Which, sir?'

'The crowd. The common crowd.' He whispered the hard consonants. Bridge raised his eyebrows, reflected in the glass.

'All customers.'

'Customers? They couldn't afford a Jew's spoon from us. They are nothing but the city, and the city is a lie, Mister Bridge. It tries to tell us that there is a commonality between us. That we are all the same at heart. The mediocre and mundane take comfort from it. I do not.' He stepped back. 'You look as if you mean to shit yourself, Mister Bridge.'

'Ah. There was something I wished to discuss with you, sir, if I may.'

'Out with it.'

'I've been considering our Commission, sir.'

Edmund nodded. 'You've costed the order. And?'

'And we cannot do it. We lack the funds and the stock, were the finest stones available. Our competitors possess better supplies. They are quicker on their feet—'

'Aye. Then we get payment in advance. For better or worse the order is ours. No one else's. I won't see it go to some jumped-up West End pimp.'

'Quite. However, I have spoken to the Chancellor and to Mister Swifte, the Keeper of the Regalia. There will be no advance. In fact,' Bridge glanced towards the backroom door, 'this is more delicate – Her Majesty may see fit to honour us with the empty frames of several older state crowns.'

'As payment? How many?'

'Three. As part payment. Naturally, we would be expected to keep those frames intact. Not to sell them, for example, to buy new stones.'

'Then we borrow.' Edmund went back to the chair and sat. Mouth shut against the pain. When he looked up, Bridge had the order in his hand.

'You have read this?'

262

He scowled. 'Of course I've read it.'

'A hundred and seven new items to be made. Fifty-six additional refurbishments. The Imperial State Crown to be reworked. *An offering sword. A ruby ring. A twelve-ounce wedge of gold. An ebony stick with gold head and ferrules. Twenty gold staves, five coronets, five cushions, seventeen badges—'*

'I said we'll borrow.'

'*Twelve Morocco cases, eight collars, twelve new Sovereigns, one silver basin, the resetting of the whole of the Diamonds and precious stones of the old Crown into the New—'*

'Enough!' He stood. Quick as he'd ever been. Leant in towards his partner. The workroom door opened before he could speak. A shopman with his hair unpowdered walked in, looked up, backed out again. Edmund shouted before the door closed. 'Mister Bennett!'

'Sir?' The shopman came back. He looked young and lax. Edmund tried to remember if he was a relative. They were everywhere in the company now, symptoms of the firm's demise: in-laws of nephews, inbred cousins, bastards of in-laws twice removed. All of them lax. Edmund talked to family as he did to anyone else. The shopman watched the door as if it might catch him, like a mousetrap.

'Get those drapes down and open up. It's high time we were doing some business.' He started towards the back door. 'And Mister Bridge? We will fill this order. Cost it again. Where is Mister Fox?'

He shouted it as he stepped from the shop into the workrooms. Down from the face, into the guts. The veins stood out on his neck. To his right were the company offices. Straight ahead, down the steps, the workshops were stripped-down basements. There was nothing comfortable in them, no softness. Only things which could scour stone, he thought. Things which could melt metal. The workshops made him feel better. The shouting too.

'Fox!'

'Here, Mister Rundell.' George Fox, shopman and smith, came up beside him. 'Just getting cleaned up for you. Are you well this morning, sir?'

'My wellness or not is my own business, Fox. You mind my wealth and leave the rest to me.'

263

'Yes, sir.' When Fox smiled Edmund could smell wine on his breath. He is starting on it early today, he thought. And then: I could do with a drop myself.

The shop around them was lit with the white heat of crucibles. To one side, a second hall and forge stood boarded up. These days, most jobs were done at 53 Dean Street. The tables here were of more sentimental value than anything. Philip had always managed the jewels himself, even after everything else was beyond him. Especially the diamonds. Edmund could understand that. He walked on down the aisle. 'How many are working here today?'

'Myself and young Bennett, that's William, and three of the apprentices. Learning all sides of the trade, they are. It's the cistern, sir.'

Edmund stopped by the lapidaries' wheels. George Fox beside him, already pulling papers from his apron pocket. 'Cistern?'

'The Duke of York's. I've the order here, let me just . . . *The Duke of York's Cistern. To be 18 and a half inches diameter. To use no more than 810 ounces of burnished silver. Figures and relief in gold matt. The neck and lip enwreathed with vines etcetera. Scenes of Romans etcetera, and two tri.* Tri?'

'Tritons.'

'Tritons peering in. That wasn't my idea. Mister Bigge's idea, they are. Four more Tritons to support the cistern base. They're on the design here. Men with scales, they seem to be. That's what we want, is it?'

Edmund began to walk again. 'We begin the Royal Commission soon, George. The coronation is to be set back a year. The Whigs will spare no cash and time to crown their young monarch. It will be a great event, so they say. Shall we be ready, do you think?'

'No one else is readier.'

'No one else has the Commission.' They reached the end of the workshop. Edmund looked back at its wheels and benches. A place built for nothing but jewels. He felt at home here. He tried to recall if he had ever loved anything else as much. 'Any other news?'

Fox crumpled the papers back where they came from. 'Not to speak of. The King is dead, but I expect you know that by now. There was two Jewish gentlemen here this morning about selling jewels. They came to the showroom door. I told them to come back at closing time.'

'Not to the showrooms.'

'No. I explained that to them clear enough. They'll be by the Creed Lane door at seven or not long after. Will you see to them yourself?'

'Aye.'

'Mister Rundell?'

He was already walking back, up past the tables and wheels. He hadn't even realised he was doing it. My body is wandering, he thought. But not my mind. 'What is it?'

'I'll see them with you, if I may.' It was less a question than a statement of fact. Edmund turned away from it before he answered. His mouth curved upwards. A stranger might have thought he was smiling.

'You think I can't manage them myself?'

'I think you can jew any pair of Jew dealers in London.'

'Good, George!'

Eighty-one, he thought. I can do better. As he walked back to the offices he muttered the words to himself, like a mnemonic or a penance.

Seven o'clock. Two Jews. The Creed Lane door.

They were an hour early by Daniel's watch, and the watch itself had always run fast, ever since Salman had bartered it from the marshlanders, stripped and reassembled it like the mechanism of a gun, and given it to his brother because they had become traders together, because he had wanted to give him something. Anything would have done. Now they sat on the green ground beside St Paul's, waiting until the end of the day.

He opened the watch. Wound it, turned it back. On its face the litany of English words, divided by numerals.

Rundell & Bridge's

He closed the lid. Salman shifted beside him. 'Time?'

'Almost.'

'By tonight we shall be rich. Tomorrow we start afresh. Fresher than afresh. Gold enough to ship Rachel here, house and all.'

The late sun was hot on Daniel's face. He listened to his brother, nervous. Talking of nothing, as if scared of the alternatives of quiet.

'Lives of pleasure. Think of that.'

'Is that what you wish for?'

'Pleasure? Aye. And money. Through commerce money becomes everything.' His voice rose a little. 'Your wishes are no purer.'

'No.' A mailcoach went by towards Ryder's the apothecary. The horses blinkered, three chestnuts and one gold bay. Daniel tried to imagine his wishes. Green turbans, he thought. It felt like years since he had wished for anything physical. If anything, he felt the opposite. He wished to be without goods, stock, cargo. Without the ballast weights of stones and gold and the smell of ink that clung to him, always, making him something he was not. Without Hardwick Place. *Too many wishes*, he thought. He shook his head, vaguely alarmed, as if he had found a bill he had forgotten to pay. 'No. You always meant to change things.'

Salman didn't reply. Daniel turned again and saw that his brother's eyes were closed, the light whitening the flat blades of his cheeks. He stirred. 'But perhaps I can't. All the miles I have brought us. All the work, and nothing has changed. We are no richer, no greater. I thought we would be great.'

The light crept down the walls above them. Across the rooftops Daniel could see hoardings for medicines and transports: *Be Bonny In Brighton! 4/- Weekdays 7/6 Weekends.* A municipal clockface. It was five to seven. He wanted to ask his brother to check the stones, but Salman was still talking. Murmuring in their old language, his voice frail and dry in the evening heat.

'Nothing has changed. It could be God's will, of course. We are bad Jews, eh. Without a congregation, without a sabbath, eating the unclean food of the English. Or should we have tried harder, do you think? I think not. Should we have gone east? Sometimes I wonder if we went the wrong way. It worries me. Do you think we should have gone east, 'Phrates?'

'It is time.' He spoke gently. His face was turned towards Salman's, so that he saw the expression when the younger man opened his eyes. He looked at the city below them wildly, as if he recognised nothing. It only lasted a second. Salman blinked it away like sleep. He stood up, brushing off his frock coat, smiling down.

'Well! Shall we go and make our fortunes?'

Creed Lane smelt of horse-shit and cabbages, old muck fermenting in the sun. The rear doors of the Ludgate Hill businesses all looked the same. On the back ramp of Rich's Bakery, a man rooting for stale bread directed Daniel and Salman the wrong way for a halfpenny. It took ten minutes to find the jeweller's entrance, the steps cluttered with oyster shells and a broken-backed invalid chair.

Salman knocked. There was the sound of a deadbolt unlocking before the door opened. In its crack stood the man who had sent them away that morning: a dab of snuff on the moustache, hair smarmed back with Macassar oil. Daniel took off his hat. 'Our pardons, sir, but we came this morning. We have jewels–'

'You're early.' The door slammed. From inside came the mingled sound of shouting and the clang of metal. When George Fox came out again he kicked the broken chair off the steps with an absent-minded viciousness and nodded towards the brothers. 'All right, in you come. Have a care for your heads. Do you have names?'

They ducked inside. The workshop was dark after the open air. Daniel stumbled, his eyes too slow to adjust. 'Levy, sir. We are brothers.'

'Levy? Christ almighty. You keep that to yourselves, now. Look lively, this way.'

On the workbench sat a basin of gilt, vines winding through its handles. Salman assessed it as he passed. Only the material was extravagant: the work itself was mundane. From beyond and around the basin, the smiths watched him back. They were young men, with thick hands and faces. Salman knew their odour. The sour Englishness of it, milk fat and cold meat, although in the workshop he could smell nothing except the sweet fumes of jeweller's rouge and molten metal.

These are men who have set diamonds, he thought, and worked gold. Seeing them, in the flesh, he found it hard to believe. He imagined what it would be like, to work ounces of gold, plates of gilt. The most obedient of metals, holding its shape like stone, soft to the sculptor's knife like clay. Not breaking like iron, or becoming soggy as hot copper. In gold, he thought, I could make wonderful things.

'This way. Directly, if you please.' A corridor, wooden stairs, a passage. At the last door of eight Fox knocked once. When there

was no answer he turned away, waiting. This close, Salman realised how short the jeweller was. Only his musculature made
him seem tall. Salman bent his head to speak.

'Sir? Is there something the matter with our name?'

The jeweller licked his lips and laughed. 'Levy?' Even with the
workshop noise echoing around them, he kept his voice down.
'You want to know what's the matter with Levy? I'll tell you.
There was a robbery here, twenty or so years ago now. Twenty-
two thousand pounds of rubies, diamonds and pearls. The rob-
bers switched them under our noses for a box of coal and
threepence-halfpenny. Wrapped in flannel.' He knocked at the
door again. Turned back. 'Levy was the name of the first thief.
Bloom was his partner. Jews, mind. Levy was the one we got. Got
him in France, good and proper. Sitting up in bed, reading at
midnight. Sterne's *Sentimental Journey*, it was. I know because I
kept it. They hanged him in good time. Do you read, sir?'

'A little . . .'

'Oh, you should.' Fox stared up at him, eyes wet as the sweat
around them. 'All books have jewels. Steal into them, Mister
Levy, like they were goldmines. You won't be hanged for that.'
His voice rose as he turned away. 'Mister Rundell? The Jewish
gentlemen are here to see you.'

'Come.'

It was a large room. Nothing else about it felt as generous. By
the narrow fireplace stood a desk and a safe, shop fittings, functional as a butcher's goods. Above the desk hung a portrait of a
man with a face like a blade. Below him sat an older figure. They
looked alike, thought Daniel. Relatives, certainly. Variations on a
theme. He tried to imagine what it was.

'Sit.' They sat. The man at the desk was writing with a quill.
The shank of it was stained with age, black at the nib, yellow at
the tip. The man didn't look up until he had finished. It took
some time. His eyes swung up, met Daniel's, and waited for
them to move away. 'You have jewels?'

Daniel cleared his throat. 'A mêlée of stones, sir, found in our
native country–'

'What are you?'

'Mister Rundell asks what is your work,' said Fox.

'I am trained as a lapidary,' said Salman.

'You know which cuts?'

'All plain cuts, also the step, table, and brilliant, the double brilliant and the scissors. I can work metals also, either hot or cold. My brother Daniel is our shopman.'

'The double brilliant, eh? Show me the stones.' Edmund stood up. In front of him, the Jews rose from their seats. Behind them Fox stayed where he was. To himself Edmund could admit that he was glad to have the shopman there. The Jews were dark-skinned, he saw. The shorter one brought out a ball of rags from his soiled coat. It looked like something peeled away from a wound. Edmund tapped the desk between them. 'Here. Put them here.'

Salman unwrapped the stones. They sat on the leather of the desk, catching the light in their curves and planes. Almost imperceptibly, the four men leaned closer. Edmund took a loupe from his pocket and went to work.

He was a jeweller by trade. He was good at what he did. In the first few seconds Edmund Rundell saw the diamond he knew it for what it was. His face didn't change with the knowledge. But then that was also a part of his trade.

He concentrated on the other stones, making himself wait. The sapphire first. Sixty or more carats of grey-blue corundum. A fine stone, excellent. Fit for a crown, although large sapphires were not so unusual: not impossibly rare, like great rubies. Edmund put it down and picked up the balas. Under the gaslight it was rose-red, violet-red, the colour uneven. It caught the illumination too slightly to be corundum. It didn't heat light, like a true ruby. Warmed and cooled, Edmund knew it would change colour, altering through blues and shades of transparency and back to red. Balas spinel, a chameleon of a mineral.

He made himself wait. He picked at the three stones with his fingers, the uncut nails clicking, flicking away what he meant to disregard. And when he lifted up the Heart of Three Brothers and held it briefly to the loupe, he showed no astonishment. Later, alone, he would weigh its thirty carats and scream thinly with delight at the great Writing Diamond.

When he was finished he put the loupe back in his pocket and sat down. The Jews stood waiting. Edmund imagined that he could smell them. They had a bitter, dry odour. Alien. He bent forward.

'Well. You are too modest about the quality of your wares, gentlemen. This is no mêlée.'

'Sir.' Salman moved forward, one step. Speaking for them both. 'We only mean to sell–'

'Are there more where these came from? No? But you work in the trade. Perhaps you know what you have here? This is a balas ruby.' He picked up the gems. Carefully now. Neither his mind nor body wandering. 'Indeed. And this is a very fine sapphire. And this, too, is a perfectly nice spinel. I like them all, Mister . . .'

'Levy, sir,' said Salman.

'Levy.' Edmund raised his face. Met the foreigner's eyes. Looked away, back down at the paper, the quill he had kept for its cheapness. 'I like them, Mister Levy. Now. These stones, naturally, will need to be recut in a proper English manner. We may lose as much as half their weight in the process. Notwithstanding that, I would be pleased to offer you five hundred pounds for the set. What do you say?'

There was a movement between the Jews. Edmund glanced up. The shorter man turned back to him. 'Beg pardon, sir. We only meant to show two. Only the ruby and the sapphire are for sale–'

'Two? Nonsense.' He didn't stand up. Didn't push too hard. 'No, you came here to offer me these stones, and I like them. I shall take three or none at all.' Edmund waited. Not for himself, he knew what he was doing. Only to give the Jews time. To let them stew. He could feel the portrait behind him. Philip, overseeing them all. He wondered if the old man would have done things as he was doing.

A polishing wheel started up next door and he raised his voice, drowning it out. 'Indeed, our only problem here is financing. No doubt you've heard that we have the Commission for the coronation. Such stock doesn't come cheap. The upshot is we have little ready money. I can give you five hundred pounds a twelvemonth from today, but if you desire quick cash, I can only find – what could I find, Mister Fox?'

'Only two hundred pounds, Mister Rundell.'

'Oh, well. Two hundred and twenty, sirs, if we scraped about. Now then, I have a second proposition, and it is this. I am sensible that you may need finances. We shall advance you fifty pounds today, and the balance of five hundred in a twelvemonth. Moreover, and to show good faith, for this next year we might find you both employment here. Apprentice wages for now, with every possibility of promotion. God knows, with the Commission we'll need your help.'

He smiled, all teeth. Still seated, the stones between his outstretched arms, the two hands poised as knife and fork. A gourmet smiling at rich pleasures. Waiting for something, some grace. 'Now. What do you say, gentlemen?'

Three stones for two lives. Daniel and Salman moved from Shoreditch into the attic rooms at Ludgate Hill. They began on wages of twenty pounds a year, Salman in the Dean Street workshops, Daniel as a shopman.

George Fox apprenticed them. All things in the trade, he even befriended them. Daniel believed it. It was never as true as he wished. Fox ate with them, at least. It was more than anyone else in England had done. Most nights they stopped at the King Lud, Salman joining them later, the opium that had sustained him all day leaving him dull. Daniel would watch the old man and his brother, leery and lamplit. Drinking until the head could forget the body's tiredness.

'Will you not drink with us, Daniel?'

'Kind of you.' He shook his head.

'Well and so. You are hard workers, I'll give you that. Slog your tripes off, the pair of you.'

'We do as we are asked.'

'And so you have what you want. Eh, Salman?'

'Aye.'

'Aye. And you, Daniel.' He veered back. 'The quiet one. Mister Stillwaters. What is it you want?'

'Nothing.'

'*Nothing?* You lie. Look around. London is thousands on thousands, all wanting something. It is a human condition. Want loves want. It grows and breeds. Why should you be any different?'

Daniel shook his head. *I want nothing,* he almost said, and did not. Knowing neither of them would understand. That both would think wanting nothing was no want at all.

'You have jewels, Daniel. Gold soft as ladies' cunnies in your hands. And tomorrow you shall want more. I'll wager my drink on it.' George raised his ale. 'Halloo, a toast! To those druggists of diamonds –' he bent across the table, almost on top of it now, reddened as a roast of meat '– apothecaries of artifice, Levy and Levy, no less, of London. Goldsmiths to the Crown.'

He apprenticed them. He made something of them. Fox worked the brothers like so much raw stuff, and he got what he wanted out of them in the end. If he liked them and they him, well and good. George Fox always made a point of being liked.

He let them into secrets. Small confidentialities, cheap bait. Interest on a larger return. Opening shop, Fox told the brothers the story of Victoria's Ropes: the legendary Hanover pearls, which belonged by rights to her uncle Ernst. How he'd slept with his sister and killed his servant, and was suing the Queen for the whole of the pearls. How Victoria had got them from Pope Clement the Seventh, whose niece was Catherine of Medici, whose daughter-in-law was Mary Queen of Scots, whose executioner was Queen Elizabeth of the hard eyes, whose nephew was James the First, whose daughter was Elizabeth of the beautiful pearl earrings, whose son-in-law was George the First, whose son was George the Second, whose grandson was George the Third, whose son was William the Fourth whose head was pointed like a cokeynut, may he rest in piss, whose niece was our dear little German Queen. How she couldn't be queen of Hanover for they were barbarians and will have no queens, there were only knaves and kings in their games. And so the pearls were his by law.

'But I reckon the Queen deserves them myself. I hope she passes those ropes along to Rundell's, and we'll break them up and set them here and there like coins under cups at a fair, and the uncle no more able to spot them than the piles roped around his arse.'

He had a wide face, street-hard. George Fox told them of Paul Storr, the great goldsmith who had made Rundell's reputation, and who had stood the Old Vinegar for over ten years – and how when he left, the company lost its greatest treasure. One night he let the brothers into the safe room to see the three empty crown frames the Queen had given as part payment. To Salman they looked ugly. Rings of sockets waiting for stones.

He told them about the company's private sale of Victoria's diamonds to pay off her family's debts. The gems big as peach stones, given to her mother's mother by an Indian prince, the Nabob of Arcot. 'Go on, ask me who they was sold to.'

'Who?'

'I can't tell you!' Fox laughed in asthmatic *ahs*, as if in pain. 'That's a whole other secret, that is. You'd have to be here years for me to tell you that.'

He told them everything and nothing. Not that he'd watched them cheated out of their stones, three jewels, good for a crowning. He never mentioned the Young Vinegar's fairground sharpness. He never thought of himself as a good or a bad man, nothing so simple. He was only ordinary. He minded his business, and his business was that of Edmund Rundell. Over the blur of the lapidary's wheel, he watched Salman and imagined him broken.

'D'you trust me, boy? Don't be a fool. How long have you known me? Trust no one. Anyone who knows how to love a jewel knows how to cheat a man to get it. And if you understand that, then I have said too much to you already.'

The Heart of Three Brothers passed on, from Levy to Rundell. It was already four hundred and thirty years old. It looked newer than that in Edmund's hands. It looked untouched and elemental. Brighter than water. Simpler than water. Fresher than fresh.

Salman dreamed of it. In his dream the stone returned to him from Edmund. He was never sure how he had regained it, by theft or purchase, or whether the stone had found its own way back. While he slept, this did not seem an impossibility.

It lay cool in his fist. He would open his fingers, loving it with his eyes, and it was only then that he would notice some change. A new flaw where there had been none, a certain shape. Salman would turn it in his palms and see that it was an egg. He wondered how he had never seen it before. The shell was cool and lucid as snakeskin.

He would bend closer and the dream would end, always. Nothing ever opened. He never saw what was inside.

He opened his eyes to the sound of church bells. For a moment he had no sense of place, the noise outside and the pallet under him meaning nothing. Then he blinked and the world came back.

Daniel slept beside him. One of his arms was flung out, as if he was asking for something or offering it. Salman got up without waking him. The dream of the jewel still hung uneasily in his mind and he pushed it away.

He went to the casement. The tincture bottle and spoon were on the sill where he had left them at midnight. He measured out ten drops and drank them off. Repeated the dose. Through the alcohol came the bitter, acrid warmth of the Turkey opium. He waited, feeling it work out through his nerves. Waking him out of himself.

The window was latched open. London was beginning to move in the light. The smog was thin today and he could see for miles. He had heard it said there were a million people here, a thousand thousand lives. All needing what they did not have. And although Salman no longer had what he wanted most of all, he felt, for a dizzying moment, as if he had everything.

This is the house with twenty doors, he thought. The house with many doors. There was stone dust on his hands, a silt of precious things worked into his skin. Levy and Levy, he thought. Goldsmiths to the Crown. Today there is nothing I would change. Today and tomorrow and tomorrow. Not even if I could.

5
The Love of Stones

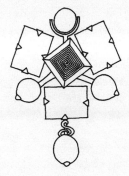

The flight is cheap and it feels it. The aeroplane smells of shrimp and dried bananas, as if it has been reassigned from cargo duties. The wings shudder in air pockets over the Baltic. I lie back and shut my eyes and think of anywhere but England.

At six o'clock London time the sun sets across Russia, but in the small hours it is already rising again. Porthole light studs the cabin walls. Time flies at thirty thousand feet. Once the in-flight film ends and the lights go down and there is less by which to keep track, I can imagine years streaming past outside. Thin and cold as cirrus.

It is an illusion, of course. Relativity is not so visible. All the same I keep my eyes on the window, the dark outside, the day beginning. Time interests me. I'm in for the long haul, after all.

At Moscow I wait four hours for the connection. The transit lounge windows are high, rained clean, and beyond them are towers and runways and the black edges of pine forests. Two Japanese girls take timed photographs. Jean-Baptiste Tavernier is here too, at the end of his seventh journey. He has been here for three hundred and nine years, buried beside a clapboard church an hour out on the Tula road. At least he got what he was looking for. My world is defined in this way. The Brethren is always ahead of me, solid as a sextant.

The Tokyo plane smells of old furniture; nothing else is different except the passengers. Beside me a woman and child eat Japanese snacks and play stones-scissors-paper for hours. They have the comfort in quietness of a functional family. The same eyes, the irises so black the pupils seem dilated with pleasure or lightlessness, the epicanthal folds turning upwards so that both mother and daughter look as if they are always smiling. Most of the time they are. They offer me pickled plums. The woman nods to encourage me.

'Please. You travel alone?'

'Yes.'

She makes a sound – *ah* – as if I have said something too sad for words. 'Have more. This is your first time to Japan?'

'Third.'

She raises her eyebrows. Three is an impressive number, and I am not quite what she expected. 'But for vacation?'

'Business. Just business.' The girl looks up at me with eyes shining. Watching me for something. I wonder what she sees and what she wants.

The plums are salty sweet. The taste stays in my mouth as I try to sleep. The oddness of it keeps me awake. I turn towards the curved wall and think of Japan.

It is a long way to go in search of stones. I can say this to myself although I do not feel it. It is further than Tavernier ever travelled, although the world has diminished in the years between us. Japan – *Jipen* to the mainlanders. Marco Polo called it the Country of Gold. The Japanese name is more beautiful, less mercantile: *Nihon*, Source of the Sun. It is a curious way to refer to one's own country. As if even the inhabitants saw their islands as the end of the world, not its centre. And not an end, but a beginning.

I have been there to sell, never to buy. In the stone trade this is how the world divides. There are countries where raw jewels are found, as if the earth is more nourishing in their climates. Then there are the places they end up. The Countries of Gold, although 'gold' is relative. Sometimes it is less than elemental. In 1893, for example, a worker at an Anglo-African mine unearthed the largest diamond anyone had then discovered. Even once the cutters had sheared it down, the stone weighed nine hundred and ninety-five carats. A diamond the size of a fist. It came to be known as the Excelsior. The black man who found the jewel received £500, a horse and harness, and a brace of pistols. Three golden wishes. I hope they got him as far as he wanted to go.

This time is different. I have nothing to sell now. The rubies were the last of my stock, and the last of those is gone. Now I am only looking for something. It is a kind of endgame. Mongolia passes below us, rivers silver in the retreating dark.

I sleep shallowly. As far as I am aware I do not dream. The woman with smiling eyes snores beside me. Beyond her, the child carves patterns with her nails into a tin food cover. Each time I wake she is still carving. She draws the English alphabet, the

Japanese syllabaries, a cartoon girl with enormous eyes. Endless noughts and crosses. Her face absorbed in her solitary games. Ex nought. Ex nought.

Ex nought

Ex

My passport is almost full. The immigration officer pores over it as if he can read something criminal into the order of visas. Outside the sky is paling towards morning, daylight returning to its natural pace.

Space waits at the end of the document for the details of my nearest relatives. Only Anne's name is entered. The officer turns back a page and rubber-stamps me sixty days. I go through Nothing to Declare and find a currency exchange. A thirty-year-old woman with a girl's voice takes my seamed English money and gives me a slimmer envelope of unwrinkled yen. Outside a Japanese family flags down passers-by to photograph its reunion.

The city shuttle costs more than I have to spare. The carriage is packed with international commuters, slack-faced from long hauls. Between their backs I catch sight of myself, reflected in the windows. Smiling. Not happy, nothing so solid. It is only that no one knows me here. It is what I am used to, this. It helps me concentrate on what I'm doing. I am tracing a man who signed his name as 'Three Diamonds'. He has been dead for some time now.

Outside the landscapes grow together, rural, industrial and urban. There is no transition. Between blue-eaved houses, the dry stubble of September rice paddies. Between factory wings, blue-eaved houses. After London they look unfinished, as if someone has left off a necessary patina of grime. Not that Tokyo is clean – already I can smell its pollution in the train's conditioned air. But its fabric is newer. Everything has happened faster here. Less has been forgotten. What took London two centuries changed here in a matter of decades.

I stay on the train until Shinjuku. Getting off is easier than getting out. The terminus itself segues into elevated restaurants, game arcades, underground shopping malls, columned aquaria through which people move, distant beyond shoals of cichlids. Crowd currents guide me to the eastern exit.

It is almost ten by the station clock. My watch is still on London time, and I turn it forward nine hours while commuters mill around me. On the wide pavement, rows of noodle stalls and telephone booths converge. For a moment I think of calling Anne again. The food stalls are nearer and I have more appetite for what they offer. I order ramen soup and bend my face into its steam, wolfing reconstituted fish. Besides pickled plums, it is the first meal I've chosen to eat since London – since, in fact, George Pyke's sliced white bread. I think of him, an old man at the edge of the stone trade, alone with his photographs. *Marvellous, marvellous.*

The pavement is crowded up to my stool. A high-school boy peers down at me. His face is like Yohei's. I remember *Eng*, his philosophy of strangers. I wonder if Yohei himself was the one I should have been waiting for. Or George Pyke. Yohei never said how you were supposed to tell. Overhead, Jack Nicholson drinks Asahi beer on a giant video screen, his smile reaching between buildings.

I pay up and go on east, into the backstreets. They remind me of Diyarbak'r, although in almost every way they are different. There is no smell of decay, only the fumes of food and air-conditioners, and there is nothing here built before the war, only strip shows, revolving sushi bars and love hotels. It is the sound of the two cities which is the same. The hubbub of crowds, the noise of trade, the underlying humanity of that. If I close my eyes I can lose myself in it. An amplified woman's voice sings advertisements for sex or food or alcohol. I understand only the desire in it, like a prayer or muezzin's song.

The day is heating up and I take off my coat and carry it. The bag chafes at my shoulder. I don't lose myself. My eyes sting with tiredness. At the next junction is a lit plastic sign for the Hundred Per Cent Inn, a man sweeping dust and cicadas off the steps. I go up past him and inside.

At reception an old woman is eating sashimi from a polystyrene tray. Above her a sign, in anglicised Japanese, lists prices for a Nap or a Night. The woman cuts the fish with her chopsticks, her arms lean and muscular. She looks up as I reach her, her features puckered with concentration.

'Good morning.'

'Oh.' Her face falls open with panic. She flutters a hand at me, willing me away, as if foreign addresses can only lead to an escalation of multiracial disasters. The sweeper comes in behind me. He calls out as if I were far away, a telephone presence on a long-distance line.

'Yes, hello? Hello?'

I force a smile. 'Do you have a room?'

'No room.' He waves the broom, a fairy godfather in Terylene shirt and wash-shrunk trousers. 'This is capsule hotel.'

'Fine. You have a capsule?'

'You want capsule?'

'Yes, I do.'

The sweeper glances at the woman. Imminent panic is spreading between them. 'No rooms, only capsules. Please.'

'Won't I fit?'

He shrugs unhappily. 'You want a capsule?'

The jet lag is catching up with me. It doesn't make me noticeably more patient than I have to be. 'I want one bed, for one night. A bed in a capsule is fine. Small is fine. I can pay now or later.'

They prefer now. The old woman motions at me to take off my shoes before she leads me away. The place feels cheap but I'm too tired to care. At the end of the last hallway she fusses over a locked door.

Inside, the dormitory is empty. It reminds me of the stone room. A Cornell box of a place, where I can be slotted away like a balla, a Tree of Diana, a lick of steel. Folded on the capsule pillow are a pair of pyjamas, homely, *Hundred Per Cent* embroidered on the breast. Down the hall there are lockers, a sauna room, a few Western showers smaller than the capsules themselves. The old woman explains details I am past interpreting. She waves dramatically at the sauna, as if it might house something monstrous.

I change and shower. It is days, now, since I have been naked. I stay under the water for as long as I can and dress in my only clean clothes, letting my skin breathe. Through the extractor fan I can still hear the advertising singers. I lock up my belongings and crawl into my private space. Quarter life-pod, three-quarters coffin.

The walls are inlaid with switches. A television is set flush into the ceiling. The mattress smells of disuse and the sweet must of a humid climate. I lie back against it and imagine, although I know they are not there, others around me. Chrysalised people. Suspended for their naps or nights, all of them waiting for something. The sensation leaves me dizzy and I breathe in, willing it away. The flat face of the television stares down. I switch it on and channel-surf.

A man eats eggs against the clock. Two samurai fight in a field of snow. The last station is pay-as-you-watch porn. A man masturbates onto a woman's breasts, his sex and her face obliterated by decal squares. His features are contorted with adrenaline or joy. I watch him make love to himself until the free time runs out and I sleep. The capsule expands into my darkness.

It is evening when I wake. There is no way to know it in here except by the clock. For a second after my eyes open I don't know where I am, or even what the choice should be.

It is as if the wind has changed on my life and I have been caught. I am lost in myself, between places. It is like a curse, although the Three Brethren carries no recorded curse. Then I turn my head and see the clock beside me. The luminosity of numbers counting themselves out.

It is 8 p.m., Tokyo time. I reach out clumsily and the television comes on in a babble of manic game-show hosts. I slap at its face until the noise goes away. My locker key is in my shirt pocket, and I go and get myself together. Nothing waits at reception except another television. There is a stack of telephone directories behind the counter, but they are out of reach, the script is beyond me, and explaining to the old woman that I am looking for Mushanokoji, the soy sauce makers, already seems like an impossible inter-cultural effort.

Outside the night air is still warm. On the hotel steps men sit in their Hundred Per Cent pyjamas, drinking and smoking. They lounge back, as if in a lazy, dreamlike way the city street has become their home for the night. As if it belongs to them. Across the road are the lit plinths of vending machines.

I cross. Cans of beer, plum wine and saké wait illuminated in the vending displays. I get a beer and walk back to the hotel. Only the salaryman on the top step nods at me. I wonder if there is a pecking order, a hierarchy of stairs. 'Good evening! Welcome to the Hundred Per Cent Inn.' He repeats himself in good French, just to be sure. He is handsome and quick with it. A tanned John Wayne face. I nod thanks. He gestures towards his friends. 'Are you American? We are regulars here. We saw that you have bought a beer. Good Japanese beer. We'll be happy if you drink it with us.'

'That's kind of you.' I sit down. The middle-step men nod encouragingly. We toast one another, *kampai, kampai*. Cicadas chirr in the road trees.

'It is good to talk in English,' says the man beside me. 'For us. A difficult language, so different. My name is Tomoyasu.'

'Katharine.' We shake hands. The lower echelons move, repositioning themselves. 'I'm glad to help. There's something you might do for me, too.'

'I see,' he says, a little drunk, seeing nothing. 'May I ask you, Katharine – I hope it is not impertinence – my colleagues and I were wondering: are you staying here?'

'For tonight.'

'*Eh?*' He says it to the other men, stretching the word out into a whole phrase of meaning. *There, what did I tell you?* On the bottom step, a man with no hair mutters. Above him, a man with a packet of Marlboro replies. There is a friction to their voices, a street-hardness, that I didn't expect. The surfaces of Tokyo are so smooth, it is easy to believe there is nothing else. No depth or shade, as if a city could be reduced to two dimensions.

'Were they talking about me?'

Tomoyasu shrugs. 'It is not so important.'

'Really. What is it,' I ask, already knowing. 'Are capsule hotels only for vampires?'

'Vampires. Ahaha.' He smiles. 'No, only men. Usually only men. Maybe it is not a rule. The staff didn't mention this?'

'Not in so many words.'

'Now it doesn't matter so much.' He stops himself. His smile has relaxed but not faded.

'Why?'

'Capsule hotels are for workers, like us. But now the bubble is bursting, the salarymen have no salaries. Maybe now they stay home instead of working late. They go and get drunk with their wives.'

'Lucky wives.'

'No, no. Unlucky bubble.' The conversation runs out into quiet. The cicadas change rhythm, their chirr breaking into a chant.

Chhhh, cha-cha-cha.

'Salarylessmen, can I say, Katharine?'

I laugh. Only because he does. He keeps going. 'Businessless. Less business, more pleasure. Personally, I am a company lawyer. These men are my colleagues. Our company makes the glass tubes for neon signs. And as for you, you are a salary-woman?'

'No, I'm just looking for someone.'

A train chatters in the distance. The company men drink their beer and don't talk, as if they are listening. The Pyjama Gang surveying its turf. They seem uncomfortable in themselves, now. Shifting, unsettled in the late summer breeze. Men caught in uncertain lives. Part of me pities them for that.

Tomoyasu drains his plum wine. In the bottom of the cup is a pickled plum. He upturns the cup, catches the plum in his hand, eats it. 'So. You are a private investigator. Investigating private things. But Tokyo is a big place.'

'Actually, it's a family I'm looking for. I think they're quite well known. The Mushanokojis.'

'*Eh?*'

Even as I say it the man with no hair looks round at me. As if the name alone makes me worth seeing. 'You know the Mushanokoji family?' asks Tomoyasu. He spits out the plum stone.

'Only by name.'

'Oh, it is a big family. Big business.' His English deteriorates with excitement. 'Condiments, *shoyu*, *neh*? Soy sauce. Very respected, *so*. Why is it you want to meet the Mushanokoji family?'

'It's complicated. But I was wondering if one of you might know where the company offices are. There's a telephone directory inside . . .'

He isn't listening to me. The bottom-step man is talking again in his matter-of-fact undertone. He is half-turned, his face in profile against the blue light of the vending machines. Tomoyasu nods when he is finished.

'Mister Abé says that he knows a place. One of the Mushanokoji men goes there. Not a top man. Middle-management.'

'What kind of place?'

'A bar.' He shrugs again. 'For men.'

'Would they let me in?'

284

He regards me. 'Forgive me, but I think they would pay you.'

They don't have to, I think. Nor do you have to forgive me. I say, 'How often does Mister Mushanokoji go there?'

Tomoyasu calls out. The bottom-step man mutters back. 'He is always there when Abé-san has been. Often, regularly, frequently, you would say? It is a very expensive place. One moment please . . .'

He walks quickly back into the hotel lobby. The colleagues say nothing while he is gone. The bottom-step man strokes his head, as if he can feel my eyes settling there. Tomoyasu comes back with a pen and paper, already writing as he sits. 'This is the bar name, *Sugi*. This is the address. It is some way from here and not easy to find, so probably it is best if you take a taxi. You should give this to the driver.'

'Thank you.' I take the paper. For a second he doesn't let it go. Then he pulls back as if ashamed of himself.

'Thank you, Katharine. I have enjoyed meeting you. You have made my conversation much better.'

They all stand to say goodbye, Tomoyasu first, the other-step men following his lead. Mr Abé waves down a taxi. The passenger door opens automatically. As I get in there is the tumble and clatter of the vending machine in the street behind me, another measure of alcohol falling into its lit aperture.

The car is upholstered in pale imitation leather. The driver wears white gloves, like a mime artist. He opens the glass partition and takes my directions and reads them without acknowledging me, as if the paper has been passed to him by an invisible presence. I imagine him drunk in Hundred Per Cent pyjamas while Tokyo passes outside.

It is an appropriate place to come, in the search for jewels. There is a department store here which sells matching his-and-hers chopsticks, forged of platinum. A hotel with a golden bath, carved in the shape of a phoenix: three hundred and thirteen and a half pounds of metal, the largest piece of gold in the world, in which businessmen float, light reflecting off their collops of fat. The capital of the Country of Gold. It is all metal and light, a landscape held in a fine balance. Like watchworks, I think, wheels resting between ruby axles. A delicate thing. Pedestrians and cyclists crowd up to the stoplights.

We head east-north-east. Back into the centre, out towards the river. For days now it has felt as if I have been heading in only one direction. But then east is where the old stones come from. Always the East, Oriental and Saracenic. When I write the history of the Three Brethren it seems to belong to Europe as much as Asia, but this is a lie. The jewel is nothing if not Asian. Its gems were unearthed more than four centuries before the diamond alluvia of Africa and Brazil were mined, or the gold ores of America and Australia. It comes from a time when the great balases still came from Badakshân, pigeon-blood rubies only from the Mogok Tract, diamonds from India. If the Brethren comes from anywhere it is the East.

The man in white gloves drives like a surgeon. Office blocks give way to quieter streets. Prefabricated houses support older wooden structures. There is little traffic here. We cross the Sumida river on a stone bridge no wider than two lanes of traffic and reach the bar after five blocks.

It is set back behind tall cedars, window lights showing through them. While the taxi pulls away I stand on the soft earth under the trees, taking in their smell. It is like that in the courtyard of Glött's stone house. I think of her, and of Hassan. I miss them, although I hope I never see them again. I make no apologies for it. I know I am selfish and self-possessed. Neither of these things is wrong all the time.

A footpath leads through the trees, lights set flush into the paving. The building at their end is half-timbered, a thatched roof sloping almost to the ground on two sides. There is the sound of water and air-conditioners and, more faintly, the familiar noises of a bar at night. Music and voices. Not all of them are male. The door is imitation lacquer and paper and it slides back automatically as I reach it.

Inside is a lobby, empty, with a cupboard full of slippers and shoes. Beside the footwear are two Lalique vases, lilies and orchids arranged in a Western style. I can smell them, funereal, as I take off my boots. It is a long time now since I have enjoyed cut flowers. They still remind me of the dead.

None of the slippers fits. I take small steps to the bar, an ugly sister trying her best to be beautiful. The room is high and raftered, the tatami-matted floor broken only by a mezzaluna drinks counter. There are a number of old men in socks and suits and varying stages of drunkenness, and three women in summer kimonos, serving and talking.

Japanese folk music is playing. The man nearest the entrance is crooning into a microphone, his eyes fixed on a karaoke screen. Lyrics scroll across it along with a montage of incongruous images: a boatload of trawlermen and a net full of tuna; a woman potter making bowls. From the sound of the music and the singer's face something monumentally sad has taken place, but apart from the fish I can't make out who it has been happening to.

No one except the women are in a state to notice much. They aren't young and they don't act it. One of them brings the karaoke man a bowl of grilled dumplings and they talk. There is little flirtation in their voices or faces. With one hand he gestures to the bottle-keeps. The woman sees me as she turns.

'*Konbanwa.*' She manages to make a question out of the greeting.

'Good evening. I'm sorry, do you speak any English? I'm looking for a Mister Mushanokoji.'

'Of course,' she says, as if she knows. Her voice is too soft, artificial as the building around her. 'Are you a guest of Mushanokoji-san?'

I lie almost without noticing. The hostess leads me around the curve of the bar to a man at its far end. He sits alone, both hands around a glass. Face set, perceiving nothing outside himself. He is tall by Japanese standards, with muscular cheeks and wiry black hair. For an old man he is still masculine, all corners and no curves. I wonder if Mr Three Diamonds looked the same.

He listens to what the woman has to say before his eyes move to me. The hostess asks him something else and he nods and doesn't talk until she has bowed and left us. Then he puts out a hand. 'Hideki.'

'Katharine.' We shake. The use of first names surprises me. I expect the old and wealthy to be more formal. 'Thanks.'

'You're welcome. What for?'

'For lying about me.'

'Well. Seeing as how you're my guest, will you join me for a drink?'

His voice itself is also unexpected. His English is American, the accent Brooklyn-broad and somehow dated. I sit down. 'I could do with a coffee.'

'Come on. This is rice spirit, have you tried that? You don't live over here, right? Oh, you should try, it's good. The spirit, not Japan.' He takes off his steel-rimmed spectacles and wipes his eyes with a napkin from the bar. 'Ah. What did you say your name was?'

'Katharine.'

'Hello, Katharine. I'm Hideki, but maybe I told you that.' We shake hands again. He puts his glasses back on, takes me in. He doesn't appear interested to see me, only resigned to it. He looks like someone used to feeling resigned. 'And I'm in the soy industry, but maybe you know that too. What's your business, Katharine?'

'Stones.'

'Stones. How interesting. Is there any money in it?'

'No.'

'Have we met?'

'Never.'

'Do I owe you money? I don't recall buying any stones recently.'

'You don't owe me anything.'

'Uhuh.' When he grins his eyes almost disappear between smile lines. 'Stones. Unbelievable. Why don't we have champagne? I always thought how champagne tastes like crystal would if it was liquid. You ever think that?'

He waves to the nearest hostess. The magnum comes in a stone cooler, pink granite, iron oxidised in the crystalline structure. Hideki Mushanokoji prises the bottle open while he talks.

'Well, I have to say this is a nice surprise. I was just sitting here, alone, thinking too much. I was almost ready to resort to karaoke, that's like ritual suicide, death by folk song. Actually, I like doing the Western numbers. I'm the only one. The other boys don't go in for them in a real hurry.'

I don't listen to him. Instead I look at his face and think of his ancestor. A similar man, nine decades ago in cold East London. I resist the desire to touch Hideki, to reach out and feel the face in front of me. As if by doing so I could close all distance between myself and Three Diamonds.

'I do U2, and Elvis Presley of course. "Rub Me Tender", as you think we say here in Japan. And now you walked in and saved me, Katharine.'

He passes me a flute of champagne. Bubbles rise inside it. Lines and spirals and double helices. It is cold and so dry it tastes almost mineral.

'Your English is very good. Did you study abroad?'

'University of Manchukuo, class of forty-five.' He smiles again. Light glares off his spectacles. 'The Americans caught me. I already spoke some English, they set me up as a radio operator.' He circles his hand slowly in the air. Revolutions of time passing. 'Afterwards they kept me at work in the States a few years. New York. Upstate.'

'I thought you were younger than that.'

'I'll take that as a compliment.'

I can place the accent better now. Mr Mushanokoji sounds disconcertingly like an American GI from an old war film. 'Stones. Hey, you're English, right? You like Sherlock Holmes? I learned English from Sherlock Holmes. *The Blue Carbuncle* – do you know that one? "It's a bonny thing," said he. "Just see how it glints and sparkles, Watson. Of course it is a nucleus and focus of crime. Every good stone is. They are the devil's pet baits." Eh?'

'Sorry.'

'Oh. Well, now you know my war story. I don't have any others, unless you want to hear about soybeans or bad marriages.'

The hostess comes and tries to refill my glass. The champagne's aftertaste is strong in my mouth. I can feel the alcohol reaching my blood already. The bar feels too hot and I sit back. 'Actually, there's a relative of yours I'm interested in. Enzo Mushanokoji.'

'Enzo.' He wrinkles up his face. 'Enzo? Jesus.'

'He used a false name in his company business. Three Diamonds.'

'He needed it. Enzo!' He puts his elbows on the bar. It brings his body closer. 'He's barely my relation. My grandfather's cousin. The black sheep of the family. Or –' he frowns, searching for words '– the wolf in black sheep's clothing. Can you say that? Did he run a company?'

'His name is on the records.'

'I didn't know that. My mother wouldn't say his name. She was very – *yashashii*, I forget the words – giving, forgiving. Enzo used to import all kinds of things. War Office contracts. These days they call it Defence. There were other customers too.'

'Who?'

'The kind of companies who wanted what he traded.' He looks around blearily. 'The kind who don't like being talked about. You want to know something about Enzo? He was the first man to bring phosgene gas into Japan. His claim to fame. Dirty business. The – who was that English guy?'

'Which one?'

'You must know, you're one of them. The potato guy.'

'Walter Raleigh?'

'Right. That was Enzo. The Walter Raleigh of poison gas.'

'He must have been rich.'

'I don't think so. He worked in the south somewhere.'

'What about his children?'

'Tell you the truth, I'm not a whole lot interested in family.' He leans closer. I can smell his breath now, the pureness of the champagne soured by his flesh. 'But listen, I'm interested in you. You're very strong, eh? Very strong. Not cold. But why are you so strong, Katharine? I have this theory that you can divide people into two types. You wanna hear it? There are business people and pleasure people. Which are you?'

'I'm the kind who keeps her business to herself.'

'Aha ha! Very good. In Japan we say, *to keep the lid down on the stinking pot.* Have another drink. What's your poison?'

'I don't have one.'

'Come on, be sweet to an old man. Drink with a drunk.'

I drink with him. When I look at my watch again it is almost midnight. A small man with a disproportionately large voice is singing karaoke and might have been doing so for hours. He doesn't look as if he's about to leave, nor does anyone else. It is as if they have no homes left to go to, these ageing merchants, only this place with its artificial warmth, mock-lacquer, imitation mothers, daughters, wives.

I ask our hostess to order two taxis. She has a neat face, powdered white as rice. Nothing dominant, eyes, nose or mouth, passion or reticence. I envy her that balance. I nudge Hideki awake. He shades his eyes, as if I have become impossibly bright, incandescent with champagne. 'I'm going now. Okay? You were great. Maybe you should be getting home yourself.'

'Wait – wait . . .' Mushanokoji fumbles money onto the counter. 'I don't want to go home. I want to stay with you. You interest me.' He sighs, drapes an arm around my shoulder. 'Katharine. My stinking pot.'

'Thanks for that.'

Half-shut, his eyes gleam. 'Enzo. I could tell you more about him. If you stayed with me.'

'Liar.'

He leers. 'But I could find out more. My wife would remember. She loves my family. Knows us better than we know ourselves.'

'Then the sooner you go home, the sooner you can phone me.'

'No, no.' His weight sags against my shoulder. 'Not home now. Only at weekends, see. She makes me stay at my suite. The Okura.' His mouth goes maudlin. 'Oh, God. Stay with me, Katharine. Just to talk, I miss talking. You're so good to me. To-morrow. I'll find out what you want. Promise.'

'Tomorrow morning.' But he is past agreeing now, and the deal is as made as it is going to be. By the time I get outside the first taxi is waiting. I roll the old man onto the backseat and follow him in. The driver doesn't turn, but in the rear-view mirror I see him observe us. His skin ghosted with moonlight, white as the face of the hostess.

'Hotel Okura.' The car starts up and I sit back into the acceleration. The old man is slumped against the far passenger door. I watch him, trying to imagine his life. The bars and hotel rooms and offices. The prostitutes, no doubt. A loneliness alleviated by paid encounters, although there are different needs to be paid for tonight, and different ways to pay. Outside the roads are almost empty. It begins to drizzle, a soft dense fall.

The hotel is beautiful and empty, half-architecture, half-jewel. In the lobby Potoro marble plaques are laid symmetrically, like golden Rorschach tests. I walk with the old man leaning against my shoulder and watch the desk clerk assessing my place. It sobers me up only marginally. Hideki Mushanokoji he recog-nises. Together we carry him to the elevator. The suite is ten floors up. The clerk leaves us, bowing, not meeting my eyes.

The lights are out. I don't turn them on. In the lounge, the entire eastern wall is glass. Beyond it Tokyo shines, slippery with rain and neon. I take off Mushanokoji's glasses and dump him in the bedroom, face down on the made linen sheets. He mutters a name, not mine. I feel no guilt about what I am doing. No one is taking advantage of anyone. There is only an exchange of insubstantial things, conversation, information. An attention to absences. I go through into the lounge, pushing the door to behind me.

I close the blinds. The moon creeps through them and illuminates a piano, sofas, a lacquered desk. I think of lacquer. The image rises up in me with a drunken resentment. It is what I would grow to hate about this country, given time, though it is also what makes it beautiful. So much is smoothed over. Surfaces, faces, precious things.

I lie down on the first sofa I come to. It feels impossibly soft. Up close, against my face, I can smell the sweetness of fine leather; the good scent of dead things. It is the last thing I think of. I sleep without dreams.

Unforgettable. Mmm, that's what you are.
Unforgettable, though near or far.

The voice reaches me first. I'm not aware of the hangover until I try to move. I go still, waiting for the pain to subside.
Like a song of love that clings to me,
Ooo, how the thought of you does things to me.
My eyes feel delicate as eggs. I open them a crack at a time and discover it is morning. Blinds cast gills of light across the walls. There is the hiss of water, a voice distorted through it. It doesn't sound like Frank Sinatra.

Never before
Has someone been more
Mmm-mmm. Uh-um, uh-um.

There is food in the room. I don't see it yet but I can smell it, toast and croissants and coffee, the bitter-sweet aromas familiar and Western. I climb off the sofa and lurch towards them.

'Hey, Katharine, have I woken you up yet? Rise and shine.'

I don't answer him. The back of my mind wonders how long he has been awake, and if he watched me as I slept. This morning I find the thought of him intrusive, although he has been nothing but kind to me. Breakfast is on the desk. I finish it all off in clumsy mouthfuls, standing to do so, hunger discovering itself as I eat. There is a carafe of orange juice, cladded with condensation, lidded with an Arcoroc glass. I drink as much as I can stomach.

The cold of the juice opens my eyes and the daylight catches them. Shuttered, it has a hard concentrated glitter. It reminds me of the effect of facets in a brilliant; and already I am thinking of the jewel. This is all it takes for me. The Three Brethren is never much more than a thought away.

I open the blinds again, narrowing my eyes, and wonder if I am also nearer the fact of it. Sometimes it seems like a delusion, the search, as if I am convincing myself of a progress that has no foundation. There are dreams like this, nightmares of going nowhere. Running without motion towards the Brethren's vanishing point.

But it feels closer. In the last fortnight there have been proofs, names and transactions and photographs. None of this is my imagination. I can prove myself to myself and there is no one else I need to believe in me. This morning I have all the evidence I want. Possibly more. I look out at Tokyo while the cousin twice removed of Mr Three Diamonds sings Broadway music in the shower:

Unforgettable, oo awoo awoo, in every way.
And for evermore I intend to stay –

'Hey, do I sound pretty good?'
'You sing like a dog.'
'Awoo. How's your hangover?'
'Fine, thank you. Yours?'
'Healthy diet.' He comes in grinning, ruddy, still scrubbing his hair. 'Work hard, play hard.' He looks proud of himself, as if he has bettered his youngers. Bulked out with a towel and dressing gown he looks younger himself. The smell of him – old skin cleanshaven – dominates the room. 'I talked to Michiko already too, that's my wife. I keep my promises, see? Here.'

He takes a sheet of paper out of the gown pocket and hands it over the desk to me. It is scrawled with minute ballpoint characters. Even if I read Japanese I doubt that I could decipher it. He sees it in my face.

'Oh Jesus, give it back here, look. This is the old guy's name, Enzo. This is the company he worked for, Mankin-Mitsubishi. I was right about the firm. You should have listened to me, see? We don't need my wife.'

'What about it?'

'It wasn't his.'

'Enzo's name was on the papers.'

'Because his name was good. The owner of the firm was foreign. It was better to have any Japanese name on the documents, especially one like mine. Anyway, here's what you want. He lived in Takamatsu, which is on the island of Shikoku. South, like I said.'

I take the paper from him, walk back to the sofa and sit. The old man comes up behind me. 'He was a wanderer, a *tanin*, you know? An outsider. Made himself into one. The family disowned him because he wouldn't settle down. That's all anyone remembers of him.'

'So he died poor.'

'Oh yeah.' He moves closer. I can feel the warmth of him against the back of my neck, his retained heat. 'He had nothing.'

'No children.'

'Nothing to tie him down.'

'I need an address for him.'

'No you don't. Houses don't last in Japan, not even in the middle of nowhere, which is just about where Takamatsu is. You won't find a whole city block that was there in Enzo's time.'

'The owner. What was he called?'

Mushanokoji clears his throat. 'Jesus, Katharine, you need to ease up. The stones business is getting to you. Relax.' His hands close around my shoulders, kneading the bones. I don't interrupt myself to stop him.

'What was his name?'

He releases one shoulder, points, goes back to work. The foreign word is written in syllabic characters, simpler than the Chinese ideograms. 'There. Mister Lewis. This is good, huh?' His hands move rhythmically. Over the shoulder bones, down to the flat flesh above my breasts. I shrug him away.

'No. Listen, I need to find out about the owner.'

'You listen. You asked about Enzo, I found out about Enzo. Favour done, okay? Done and dusted. Now you do me a favour. Lean back.' His hands come at me again. They hurt where they grip and I knock them away.

294

It surprises him, I think, as much as he had surprised me. Neither of us is what the other expected. He mutters, I don't hear what, and steps back as I stand. He is still ruddy, his face full of blood, and he is breathing too fast. It has nothing to do with the shower.

No one moves. Voices go past in the corridor, a tail-end of laughter. Then the old man grins. 'Come on. What's your poison, Katharine Sterne?'

He steps round the desk. Big for his age, all corners, no curves. I think: I am a fool to have ever been here at all. I must be blind, blinded by something. A sofa is behind me before I know it. The old man tries to push me and I step away from the outstretched palm and into his fist.

I see it in his eyes more than I feel it. My head goes clear before my sight fills with stars. I am not aware of falling, only of the carpet under me. Quick as a conjuring trick. Mushanokoji is talking overhead, but I can't hear what he is saying. My mother's voice is more interesting. I listen to her instead.

Her hair flickers down around me, white and mineral. Behind her, distant, is the sound of the sea. I would turn to see her if I could.

Katharine, you've been touched by the moon!

I smile for her. None of this is her fault. My mother the magician. She is eager and sorry and full of love.

Come here. Come. My little moon face.

A hand turns me. A different voice whispers of want in a language I don't understand. All I need is to get rid of them, the hand and the voice. I get hold of a forearm, then a wrist. The veins and bones protrude, made half a century before I was born. I come to the old man's fingers and go through them, looking for a weakness. The thumb and the index, also called the toucher. The middle and ring, down to the smallest.

My little wishbones. When I have a grip on the last two fingers I begin to pull. I have done more difficult things. There is some resistance from the ligaments. I don't let go until the bones crack.

Mushanokoji shrieks once, twice. It brings me back to myself. I take care of my body first, not bothering with him. My shirt is ripped but I am still dressed, unhurt if not untouched. One cheek aches with a slow rhythm, as if the old man's hands are still at it.

When I look up he is doubled over, hands between knees.

295

Blood has crazed the skin of his wrist and is now, presumably, staining the plush cream Okura carpet. I go over to him and he peers up, motioning me back with his head. Comical in his agony. I have to laugh.

'Goddamn foreign bitch, oh you . . .' he gropes for words '. . . damn limey pig. Get away from me. Get away!' He begins to scream again in Japanese, a cacophony of rage and outrage.

I leave him. The sound of his voice follows me away into the city, the light hot on my skin, my belongings heavy and getting heavier. I walk until I am alone in the crowd. Adrenaline aches in the pit of my gut.

His voice is what stays with me. I think of it again, much later. It is night, and in the dark the hotel room could be anywhere, assume any proportions. My arms close around myself like those of a lover. I have been here before, many times. I have never been here before.

Stones, I think. My poison is stones.

苂

To Edmund Rundell from Edmund Swifte.
Jewel House. The Tower.
October 10, 1837.

My dear Sir,
I hasten to transmit to you, and in order that you may hear before the Lord Chamberlain communicate it himself, the discussion that has been had between the Queen, the Marquis and myself, concerning the Crown. I will not undertake to say that my account is verbally quite accurate: for I was at the time quite painfully occupied with the Mump of the youngest of my children: but I am sure it is intentioned, and with a few variations of the phrase only, quite the same.

This morning the Marquis and I met Her Majesty at the Jewel House, the Regalia in its entirety being laid out for the purpose. The Lord Chamberlain having gone over the outlay of previous coronations, the Queen proceeded to say that the Imperial Crown seemed to her a very poor and stuffy affair – these her words. I begged to state that I believed the crown excellently made, by the Crown Goldsmiths. The Queen then noted several particulars that were not to her taste, namely, the blue Strass glass presently occupying the rear socket, and replacing the sapphire hired from your company for the last King George's coronation: the state of the brilliants: and the monstrous weight of the piece. Indeed, I am sorry to say that when the crown was tried for size, as it were, it was found to be too great a burden for the young Queen's neck, and I have no doubt that any other eighteen-year-old girl would have felt it the same.

The Queen then wished that, firstly, a glass model of the new crown be made up, showing the position and quality of all new stones: and that secondly, the presentation of this model to Her Majesty occur no later than the end of this next month: this in order that Her Majesty may make such amendments to the design as Her Majesty wishes. The Queen also desired that some of those who are to work on the crown be presented to her at that time.

The upshot is that a deal of work must be done to renew the crown, as you know: this I have no need to write to you. More unexpected, or so I find it, is that on this question of jewels, the Queen has very much her own ideas. In this vein Her Majesty has said things of your company, sir, which I shall not wish to repeat. My great anxiety is that there may be work to be done both in the refurbishment of the crown, and of your own Royal reputation.

I hope and trust that I shall not be considered to have gone out of my duty in this matter.

Believe me, my dear Sir,

　　Your truly obliged and thankful servant,
　　　Edmund Swifte.
　　　　Keeper of the Regalia.

To Edmund Swifte from Edmund Rundell.
Rundell and Bridge. Ludgate Hill.
October 17, 1837.

Sir,

In reply to your numerous missives, herein the costs for the crown and all else. The Lord Chamberlain's department has already received the same. The glass maquette will be ready by Advent at the latest. A party of salesmen and those involved in the crown's facture will be present on the first Monday of December, as Her Majesty and the Lord Chamberlain have advocated.

I have talked to the Queen. I thank you for your concern.
  Your servant,
    Rundell and Bridge.

To J. G. Bridge from Edmund Rundell.
9 The Crescent, Bridge Street. London.
October 29, 1837. By hand.

Mr Bridge,
  I trust this finds you less liverish. Health must not be allowed to keep
you from your work. Therefore some matters for you to consider abed.
  A Monsieur Lambert has been making enquiries as to the company's
future. Where he learned there is something to be had is not known:
whether he is worth our while is no more certain. Fox says he has
money. He looks well cut. The man is French from hair to bone, yet certainly on the look-out for London business. More of this in good time.
  The Crown. For the cash they will be good brilliants though, as you
say, not of the best. Mr Swifte, who is old and much given to concern,
says the Queen is anxious for a sapphire. The Jews' table-cut is a better gem than that last hired, and Swifte at least knows his gems, and
will tell the Queen as much. Her Majesty herself, you will find, has no
small appetite for stones.
  This leading to a final business. I have looked into the Jews' Writing
Point. Money through and through. A pedigree markedly nicer than
that of our young sovereign. I anticipate there may be a small order to
be made up, in private, for her Majesty, and for this purpose the
Ludgate Hill workshop will suffice. The size of the order may bear no
relation to the magnitude of the gain from this last venture. Fox alone
will do the work. This particular transaction to be kept confidential
from all others. When you are well again, you will see it done.
  Yours &c.
    Rundell.

To Queen Victoria from Edmund Rundell.
9 The Crescent, Bridge Street. London.
November 7, 1837.

Your Highness,
  I had been indeed deep distressed to hear that the Imperial Crown
was not entirely to Your Majesty's liking. Having now met Your Per-

son, and on inspecting the piece first-hand, I must confess to feeling no surprise that Your Highness's taste in jewels should be so keen. My opinion is at one with Your Majesty's. As Your Highness knows, it is 17 years since the crown was last worked by Rundell and Bridge. King Edward and his government neglected to award us the contract for his own coronation, and I believe the crown has suffered ever since.

The model of Your Majesty's new Imperial Crown is now complete, and my colleague Mr Bridge will have the great honour of presenting it to Your Majesty. I have high hopes that Your Majesty will like the adjustments. Notwithstanding its lightness, the crown will bear 425 new jewels: these in the main brilliants and pearls. In addition, a great sapphire shall be placed in the back: and this, as Your Majesty observes, will serve to balance those historic sapphires at the front and mound.

Plain glass will not capture the quality of this sapphire. It was carried to England from Mesopotamia by a pair of Babylonian Jews – so they refer to themselves. These gentlemen now work at Your Person's Goldsmiths, and I believe Your Majesty might find them curious or of some interest. Therefore, and since they will contribute to the crown, Mr Bridge will bring the nicest of the Babylonians to Your Majesty's presentation.

If I may also bring to Your Highness's attention an unrelated matter. A considerable stone has come into our company's possession. My own researches, in the pages of various lapidaries, lead me to believe it has at one time or another, some centuries in the past, played a bit part in the settings of England's Crown Jewels. Mr Bridge will be happy to show this jewel to Your Majesty at the earliest opportunity. I would be most interested to have Your Majesty's opinion, both of its worth, and of what might be done with it.

Believe me, Your Highness, to be
Your most sincere and obedient servant
Edmund Rundell.

A Preliminary Account of Expenses to be incurred in the Lord Chamberlain's Department on Account of the Coronation of Her Majesty Queen Victoria, November 24, 1837.

6 To Stratton and Wilson, for 60 Damask Napkins – £21/-/-
7 To Osmond, for 264 Yds of Scarlet Cloth – £221/12/-
8 To Cooper, for 80 Yds of Crimson Genoa Velvet – £104/-/-

20 To N. Lewis, for Embroidering the Royal Table Cover – £70/10/-
21 To Sir G. Smart, Payment to all the Performers Vocal and Instru-
    mental, and Disbursements – £275/9/6
22 To Roberts, Payment to all Coachmen of the Procession – £11/3/9
23 To the Apothecary to the Person, for Anointing Oil – £100/-/-
24 To Mr Chipp, for the hire of the Kettle Drums – £2/2/-
72 To Rundell and Co. for a Ring composed of a Violet Coloured Ruby
    with a Ruby crofs of St George and set with Brilliants – £155/10/-
73 To Rundell and Co. for a Hedge of 22 Carat Standard Gold for the
    Offering – £50/-/-
74 To Rundell and Co. for a Silver Gilt Inkstand for the Oath, com-
    posed of a Greek Triton with an Altar for Ink with a Crown on the
    Cover and the Royal Arms chased on the sides of the Altar, and a
    Wainscot Case for the above – £46/-/-
98 To Rundell and Co. for the Resetting of the whole of the Diamonds
    and precious stones of the old Crown into the New Imperial
    Crown with the addition of Brilliants, Pearls, and a Fine Sapphire,
    and for the replacement of 4 Large Pearls, known as Queen Eliza-
    beth's Earrings, with 4 Good Pearls, and all with a Rich Purple
    Velvet Cap lined with white Satin and Ermine Border, and a Mo-
    rocco case for the above – £1,000/-/-

Losses and Reimbursements.

– To E. L. Swifte Esq. keeper of the Regalia at the Tower, for the loss to
   be sustained in the armed removal of the Regalia to Rundell and
   Co., on Account of Her Majesty's Coronation – £150/-/-
– To Mrs Wombwell and Mr Redfearn of Wombwell's Circus for the
   loss of audience to arise from the provision of 80 white fantail doves
   – £14/5/5
– To Her Majesty the Queen and the Jewel Office, for the joint loss to
   be sustained in a Disbursement – £14,000/-/-

☒

Tokyo is an easy place to be lost. It has no limits. Instead of end-
ing, it continues on into other cities, a megalopolis twice the size
of London. It has no centre, either. There is only the invisible
presence of the Imperial Palace, lost inside a hollow green man-

dala of moats and cryptomeria. And the streets have no names.

Step off the roads here, into the places between buildings, and the city changes. The glass walls of high-rises – mirrored, smoked, polarised – give way to anonymous footstreets of small shops, ink brushmakers, tunafish dryers, old traders. A place less assured, or so it seems to me, less certain of where it is going. The rural Japanese leave the night trains at Tokyo Station and stand bewildered under the glitterboards and advertising Zeppelins, scraps of paper held tight in their hands. On the paper, instructions to reach the neighbourhoods of their city relatives.

I take comfort in all this. It suits me. It means I'm not alone.

It reminds me of a letter Anne once wrote. Nine double pages. I didn't keep them, but they've stayed with me all the same. She wrote things I tried not to think about at the time. In Japan I've had time to think about all kinds of things.

'I watch you looking for this jewel, the Brethren, (blue paper, the colour of litmus without acid. Her handwriting is clear and hard-pressed, like mine.) *and I wonder why. In the picture you sent, it looks like pure blue-rinse kitsch. One of those breast ornaments Tory Ladies wear to divert attention from their facelifts. So what am I missing? What is it you see that I don't? Then I wonder if it's you, not me, who is missing something.*

Sometimes I think you must be making it all up. That 'Three Brethren' is just your little Freudian Slip. Iz zere something you are hiding, my little one? An eternal triangle of lurve? Worse: bigamy? Conversion to a Mormon brotherhood? I know the jewel means a lot to you, I don't want to belittle it. But you are more important to me than it will ever be to you. Promise. You're more important than the jewel.

You send me these copies of old pictures, your notes I can't even read anymore. You joke about your 'Obsession'. But obsession is a clean word, Katharine: admirable, under certain circumstances. This jewel is an addiction. Addiction is a disease. But call it obsession; well, even that's a sour way to live. All the good things in you, the drive and love and the cleverness, they turn back on themselves.

I see nothing to admire in what you are doing. You say you've hurt people. I can't imagine what would make you do that. You were always the gentlest of us. This search isn't a life, it's more

like a way of losing life. You're just digging yourself into a hole.
I'm afraid that one day you'll go so deep, you'll never come back.

It is evening on the last day of September. I eat supper in a Korean grill on the port's eastern waterfront. Outside, a boy with orange-bleached hair pushes a flyer into my hands. Rain has smudged the words together.

HEY, ARE YOU FOREIGN?

Then Why Not Come To

The Pleasant Palace.

We are enthusiastic lodging house for unique people.

Close to Urawa transport and amenities.

It is always Pleasant here.

¥1000/ Night (Bed in Shared Room).

Kitchen. TV. Comfortable. Don't be a Peasant, be

Pleasant.

I take a local train north, out towards the grey subcity of Urawa. The Pleasant Palace is a rusting hulk by the bullet train overpass. The name suits it to the same degree that Greenland suits Greenland. It is all I can afford and all that I need. The room has two cohabitants, New Zealand girls with bottle-blonde hair and Karrimor rucksacks. Mel Twentyman models in car show-rooms, Nicola Wu sells street jewellery. They met only a day before I arrived but they talk as if they have been friends for years. They are communal people, easy in themselves, capable. I watch them go about their lives.

'You know what I really love?' says Nicola. 'Background music.' She is repairing her jewellery, nephrite earrings bought cheap on the mainland. She bends the wire with her teeth. 'Life would be so much easier with the right background music. Don't you reckon?'

'God, yeah.' Mel is unpacking a Sony Walkman. It is a present from her employer, a Korean who has already fallen a little in love or lust with her. He isn't married. She doesn't mind him.

'What would yours be?

'Depends.'

'On a good day.'

'On a good day? Counting Crows. Isn't that sad?' Nicola hums her tunes. Mel joins in. They look at me and I smile for them. They are two or three years younger than me. It feels like more. And again, I find myself remembering what I meant to forget. Eva, drunk in the stone room, trying to give me something. *You are remarkably old.* I wonder if it is true, and if it is something I can change.

I sleep long hours. My room looks out onto the stanchions of the railway. At night I lie awake and listen to the wires. They whisper minutes before the bullet trains pass.

Only once do I think of Mushanokoji. I am coming back from the coin-laundry by Central Urawa Station, my arms full of cleanness, when something falls from the bundled clothes. It is a wad of paper, the ink leached through the pulp, but I recognise it even so. The indecipherable and useless details of Mr Three Diamonds's life.

The autumn breeze is warm against my arms. The pulp edges away and I stop it with the tip of one boot. I think of the old man's touch, his touching finger, the blood on his wrist like veins in marble. He has pushed me off course, and now I can't find a way back. I'm no longer even sure if I want to.

My arms are full. I step over the paper and keep going. It is late, between dusk and nightfall, and the last cicadas have gone quiet in the road trees. When I get back Nicola offers me a beer, and we drink together, looking out at the overpass, the sun setting behind it. Talking about her work, the money she has saved, her country, my country, nothing, nothing.

The flyers work. The Pleasant Palace fills up, three to every room. No one has a working visa. Everyone except me could do with one. Once I take the train back to Tokyo Bay, as if I could have left something behind there, a findable energy. I come across nothing except Tsukiji, the city's market, where giant bluefin are tailed and flash-frozen, mist rising from their ranked amphora, buyers stooping between them.

I have nowhere to go. Most days I sit alone under the unpleasantly grime-caked air-conditioner, the notebooks spread across the floor. They cover half the room, worn as old basalt. Opened, their diagrams and transcriptions seem to come together, to make a complete and complex pattern, although this is a lie. They will always be incomplete. They remind me of a man I once saw, in Ephesus, stealing tesserae from a thousand-year-old mosaic. He picked out the squares of travertine and azulista and put them in the pockets of his empire-building shorts. His face blank, as if it could deny what the hands were doing.

No one saw him except me, and I didn't stop him. Now I wish that I had. He stole the tesserae, not as if he was destroying something, but as if he could carry the mosaic home in his pocket. There was a need in him directed towards something impossible. When I have finished with the books I put them away and sleep. The bullet train shudders through its shackles in my dreams.

A drunk takes up residence under the stanchions. Every morning, from the bedroom window, I check to see if he is still there. He is always in the same green creaseless nylon suit, leant against the torus of a pillar, or hunched into himself like a netsuke carving. He is almost completely bald, with only shadows of hair left above each ear.

Then one day he is gone. I wake early. It is half-dark. My cheek aches where the bruise is fading. The New Zealanders breathe softly in their safe dreams. I get up and cross to the window.

The overpass is uninhabited. A wish creeps up on me, softly, like wakefulness. I want to know where the drunk has gone. Which doorway he is sleeping in, or what kind of life he has gone back to. His face cleaned, the eyes calmed. I wonder who would take him back. The man in the creaseless suit, unremarkable in a shopping crowd or on a rush-hour train.

I dress quietly. I am thin, and shadows catch in the hollows of my collarbones. My boots are in my bag. I go downstairs and put them on by the house door. Outside, the air feels new and cool. I walk, not quickly. Settling into the familiar rhythm, looking for something I know I can't find.

It is miles into Tokyo. I follow the bullet train line south-east through the quiet suburbs. Dawn traffic accumulates around me. By the time I reach Asakusa it is noon. I go into the first department store I come to, a riverside high-rise, letting the crowd carry me past pearskin lacquer furniture and cobra-top ghetto blasters, orthopaedic mattresses and sumptuous silk underwear, bean cakes and gold leaf jellies, the half-timbered Piccadilly Pub, the pufferfish eatery and Haagen Dazs ice-cream parlour in one building, the open atrium where stallholders sell turtles'-blood elixir, seaweed tea, cyberpets and boar-tusk seals. There is an energy here, a sense of purpose. A belief that anything can be had, at a price.

It has been too long since I walked. It helps in a way I had forgotten it could. Mushanokoji is a fortnight behind me. I stop at a Circle-K, buy a rice parcel seasoned with salmon eggs, and eat without stopping. At the Sumida river I cross eastwards, away from the high-rises, into the wooden back streets. It is some time more before the road softens underfoot.

I look down and find I am walking on yellowed grass. I am in a municipal park, boulders and ornamental pines between cheap fifties conurbations, prefabricated buildings that should have been demolished decades ago. Immigrants sit on the benches or walk together. At the far end of the park, shielded by gingko trees, a motorway cuts across the sky.

There is a fountain ahead of me. Koi carp lip at pondweed. The fountain spout is rusted and dry. Foreign men sit around the pool's rim. They have dark hair and olive skins, and I am reminded of Diyarbak'r. They smoke steadily, looking at the ground and their own cheap shoes.

I sit. Now I have stopped moving, the drive goes out of me quickly. It is a long way back to the Pleasant Palace. My feet ache and I look down at them and at my hands. Turning them.

'Excuse me.'

He has dark skin with dark hair and beard. Dirty nylon suit trousers and a fake Gucci belt. He is holding out a packet of Fortuna cigarettes.

'No. Thanks.'

The man sits down. Takes out a cigarette, then puts it back. I feel him lean towards me across the pool. 'I had to introduce myself. You have the most lovely blue eyes of any Japanese woman I have seen.'

'I'm not Japanese.'

'Really?'

I smile a little. Despite myself.

'I am also not Japanese. My name is Pavlov.' He holds out his hand.

I raise mine. Pull back instinctively. There is a frog on his out-stretched palm, small as the ball of his thumb. It blinks at me, green with gold irises. The man talks fast. 'My name is Pavlov, and this is Pavlov's Frog. This frog is famous to science. If you ring a bell, she will roll out her tongue.'

'You're hurting it. Your skin is too warm.'

His grin falters. The frog hops back into the pool. Under the beard his face is older than I would have guessed, seamed with smile lines. 'I am sorry. I meant to make you laugh. Laughing is good for the soul.'

'Even for frogs?'

'Especially for them. Where I live, the frogs laugh all night.' He cleans his hand on his trousers. Gets out the cigarette again, lights it while I watch. The lighter is slim, plastic, patterned with red and green glacé cherries. A woman's accessory, or a child's.

'Where are you from, Pavlov?'

He shrugs. 'Not Japan.'

'What do you do here?'

'When it rains I sell umbrellas.'

'And when it doesn't rain?'

'Then I sell parasols.' The beard pulls up around his lips.

'You have a family?'

'Yes.' He nods. 'You have good eyes. And what do you do . . .?'

'Katharine.'

'Katharine. I think maybe you come to Japan to teach English.'

'No.' A siren goes past. The park men move, as if a wind has passed through them. 'I came here looking for something.'

'World peace? Happiness for all people?'

Now I smile. 'Nothing so unselfish.'

'That's good. Because then I can help you.'

'You don't even know what it is.'

'Yet still I can help you. Isn't it good? I am Mister Lost and Found. The secret is this: computers. I have the best in Tokyo. Tokyo has the best in the world. So, if you look on my computer, you will find what you have lost.'

'I haven't lost anything–'

He raises a hand. 'No, I will not hear it. This is the modern world. The morning of the new millennium. If you can't find what you are looking for, you are not using the modern world correctly. You are not following the instructions on the box. Why do you hate computers?'

'I don't.' I look up, feeling the sun and wind, harsh against my face. 'Do you really have parasols?'

'Listen, I have whatever you want. Eh?' He is extracting a bill-fold from his trouser pocket. Inside is a wad of business cards. No cash. He holds a card out. 'Please. An invitation. We will put your question on my computer. In no time you will have a thousand answers, from all over the world. When a good answer comes in I will telephone you, and then we will celebrate, and then you will find whatever you are looking for. Yes?'

I take the card. On it is a name in tiny italicised characters: *Pavlov Bekhterev, Trader*, and, larger, an address in Japanese, English and Cyrillic.

'Two blocks from here.'

'Thanks. It was nice to meet you, anyway.' We shake hands. He looks at his watch. 'You have a business appointment?'

'Ah, no. This park is next to the nursery. I must pick up my children.'

'Pavlov's sprogs.' His face remains blank and I laugh. 'It means children.'

'Sprogs. Exactly. Ring a bell and they all at once shit their nappies.'

At the park gate he waves goodbye. With the card I wave back. Later, in the Pleasant Palace, I turn its thin possibilities in my fingers and wonder what I have to lose.

Screenlight bathes his face. Softens it. 'So, now. You will have to tell me what you are looking for.'

'A jewel.'

'A jewel.' He types as he talks. 'And what do we call it?'

'Lewis.'

'Lewis. An unusual name for a stone.'

'I want to know about everyone called Lewis on the island of Shikoku. To start with.'

'No problem. It is also a strange name for the Japanese. And then we will eat. Anna is cooking now. Do you like *okroshka*? I love it. In summer I pick the cherries myself, in the park.'

'I don't even know what that is.'

'Then I will introduce you. *Okroshka*, Katharine; Katharine, *okroshka*.'

The apartment has a kitchenette and bathroom, a squat toilet, two bedrooms floored with worn-out tatami. It overlooks a rice field, the field in turn overshadowed by the Morinaga Milk Caramel Factory. The children, Alexander, Valentin, Elena, are one, two, three and a half, each with the same bow-lipped face, like Russian dolls. Anna is tall and sallow, her smile sweet as Pavlov's but more halting, as if it remembers more. She has no English and no Japanese. At supper we talk in broken German, the children already put to bed. I wonder if they are refugees, but I don't ask from what and they don't say.

The best computer in Tokyo is a Toyota laptop with a cheap modem attached at the back. After pork cutlet and chilled cherry soup, nursing coffee and vodkas, we go to see what Pavlov has caught.

'Nothing.' He shrugs. Adjusts the flat blue screen. 'But this is only a kind of search engine we have used. The Internet is like an ocean, very wide, and there are other ways to travel. On it, in it, or under it. If there are Lewises on Shikoku I can find them, undoubtedly. They can run but not hide. With this mean baby I can check all bills, the working permit, Alien Registration Card, the driving licence, the registered parking space, the multi-generation mortgage. Birth certificate, death certificate. All the ID in a life.'

I sip the coffee's sweet tar. 'Can anyone see you doing it?'

'See? No.' He moves through boxes, screens, indexes. 'What kind of people?'

'Anyone.'

He rolls his eyes. 'In computers, with money, one can see anything. Do these people have money?'

'I don't know. I don't know anything about them.'

'Those are the worst kind of people. The anyones no one knows anything about.'

He turns out of the screen's illumination. The apartment is dark. It smells of Russia. Somewhere a child cries. 'This will take some time. When I have your names, in a few days, I will call you.' His face breaks into a grin. 'Now, did you ever play chess? Chess Katharine, Katharine chess. Sit down, sit. Pick a hand.'

It is late by the time I leave. Pavlov offers to drive me home, but it is too far, his eyes glisten with drink, and when I turn him down Anna gives me a shy glance of thanks. I imagine us careering into the rice field, sinking into the fresh harvest mud. The last of the bog people in the last of their bog Honda.

Outside the air is warm with the smell of cooking caramel. From the field beside me comes the sound of frogs. There are fewer of them now the rice is gone. Pavlov says they are laughing. To me it sounds more like singing. Listening to them, I cross away from the light of the flats, through the dark, up to the far shore of the factories.

The last train waits for me at Cherry Blossom station. The seats are hard and straight-backed and I'm glad of them. I don't know how far I could go if I slept, or where the line ends. My eyes close only once, not for long. In the dark, it seems to me that the carriage fills with people.

I can hear them breathing. Aslan the driver sits next to Aslan the waiter. Leyla leans by Araf, still smiling without understanding. There is Graf the auctioneer and beside him, the Japanese woman, searching for her father's sword. Hassan and Eva, R. F. von Glött and the moon-faced hostess, their hands on their knees, like old gods. George Pyke, his shoes scrubbed as church steps. Ismet with his assessor's eyes.

They are waiting for me to look at them. All the people who have brought me here, even if they didn't know it, even if we have never met. In the dark of my head I realise they are like Anne's letters. They have all stayed with me, all this time, although I will never see them again.

水

'They say she is small as a child.'
  'So she is.'
  'You have seen her?'
  'Just the once.'

'They say she speaks only German.'

'Now William, not nervous?'

'No.'

'You, Daniel?' George Fox's voice in the leathered dark. It was 1837, the first Monday in December. The window up, the cold shut out.

'A little.'

'Any man might be nervous, going before a queen. They say her first English was: "Off with his head".'

Laughter. The flare of a match. Fox bent over the business of his pipe. In the company carriage, George Fox, John Bridge, William Bennett, Daniel Levy. Knee to knee, Rundell's door-to-door salesmen. Picked for their charm, sweating in tails. Bridge in breeches. William's hands holding on to themselves.

Daniel turned away from them. In the packed space he could smell their anxiety, like that of animals. The carriage window was fogged with breath and he cleaned a space and looked out at London in its element. Snow had fallen overnight. There is more to come, he thought. The light felt defined by its imminence.

London. In four years he had grown to like the city. He had never expected that; nor had he thought Salman would come to hate it. His brother had no time for the capital's dark months, the clip of English on the tongue, the promise written on a banknote. When he was paid Salman took it in coin, as if he trusted only the physical value of things. The equivalence of worth and beauty. At Rundell's he worked long hours and spoke little when he was done. Daniel missed him. Once he had come awake to see his brother sitting upright, shouting curses at the empty air. Not English, but their old language, its Hebrew, Persian, Arabic. Daniel no longer thought of it as his own.

He blinked and the world outside came back. Workmen stood in Trafalgar Square, killing time by a brazier under work-site hoardings. Daniel took out his spectacles, hooked them on. As the carriage turned onto the Mall he could see Marble Arch ahead, a squat sentinel over frozen parkland. Buckingham Palace rising beyond it.

'Watch Mister Bridge, boys. Do as he does and you'll cope nicely.'

'Now, George.' The Young Oil an old man in old-fashioned

clothes. His skin damp with the remnant of a winter sickness. A deal case in his hands, deep as a hatbox.

'You'll see that his back is remarkably flexible.'

'Really, George, you do me—'

'No man in London, I'm sure, can bow lower or oftener than Mister Bridge.'

Laughter again, sharp with tension. The arch gates were locked. It was only when the carriage started up again, the gravel giving way to smooth sand, that Daniel felt any unease.

The palace loomed overhead. He followed the walls upwards with his eyes. The windows were net-curtained blanks. He thought: I don't belong here. This is Salman's dream, not mine. It is my brother, the jewel worker, who wishes for palaces. This is what he meant us both to come to, but I have arrived without him. And it is not what I want.

He leant forward, as if the feeling of guilt were something he could leave behind. He wondered, suddenly, what it was he did want. All he could think of was Rachel. And already the wings of the palace were enclosing them, the carriage turning in its court, and the warders were coming in their red tails, the maids of honour stooping to lead them inside.

Vistas of red carpet. Rooms of white and gold. A butler stepping out of a mirror, the door closing softly behind him. The salesmen were ushered inwards so quickly that Daniel was left only with faint impressions of the complex around him. Forms in white marble. Faces in oil.

The waiting room smelt of sewage. The fire stood empty, although the wall above it was stained with soot. A servant came and took their hats and coats, leaving William and George stamping in the cold. John Bridge sat down, laying his case on the chair beside him. He looked tired already, sweating with slight fever.

Daniel walked to the window. It was sealed shut with congealed layers of paint. He resisted the urge to try to open it, to cut the stale air with that outside. The sky had brightened over the whiteness of Green Park. Reaching into his waistcoat he took out his watch, and opened it in his palm while Fox sucked his teeth and rubbed his hands and talked of nothing.

'Just like them, to skimp on a pennyworth of coal. Now we wait while she washes her dogs, no doubt. William, your choker. No, and no. Now! There stands my gentleman. What have you there, Mister Levy?'

'Nothing but the time.' He closed the out-case.

Fox clicked his outstretched fingers. Daniel unhooked the watch chain and handed it across. The jeweller cocked his head.

'Well. This is our work.' He grunted. 'Not bad. Not one I did myself, mind. A little beyond your station this, Daniel. *Tempus metitur omnia sed metior ipsum.* Read that, can you?'

'I have no Latin.'

'No. How is yours, Mister Bridge? *Tempus metitur omnia sed metior ipsum?*'

'Time measures all,' said the Young Oil, distracted, a handkerchief clenched in his hand. 'But I measure it.'

'So we do.' Fox spooled the watch chain into Daniel's palm. 'Ten after ten. No one knows time like the jewellers who sell it. *Time is, thou hast, employ the portion small. Time past is gone, thou canst not it recall. Time future is not, and may never be. Time present is the only time for thee.'*

They fell quiet, four salesmen in a room without customers. From beyond the door came the echo of footsteps, an old man coughing, the shudder of ancient pipes and cisterns.

'High times we had here, in George's time.' The Young Oil smiled faintly. 'William's also. Scunging business from half of Europe and the Indies. Still, you will find Victoria is already a fine monarch.'

'A Whig,' said Fox, 'this one.'

'She's young. Give her a few years, George. As a queen she is already excellent, although all trades must be learned, of course, and nowadays the trade of a sovereign is a very difficult one – Ladies!' He rose, already bowing as the door opened. 'Miss Rice, Miss Hastings.'

'Gentlemen.' A hiss of silks. A warm voice. Two faces, one pretty, the other sexless as a child's. 'Mister Bridge, you were speaking of our queen.'

'Of the crown we bring her, Miss Hastings.'

'And what jewels do you bring us, sir?'

'For you, ladies, I offer these young men at a cut-down price.'

'Young men make fine jewels.' Flowers in their hair. The smell of rosebuds and jasmine. Daniel wondered how that could be possible. 'And how are they cut, Mister Bridge?'

'I am afraid to say that Mister Bennett and Mister Levy are poor steps. They pale beside your brilliant facets.'

Laughter. 'So. Her Majesty and my own mistress the Duchess are eager to see your proposal, gentlemen. We must hurry back to them, if you please.'

The smell of sewers followed them. From the state chambers, the maids of honour led them through a room defined by staircases, a hall cluttered with empty pedestals, a passage where wardens hurried past and the windows were dark with grime. The palace is hollow as a ruin, thought Daniel. A great stone block full of throne rooms and servants' backways. Palaces inside palaces.

They emerged into a space of white and gilt Tuscan columns, the chandeliers quarter-lit. A room that seemed identical to the palace antechamber, although Daniel felt as if he had walked a great distance. He paused, dizzied, trying to find some distinguishing feature by which to reorient himself. The natural light gave no direction, and the paintings were the same unidentifiable, smoke-darkened oils.

He looked down. On the red carpet was a mess of small footprints, as if a child had walked into Buckingham Palace with street mud on its feet. They began by the fireplace and dwindled across the floor. In the dimness they looked bare. It was hard to follow their smudged succession.

He turned, reaching to adjust his spectacles, but the others were already ahead of him. For the second time, he was in danger of being left behind. He caught up with the salesmen as they reached a pair of high, damp-stained doors, a footman with white skin and a port-wine mouth already admitting them, the crowd absorbing them into its distracted noise.

A morning room, still candlelit at half past ten and needing it. The smell of dogs, cigars and scented violets. In one corner an old man sat bolting down a plate of bacon. At a marble table the cigar-smoker looked over dispatch boxes with slow distaste. There were animals under the furniture, Daniel saw. A black spaniel in red clothes better than those Daniel wore. The serpentine curl of a greyhound.

Above them all, the curtains were moving by themselves. In the shadows of the ceiling Daniel thought he could make out a figure, something alive but shrunken. It was clambering from one drape to the next. At the window stood a tall man with benign eyes and beside him, a child in a woman's dress. The man was smiling. The child was calling out a name. Their voices distant and dreamlike.

Well, and now you must coax him down.

Sindbad. Oh Sindbad! He will not come.

The room was full of women dressed as queens. There were queens playing whist, playing an Italian duet, drinking chocolate. Queens bent over embroideries, needles poised. The candlelight reflected from their raised eyes. Daniel looked back at them and felt his own shabbiness. He tried to recall Victoria's face, and found he remembered nothing.

'Bow, man!'

A voice, Fox's, hissing beside him. He bent, the salesman in him quicker than thought. When he peered up again the room had shifted around him, as if its natural rules had changed. He realised that he had been standing alone. That the creature roosting on the curtains was a monkey, like those in the market of Khadimain. That the child was a queen.

The music stopped as she moved through the crowd. The tall man came with her. Head down, Daniel saw nothing except their feet and those of the attendant crowd. A girl's voice reached him, sweet and petulant.

'Who is this?'

'This gentleman is your jeweller, Majesty. John Bridge of Rundell and Bridge's.'

The Young Oil coughed nearby. 'Your Highness, and may I humbly present Messieurs Fox, Bennett and Levy, also Goldsmiths to Your Person. These gentlemen and myself—'

'Where is our crown?'

Her voice was beautiful, thought Daniel. Years later, he would remember it when all other details of Victoria Guelph had faded. The voice of a queen, like that of a singer about to sing. He felt Fox and Bridge rise and stood with them.

'Of course, Your Majesty. I have brought it here in this box.'

'Then you must take it out.'

314

A murmur of laughter. The sound of the cigar-smoker still writing, caught in a sudden hush. Light played across the floor at Daniel's feet, red, white and blue, and he looked up.

George and William had lifted out the crown and set it on the card table. Even modelled in glass and tin it was overpoweringly precious. Gross as a wad of banknotes. The candles caught its thirty thousand facets. Outside, it had begun, at last, to snow.

'The Imperial State Crown, Your Majesty.'

Her small hands clenched and unclenched at her sides. Her mouth was slightly open. As if, thought Daniel, she might eat the crown and spit out the stones. She walked around the table as John Bridge began to talk. His patter easy, addressing the Queen but working the crowd, unctuous as a masseur. 'Jewels, Your Highness, are marvellous things. They are the majesty of the earth, and the mark of all true earthly power. This model is a simulacrum, a confection of glass. However, I believe that jewels wait in every mind's eye, and so I hope I may appeal to Your Majesty's imagination. Here, then, above the ermine, is the rim. Clusters of sapphires and emeralds are enclosed in shells of diamonds. These clusters, like fruit among vine leaves, are separated with trefoil diamond designs, and set above and below with pearls.'

Motion in the audience. A shiver of something vicarious.

'If I may then draw Your Majesty's attention upwards, to the eight *fleur-de-lys,* which hold pigeons'-blood rubies, and the eight *crosses-pattées,* of which seven hold emeralds, and the frontmost the ancient Black Prince's ruby, with the Stuart Sapphire in its company. Now the rear of the crown, and at Your Majesty's express wish, we have allocated here a considerable new tablecut sapphire. Continuing upwards, from the *crosses-pattées* rise eight arches, set with new diamonds in oak-leaf designs, with drop pearls as acorns . . .'

From the crowd a collective sigh, a sound to accompany fireworks.

'Aha, thank you, ladies – and here, where the silver arches meet at last, depend four great new pearls. Rising above these pendants is the mound and the great *crosse-pattée,* sheathed entirely in brilliants, and at the nearest point to heaven is set the sapphire of Your Majesty's ancestor, our nineteenth king, Saint Edward the Confessor.'

The Young Oil's voice warming to its business. 'On the day of Your Majesty's coronation, when the light falls on your brow, it will be captured in this prism of three thousand one hundred and three jewels. The sun itself shall put on the colours of the British flag. This crown, Your Highness, will be the most valuable, and we may safely add the most beautiful, in the world. Worthy of a sovereign on whose Dominions the sun never sets.'

A waiting silence. Victoria's eyes moved from the crown to take in John Bridge, as if she had noticed him for the first time. 'Where is the Keeper of the Regalia?'

'Here, Majesty.' The old man stepped forward, still swallowing with anxiety. A sheen of grease on the innards of his beard.

Victoria pulled the model towards her. There was something wrong with her lips, Daniel realised. A twist that was almost a deformity. Snow tumbled against the glass beyond her. 'How do you like the crown, Mister Swifte?'

'Like?' For a moment, as if in fascinated imitation of the Queen, Edmund Swifte's own mouth gaped open. 'Oh, it is matchless, Majesty. Matchless.'

'Lord Melbourne?'

'Fair work.' The tall man nodded. 'Certainly.'

'Baron?'

At the marble table, the cigar-smoker raised his head and glanced in the direction of the crown. 'I am out of words for it, Your Highness.'

John Bridge stood half-bowed, still waiting in the posture of his last words. Now Victoria leant towards him and smiled. 'It is most beautiful, sir. Most impressive.'

The applause began, languidly, as if it had not been waiting for this exact moment. A foot in front of him, Daniel saw John Bridge's arse visibly relax. The voices echoed in his ears, like a chant: *Majesty, Your Majesty, Majesty* – as if the word were a necessary protection against her. At the card table, Victoria was still fingering the false diamonds and sapphires. When she spoke again her voice was indiscernible, and her face creased into a frown as she repeated herself. 'Where are the Jews?'

Melbourne bent beside her. 'Your Majesty, I'm not aware–'

'Ah!' The Young Oil straightened. 'Forgive me, Lord Melbourne, I must explain. This new sapphire, as my colleague Mister Rundell has informed the Queen, was brought to England by a pair of Mesopotamian Jews. I believe Mister Rundell promised the Queen that one of these brothers would be presented to Her Majesty. And so he is. This man is Daniel Levy, one of two Mesopotamians in our employ. They call themselves Babylonian Jews–'

'Where is the other?'

'Hard at work on the refitting of your crown, Majesty.' Bridge smoothing the facts out. At home in the room as the spaniel in its buckled coat, the women with their needles and flowers. 'Now, as they tell it, the brothers were given an ancient jar. At any rate, the vessel came into their possession. When it was opened, it proved to contain a fortune in jewels.'

'A jar of jewels!' The child's eyes lit up with a new animation. There was a rash of acne on her forehead. The sense of disorientation rose up in Daniel again. He wondered if this was a game at his expense, the Queen of England hidden in the crowd, watching.

'So the story goes. With the jewels they had wealth enough to reach England. Here Your Majesty sees the older of the pair. A fine salesman we've made of him too, eh, Daniel?'

He felt the court's eyes on him. This is what I have become, he thought, after all these years. A fairground exhibit. A strong man, a Saracen, a living skeleton.

'Ah. He is speechless with honour, Your Highness.'

'Why, this jar is like some Aladdin's Lamp.' She smiled widely. Daniel realised he could see her gums. 'Where is his brother? We wish to speak with them together.'

'Alas, the younger of the two–'

'Together. We asked to see those who will work on the crown. You will arrange it.'

'Yes.' The Young Oil caught off guard. 'Your Highness, of course. The Lord Chamberlain and I will fix a day. Excellent. Well. In the meantime there is other business to discuss, with which Mister Levy and Mister Bennett need not concern themselves. If they may–'

She waved them away. Bored of them all, already, of the glass crown and the story of the Jews' jar. As he reached the doors, unable to stop himself, Daniel looked round.

The card game had begun again. The cigar-smoker sat at his table. Nothing had been significantly interrupted. Only the animals seemed changed, the greyhound uncoiled and crouched avidly over a dish of greens, the spaniel vanished, the monkey caught. The Keeper of Jewels held it on a fine neck-chain, and beside him the Queen was smiling down at it, its own teeth smiling back.

The doors closed them in. Daniel turned back into the underlit hallway. Beside him, William stood bent forward, hands on thighs, breathing badly.

'William?' Daniel put a hand on the younger man's shoulder. The tailcoat was warm with sweat. 'Give me your arm.'

'No, I can manage myself. Oh God.'

There was a muted sound of retching. The footman stepped towards them, his white face relaxing into dourness.

'Allus the same. Here. Wipe yourself.' He pressed a handkerchief into William's hands. Stood over him while the shopman cleaned his mouth and the floor between his feet. Waiting on him as if he were not quite staff, not quite state, Daniel thought. Jewels place us somewhere in between.

He took out a shilling, a day's wages. Passed it over William's head. 'I'm sorry for the trouble.'

'Aye. Allus the same, the men. Halfway to relieving themselves with relief.'

A woman's voice cut across them, cool and sardonic. 'There is no need to apologise, Mister Levy. William Bennett isn't the first gentleman to be overcome by the Queen.'

He looked round. Outside the morning-room door stood one of the maids of honour. A plain face made pretty by intelligence. He bowed, trying to recall her name.

'Miss Rice, Mister Levy.'

'The brilliant.'

'The step.' She smiled tightly. They waited as William straightened up, balled the stained cloth and stuffed it inside his best coat. He took a deep breath and smiled weakly. 'Miss Rice. An honour to meet you again.'

'Mister Bennett. I have been sent to lead you out. The sooner the better for you, I think.'

'Kind of you, madam. Very.'

She walked ahead of them, not looking back. Outside the sky had snowed itself out. A faint natural light fell into the halls and passageways, the nearest London in December could come to sun.

'All done, then,' said William. He talked fast, for the sake of it. Relieving himself, thought Daniel. 'The whole business is done and dusted. How was I?'

'Very fine. All gentleman.'

'I remember almost nothing of it. To tell the truth, I was a little scared of her.' He smiled, shy and ashamed of it. Daniel caught the pungency of vomit on his breath. 'She approved of our crown?'

He thought of Victoria, her hands clutching and unclutching. 'Aye. She likes all jewels, I think.'

'Good luck to her. There are days when I cannot stand them myself. I need a drink. An oyster lunch to celebrate, eh? I'll wine and dine you.'

'They wait for me at Ludgate Hill.'

'Let them wait. If we hurry, we can make Haymarket while the sun still shines.'

'I—'

'I know a Jewess there, if you like your own. If not, there is no end to the choice—'

He broke off as they caught up with Miss Rice. She stood watching them, amused, not impatient. Beyond her stretched a marble colonnade littered with boxes. The windows had been boarded up from the inside.

'Well, now.' William went forward into the gloom. Daniel watched him look around intently. Between them stood a dark hulk, tall as either shopman and wider than both. It was a bell, Daniel saw. His eyes adjusted. There was writing on the massive flanks, an inexplicable script composed in vertical lines. William raised one hand, then the second, feeling its substance.

'This is cast silver.' He sounded sharper now, in his element. A young echo of the Young Vinegar. 'I'd put money on it. Where have you brought us to, Miss Rice, the Jewel House of the Celestial Empire?'

'This is Buckingham Palace, Mister Bennett. I am quite hurt you would forget us so soon.' She began to walk again. 'All you see here are gifts to Her Majesty. They are becoming something of a problem.'

Daniel followed her voice. Paths ran between half-opened crates of exotica. A throne set on elephant's feet. An Ottoman clock, its glass dome cracked open. Somewhere here, he thought, there will be offerings from Iraq. Rotting cauldrons of *halqûn*. Gold robbed from the old cities.

'The dignitaries bring presents from every corner of the globe. There is no longer space to house them, nor even time for the Queen to enjoy what she is given.'

Rice's shadow moved, William's a step behind it. In the slight light they left behind Daniel could make out marks on the floor. He stooped down. They were old, scuffed in with others. Only their outline suggested bare footprints.

'It is the price of royalty. Its punishment.' Rice's voice was hushed with distance. 'A very small punishment in a very lovely Greek Hell.'

'And she is, after all, a very small queen.'

'You would not say that in her presence.'

'But not so very lovely as you, I think.'

'Oh.'

Daniel laid his hand on the floor. The nearest print measured from his wrist to the curved line of his middle knuckles. Half a foot. He touched the impression with one finger. Raised its black spot to his face. From its grain came the unmistakable sweet odour of coal.

'William, see here.'

There was no answer. He stood up. Called out again. 'William. William? Miss Rice?'

Nothing came back to him but his own rising echoes. Daniel stepped out between the boxes and walked fast to the end of the colonnade. Beyond the last columns a staircase curved downwards, lit by grimy windows, and two panelled passages ran off into darkness. He took the staircase down, followed a hallway carpeted with dust past a roped-off stairwell and a room with bloodstone fireplaces, the walls stained with entrenched damp, the floorboards groaning underfoot. Immediately he was lost.

He stopped, listening. There was sound everywhere, none of it close. A background noise of people, echoes of whispers, whispers of echoes, the clatter of distant dishes. He wondered how long William and Miss Rice would look for him. Or if they had lost him on purpose. William leaving Haymarket for a rainier day.

He had guessed he'd come down to the ground floor, but it felt as if he were underground now. Ahead the floorboards had given way completely, the carpet sagging into the space under them. Further on, the passage darkened, and Daniel could see nothing. He turned back, trying to remember his steps. It was a moment before he saw the figure waiting for him.

It was no more than ten yards away. It was all dark, skin and clothes, camouflaged into the dimness. In the absence of light it seemed too small to be human. He thought of Victoria, as if she might have followed him. Only as the figure began to walk towards him did he realise there was something in its hands. A length of metal.

It stopped in front of him, waiting. He saw it was a child. It was dirty in a way Daniel had never seen, even on chimneysweeps. Soot had worked its way into its nostrils, the insides of its ears. Only the eyes were still white.

'You've lost your way.' It was an old voice, deep and breathless. Odd in a child. Out of place, Daniel thought, as a ship in a bottle. It repeated itself. 'You've lost your way. I saw you do it. You was looking for me.'

'The footprints.'

'Aye.'

He hesitated, lost for words. The child's feet were bare, he saw. Only the nails stood out as pale half-moons.

'You live here? In the palace?'

'These last two years now.' It shifted the metal length from one hand to the other. Daniel saw it was a candlestick, old and tarnished.

'And no one finds you?'

The figure hawked and spat. Daniel caught a flash of teeth. 'They knows I'm here. They don't see me. I knew you, else you wouldn't have seen me. I kept my eye on you and all.'

'You say you know me?'

'I seen you afore. In different clothes.'

Daniel put a hand out. The figure stepped away from it. Under the hoarseness of the voice there was an accent. A brogue, something Irish. He had heard it before, once, at a time when he had no name for it.

'I thought you was Joseph and Mary.'

He bent down, staring into the blacked-out face. 'Martha?'

'I didn't think to see you again.'

He stayed there, on his haunches, facing her. He tried to guess how old she was. But it had been years since he had seen her, and she was too small, stunted with malnourishment. He shook his head. 'You had a mother. Brothers.'

She stepped back again. 'I make do for myself now.'

'How do you eat?'

'I make do. I forgot your own name.'

'Daniel Levy.'

She cocked her head, gesturing backwards. 'Shall I lead you out, Mister Levy?'

'That would be very kind.' They began to walk. Light outlined the figure in front of him. Her thinness was like that of the creature roosting in the morning room. 'It is good to see you, Martha. How did you end up here?'

'Fergal showed me. That was my brother. He was a skivvy for the footmen here. I don't know where he is now. Maybe the workhouse. After I found my own ways. Tom showed me his ins and outs when I came.'

'Tom?'

'He's gone now too. He lived here. They caught him a year ago now. I don't know what they done with him.' Her head turned, rat-thin, grinning. 'I seed the crown. The Queen liked it, did she?'

'You were there, this morning?'

They reached the roped-off stairwell. Martha ducked under it. 'I seed from the fireplace. I sleep up the chimneys. There's space aplenty. There's shelves and nooks big as rooms. The sweepers' boys know my places. They say nothing. I thought your crown was beautiful.'

When he looked up Martha was waiting for him. Her expression was the same, he realised, only hardened. Still anxious, as if there was something to say and no time to say it. 'There was two of you.'

'My brother and I, Salman. Yes.'

Martha turned and began to walk again. 'Are you jewellers to the Queen?'

'We work for the Crown Goldsmiths.' They came out at the top of the stairs. Tail-ends of candles illuminated a distempered corridor. To the far left he could see a broader chamber, better-lit, cluttered with empty pedestals.

'At last! I know my way from here. Without you I would have been lost for days.' He took out his purse, felt for the half sovereign he knew was there, extracted its heavy weight and passed it to Martha. She bit into it, hungrily, as if gold were edible.

'Can I work for you, Mister Levy?'

'I . . .' There were mirrors on the passage walls. He caught sight of himself as he struggled for words. His spectacles opaque with candlelight. 'I am a shopman. The company is not mine, Martha. I have no jobs to give—'

'I can fetch and run. I can clean. I can copy newspapers. If you give me a needle, I can stitch two ways.' She watched him, waiting. 'I should live here as I have done. I should like to work for you, Mister Levy.'

He felt his heart lurch and give, falling away inside him. He leant back against the palace wall. 'You say you can read?'

She lowered her head. 'Some.'

'Do you know Ludgate Hill?'

'Well enough.'

'There is a sign above my shop, a golden salmon. A gold fish. Come on Sunday, at noon, to the back door. Creed Lane. Half a shilling for a half-day each week, is that fair to you?'

She raised the candlestick in her hand. 'I can get linen and candles and more.'

'No.'

'Aye. Then what?'

'Then you shall learn to write.'

Midnight. London clean with snow. The sky above it emptied out into a broad black vacancy.

'Tell me what else.'

'There is nothing else to tell. The Queen, the child.'

'Damn the child, Daniel.'

'There is nothing else. Bridge said he would fix a day next month. William and I walked back. He wanted me to go with him to the Haymarket.'

'Why?'

'He was happy to have seen the Queen.'

'And you were not. In four years this is the best news we have had.'

'I'll not go back there.'

'Why?'

'I felt ashamed.'

'Ashamed of what?'

'You were not there.'

'Of being unable to afford the expense of a fire? Ah, Daniel. Ashamed of chance? In this trade no word carries more weight than hers. With the right thing said at the palace, we will be set clear for life. Wake up.'

'I am not asleep.'

'You lie. You remember how it was when we arrived at the docks? The English looked at us as if we were Ali Baba and his last thief. And nothing has changed except our clothes. Inside we will never be like these people. Are you ashamed of that?'

'No.'

'We are always *dhimmi.*'

'We have been here four years, Salman.'

'Aye, four years, and no one yet has rolled out the bloody red carpet. Eh? We have had no chance until now. The Queen of England wishes to see us. What more do you want?'

'I don't know.'

'Why will you not go?'

'I don't know.'

'Say you will come with me, Daniel.'

On the window sill, three ale bottles, emptied. An end of bread still uneaten. The tincture bottle turning the moon blue. Two men on the pallet bed, not sleeping. Light reflected in their eyes.

'Daniel. 'Phrates. Please.'

'If that is what you want, then I will come.'

> *A was an Archer's Arrow;*
> *He kept it very nice;*
> *He hunted Buck and Calling Birds,*
> *And Frogs and Harvest Mice.*

'Good. You have copied the first line?'

'Aye.'

'Let me see.'

January, the first Sunday to have sun. Two figures sat on the

324

steps outside the Creed Lane door. The child reading slowly, painfully, each word a step trudged forward. Her writing a cipher.

'Good. What is a calling bird, do you think?'

'I know not.'

'Nor I. Go on now.'

> B was a Butcher's Dog,
> Which was not very small;
> The Butcher fed it Sausages,
> Until it would not growl.

Laughter. The girl leant into it as she began to cough. Daniel took the chapbook from her. 'There. Enough this time. You've done well.'

'I'm not tired.'

Her face looked weary from coughing. He held out five pence. 'It is too cold.'

'Not for me.' She took the coins. Squirrelled them away.

'For me then. I'll catch my death from letters. In the spring we will study longer.' He wondered if Martha had ever had a teacher of any kind. There were schools, he thought, that might still take her. He would have to look into that.

There was the sound of the bolt being drawn back. They both looked up as Salman came out. He smiled down at the child absently, pulling his black coat closer. 'Good morning, Martha. How is your reading?'

'Middling.'

Daniel made room for him as Salman sat down. 'It isn't so long since I was learning myself. My brother is a fine teacher, eh?' He turned to Daniel. 'A little bitter to study out of doors.'

Daniel lowered his voice, tucking the alphabet back into his pocket. 'George will not let her inside.'

'Still? She is cleaner than him. She has never been mucky as George Fox, have you, Martha?'

She giggled, teeth chattering in the wind. 'When I was mudlarking.'

'Mudlarking?'

'Afore the palace. My mother made us.'

Daniel watched them as they talked. The child's profile alongside his brother's. Martha's face was clean but grey, as if the coal dust had indelibly marked her. Beside her, Salman looked washed out. His skin had lightened, as if the white heat of the crucibles had affected its chemistry. His eyes were still dilated in the winter sun.

'Raking the mud. Scunging down the pipes. There was rope and bones and iron. I don't think you've ever seed anyone so mucky. I know places where you'd go head over ears in mud.'

'From sewers to palace. In a fortnight, you know, we shall be under Her Majesty's roof ourselves.'

'Mister Levy said.'

'Oh, and am I not Mister Levy? What do you call me?'

She squinted up at Salman. 'The little Mister Levy.'

Daniel sat back. 'How was your sleep, Salman?'

'Dreamless.' Salman turned away from him. 'There's an errand you could run for me, Martha. James Ryder, across the Hill. Look for the apothecary's sign. There's a penny for you and five shillings to settle with him. Bring what he gives you.'

She stood up and took the coins. Her smile fading, as if money were serious business. Not happy, Daniel thought. Nothing so careless. Contented, though, and that was something.

She nodded goodbye to him and went without looking back. He felt Salman rise beside him, still talking as he went inside, although Daniel was no longer listening. After they were both gone he hunched forward, the cold working into his hands and feet. The backstreet lay silent around him. Even the rats had been driven in by the cold.

I am ashamed of jewels, he thought. The realisation came to him out of nothing, for no reason; or as if it had been waiting to find him alone. It was what he had meant to say, three weeks ago, in the attic room. *What are you ashamed of?* Salman had asked him. And he had not known what he meant to reply.

I am ashamed of jewels. It felt as if it had always been waiting to be said. What Salman wanted most of all was something he wanted nothing of himself. He remembered Jane Limpus. The candle between them. His life had been decided by his brother's desire.

He shook his head, stood up and went back into the workshop, bolting the door behind him, locking it. The benches and wheels stood quiet for the Christian sabbath. Daniel went on through into the showroom. The blinds were drawn. In the

326

gloom he stood, feeling the displays around him. Silver and car-
buncles in domes of glass. A lick of bile rose up in him.

He thought of what was done for jewels, and what was felt for
them. The way the doing was bound up in feeling, the feeling blind
to whatever had been done. Victoria Guelph's clenched hands: he
thought of that. Rachel's abandonment. For days he thought of
these things, the spectacles hurting his eyes, his back stiffening as
he waited for custom. By then it was already years too late.

ᛉ

Pavlov has strange ideas of days. I wait in Urawa while the long
Japanese autumn begins to cool and Mel and Nicola pack up and
go home to New Zealand. Weeks go by, whole slippages of time,
although I have nothing to measure them by except the slow de-
pletion of my money. Once I walk the grey miles to the Bekhterev
home, the city air pungent in my throat, but there is no one in
and no one answers the note I leave. Once I telephone my sister.
She says I'm so close, just around the corner, why don't I stop by.
Come and stay, Anne says. *Why don't you come and stay?* And I
have no answer any more, no reasons. She doesn't ask about the
jewel. I would thank her for that if I could.

In November the weather turns cold for good. The day Pavlov
rings it snows for the first time. I take the train across Tokyo and
walk from the station, listening to snow clomp off the cherry trees.

He opens the doors and grins. There is a precision screwdriver
behind his ear. 'Checkmate, Katharine! Fun and games. Come in.
Come.'

'I don't have time for chess.' I follow him inside. Someone is
cooking in the flat upstairs. The smell of grilled meat and soy fills
the unlit rooms. Only the computer is on, a blue plaque in the
gloom. I wonder, too late, how much time Pavlov has spent on
my behalf. Looking for something I no longer believe can be
found. Guilt twists its way into my stomach. 'How have you
been? How is the umbrella business?'

He waves me over to the laptop, his eyes catching its light.
'Now, you will see something to make you happy.'

His hands move fast over the keys. I sit down in the only chair.
There is a smell of mould in the bedroom, overriding that of

327

cooking. Cups and plates are stacked around Pavlov's hardware. The unease rises up in me again.

'Where are Anna and the children?'

'Oh –' he shakes his head, preoccupied '– look, please.'

When I turn to the screen a woman is smiling back at me. A lean, tanned face. Incautious eyes. A passport booth photograph, an orange curtain corrugated behind her curly hair.

'Who is this?'

He points at the Japanese text. 'June Patricia Lewis. For five years she has worked on the island of Shikoku. Her employer has been the I Wish They All Could Be Californian English Conversation School, Takamatsu. Her working visa ended when she left this company ten months ago. But, you see here, she is still in Japan. Living in Takamatsu. She has worked illegally as a teacher and a hostess and also doing some – dancing, maybe. The police are very cross with her, and soon they will send her home. She is twenty-eight years old, divorced, American citizen, degree from San Diego University in Spanish. Every week she telephones a number in Oakland.'

'Pavlov –' I look at the woman on the screen, the apparatus of her life laid open '– how long have you spent working on this?'

He squats down. 'This is nothing. Wait and see.' He drags down the cursor. A second page appears. There is no photograph this time, only a solid wall of script. Pavlov smiles between us, the computer and guest, waiting.

'I can't read Japanese.'

'Oh, well. This is the story of the other Lewis. On Shikoku there are only two. But this Lewis is different from the first. Here, I found the death certificate for Mari Murasaki. She died in Tosa in 1987. Her maiden name, this is Lewis.'

I lean into the blue light. 'Tosa.'

'Not really what you would call a city. It is very remote. The far side of Shikoku, the Pacific side. So now, you see, here is a signature on her death certificate. This name is Hikari Murasaki. This says he is her son. A Lewis in disguise. Here is the address he gives for funeral arrangements. Near Tosa, just along the coast. Do you want vodka, Katharine?'

'No, thanks.'

'Okay, sure. So next I look for bills. This name, Hikari Murasaki, and this address. But there is nothing. The house has no telephone, no registered parking space, no electricity or gas. The man has no tax record. For twelve years they are invisible, this man and his house. No one is invisible by accident.'

He reaches out, switches the computer off, turns to me in the dark. 'He is hiding from something. Maybe it is you, Katharine.'

I sit still, thinking it over. Pavlov goes into the kitchen and comes back with sweet tea in tulip glasses. He watches me warm my hands as he drinks.

'It could be me,' I say eventually. 'If not, there are others.'

Pavlov nods and smiles. 'The people with money.'

'The people with money.'

'But then you think this is the one? I have found what you are looking for?'

'Maybe.' I say it quietly. Admitting it only to myself. Pavlov stands up and takes the tea glass out of my hand before he claps me on the back.

'Just as I have said all along! If you are looking for something, you must come to Pavlov. And now we will celebrate.'

We sit in the kitchen, drinking vodka, eating Tuc crackers from a plastic plate. There are pictures of the children on the grease-stained wall above the mini-cooker. I look at them while Pavlov talks, drawing in the air the infinite methods of his ingenuity.

Alexander, Valentin, Elena. Their father gets up to find more food, opening bare cupboards. I talk while he is turned away. Giving him time to choose how he will turn to face me. I am becoming Japanese, I think. 'It's great to see you again, Pavlov. Will the children be back soon, and Anna?'

'Anna. Yes.' He turns back. In his hands is a can of sardines. His eyes are lowered, although his face is otherwise still smiling. 'You see, I myself have political asylum. The police of Japan, however, have decided that my family do not. They are not "high risk". It's okay. Every month I will send them money. In Georgia they will be rich as thieves with all the things I send them.'

He sits down and begins to open the can, scrolling the metal back. When he is finished he puts it down carefully, gravely, as if there is nothing more to be done with it.

'I'm so sorry, Pavlov,' I whisper. 'I didn't know. I wish you had called me. What can I do?'

He shrugs. 'Nothing. Perhaps I should be looking for a jewel, like you, instead of a place for my family to be with me in safety. I think it would be easier.' He starts to smile again and then thinks better of it. The vodka is on the table, frost congealing on the bottle, and he pours again for both of us, his face lengthening into a terrible sadness.

'Pavlov.' I reach out. His hair is coarse. I cradle it. 'You have done too much for me.'

'No, no.'

'If there was something I could give you back . . .'

But I have nothing left, I almost say, and stop myself. The man who has less than nothing smiles again. The sun comes in, briefly, across the Formica table. 'You gave me work. This month, I needed to work. But you do not have to give back anything, Katharine, just because I give you something. This is not America. We have free lunches here.'

'I need to help you too.'

He reaches across, takes hold of my arm, shakes it. 'Then you will keep in touch. I need friends, my dear. So you will call me when you have found what you are looking for. Will you do that for me? Will you promise?'

I promise him.

The bullet train south costs almost everything I have. From the window I watch the climate changing. The snow receding into rain, the rain to late autumn sun. Farmers in the fields round Himeji still burning old scrub to stubble. From downtown Okayama, a night bus runs across the Great Seto Bridge where it arches over the Inland Sea. There are children awake in the seats behind me, their eyes and mouths reflected in the glass. They whisper of pearls and monsters and whirlpools.

At Takamatsu I sit in the town square, drowsing, and wait for the morning bus. When it leaves I am the only passenger. The driver sings along to taped shamisen music. He motions me up to the front. 'Shikoku is green,' he says, gesturing out at the hills of unbroken pine forest; as if, being foreign, I might also be terminally colourblind. *Aoao*, he says, smiling – green-green – and it is. The road smells of tar and cedars, figs and oil. Bush warblers sing in the trees. The driver gets out a timetable and writes notation for their call, one-handed, as he drives. He waves it at me, nodding, as if written birdsong is what I have been travelling for. I take it. We stray towards the road's edge and away.

At noon he stops at a hill town that clings tight around a river gorge. From the only shop he buys us fried chicken and seasoned rice. It is the first food I have eaten in two days. The rush of it leaves me dizzy and I close my eyes, hearing warblers in the forest, wind-chimes in the town station.

I am asleep when we reach the coast. The next time I open my eyes the trees are gone, and seabirds wheel overhead. There are orange groves beside the road, and then, as I pull myself upwards in my seat, the Pacific Ocean. Waves crash along dark sand. At times the forest comes down to meet it, the road verging back into the pines. By the time we reach Kôchi city it is late afternoon, and I get out and walk between the resort dive shops, the souvenir emporia full of nudes carved in coral, turtleshell perfume bottles, Tosa fighting-dog figurines. I buy a bag of dried octopus and a can of hot coffee for the driver and sit with him on the sea wall, while he talks about his love of music too quickly for me to understand.

There is no scheduled stop in Tosa. The driver drops me on the main street and U-turns away, grinning madly back, the bus swerving a little on the empty road. The sun is cutting off early behind the inland hills, and I take my jacket out of my bag and put it on. There are shops at the roadside, a post office, a bar, nothing open. There is still one light showing faintly at the end of the street and I walk up to it.

The sliding doors are unlocked. Inside sits a sealmaker. He looks up at me as I come in, nods as if I am a regular, goes back to work. He carves name-characters into a length of onyx. On the wall above him are a pair of tusks, the grain still white: black-market elephant. The hooded work-lamp shines through the old man's fingers. Their pink flesh lit down to the bone.

When he has finished he smiles up at me and I give him the address on its computer-printed paper. He motions me to sit, takes parchment from his desk. An old woman comes up from the back with green tea and bean cakes. The sealmaker pours ink into a writing plaque, wets a brush, and draws me a map. It takes half an hour. I cover the distance it shows in twice the time.

The main street rises out of town. I follow it up over the hillside and find, not marked on my instructions, the beginnings of a seaside attraction. A Ferris wheel and hot-dog stands are lit up in the semi-darkness. Beyond them, dark on dark, a promontory curves away to the east. There is only one light, at the tip, demarcating it from the sea.

It begins to rain, warm against my skin. I put the map away, folding it between the pages of my last notebook. When I look up, the promontory light is still there, fixed. I go on towards it, following the coast road out onto the headland.

茶

The Palace, 1838. The forecourt sand frozen to ice; the waiting room still stained with soot. Along the servants' passages, the echo of unanswered bells. Stairs broad as cathedral steps. A hall of mirrors and nine clocks. A salon at the end of it busier than Ludgate Hill at noon.

Daniel and Salman standing by the door where the maids left them. A stranger would not have recognised them as brothers. One stood with his head cocked, his back stooped like a servant, or a man uneasy with his own height. The other waited with his hands folded behind his back.

Worker's hands. Salman knew it. Next time I am here, he thought, I shall wear gloves, like a gentleman. He watched the room, the crush of sexes at tables of waisted decanters, brandied cakes and crystallised fruit, and thought of his hands. The right was stronger than the left. The backs of both were marked with burns, like liver spots, as if jewels had aged them. Eight months ago, a spilt crucible of silver had caught his left wrist. *Now you are hallmarked, sir!* George had shouted across at him.

Hallmarked. Salman watched the ladies, the sleekness of their ringleted hair, and wondered what their marks would be. Where they had come from, and how far, to reach lives of pleasure. Un-called-for, Jane's voice echoed back to him. *You are a jeweller, you should know pleasure.*

And I will, he thought. I am almost there now. Crossing the palace threshold, he had felt the thrill of money like a tug of static. An undercurrent of raw financial power. He held his hands tighter. 'Why do we wait?'

'Because we are nothing here. Be calm.'

'Look at them.' Salman's lips hardly moved as he spoke. A ventriloquist hiss. 'Livestock at a trough.'

'I thought this was what you wanted.'

'It is what we are entitled to. Whether these deserve it is another matter entirely.'

A bout of men's laughter drowned him out. At three o'clock, the air was already inked with the sepia of cigars. A man in foreign-tailored clothes stepped towards them through the haze.

'Baron Stockmar.' He straightened, neat as a cocked gun. The man at the marble table, Daniel remembered. He was so thin, it made Daniel cold to look at him. Beside him, his brother bowed from the waist.

'Salman and Daniel Levy–'

'Goldsmiths to the Crown, yes.' He looked at them as if he found it hard to believe. 'Yes. Will you have a drink? Something warming. This way. This way.'

The chandeliers were lit. Outside, Salman saw, it was already dusk. A pipe had burst, and spars of yellowed ice hung down beyond the windows. Stockmar paused at a dumb waiter to pour them brandies. Salman watched his brother drink too quickly, tasting nothing himself, only feeling the burn as they began to walk again. Conversations reached him through the crowd in mislaid fragments.

' . . . A hundred days of ice . . .'

'And the northern poor, you say, believe the Queen poisons their bread?'

'Disraeli! So articulate that he articulates nothing. I was . . .'

'Elle a peut-être du sang bleu mais elle pisse jaune . . .'

A door set flush into mirrors. A servants' hallway without natural light. The Baron stopped at a bare wall, produced a key, and led them through.

The noise of the court was shut out behind them. They had come into a sitting room, poorly lit, stagnant with the smell of locked windows. Salman let his eyes adjust. In the window seat an old woman slept, a book slumped open on her knees. Victoria Guelph sat straight-backed in an embroidered chair, a silk glove on her left hand, rings on her right. On the sofa opposite her a man was talking, a tray of limestones in his lap. As Salman watched he smiled and raised one to the Queen. Delicately, as if it were a cupcake.

'Your Majesty?' Baron Stockmar bowed. She looked tired, thought Salman. Owl-eyed as a child kept without sleep. It seemed curious to him that a queen should be so human.

'Mister Chambers. Your pardon. The Queen has further visitors.'

The man with the limestones glanced up at Stockmar, taking him in, still talking in a deadly monotone. 'Extinction is all, Your Highness. Extinction makes a necropolis of the earth. These impressions of lost creatures are the proofs and epitaphs of a scientific truth. Christians, Mohammedans or Hindoos, we stand on the bones of more lost species than will ever walk the earth again–'

Stockmar took a step forward. 'The brothers Levy, Your Majesty. Goldsmiths to the Crown.' The Queen blinked wanly at him. 'The Semitic jewellers, Majesty.'

'Oh?' A light crept into her eyes. 'Oh–' She stood up quickly. Flurried, brushing her skirts out. 'We had forgot all about it. We have waited so long. Please, will you sit? Mister Chambers, I am sorry. It was so kind of you to explain about the necropolis . . .'

With the expression of a man who knows he has lost, Mr Chambers stood and bowed out as the brothers took his place. When Salman looked up Victoria was smiling at him. 'Now. You must tell us your story. Stockmar says you are from Babylon.'

'Baghdad.' He sat still, observing her plush and glitter. The way it made her seem both smaller and unreal, a five-foot doll in champagne satin. A lapdog under the chair, a rim of teeth smiling up at him. 'A more recent city, Your Majesty.'

'And you were given a jar. With jewels in it. And you came here to work for us.'

His life reduced to sentences in a foreign tongue. Salman nodded.

'Such a wonderful story. Where is the jar now?'

'Broken, Your Majesty. Left behind.'

She turned to Daniel. 'And how do you like London?'

'We—' Daniel coughed at the sound of his own voice. 'Well, Your Majesty.'

'Indeed.' Close up, her eyes were protuberant. Her mouth twisted, almost hare-lipped. While his brother spoke, Salman looked at her rings. Assessing their quality, as if that too were part of her; and it was. 'You do not note the extreme weight and thickness of the atmosphere?'

'No, Your Majesty.'

'Recently we have found we prefer the countryside. Do you know Scotland?'

Daniel shook his head, wretched. 'No, Your Majesty.'

'Oh.' Abruptly she turned back to Salman. 'You admire our rings. What is your professional opinion of them?'

He smiled. Given his own ground, and ready for it. He narrowed his eyes to the rings and paused, making her wait, making them all wait for him until he sat back, a doctor giving diagnosis, tasting old opium on his breath.

'They are in excellent taste, naturally. This and this —' he pointed, not touching '– are European. Made this century, and most likely in France. The diamond was recently removed and recut in London, to the English fashion. It is –' he breathed in, close to the jewel '– Brazilian, though the structure is almost as fine as an Indian stone. Mined in the highlands, perhaps at Tejuco. Here now, in the pearl ring, the gold is of a purer carat. It is either Saracenic or Oriental. I believe it is from India, and an heirloom of Your Majesty's grandmother. The brilliant is well balanced. Most of the pearls are passable.'

'And the emerald?'

Salman held out his right hand. As if she had been prompted by a tutor, Victoria began to take off the rings, tugging them over her thick knuckles. She dropped the emerald band into Salman's palm and looked up as he stood. Holding the jewel to the chandeliers, turning it under his lapidary eyes. Left bare, her fingers closed into a fist.

'With respect, Your Majesty, this is not an emerald. You will note the dullness of the colour and the absence of flaws. All

335

emeralds have imperfections, called gardens, which enhance their beauty.' He returned the ring and sat. 'That stone is olivine. A superior specimen of an inferior gem.'

She leant forward avidly. 'What is your favourite stone? Mine is rubies.'

'In India, the ruby is known as the Lord of Stones.'

She paused, her mouth gaped open. As if, he thought, I have performed magic. Read minds. In the lapse he could hear the older woman sleeping. His brother shifting, insignificant beside him. From outside, distant, the echo of clearance work from the waste grounds of Parliament.

'Stocky? Be very kind, will you, and wake Lehzen. We wish her to fetch the new jewel.'

Her mouth had shut tight. It changed her face, thought Salman, bringing out something else in her. More of a hardness, less vacancy. He felt the Baron step closer behind the sofa. 'Majesty?'

'The ruby brooch.'

'Yes. If Her Majesty would consider some less important jewel.'

'Indeed not. We wish to show the brooch.' Her eyes swivelled up and settled on Stockmar.

'I find the idea ill-advised—'

'Enough. We wish it. Lehzen?'

'Eh.' There was a thump. Salman looked up in time to see the woman haul herself out of the window seat, winded by sleep, her book fallen to the floor. Hooper's new tragedy, he saw. 'Your Highness?'

'Lazy Lehzen, you are always asleep. The ruby brooch. Bring it quickly please.'

'As fast as I am able, Your Highness.' Her voice was accented like Stockmar's. She slowed as she crossed the room, peering back at the visitors, reaching to adjust a forgotten pair of spectacles.

'If our story interests Your Majesty,' said Salman, bowing forward, 'there is more to it.'

'Oh?' Her eyes left Stockmar reluctantly, her cheeks flushed. Salman saw that her anger receded more slowly than it had begun. He talked smoothly, treading with care. His hands opening together, like pages.

'In Baghdad I was trained by an Arabian lapidary, a man

336

who worked in the city's old bazaar. It was through this Arabian that I was given the jar of jewels. Thus when we came to London, my brother and I were already trained in the business of jewellery. Our work here was not at first with Rundell and Bridge's. We owned a small jewellers on the new Commercial Road, where my brother was shopman and I the smith. You see, Your Majesty, we were goldsmiths in our own right. We intend to be so again.'

There was a sound from the servants' door. More visitors, thought Salman. My time is almost out. His brother shifted on the sofa beside him. Daniel in the limelight, already dying to be out of it.

'In which gems did you do business?'

'Cairngorms, amethysts, topaz.' He held the names out to her like confections. Her lips, he saw, were wet. He felt the proximity of success. A champagne sensation of elation, his chest filling with its ribbons of bubbles. 'Jewels tailored to our customers, who were poor people, as we were also. Our best cargoes of stones were brought in by the East India docks, just as we had arrived ourselves . . .'

'Yes.' She was watching him, fascinated. Salman could hear her breathing. 'You are good men. Good men. We know how to appreciate real worth.'

'You are most kind–' A movement at the door interrupted him. The woman, Lehzen, had come back already. She was breathless, a case in her pale hands. Salman leant forward, trying to hold the Queen's attention. Meeting her eyes, but already she was turning away. He smiled, all teeth.

'Lehzen?'

'Yes, Majesty, I have it.' In two hands, Lehzen held a box that could have been carried in one. It was triangular, each panel filled with cloisonné. A fashionably medieval style, Salman observed without caring. Knots of flowers. Iris, convolvulus, narcissus.

'Really most kind, Your Majesty. If we might inform you when we have our own premises. It would be an honour for us to present Your Majesty with our first–'

He broke off. The Queen was opening the box. Smiling into it, as if there was something inside which could understand expression. Extracting a weight of stones and gold. She was

337

speaking again as she put it on. Salman found he could no longer follow her voice.

The air sang in his ears. He bent towards the jewel. It was a massive arrangement. A triangle of rubies, but also of pearls. A double geometry. The organic jewels were fastened with gold spines and bows, hooklets and wires. The balas rubies were held in by claws. At their centre was a clear stone. Cut in the shape of a pyramid.

'Is it not beautiful?' She was smiling at him. Eighteen years old, alive with it. 'We knew you would appreciate it. Bridge says the diamond alone is thirty carats.'

'The diamond.'

'The finest water he has ever seen. The Heart of Three Brethren. Mister Bridge says it is very old. Is something wrong?'

He felt his mind knocked sideways, tried to stand, and staggered back. Too quickly, the room began to fill with rising figures. His brother's voice called out to him. The Queen's face swam up, her mouth an 'O'.

He muttered something, a rejection. The beat of his heart was too fast. His body was suddenly an excess, a hulk of muscle. Not making said what he meant to say. He tried to bow.

'My stone. Please.'

'*Yours?*'

'Majesty, if you will just give me my stone . . .'

Daniel's hand on his shoulder. The women's voices calling out. The sound of running footmen. Not coming to help him, he knew. Not there to roll out the bloody red carpet. Something seemed to burst in his head, filling his eyes with its shadow, and he sank back into a chair. When he looked up, there was nothing to see but the jewel from the jar.

It seemed lifeless. The facets had no brilliance. Even in the primitive mathematics of the setting, they were too simple. The pearls had more lustre, the rubies were brighter. Better, he thought; I could have done better. They should have let me cheat myself.

Victoria Guelph stepped back from him, a small figure becoming smaller. From a distance he watched her raise her hand to the jewel – as if, he thought, she feels herself naked. As her fingers tried to cover it, the diamond caught the light.

It glared out at him. He blinked, dazed. The image stayed

imprinted on his lids, dancing there. It was how he would always remember the jewel. Even after the world itself became frightening, impossible in its thinness, Salman would recall the way the Heart of Three Brothers had opened to him. In the house of Judah the Rabbi this was what he whispered, a knowledge to drown out the sound of Daniel's mourning. That the diamond had come alive. He had seen it. He had seen it. It had looked at him, cold, human with age. An eye opening in a dead head.

'A fit. Nothing more.'

'A fit? A disgrace is what it was. We can have no more of it. Five footmen. Five, damn it, to hold him down.'

'No.' Daniel shook his head wearily. 'No one held him. It was not necessary.'

George Fox lunged towards him, hissing. 'And that is not the point, Daniel. Five servants is the point. Five mouths to shut up before they reach Fleet Street. Do you know what this has cost Mister Rundell?'

It was noon. A fire was still lit in the narrow grate. Daniel sat in front of the office desk, Edmund behind it, white hands dovetailed under his chin. George did the talking, as he paced. 'An expensive day's work you had, on behalf of our reputation.'

'My brother says the diamond is ours.'

George waved him away. Daniel tried again. 'This is what he believes. He knows his jewels.' He turned, speaking to Rundell now. 'Perhaps, sir, if you showed him the spinel. The stone that we sold to you, surely that would set his mind—'

'Now.' George was in front of him again, pointing. 'Have a care, Daniel. This is no time for accusations. Not from you.'

The fire buckled and muttered in the grate. Daniel turned towards it. There were no windows in Edmund's office, he saw, and wondered how he had not been aware of it before. A miser's room, the safe made safer. Today the absence of light felt like a withdrawal to him. He thought of the stone. The jewel from the jar or from the palace, Daniel wasn't sure which. Light in the ridges of its script. *To keep one from ghosts.*

He shook his head. 'I'm sorry, George. Truly.'

'Well.' The shopman sat down. 'Well then, so am I. When will he be fit to work again?'

Daniel raised his head. 'You'll have him back?'

Fox scowled. 'He knows the crown. It'd be no small job to find another who could take his place, so late in the day.'

Rundell raised his hooked face. 'Has he slept?'

'Little. Last night he walked.'

'Walking at night, in this winter. There is something loose in him—'

Edmund waved them both quiet. He blinked across the desk at Daniel. It seemed to him that there was something reptilian in the old jeweller. A dry appetite, slow with torpor.

'Tell your brother —' he picked up a worn quill, dipped it, began to write '— that today is his, but tomorrow he works or goes. If the latter, he breaks his contract. In that case, any moneys owed by us may be forfeit. There is a crown to be made, and your brother will make it. If not, we may be justified in paying nothing, or only some part, of any debt owed for the three – minor – jewels which I have bought from you and your brother.'

He stopped writing, reached for the sand, and let it skitter across the page. 'Tomorrow I will know exactly how the ground lies, when my lawyer replies to this inquiry. In the meantime, I hope I make myself clear. Good afternoon to you, Mister Levy. You know your own way out.'

At the news-stands on Fleet Street the afternoon papers had just been delivered. Daniel bought the *Sun* and the *True Sun*, tucking their slight warmth under his arm. Thinking of Rundell, as if he was still with him.

The Crown Goldsmith had cheated him. He tried to believe it, tasting it for truth. He felt nothing at the idea except anger and a certain curiosity, nothing in comparison to the nausea of loss he had seen in Salman: the flood of panic, as if he couldn't live without the stone he had already sold. Daniel tried to imagine what there could be left for a man like Rundell to want. But then no one had such an appetite for stones. He had heard George say that. Mr Fox, talking about what he knew best. *Want loves want. Why should you be any different?*

The air was bad, the smog worsened by winter fires. Half the shops were shut, as if they had decided winter had become too cold for commerce. On Stonecutter Street Daniel bought apples and yesterday's bread, sharp cheese and a bottle of sweet wine, hugging the foods inside his coat as he trudged through the mucky snow. Uphill there was light in the window of James Ryder's, and he pushed inside and waited while the apothecary made up Salman's opium, his druggist's cough loud and fumy between the shelves of bottles. Tinctures of saffron and digitalis, wines of aloes and iron, ointments of tar and black pitch. For nausea, for febrile disease, for the relief of nervous dreams. Daniel paid and took what he had up the backstairs to the attic room.

'I hope your walking has made you hungry—'

Out of breath, he opened the door and froze. A figure stood silhouetted against the window. Its bulk blocked out most of the light. In the dimness Daniel said its name, but softly. Hardly meaning to say it at all. *Tigris.*

Salman turned. As he did so Daniel saw that his eyes were gone, his mouth slack. In profile his face was scoured out, so empty it seemed like a violence in itself. Then it had turned on into shadow. Daniel felt a fear rise in him, physical as vomit, and he sat down on the bedclothes, clumsily unbuttoning his coat to the goods inside. Swallowing, opening the newspapers he had no interest in reading.

'For what it's worth, you have not made the papers.'

There was no answer. Daniel took out his spectacles, put them on with his cold hands, and began to read aloud. Salman's stillness at the periphery of his vision.

'The *Sun* goes on with the fire at the Royal Exchange. The engines were so cold, it was necessary to thaw them before water could be thrown on the burning building. Other excuses etcetera. And in the *True Sun*, let's see, we have Spring Heel'd Jack.' He made himself laugh, not looking up from the columns. Not thinking of the moment he had not recognised his own brother. 'Who is a monster, it seems. "Spring Heel'd Jack's reign of terror has been brought to the attention of the Lord Mayor of London." Blah blah. "Having appeared at Barnes as a white bull, at Finsbury as a dragon breathing flame." Blah blah. "At Kensington Palace as a white baboon, climbing over the Queen's forcing houses."'

'Where is the dragon?'

Daniel looked up. His brother had stepped up to the bed soundlessly. His eyes were glassy but his voice seemed sensible. As if, thought Daniel, what I am reading means anything at all. He put the newspaper down. 'At Finsbury. Salman. How do you feel?'

He frowned, as if searching for an answer, then yawned suddenly, hugely, and sat down. 'Well. Better than I have felt in months. What food did you bring? Bread?'

Daniel watched him begin to sort through the paper packages, tearing them open. 'Aye. Your tincture also.'

Salman nodded. 'I won't be needing it. Ah. And cheese.' He took the loaf and broke it in half, shepherding crumbs onto the shop paper.

'You feel well, truly? How long did you sleep?'

'A hundred years. Truly I feel well.' From his coat he took out a tarnished iron penknife, hinged it open, and began to cut cheese. 'I walked to the docks last night. And back. The ships were frozen at anchor.'

'I have talked to George and Mister Rundell,' Daniel went on cautiously. 'They say the diamond is not ours.'

'They lie.' Salman glanced up at Daniel, smiled, and went back to the apples.

'They say you must finish the crown. Else our contracts are broken and any money they owe is forfeit.'

'A bluff. They lie and lie.'

'Then you will not stay?'

'No.' His voice was mild. In his palm, the apple hissed open to a sweet whiteness. 'I would not leave now for the world.'

He smiled up at Daniel again, waiting for him to smile back. They sat together in their coats and ate.

> J was a Judas Kiss,
> Which sold the Lord for pelf.
> He sneaked away from Jesus Christ,
> And then he hanged himself.
>
> K was the good King's Crown;
> He wore it on his head—

She broke off, coughing, the small lungs hacking themselves empty. Daniel leant towards her, but already she was finished, worn out. She sat back on the pew. The sound of her carried on, out from the transept to the nave, the whisperings of the dome, the grey spaces of St Paul's.

'You must not catch cold, Martha, even for the sake of reading.'

She shrugged. Her face white. 'Warmer here than out. Better with the candles. Was I good, sir?'

'Better every week.'

'I like it here. Learning.'

He smiled at and past her. In the nave, worshippers were putting on coats between the crowds of statuary. 'Churches are beautiful things, Martha,' he said softly. 'But only with people in them. Without us they are nothing but stone.'

'I never came here, before.' She began to cough again, held it back.

'You mean with your family.'

He watched her scowl. Reluctant, always, to speak of her own. They had been Catholics, Daniel supposed; their places of worship elsewhere, like his. He lowered his voice. 'Are they still alive? Could they take you back?'

'I don't need their taking or giving.'

He wondered if he should ask more. If that was the way to help her best. There was a tray of candles beyond Martha. The light flickered in her eyes, against her sallow cheeks. By her hand it winked off something metallic, and Daniel leaned forward. 'What have you there?'

She made to hide it instinctively, then stopped. On the wrist was a charm bracelet worked out of flat tin. A frog, a crab, a dragonfly. 'Jewellery. You are getting airs and graces. You bought this?' he said, already knowing.

'The little Mister Levy.' Her eyes were smiling now, if not her mouth. 'Did he not tell you? For Christmas.' She lowered her arm, suddenly sober. 'I heared about him.'

'What did you hear?'

She muttered. 'Heared he tried to kill the Queen.'

Daniel breathed out. 'That isn't true, Martha.'

A group of workmen went by, talking in a soft foreign tongue. Martha waited, her face full of anxiety. 'Then what?'

He took a deeper breath. 'There is a jewel the Queen has. My brother believes that it belongs to us.'

'Does it so?'

'I don't know.'

343

'What kind of a jewel is it?'

'A diamond. In a brooch shaped liked a triangle.' Absently, he traced it out on the pew between them. 'Rubies, and pearls, the diamond here. It is very beautiful.'

When his hand stopped moving she looked up. 'What will you do?'

'We have no proof. I think no one would believe us.' He shrugged and smiled. 'Who would you believe, Martha, the Queen or Mister Levy?'

She looked at him. Surprised, as if she was not used to him saying anything so obvious. 'Mister Levy.'

'Bless you. Now, where are we up to in this nonsense of an alphabet?'

It was a hard winter, the worst for years. When Salman dreamed of it, everything began as it was. He would find himself walking on the Commercial Road. It was nearly morning. He could feel the cold against his face.

The jewel was gone. He arrived knowing this, and also knowing that he dreamed. There was a tightness in his chest, a sensation of vertigo. It was the feeling that came to him in opium trances, and as he walked Salman knew he no longer needed the tincture. It was inside him now, implicit, under his skin.

He could make out terraces of houses. Honduras and Hardwick Place. Road trees grew above them now. When Salman looked up it was as if he had never seen trees before. Their forms were drawn out by want. Extended between water and light. They were alive, he saw, with immense and cold properties. *Like the diamond*, he thought, and thinking of it he opened his hand and found it had come back to him.

There was something wrong with the jewel. Two fractures ran across one another through the pyramid. He touched the point, wanting to make it right, and the stone fell open. Inside it was hollow. He stepped back, dropping it quickly like an insect or scorpion.

And when he looked up everything had changed. The air had thickened, tinctured with fog. There were noises under the trees. He began to walk, not looking back. He thought of Mehmet and his blood crimes. The jar, full of the smell of rot. The diamond which was not a diamond, but something waiting to be hatched.

There was a click of claws on the stone pavement. He cried out and began to run. Behind him, under the trees, the sirrusch came on its ruined feet. He cried out again, yammering, and in the attic room Daniel held him, cradling his head. He listened to Salman's voice, trying to hear what his mind was saying. The jewel haunting his nightmares, taking from him more than he had ever gained from it.

⚶

There is a boat out to sea. From the foot of the headland I hear it: the mutter of an outboard motor, coming over the waves without light. The sound keeps pace with me for a while as I walk, until the sea wall gives way to rocks, the rocks to beach, the road underfoot becoming a concrete causeway in a landscape of scrub and dunes. When I hear the boat again it is far away, the lamps of squid fishermen visible back beyond Tosa.

At its end the promontory rises, the road running out to a patch of levelled ground with the sea on two sides. I can make out a quay, two boats moored, a vending stand shut up for the night. There is no house to be seen. An hour too late, I wonder whether the illumination I saw from Tosa was a ship after all, or a car of lovers out to watch the ocean. Then a light winks through the inland dunes. I move my head back to it and start to walk again. Following its navigation point between hollows and outcrops of sea thistles.

The wind is behind me. It rises as I crest the last dunes. In the lee it falls away again, so that as I come down towards the house I hear its people. Somewhere children are playing. In the dark almost nothing is left of them but the sand's scuffle, a yell of laughter, the panting of an animal. Another ten yards and I can see them over the measured darkness of an allotment. Two children, one dog, shadow-dancing.

It is a clapboard house, the windows shuttered. A clearing out front, a clinker-built dinghy upturned under the shade of a ginkgo tree. At the near edge of the worked ground a man is digging. I see him before he hears me. A lamp on the porch illuminates his face as he works. It is like something from a painting, a

Dutch oil. The fierce expression, its muscles and bones, thrown up into relief. Halfway down the path he sees or hears me and he straightens, his face turning into the dark. It is unreadable by the time I raise my hand.

'*Sumimasen*,' I say – Sorry, excuse me, sorry. '*Sumimasen*.' An Englishwoman pushing through crowds. The man stands with his arms at his sides. Not waving me off, not doing anything, in fact, while I struggle to string together a sentence he might understand. '*Murasaki-san desu ka? Murasaki-san no otaku desu ka?*'

I can see him breathing. The spade is still in his hand. The blade shines clean from the sandy soil. There is sweat along his temples. He is wearing a blue short-sleeved shirt and trousers, and a Japanese labourer's cloven shoes. The wind drops between us. In the quiet there is a yell of laughter across the dunes. Somewhere, the chug of a generator. As if the house itself is out to sea.

I try again, my voice too loud and alien. '*Murasaki-san no otaku–*'

He sniffs back sweat and walks away, out of the radius of the light. By the corner of the house he squats down. His head dips, hands catching up water from a standpipe. Once he looks round at me, and I catch the whites of his eyes. He strips off his shirt and begins to wipe down his chest and hands.

I watch him, half-concealed in the dark. When he stands he is taller than me, well over six foot and built like a wrestler, more muscle than sinew. There are curls in his chest hair, hard with salt, although his head is shaven. Even his face is something less simple than Japanese, the nose aquiline between Mongol cheekbones and epicanthal eyes. Features to cut winds on.

'Where are you from?'

The voice comes out of the dark, reading my mind. I begin to look round, and catch myself. The man's English is startling. The words are stilted but not broken. The intrinsic grammar forms without effort. 'London,' I say, and he walks back to me. His sweat is sweet and peppery. The shirt is bunched in one hand. The spade is gone and I'm glad of it.

He frowns. 'No. What company?'

'I don't work for any company.'

'You have no business here.'

'I was looking for Hikari Murasaki.'

'Who?'

346

'Is he here?'

He stands stooped, head cocked. As if listening for something other than a question answering a question.

'I've come a long way to find him.'

'Everywhere is a long way, from here.' He puts the worn shirt back on. An uncomfortable gesture. His eyes don't show it. 'Our name is Mura. This is my house. We have lived here for a long time.' He looks past me towards the voices of the children, as if glancing at a clock. 'Eight years. I don't know any Murasaki.'

'Are you a fisherman?'

He shrugs. 'Sometimes.'

'Your English is very good, for a fisherman.'

His eyes flicker. 'I am *sansei*,' he says, quietly, reluctantly. 'Third-generation immigrant. I learned English from my family.'

I'm sorry, I almost say, and don't. He expects it in every sense. 'Do you know who lived here before you?'

'A man.'

'What was his name?'

He shrugs again. 'It was a long time ago.' He scratches the stubble at his hairline, then nods. 'Maybe Murasaki. I can't say.'

He is lying, I think. Of course he is, I need him to be lying. But even as I think it, the sense of failure is beginning to rise. It is quicker these days, its channels running deeper. As if a part of me has been worn away.

'I'm sorry.' He gestures towards the porch. Beyond the lamp, the interior is unlit. 'We will be eating soon. You must be tired.'

'I–' I look back towards the dunes. Faintly, I can smell pine trees. The sea has carried their scent, out from the coast on the low tide. It is a long way back there. I have come as far as I can go.

'Where is your car?'

'I walked.'

He clicks on a light. We go inside. 'The forecast is for rain. Sometimes the road floods. You should not stay too long. Your shoes. Please, sit by the fire. Are you staying in Kôchi?'

'No.' I am too tired to lie. The miles south and east are beginning to catch up with me. The room is big, well lit by the kitchen and hearth, fading to shadows by the staircase and shelves. There are the smells of tatami matting and sea tar. A house lizard zigzags up into the roofbeams.

347

'There are guest rooms in Tosa. We will eat first, then I will take you back.' At the door Mura leans out, calling two names. *Tom. Iren.* When he is satisfied with what he sees he goes to wash his hands with soap at the kitchen counter. Pots and spoons hang around his head. Beside the counter are a refrigerator, canister gas stove and rice steamer. The white goods so battered they might have been salvaged from a shipwreck.

It feels as if I have walked to the end of the world. I watch the man in silence. His age is indeterminate, anywhere between forty and sixty. Certainly the sea has aged him. The lines of his mouth are not unkind. He lifts the lid on the steamer. Opens the fridge, brings out raw fish, burdock and lotus root. Picks up a knife. A radio sits on the counter beside him, a long-wave signal turned down low.

'You can call me Saisei.'

'Katharine.'

He nods a formal hello. Two children come in hand in hand. The boy eight or nine, the girl half that. They have their father's eyes and their hair, too, is not quite black. A foreign lightness. They stop dead at the sight of me.

'This is Katharine,' says the man. 'She is eating with us tonight.' And then, as if they need a motive, 'She speaks English.'

Keeping a distance, like his father, the boy heels off his shoes. But the girl is already moving, up onto the matting. There are butterfly barrettes in her hair. One is loose. Her eyes shift. As if they are trying to see behind mine.

'Her name is Iren,' says the boy. Sizing me up. 'She's only five. She doesn't speak so much English. She understands it as well as you do. Are you from New York?'

'England.'

He glowers at me. 'I don't know that.'

'It's a country. Where English comes from.'

'Do you have zebra in England?'

'Only the kind without stripes.'

He stops glowering to consider the possibility of stripeless zebra. The girl puts her hand up to my face. Her father glances up from the cooking. 'Tom, take Iren upstairs. You need to wash before we eat.'

Iren looks round with narrowed eyes, whining. Her brother

takes her hand again and leads her away. The man nods at me from the chopping board. 'Do you find people professionally?'

'No.'

He turns off the radio. 'What is it that you do?'

'I'm in the stone trade.'

'What kind of stones?'

'It doesn't matter.' I can hear the children upstairs. The sound of water and laughter. Their presence, the joy of it, runs out of me as quickly as it gathered. I look down at the fire. The ash is just warm. 'I'm sorry.'

'No. But I'm interested, since you are here.'

I look up. Too many questions, I think. Somehow, they have become one too many. I examine the man's face again. The fisherman who is third-generation Japanese. I wonder if Pavlov ever checked boat licences.

'I buy and sell. Precious stones, gems, jewels. Diamonds and rubies and pearls. There is not much more than that to tell.'

'It sounds very interesting.'

'It's just a job.'

He is cutting tuna, combing the skin out from under the flesh. 'It is always hard, working alone.'

'I never said I worked alone.' The room realigns itself around me. Its atmosphere changes. I see that, perhaps, I have been shepherded inside. The children have been herded away. The man with the knife is between me and the door. That perhaps it has been the gentlest of interrogations.

'But you don't work for a company.'

'No.'

'Why do you come here, looking for stones?'

I answer him with questions. 'The man who lived here. Do you remember anything about him?'

Without looking up he shakes his head. 'I'm sorry.' Iren comes carefully down the stairs. Tom behind her.

'Where did your family come from? Can I ask?'

He grunts. 'They were traders. They lived in many different countries, many years ago.' He turns on the tap. Runs hot water over the knife. 'But now it is time to eat.'

The table is barely higher than the tatami mats, space recessed beneath it. I sit uncomfortably while the man serves miso soup, vegetables stewed in soy, bowls of rice topped with sashimi. The fish is so fresh it tastes of nothing. Only sweetness, like iced fruit.

'This is good,' I say, and realise I mean it. The man nods. Iren is learning how to use chopsticks. Her father teaches her, his fingers opening and closing in slow crab-motions. Her hand is all thumbs. Tom jibes at her in Japanese. She looks at him mournfully.

'Have you heard of a man called Enzo Mushanokoji?'

'No. Why?' He is still teaching. Iren's hand copies his, the chopsticks desperately waving. Clumsy as an upturned insect. A finger-bug. I keep myself asking questions.

'Mankin-Mitsubishi?'

'No.'

'I am looking for a jewel called the Three Brethren.'

He pauses. I see him do it, the small fact of it, before he shakes his head and begins to eat.

'You asked about the stones I work with. I'm telling you. The Three Brethren is a knot of gold and jewels, made to hold a cloak at the shoulder. It is very early fifteenth century. For hundreds of years people have believed it has been lost for good. I'm going to find it again.'

'That is all you do? You have an easy life.' The man is watching me as he eats. 'Iren,' he says, without looking away. 'Please don't play with your food.'

Her face crumples up with misery. I talk over her head. 'A century ago there was a company on Shikoku called Mankin-Mitsubishi. A worker called Enzo Mushanokoji bought the Three Brethren for this company. The owner of Mankin-Mitsubishi was a Mr Lewis. A Mari Lewis died in Tosa in 1987. Her son was Hikari Murasaki. He lived in this house. I've spent five years trying to find this jewel. Please. If there is anything you remember–'

'I am sorry. I said I can't help you. Iren, please.'

The girl smiles up at me. Craftily, as if she has done something a little wrong but pardonably clever. 'But you must remember–'

'Iren.'

Out of nothing his voice is sharp as his face. I look between him and the child. Her features are wiped clean with surprise. The chopsticks still droop in her fingers. Her bowl is an edible sculpture. The man reaches across me. For a moment it isn't clear whether he means to grab the bowl or the child. I look back at them and see what he sees.

It is an illusion. The duck which becomes a rabbit, the black chalice which is also two white faces. In the centre of Iren's bowl, three pieces of tuna have been drawn together in a triangle. The girl begins to cry in deep sobs. A child who understands English, playing with her food. Between the red slabs, rice has been kneaded up to a point.

'Please,' says the man, and shakes his head, bewildered. He mutters to Tom in Japanese. The boy stands up uneasily, reaching out for his sister.

'You lied to me,' I say, as if I feel betrayed. Instead it feels as if I should apologise. It is as if I have broken the family china. Something precious. I don't know what to do any more than the man across the table, or the children between us. As I watch, his hand picks up the chopsticks and tightens into a fist.

All this way, I think, to be alone at the end of the world. I try to stand. My foot catches under the table. Quite slowly, I fall backwards onto the matting. The boy watches me with his mouth open. Iren gapes, shocked into quiet. The man whispers to them again, rising easily as he does so. Before I am on my knees he is at the kitchen counter.

'Sit down. You are not leaving yet. Tell me who you work for.' When I look up he has the sushi knife in one hand. It is a large blade, black oxidised metal, an edge tempered in waves. I walk straight past him into the shut door. My head knocking to get out. He steps round the counter. 'I said wait, Katharine. I need to know who it is you work for–'

I get the door open and start to run. Crickets chirrup in the marram grass. Creatures with traps instead of legs. The man calls out after me. The night air is warm against my face. There is a smell in it which might be rain. At the top of the dunes the sand collapses under my weight, and I climb over and crawl down between the sea thistles. When the man calls out again it is neither of the children's names, nor mine.

I try to remember how far it is from the house to the coast road. To gauge how fast the man can run. I wonder if I could hide, and for how long, and if anyone would find me but him. In the distance I hear him swear and shout out the same name again. *Lyu.*

The beach looms up, lines of waves white in the dark. The sand is compact at the water's edge. I turn inland, settling into a barefoot rhythm. Over my own noise and the crash and hiss of surf I listen for the man's steps, but there is nothing. The waves are high, spume blown from their tips. The Ferris wheel still turns above Tosa. It looks so close that if I called out, now, the wind might carry my voice to its top.

There is a dull pattering behind me. It is some time before I realise it is getting any nearer. It is less like the sound of feet than rain. For a moment I wonder if it is the boy, Tom, and I look over my shoulder.

A dog is pacing me along the beach. It is the size of a Dobermann but much heavier. Barrel-chested, with the head and jaws of a fighting animal. A Tosa, I think. The Kôchi figurines made flesh. Its black and tan coat is grey in the moonlight. It makes little sound as it closes the distance between us.

I turn back to face the coast and run harder. The dog is no longer getting closer. Its breath shudders under its own weight. I begin to feel a little sorry for it. Only a little. It is almost companionable, the chase. A woman and one man's best friend. The Tosa is not built for speed, after all. Running is secondary to what it is designed for.

'Help!' I call out, faintly comical with exertion. I might as well be on the dark side of the moon. Bladderwrack coils around my feet. For a second I lose my rhythm, its alignment of breathing, heartbeat, footfall. When I find it again, the air hurts. I keep going, but now I can feel the weight of my clothes, the wind tugging them. The dog is still coming. Not closing the gap between us, but seeming to wait in motion, as if it knows it only has to be patient.

The coast is far away, distant as a fiction. For the first time, I allow myself to realise I am never going to reach it. I wonder if I will die here. I wish it was the man behind me after all, then I could ask what happens next. A last request. It seems to me that I should at least be allowed to ask.

The sea crashes beside me. I look at it as I run. Where the water hits the beach it draws back hard, hissing. Undertow strips the sand away to steep black shingle. It looks stronger than me, more cunning and more vicious. Pulling the ground from under it.

I struggle with my jacket, the wind helping me get rid of it. It is harder to make myself slow down. I close my eyes to do it, bent over, taking deep, ragged breaths. There is time for three, then another. To half-turn, before the animal reaches me.

It barrels into my side, too out of breath itself to leap. I reach for it, find a collar, and fall backwards. The movement lifts us both down over the incline towards the waves. We hit the ground rolling. The head snaps at me, all froth and foam. It has time to gasp once, staring upwards with the whites of its eyes, before the undertow takes us both.

The world changes. Phosphorescence blooms around us. It is a halo of violence, a sheen of light around our limbs. The sea drags us down and out. The storm of breakers fades away southwards, until there is no sound but the submarine tick and skitter of sand. The undertow's propulsion begins to fade. My ears pop with pressure. The animal is still in my arms. It thrashes, muscular as a shark, forcing itself upwards, and I press against its ribs. A heart massage. Life to life. Hugging the last air out of it.

And then it is also changed. The sense of it is too smooth. The scales slip through my cold hands. The neck turns, serpentine. It gores at me with its spurred feet. A head snakes round to face mine and the eyes are old. Old as stones. Teeth grin for me in the salt dark.

I hold it away. It begins to spasm. Only when it stops moving do I let it go. It drifts upwards with its own valency and I follow it. The surface current is with me. I turn onto my back and scull south, a pale human star. Not looking at how far I have to swim. Keeping the moon westwards.

It takes immeasurable time. The sea is quiet. There is blood in my clothes. It warms my skin and I'm glad of it. The sea washes into my cold mouth and I cough out the taste of salt and iron. The breakers begin to pick me up and where they leave me I dig in my hands, anchored to the shore.

The tide is going out. For a while I sleep. Later the rain wakes me, warm, falling into my eyes. I open them and the man is there. He leans above me. His hands are empty. I cry out and re-member nothing else.

茶

Jenny bright as the day,
And buxom as May,
I happened to kiss; when she angry did say,
'What liberties, Sir! Why these freedoms I pray?'

George Fox, drink on his breath, singing to the pedal of the wheel. It was June. Two weeks until Coronation Day.

Dear Jenny, I need no apology use,
Your charms for my crimes are sufficient excuse,
Your charms for my crimes –
Are sufficient excuse.

Apprentices worked around him. Aproned, like butchers. George himself was down to shirtsleeves. In the morning the Young Vinegar had been in, but these days the work went quicker without him. The workshop was rank with the smell of men. More faintly, like fresh air, Fox could smell meat from the Dean Street chop houses.

He was correcting a brilliant, cleaning down the facets. Between the skew and skill he looked up, searching for Salman in the bad light. Hoping he was gone: George could admit it to himself. Hoping he had gone back where he came from overnight. It was not a malicious thought. He knew that he was not a malicious man. It was only a question of good business.

There were new faces in the workshop. Outside men, drafted in to break the back of the coronation order. George would have drafted out Salman if he could. It worried him that Mr Rundell didn't see it. The Jew was an element in an old transaction. He was too quiet. George watched for him as if he might hurt himself, or go home with crown jewels hidden in his pockets. As if he might burn up with anger at the work table, leaving nothing behind, like a diamond.

He sang again when the work let him. His voice was rough but sure of itself. Not good, not bad. An ordinary voice for an ordinary man.

What followed, ye lovers, must never be said,
The sweetest of fruits, they will always be hid,
But 'twas all very fine, very pretty indeed.
It was all very fine, very pretty indeed.

354

Cheers. An applause of hammers on benches. Fox spoke up into it. 'Now, sirs. Too kind, too kind. William Bennett, now, has a drawing-room voice. Where are you, William?'

William half-rose, shy as a ghost in the crucible-light. 'What shall I sing?'

'A request, then,' said George. He scanned the new apprentices. Young men, mostly. Not without desire for the gold they hammered out to leaf; but not understanding, either, what people would do for jewels. The lengths and stakes. They looked innocent to him. 'Gentlemen, something to work to. Eh? Come on.'

'"I Locked Up All My Treasure."'

Salman's accent. George could see him, dark in the dark, still bent over his work. His face fierce with sweat and his hands working together, like a surgeon's. He is the best smith I've ever had, George thought. Perhaps the best I've ever known. No one has such a feeling for stones. He blinked, not hearing, for a moment, that William had begun to sing.

> *I locked up all my Treasure,*
> *I hastened many a mile,*
> *And by my grief did measure*
> *The passing time the while.*

Mister Levy, back from the palace! he had said, two days after the accident. *Are you recovered from the spectacle of the Queen?* And Salman had said nothing. Nothing to him, then or since. As if he knew it was nothing or everything, and knew what everything could be, and how far it could take them beyond words.

> *My business done and over,*
> *I hastened back again,*
> *Like an expecting lover,*
> *To view it once again.*

He was working on the crown, George saw. Most of it was still unfinished, all sockets and bones. Only the lowest tier was complete. The patterns of flowers and leaves lost in an excess of brilliants.

He thought of the jewel he had made, working alone, at night. The Three Brethren, Rundell called it. It had been lovely in ways a crown could never be. Its great stones coming together like fea-

355

tures into a face. Finding their own balance, as if they had been waiting for one another. I have no reason to feel guilt, he thought. No one should be guilty for having made something so beautiful.

> But this delight was stifled,
> As it began to dawn,
> I found my Casket rifled,
> And all my Treasure gone,
> And all my Treasure gone.

'Very good, William. Very good.' He reached for his beer, swigged the warm alcohol, coughed it back. When he was settled again he began to pedal, leaning into it. Seeing the stone and nothing else. The wheel quickening.

The workshop closed at ten. Salman walked away down Haymarket, turning east towards the river. It was a light evening, dank with the smell of summer rain. On the ferries, the watermen and their women were already hanging bunting. It felt as if the city had taken a holiday.

June had been the month of coronation madness. At Rundell's, tiara sales had risen tenfold. Outside the Ludgate Hill showrooms, crowds had waited in the rain to see the glass maquette exhibited. Bakeries were doing good business in New Imperial State cakes, rum-soaked and marzipanned. For weeks the Queen's route had been lined with models of the crown. My crown, Salman thought. At night they shone, gas flares muttering in the wind.

He followed the river eastwards, unsure whether he was turning home yet, or walking for the sake of it. In the last months he had done this almost every night. It took the place of sleeping. He walked like a man who no longer trusted his dreams. Tonight he felt calm, but often when he did without sleep he found himself thinking of other states of mind. His head gnawing at itself. The city echoed his fear in ways which seemed to him a kind of proof.

In April, coming through Green Park, he had found a dead monkey under the trees, its belly cut open. Between overturned caravans, the performers of two circuses had been fighting over the prime coronation ground. Two peelers had gone past with a clown between them, his face twisted up with rage.

A week later, the moon had been eclipsed. A cast of shadow had closed over it as Salman watched from Wapping Stairs. A lighterman had shouted that the Queen was to blame. His voice high, wild with moonlight. When she was crowned, he had said, London would sink into the sea. And then always, every night, there was the sense of being followed. The stories of Spring Heel'd Jack, sold at the news-stands in ten parts. Salman put it out of his mind. Instead he thought of the Queen, taking off her rings. The diamond. Coronation Day.

The light was going. At Blackfriars, children were combing the mud under the crumbling sewer mouth. Salman turned up Bridge Street, past its handsome crescent. There were more street children around Ludgate Circus, crowding the slow traffic. It made Salman hungry to look at them. He tried to remember the last time he had eaten. The King Lud was still open, and Salman crossed between the carts of coalmen, feeling for his purse.

'Mister – please, Mister . . .' The children were following him. One of them pulled at his arm, a girl. He shook her off. At the pavement she reached for him again, and he felt the anger boil up out of nothing. His head drowned out in its busy flood.

'I said whore yourself elsewhere!' He pushed her away, the wind snatching at his voice. The girl staggered back towards the traffic.

'Mister Levy–'

It was Martha. Her eyes wide in her dark head. A horse snickered and sidestepped around her, the coalman shouting down unintelligibilities.

'Martha! I am–' He stepped towards her. His heart running on without him. 'Oh, forgive me . . .'

She came back with her head down. Salman realised he was sweating. He wiped his mouth dry, smelling his own acrid tang. 'Martha, I'm sorry. I was somewhere else, my mind was on other business. Are you hurt?'

She shook her head, mournful.

'Did you come to see my brother?'

'Nay.' Her voice was small. He leaned down to catch it. 'I need to ask you something.'

'To–? Of course, then. Of course. Will you eat with me? I was about to have supper. Are you hungry, Martha?'

He sat in the booth and watched her eat. Uncomfortable with the guilt that made him want to make up to her. She used no cutlery, holding the chop delicately, eating round the bone. Too quickly, Salman saw, getting it down while she had the chance. She had bought clothes for herself in the last few weeks, a worn camlet coat over her dress. It made her look older, as if she was growing too quickly into the wheeze of her voice.

He tried to remember the last time he had looked at anyone properly. Taking the care to see them, as he took care of stones. He wondered if he was changing, and if so, what he was becoming.

'There.' He cleared his throat, his voice still gruffer than he intended it. 'I feel better for that. You too. No doubt.' She ignored him, busy with the last meat and fat. 'How are your lessons with my brother now?'

She looked round, as if Daniel might be there. 'I can read better. The other Mister Levy is showing us how to write.'

'You have a head for letters. Better than mine.'

She smiled so quickly the expression was gone before he could respond. 'He says you'll be leaving. After the crownation.'

'Coronation, Martha.'

'Is it true then?'

'We are owed money, it'll come to us this summer. We'll put it into a business of our own.'

She bared her teeth, dug between them, worked out a tassel of meat. Observing him. 'Will you be jewellers like Rundell's?'

'Better than them. Bigger, once we pick up steam.'

She nodded as though she believed it. 'Then I can work for you. I can come along.'

'Work? Aye, well.' Salman sat back. Uncomfortable, as if his ambition had been overtaken, suddenly, by another. Already the child was talking again.

'Do you have jewels enough?'

'Jewels!' His glass was almost empty. He drank off the ale. 'We have a way to go before summer, Martha. The details are not so settled.'

She stood and began to button her coat. Wrists stick-thin under the bulk of clothes. Salman put down his glass. 'You're leaving?'

She glanced up at the bar, then surreptitiously reached for the meat bone. Tucked it into her pocket. Salman stood up.

'I'll walk you home—'

'I can make do for myself.'

He stopped at the conviction in her voice. Again it seemed too old in the child, the mind prematurely aged. 'Well. Then I will see you for the coronation, if not before.'

She watched him. 'There'll be fireworks. The other Mister Levy said so.'

'And the other Mister Levy is always right. Goodnight, then, Martha.'

'Night to you.' He followed her to the doorway. It had begun to rain again, steady as a fog. Martha walked out into it, southwards down Bridge Street towards the river. Small and framed and certain, it seemed to Salman, as if she belonged out there.

'Goodnight.' He said it again, to himself. Under his breath, like a resolution he had no faith in. Only when Martha was already out of sight did he wonder what she had meant to ask.

It was eleven by the King Lud clock. He went back inside, ordered spirit, drank alone until closing time.

Thursday, the last in June. The night was short and it suited him. By first light there were figures in the street, stragglers from the country in damp walking clothes, locals in umbrellas and best. Two gypsies outside Ryder's with a hot wine stall already lit. Salman dressed at the attic window, watching them shelter from the rain. Ready to make a killing on Coronation Day.

A report echoed off the rooftops, then a second, deeper. Behind him his brother shifted in his sleep. Salman went back to the pallet bed. Sat, the straw pricking through its sacking. Daniel slept with his mouth open, as if he was listening to something. Over his hollow breath Salman could hear the watch tick on the pinewood table.

He reached out. Laid his hand against Daniel's cheek. The hooked profile, which Judit had said was like their father's. The sayer and the said already dead, and only this man left, his gentleness, his want for nothing. Complete, somehow, in himself. Salman narrowed his eyes, leaning closer, as if he might learn that secret even this late, or keep what he saw for good. As if seeing alone could do either of those things.

'Daniel.'

He woke at the sound of his name. Alert, pupils retracting. 'I heard thunder.'

'Guns in the streets. Artillery in Green Park.' He talked quietly, as if something were still sleeping in the faint light. Daniel sat up against the distempered wall. He had grown thinner, Salman thought. Gaunt under the eyes. Paying the child what they could not afford.

'A little early for the revolution. Eh?'

Salman lifted the watch by its chain. 'A quarter before four.'

'Martha will be here soon, then. George has promised to allow her in today, on account of the occasion. A small coup there.' Daniel put his hand out for his watch. Wound it tight, gauging Salman over it. 'You haven't slept.'

'Like the dead.'

'God help us, then. We shall be overrun.'

They sat quiet for a moment. At ease, as if they were unchanged after all. Transit and disillusion stripped away to an old fraternity, 'Phrates and Tigris, the river brothers, a balance of opposites. Then Daniel put the watch down, leant forward. 'We should be proud. Today at least.'

'Then you will have to be proud for us both.'

'I always thought this was what you wanted.' He sighed, seeing his thoughts through. 'Today the Queen will wear our crown. Our sapphire. A million will see it and remember. The imperial sapphire as our emblem of trade. Think of that.'

'I think of it all the time,' Salman said gently. 'As you sleep easy.' There was a foetid flavour in his mouth, like an aftertaste of opium. His throat clicked. 'I think of the jewels she will wear, and those who will see her. And how they will laugh at us down the years. The Jews who were jewed out of their great diamond.'

He got up and went back to the window. The rain had eased against it. Daniel's voice followed him. 'You said you wouldn't leave for the world.'

'Aye, and here I am.' A carriage went past. A Derby insignia, the coachman hunched in his oilskins. 'I meant what I said. They deserve a chance.'

'Who?'

'Rundell. Fox.' He listened absently as Daniel dressed. The cuffs and hooks of his foreign clothes. 'The Young Vinegar and the Old

Fox. There is still time for them to make some – reparation.'

'You still believe the diamond was ours.'

'I know the stone.' He glanced round at Daniel. 'Better than they do themselves. They might as well tell me that you are no longer my brother.'

Daniel reached for their umbrella. Opened the attic door, smiling in its skewed shadow. 'I wouldn't be worth the lie.'

Downstairs William and Martha were already waiting, pallid in the half-light. Other smiths stood at the Creed Lane door, shouldering on coats. A kettle stood steaming over a crucible burner. The shop was scrubbed clean. The work worked out of it, like a good kitchen.

'Morning, William, Martha.' Salman walked over to the child. She was sitting by the benches, drinking tea.

She peered up at him. 'You've slept too long. The best places are gone. I can sign my name. I have my pencil. If you have paper I'll sign it for you.'

'Well now. A signature would be–' He looked past her. William had gone over to Daniel. Had taken his arm; was talking to him, Salman saw, in a hissed undertone. 'William? What is it, has the coronation been cancelled?'

They turned to him together. Daniel frowning, as if Bennett had told him something nonsensical: that the Queen had been lost, or the crown pawned. Salman saw, now, that the men at the door were talking with their own quiet intensity. That everybody knew the facts but him. Daniel shook his head. 'William says the company is to close.'

'The company?' he said, already knowing. 'Rundell and Bridge's?'

'It is only a rumour–'

William cut him off. 'I have it on authority, mind. There is a Frenchman – a buyer for the business – and the bulk to be auctioned off. The winding down will begin any day.' He wiped his face, grimacing. 'I shall have to find work. Me and forty other bastard jewellers. You excepted, sirs.'

'But we are owed money.' Salman felt the blood running out of his face. 'There are two months to go on it.'

'So there are. I'd clean forgotten. Well now.' William leant closer, curiosity getting the better of his own anxiety. Smiling a

361

little, necrophagous. 'What was the sum?'

'Four hundred and fifty pounds,' Daniel whispered.

The Englishman whistled softly. Eyes finding their smile. 'Christ bleeds for you, I'm sure. If I was you, I'd get hold of Rundell before the old jigger dies himself. They say he only lives because the Devil won't have him.'

Daniel looked up. 'Will he pay us?'

'Aye, if you push him. He's still about here somewhere. His carriage was late coming round – Salman–'

He ran, not waiting for Daniel. Past the men at the Creed Lane door, out through the cluttered backstreet. The pavements of Ludgate Hill black as slate with rain as he rounded the corner and saw the barouche at the kerb, already pulling away. Salman ran level with it, calling up at the hammer-cloth, the coachman easing the horses in. A white hand appearing at the window, un- hooking the blind. The past repeating itself.

'Mister Rundell, forgive me, I–' He leant against the dark com- pany livery, out of breath as the window came down.

'Take your hand away, sir!' the old man barked at him. Salman pulled back instinctively. He doesn't know me, he thought. After what he has stolen, I mean nothing to him. Absently, he wondered if that increased the crime or lessened it. Above him the jeweller's face relaxed fractionally. 'Mister Levy. I hardly recognised you. Please remove your hand. Else I will drag you to Westminster.'

'There is a rumour in the shop. They are saying that Rundell and Bridge's' – He felt the violence uncoiling inside him. The street wavered around him, a mirage of London. Out of nothing he found himself remembering the sea, gleaming like something cut open – 'is to be wound down,' he finished. Edmund Rundell leant out towards him. As if he might bite.

'Here is one half of the equation. Do I seem wound down to you, Mister Levy?'

'Sir, there is still money owed to us,' he heard himself saying. 'For the sapphire in the crown and also – for the other stones.'

'Ah, yes. The jewels of the Babylonian Jews.' Rundell frowned gravely. 'You must think yourself hard done by. Eh? The money comes due in August.' He blinked, autodidactic; remembering the money quicker than the man. 'Four hundred and fifty pounds, is it not?'

'Sir.'

The jeweller nodded down to him, hand reaching for the window. 'Come to my office, you and your brother. Tonight, after the coronation. Late as you like. Good day to you. Driver!'

'Thank you. Mister Rundell, may I say how happy I am –' he felt the sweat break out on his skin '– happy that we can come to an agreement. That there can be some reparation between us.'

He stood in the street as the carriage moved off, hunched over its occupant. Relief washed through him. His shoulders slumped, leaving him smaller, as if something had gone out of him. He realised that reparation had never been a last chance for anyone but himself.

He turned back towards Creed Lane. Daniel met him at the corner, William and Martha behind him, a diminishing procession of patent black umbrellas. Above them the rain had stopped. Salman reached for his brother, his hand, arm, embracing him tight. Rocking together while Coronation Day echoed around them, its gunshots and trumpets, vendors and fog drums, cannon and children and church bells.

'Can you see, William?'

'Aye.'

'What is there?'

'A great deal of lice and bad hair. Hold on to your hats.'

'What about the Progress?'

William leered back at them with difficulty. In five hours they had got as far as the west end of the Strand. Now the crowd had become too thick to move. An early firework spiralled overhead, dim with daylight. 'Progress is out of the question, I think. Did any of you think to bring a drop of something? Damn.'

He turned away. Daniel arched round, looking for his brother and the child. Salman waved back, a yard behind him. The air smelt of sweat and gunpowder, rain churning the smoke down over the masses.

'Mister Levy. Mister Levy?'

There was a tugging at his coat. He looked down, checking for his watch chain. Martha was pressed in beside him. Holding on to him, Daniel saw, tight as a limpet. Close as a child of his own.

The crowd jostled against them and he smiled. 'Martha. Are you still afloat down there?'

'Aye.' She grinned back. A man pushed between them, florid-faced, waving a hip flask, bellowing names. *Flossie? Inie, my heart!* Martha narrowed her eyes against his noise. 'I want to give you something.'

'Now?' Daniel watched her keeping her ground. In the far distance there was the sound of cheering, disembodied as a rainstorm. The Progress has begun, he thought. Martha shook her head.

'Tomorrow. For the letters.'

'Letters are free, Martha. You don't have to repay me for that.' A wave moved through the onlookers, lifting them briefly off their feet. Desire made visible, Daniel thought. The impulse of want loving want. By the hoardings of Trafalgar Square someone screamed. A woman's laughter, high and bright with hilarity.

'I'd work for you always.' Martha squinted up at him. 'If I could. I like learning. I'd give you something, if I could.'

'I – thank you, then.' He tried to bow for her. An elbow caught him in the ribs and he scowled. 'Nothing expensive, mind.'

'I'll write to you what to do. Tomorrow night.'

'Tomorrow night it is.' A gun went off a yard ahead, the crack of a pistol, so that before he could ask her what she meant to write Martha had turned away. The faces around them turning with her. The cheering creeping closer.

They saw almost nothing. The mounted peelers eight feet tall, sabred, immobile as statuary above the crowd. The second Progress at five, chariots gridlocked all the way to the palace. Not Victoria Guelph, certainly. Not the crown as she knelt to receive it.

They never heard the way the Abbey filled with a great word-less rush of movement, the peers and peeresses raising their coronets together. The crowning a mime of possession, a physical need echoing through the eyes of two thousand people. Daniel and Salman didn't see the way the light fell just then, catching it-self in the crust of stones they had made. Desirably divine. A halo above the head of a queen they would never see again.

They were part of the crowd, and the crowd celebrated in sight of nothing but itself. In Green Park they bought sloe gin and boiled beef, hungry for everything, eating standing as the dusk

364

came down. Gunsmoke gave way to night-time illuminations. William pulled Daniel's forehead against his own.

'I love you and leave you, sir.' He was shouting, extravagantly drunk. 'I have a fuck to find now and a job when I can. Where's your hand? Give it here. A fine jeweller. Goodbye, goodbye.'

'Good night, William.' Daniel watched him lose himself in the crowd. Fireworks overlapped above the trees. Under their blossoming light he looked around for Martha and found he could only see Salman. His wide face upturned, broken open with its smile. Daniel pushed through to him. 'Where is Martha?'

'Long gone. Back to the palace.'

'Alone?' It surprised him often, now, this concern for the child. The way it had crept up on him, like Martha herself.

'Tch. She can take care of herself. It's a stone's throw.' Salman peered sideways at him. His mouth pulled down into a smile. 'Look at the sky. It's beautiful. Look at it. We have thrown jewels up to God tonight.'

Daniel followed his gaze. They stood like that, together, drinking until the last of the gin was gone. At midnight the Queen could still be made out on the balconies of the palace, watching rockets bloom over Mayfair, but the brothers never saw her there. They headed east, following the river home. Drunk with alcohol and the euphoria of the city around them. Moving of their own accord, free of the crowd's muscular dynamic. Singing sometimes, sometimes not, half-forgotten lines under their breaths. Shanties, work lays, love songs.

Ludgate Hill was still busy, the gypsies unsmilingly making their killing. A uniformed horn and two clarinets sat outside Rundell's, playing drunken anthems. Daniel stepped over them to the nightwatchman's door. Indistinctly, as he knocked, he could see a bill nailed to the panelling. He leaned towards it and stopped, the smile fading in the shadow of his face. Quite still, reading to the end.

Another firework opened above them, crystalline and thunderous. Salman leant over his brother's shoulder to cheer upwards. Daniel's voice drowned out. He spoke again. 'It is closed down.'

'Closed?' Salman looked down. A figure shouldered past him. Then another, pushing him back, as if he had lost the sense of the crowd. 'How can it be closed when Rundell is meeting us here, tonight? If you will just put some back into your bloody knock–'

He hammered at the door. Harder, light blooming behind his eyes. 'This is not right. Jigger it, we have come to the wrong house–' Salman stepped away into the street, staring up at the unlit building. At the periphery of his vision the darkness seemed to be thickening. As if it could fall further than midnight. He shivered in the breeze. 'We have gone wrong somewhere. Daniel?'

The bill fluttered on its nails. Daniel reached up, smoothed it out. Not thinking of himself, or jewels, but of turning points. Of how quickly lives could fall back into themselves.

'We have gone wrong. We should have gone east, I think. We took the wrong ship. I knew it all along.' Salman's voice low and venomous. The horn player crab-stepping away from him. 'Why did we come here? We were lost the day we arrived. The English are all bastards, fucked out of cold bitches.'

'Listen.' Daniel took his arm. 'Nothing keeps us here now. We have no ambition here and no contract. We can go east.' He watched his brother's face begin to clear. 'We can always go east. Back home. Salman?'

He was frowning. Not looking at Daniel, but past him. Daniel turned, short-sighted, seeing nothing. 'What is it?'

'The Old Fox.'

'George?'

'Pissing around his hole.' Salman was already moving, pushing through the last of the crowd. Daniel followed him, a step behind, a long shadow. Only as they reached the King Lud did he make out the shopman, urinating against the pub wall.

He nodded cheerily, tucking himself away. 'My boys! Good to see you. Very. Will you buy a round? They'll sell me no more, but you look fresh–'

'Where is Rundell?'

'Salman! There is a voice I never hoped to hear again.' He grinned, port-wine and vomit on his breath. 'Oh my stars, I have had such a night. I've drunk hock from the mouth of a pretty girl. The Queen is crowned. The company is to be wound down. And all the world celebrates.'

He had been crying, Salman saw. Up close the shopman's face was mired with snot and tears. He mumbled to himself. 'A company such as Rundell and Bridge's, it's no overnight job, there are years of orders to farm out. But it is all ended tonight. It is finished for the likes of us–' Salman leaned down to the lapidary. 'The shop is locked up. Our room is there. All our goods.'

'Aye well, no one goes in now.' George belched at him, his eyes swimming. 'Except me. Stay at mine tonight, if need be.'

'Yours? I thought you lived here.'

'Ahaha, no indeed. Eight Bread Street. In the morning I'll fetch your things myself. And tonight I'll have two young scallies to walk me home.'

'We are owed money.'

A maroon exploded overhead. George closed his eyes and began to sing faintly. Fast, too fast for Daniel, Salman pushed the shopman backwards. There was a dull crack as his head hit the wet wall.

'*Tigris!*' Daniel reached for them both. Salman shouldered him away. George opened his eyes and smiled blearily.

'My boys. Were we talking of money, Salman?'

'Payment for the jewels. For God's sake, the crown sapphire.'

'The sapphire.' Fox blinked. 'That had slipped my mind. You're best taking that up with Mister Rundell.'

'And where is he?'

'At home, if I know him. Ninth in the crescent, Bridge Street. Just there.' He pointed shakily towards the river. 'It would do me no harm, mind, if one of you walked me back.'

'Enough of this.' Daniel shook his head. 'Here. His arm.'

'The jewels are mine.' Salman's voice rose.

'You are in no state. The jewels are gone, Salman. Tigris.' The name a warning. Salman took a step away from him.

'I said I will do it myself! Get in my way and you are – I will–' He stopped. Hawked into the gutter. 'And take him with you. I mean to get back what we are owed.'

And Daniel shook his head again. Keeping his thoughts to himself. Thinking of the jar split open. I have never changed my brother's mind, he thought. In there, the earth is still flat. 'I'll see you at Bread Street?'

Salman watched them go. Fox legless, Daniel stooped against him. Once they were out of sight he began to walk again. Not south, down Bridge Street, under the eyes of the crescent houses, but north. Back up Ludgate Hill, head down, the crowd thinning around him. Outside Ryder's he stopped. Above the shop a window was still lit. Salman lifted his hand and knocked, eyes shut, until the door opened.

'Mister Levy.' Ryder slowly craned out. Looked left, right. 'A pleasure to see you, after so long. Do you have any idea of the time? If I had not been up comparing the Edinburgh and Dublin Pharmacopoeias–'

'I need something from you.' He pushed inside. In the pungent dark of the shop he watched Ryder nod as he closed the door, a silhouette against the jars and tinctures.

'An extract of celebration. There you are not the first tonight.' The apothecary's voice was husky with chemicals. He moved easily through his ordered shelves. 'Though I sincerely hope you are the last. I had thought –' he turned, a blue bottle in his hand '– that you were finding other remedies for your nightmares. Hoped, even. But evidently not.' He smiled at Salman. His mouth all gold. 'Nine shillings. One for the hour.'

'I have no more need of that,' Salman whispered.

'Ah?' Ryder took a step towards him. Then another, as if he were attracted to something almost imperceptible. The shadow of smoke from a volatile compound. 'What is it you want from me, Mister Levy?'

'I–' Salman looked around. 'Not I. An order for Rundell's. Something to clean stone. To clean metals. And stone.'

'An acid?'

He nodded, feeling the yammer of his heart as the apothecary stepped away. 'Not an order I take every Coronation Day, certainly. That will be the muriatic, I think.' Ryder raised the gaslight. 'The powders I have sold tonight, those I can put up in paper. But this, now –' he went to work, decanting a ceramic jar into a clear bottle, smiling with effort '– this I will have to dispense in glass. Cork, you see, blackens the sulphuric acid, and is dissolved by the nitric and muriatic. There! Have a care, Mister Levy.' He righted the jar. Stopped the smaller vessel tight. Held it out. 'I hope to see you make something beautiful of this.'

'How much will it be?' The bottle fitted inside Salman's calloused hand. Ryder walked him out. The street was almost empty.

'The Crown Goldsmiths have their own account here. This I'll chalk up with the rest. You, Mister Levy, owe me only a good night's sleep.' He stopped in the doorway, smiling. 'Goodnight, Mister Levy. Goodnight.'

He watched the apothecary go, the gaslight fading out. A rider went past, the horse champing. Salman turned away suddenly, as if the ring of metal had woken him. He began to walk again, downhill into Bridge Street.

Steps led up to the door of number nine. Salman rang the bell and turned, looking out over the Thames. Not my river, he thought. There were lights on the water, vagrants' fires reflected from the riverbank. Blackfriars Bridge stood empty over its stone piers. In the mild June air, he could still smell the residue of gunpowder.

'Who shall I say is calling?'

He turned. The door had opened onto another world, a hallway filled with ruddy light. A butler stood half-bowed, clean-shaven at midnight. From beyond him came the sound of a piano. Laughter. Salman stepped back.

'Levy. I work for Mister Rundell.'

The butler turned, waiting with invisible patience. 'If you could come into the hall, Mister Levy. Into the hall. Please come in. Mister Rundell will be one moment.'

He stepped inside, blinking. The hall was furnished entirely in red. A crimson Turkey rug, wallpaper embossed with rosebuds, gaslights hooded under Bohemian glass. He looked down at his own hands, turning their discoloured skin. The bottle ruby between index and thumb.

'Good morning, Mister Levy!'

Salman looked up. Edmund Rundell was coming down the stairs, livid in the light, bright with energy. Fiendish with it. 'Now then. Salman, isn't it? What can I do for you, so early? Shall we drink to the end of Rundell and Bridge's?'

'No.' He lowered his hands, closing them at his sides. 'Thank you, I am here on business.'

'What's that? Speak up. Business?' Edmund stopped in front of him. He still held a liqueur glass, though it was empty, inverted, alcohol trembling at the rim. 'Heh. There will be no more business in this house. Come. Watch me make another toast.'

'No, I–' His voice found itself. He looked up, searching the old man's face. 'You owe me money, sir. For the three jewels.'

'Jewels?' Edmund barked with laughter. 'Jewels! Jigger it, I thought you said Jews, sir. God knows I wouldn't pay money for those. Aha.' He wiped his mouth, eyes sobering. 'And what jewels would these be?'

'The sapphire. The diamond.'

'The diamond, sir.' Edmund licked his lips. 'The diamond was not yours. I had thought that was made abundantly clear.'

Salman shook his head. His face florid in the unnatural light. 'The sapphire, then. The jewel in the crown, and the balas ruby. Four hundred and fifty pounds is what is owed. You were to meet us tonight. You cannot tell me–'

The Young Vinegar leaned into his face. 'Do not presume to tell me what I can or cannot do, sir. In this house or any other.'

Without meaning to, Salman found himself stepping back again. Stuttering. 'The business left between us–'

Edmund spoke through him. 'How old are you, Mister Levy? No, don't tell me. I am four times your age at the outside, but I will have you, sir, if you speak that word here again. I am done with business.' He snarled, following Salman, increments of light passing over his face. 'You believe you matter, young man, eh? But you are wrong. Today matters, because today sees a line drawn under all my business. It is the end of my uncle Philip's concern, which the world has been privileged to know. His time has wound itself out now. And mine has not.'

He reached Salman and stood over him, his voice exhausted with its own anger. 'Philip. I am talking about Philip. I outlive everything that he made today.' A river drum sounded outside, distant. The fog is coming down, Salman thought. Above him, Edmund shook his head. 'Do you understand any of this? Of course you don't. Get out of my house, Mister Levy. You have no business here.'

He began to turn away. Salman reached out for his shoulder, feeling the worker's sinew under the tailored cloth. There was a sound, not a word so much as an explosion of air, spittle dotting the old man's lips as he veered back, and Salman raised the bottle and broke it across his face.

For a moment there was no sound. The smell of acid filled the hall, sour and acrid. Edmund bent over, his hands going together to his face. As if he wept, Salman thought, and as he watched, something did begin to weep between the jeweller's fingers. He knelt down beside him. Leant back against the wall, not touching the old man, not quite whispering.

'You took everything I loved, you see. We are not so different, Mister Rundell. We loved the same thing.'

The jeweller began to whine. Distant, close enough to touch, Salman saw there was flesh running down his chin. He moved closer. Matter of fact. 'We are alike, sir. Anyone who knows how to love a jewel knows how to cheat a man to get it. And you have cheated me of everything I had. We are brothers to dragons, and companions to owls. Our skin is black upon us, and our bones are burned with heat.'

Against him Edmund began to move, rocking on his heels. A sound escaped between his teeth, something like laughter. Salman put his mouth against the jeweller's ear. Saying nothing. Resting there until there was no sound left.

Smoke rose from the juncture of the hands and head. Salman stood and opened the door. A light mist curled in around him, incandescent in the porch-light. He stepped out into it and began to walk. Eastwards, towards the docks.

I will break, he thought. *I will break open, now, like a vessel. And out of me will spill a horror of jewels.*

Edmund's silence rising and rising behind him.

Bread Street, first light. In the doorway of number eight, two men stand talking. The shorter leans against the street wall, bare head crooked up. His hands open and close, raw with gurry sores or burns. He looks tired, and he is, he can feel it in his bones. Tired of doors. Even so, as he talks it is the second man who cries out. He sinks to his knees, his stature bent back into itself. At number five, Adams the fishmonger looks up. It is Friday, the best of days. He watches for trouble, as he guts.

There are no ships east. If there were, the brothers could not afford them. A schooner will take them as far as Lisbon for all the English money in their pockets. From there they will have to work their way. For good labouring men it would be five months at best. It will take them eleven. Only one will ever pass as a labouring man.

They stand on the export wharves, waiting for the ship at noon.

No one comes to see them go. They have nothing except the clothes they stand up in. They have lived in the city for five years. The shrieking of gulls rises above them, full of hunger. The shorter man stares after the sound. Only when his brother stoops to him does he turn away. The ship is ready for transit, and besides, he can't see what he was looking for.

Buckingham Palace at high tea. Alone with a decanter of Madeira, Lehzen is brooding in the chambers of Victoria Guelph, the child she once governed, when she sees the footprints for the first time. Naked and charred black, they criss-cross the Queen's rooms, as if a small devil has come searching for sinners. Long before anything is found missing the warders have already been summoned by her screaming.

Martha is already well away, down in the basements of the palace. It comes easy to her, what she does, easy as learning letters, her feet as quick as her mind. The warders in their red tails make it only a little more difficult than she expected. It is like a game. Three times she has to hide, the box held against her wheezing chest. It is later than she would like when she comes to a roped-off stairwell, a room of bloodstone fireplaces, a corridor where the carpet sags down, rotting into the space beneath.

She climbs down into the sewers. It is a way she has gone many times: the way she first came to the palace, years ago. Now the water is high around her ankles, but she knows the tides, knows how dangerous they can be. Even in the dark she is certain there is time to spare.

It is the sound of the water which gives her away. The echo of it ripples back into the abandoned rooms. Somewhere under Haymarket she realises there are voices following her, the sounds of men distorted against the crumbling brickwork. Rats wheedle in the sewage of the Queen. Martha goes east, northeast. She is heading for the Fleet, the great sewer mouth of Blackfriars, a pipe which was once a river itself. She knows the way like the back of her hand. Better, even.

The water rises. The men behind her have the advantage now. She thinks they do not know it yet. She is swimming, almost, the box fisting up one hand. Her breath makes her sound as if she is drowning. *Martha, are you still afloat down there?* she remembers, and laughs. Behind her the men slow, imagining monsters.

There is a passage to her side. She feels it with one bare foot, the mouth of it quarter-hidden by the waterline. Martha pulls herself back and into its bolthole. Holding her breath, not letting out its sound of frightened birds. On all fours, and not knowing, now, where she is going, but only going. The passage is tarnished black with slime. It leads her upwards, turning once to reach its dry dead end.

She sits back against the wall. The air hurts as she takes it, raggedly, the tears squeezing out of her eyes. The water is at her feet. The men she can still hear. In the dark, she can no longer tell if they are approaching or receding. Her lungs pitch inside her and she coughs up something foul, a bitter clot against the back of her hand. Its warmth feels good. She doesn't wipe it away.

She opens the box. Inside it lies the jewel, a form with three eyes. It feels beautiful to her. She touches the diamond. It winks, only once, catching photons of stray light. Beside it is the note she has written for the Mr Levys. She thinks of them. Mary and Joseph. Their kindness, which was the kindness of strangers, and is everything to her now. The way it has made her love them.

She blinks, dark on dark. The voices of the men are gone. She didn't realise. She feels for the water. It is at her waist, warm as her skin with faeces. The passage curves down into it. If she could hold her breath, she could get out. But she cannot hold her breath again. She listens to herself in the pitch blackness. She sounds monstrous. She feels her smallness.

She feels the jewel, its outline. She thinks of giving it to the Mr Levys, and smiles. Water drips against her teeth. Martha thinks of summer, when the Mr Levys will have their money. It will be big when it picks up steam. There will be work enough for her. Work enough for her lifetime. The little Mr Levy will make the jewels. Mr Levy – her Mr Levy – will sell them.

She tries to think what she will do. But she knows. She will write the letters. The water is at her chest. She closes the box. The water is at her throat. She closes her eyes.

The box covered in flowers. Iris and convolvulus and narcissus, gripped in her fingers. The jewel held tight as someone loved.

The tide rising and falling with the hiss of her disease, an emphysema which would have killed her in her first thirty years. Never knowing, at least, that she had been left behind. Spring and neap rising over her for seven decades. A lifetime before a man comes whistling through the dark.

His lamplight arching across the brick. The radius, swinging down to Martha's face. The whistling stopped. The light increasing. The box gripped in the cagework of her hand.

⋊⋉

I open my eyes. I am alone in a room that is not mine. There is bedding under me, a low table to one side. There are animals on the walls. Parallel processions of zebra, lions, elephants. As far as I know I have never been here before. The sensation is not unfamiliar.

It feels late. Certainly it is less than dark. There is some kind of daylight outside the shutters. The smell of tatami reaches me, sweet as hay. Everything is external, the details withdrawn. My head is empty as the volute of a shell. After a time the sound of breakers reaches me, and I remember the breakers and what brought me to them.

It is an effort to look sideways. On the table is a blue cup with no handle. I reach out. Tip it to see inside. Water slops across my nose. I drink what I can get. The cold of it moves through my supine body.

There is a noise in the house around me. The creak of stairs. I try to sit up and fail. There is a pain in my chest, something that might be a broken rib, although I have never broken a rib before, cannot be sure of my own breakages. For a moment it hurts so badly I can't breathe. The cup tips over and the last water blooms coldly round my hair.

I watch the door open. The fisherman is standing in its aperture. When he sees I'm awake he comes in. He goes over to the shutters and folds them back, flooding the room with light. He goes back out, not closing the door.

He comes back in again. It is like watching a tennis match. I do it without moving my head.

374

'What time is it?' It seems important. The words hurt. I cough at the pain.

'Two o'clock.'

'Who are you? Are you Hikari Murasaki?'

There is a bowl in his hands. He comes and picks up the cup. Rights it.

'You should have taken me to a hospital.'

'We did.'

Another cough begins and I choke it back. 'I've been to hospital?'

'You have two fractured ribs, bruising, lesions. There was some concussion. After you regained consciousness they said you were ready to leave. The practice is small here, and busy. They say you must rest. I did not know where else to take you.'

'I don't remember that,' I say. As if he might be lying, and he might. He sits next to the bed, cross-legged, watching me. We watch each other. Outside the sky is bright white, a marine lucidity. A seagull begins to laugh in the distance. I close my eyes and think of Punch and Judy. Southend, the pier a road to nothing.

'How long have I been asleep?'

'A hundred years.'

'I want to know,' I say, but when I look up he has gone again, busying himself. Embarrassed at something, possibly, although it is hard to know, his face is not one which gives up emotion easily to strangers. The whirr of an electric fan begins.

'Two days,' he says, and straightens.

'Why didn't you leave me?'

He comes back. Picks up the bowl. 'This is a soup made from crab shells. You should eat something.'

'You could have left me. The sea would have come back up. I wasn't going anywhere. No blood on your hands.'

I sip, a spoonful of soup. It is nothing but taste, barely a food at all. My stomach groans with it. Quite suddenly I am avid with hunger. I can smell the man's sweat as I empty the bowl. Pepper and sea salt. He is still watching me. 'You are arguing for your own death.'

'No.' Talking with my mouth full of sweetness. 'Just curious.'

'I have never killed,' he says. As if it is a reason. He takes the bowl back and stands to go. His eyes are sanguine. The colour of old blood. At the door he pauses. 'Have you?'

'I don't know,' I say, and close my eyes. Turning away from him and his talk. Sleep breaking over me.

Every day he cooks for me. Warm rice with broth, white miso soup. Each meal a step back. Soft rice noodles, steamed eggs with fern. Comfort foods and temptations. Raw sweet prawns. Salt-baked bream. Scallops grilled with their corals. His nourishment draws me out of myself. I watch him and wonder if he knows what he is doing.

The porch door wakes me each morning, banging shut before first light. From the bedroom window I can see the man, walking the dune path to the quay. His boat starts up, turning out to the open sea.

By seven he is always home again. He cycles the children to school. Tom frowning to keep up, Iren happy as a Buddha in her child seat. They are visible on the empty coast road, all the way to Tosa.

No one comes to the house. The postman stops at the mailbox by the quay. Sometimes, at low tides, an old woman appears further down the beach. She is thin and bent, always alone, raking for clams or razorshells. I watch her searching. The strand reflects her back.

For three days the stairs are beyond me. I make myself exercise, pacing the room, under the watch of the elephants. Everything here is watchful, waiting. The man brings up my belongings, the bag I once left behind. When I don't open it he leaves me books instead. Only three are in English. The rest overestimate my Japanese. I sit by the open window and read the King James Bible, the 1892 Pears Cyclopaedia with its arguments for a flat earth, the poems of Robert Louis Stevenson.

> *Mother, speak low in my ear,*
> *Some of the things are so great and so near,*
> *Some are so small and far away,*
> *I have a fear that I cannot say . . .*

Odd things, desert island books. Heirlooms inscribed with half-familiar names. *To Hikari. From his grandfather, Michael. To Mari, 1946. On her wedding day.*

There are thirty stitches in my left thigh. I cover them with one

376

hand as I wash, bent over on the bathroom stool. The bruising is deepest below my ribs. In a week it begins to fade. The trapped blood sinks to a livid belt above my hip bone.

It is late November. Only the nights are colder. I spend the evenings downstairs, glad of the liberty and the warmth of the hearth. The radio whines through Japanese and Korean. The children are sullen, venomous with hurt, wanting me gone. I stay out of their way when I can. Listening to their games and arguments, their private comings and goings. Beyond them, always, the sound of the gulls, and their correlative, the sea.

We talk carefully. Always of the present, avoiding futures and pasts. Never of why I came, or why I stay. Never of what he is doing, and for whom. Circling the periphery of accidents.

'You have a lot of books.'

'I like to read.'

'No photographs. Nothing of your family.'

'I could say the same about you. Hold this.'

'What is it?'

'Something for killing fish.'

'So what's that?'

'Also something for killing fish.'

'They must run a mile when they see you. The Great White Hunter of the eastern shore. What do you have against them?'

'Nothing. I need a living. They don't run.'

'Still, I'm sure you'd make them if you could.' Waiting for him to smile, his face relaxing into its lines. Wanting it. I can admit these things to myself. 'What about this?'

'Something Iren made.'

'Don't tell me.'

'For luck. For my boat. She is good with her hands. Do you like it?'

'Especially the glass. It looks like you could kill many fish with it. You must be proud of her.'

'Of course. There. Fixed.'

'You don't sound sure.'

'Why don't we find out?'

He turns in a circle out of the harbour. We head due south-east into the Bay of Tosa. It is a beautiful day, the sun and sea both so blue that the horizon is almost invisible at their juncture. I look back for the promontory and it is already distant. The island rising above it, greener than green.

He watches the sea as he steers, eyes running over the seams and glassy flats that demarcate currents and submarine geography. At a point that seems like all others to me he cuts the motor. We sit, drinking Sapporo beer from a cooler, fishing for sea bass and black bream.

'This is nice.'

'I'm glad you think so.'

'Is this all you do?'

He grunts. 'I go to market in Kôchi. I work on the allotment. I look after my children.'

'Did you ever want to be anything else?'

'No.' He drinks his beer, eyes narrowing.

'You must have had ambitions. Fire-eater, international playboy, prime minister of Japan.'

'No.' And then, more quietly, 'I wanted to be a teacher.'

'You would have been good.'

I don't ask him why he never tried. To be a teacher would mean living among people. To live among people would risk the Brethren. I know, as clearly as if he had told me, how the jewel can split a life in half.

A fish jumps, then another. I catch a horse mackerel, making hard work of it. The man squats beside me, gutting it against the deck. He grins. 'Congratulations. There is packing ice in the cabin.'

'Where?'

'Under the seat. The blue box.' He calls after me. 'Kaori-chan–'

I stop by the cabin door. He is still bent over the fish, face in shadow. Wind hums in the radio mast. 'Who's Kaori? Is that your wife?'

And already we are too close. We have crossed the line into the circle. Hikari Murasaki shakes his head. He stands up. Reaches for our rods.

'We should go back,' he says. The reels sing in his hands. 'There is rain on the way.'

I think of him at night. His hands dabbed with fish blood. The way his eyes are always on me. Watching me for something, like the child on the aeroplane. Not like a child.

Sleep stays away from me. I have had too much of it. I sit at the window until morning, watching the sea. Out across the dunes, the waves advance and advance without ever coming closer. Soft and phosphorescent, like lines on a computer screen.

Sunday. At dawn he is out by the ginkgo tree, caulking the dinghy. I sit on the porch and drink his coffee. The first of the sun falls across us.

'Thanks for taking me fishing.'

He nods. There are nails in his mouth. A skylark goes up over the dunes.

'Have you always lived here?'

He takes the nails out of his mouth. 'Not always. You look better.'

'I feel better,' I say, and I do. Even the ribs are mending. 'I never asked whose room I've taken.'

'Tom's.' He works out a tuft of oakum from its sack. 'He can share with Iren while you are here.'

'I don't need to stay much longer.'

Nothing changes in his face. Delicately, smiling with effort, he chisels the oakum in between planks. 'Where will you go?'

'I don't know.' I wrap my hands around the mug. 'They won't talk to me. Tom and Iren.'

'No.'

'Is it the dog?'

'Lyu.' He straightens and comes back to the porch. Sits down and drinks my drink. It steams in the sunlight. He is wearing a plaid shirt, short-sleeved. It makes him look older.

'Can we talk about it?'

He turns to look at me, considering the question. 'If he was alive he would have come back by now.'

'I'm sorry.'

'It isn't your fault.' He is still looking at me. His pupils narrowed to my proximity. 'I shouldn't have sent him after you. I didn't know what else to do.'

'No.' It is only the second time we have talked of that night. I think of how slowly we turn towards one another. Imperceptibly, like hands on a clock face.

'I have explained this to the children. It is easier for them to

379

blame you.'

'What if I spoke to them?'

'How fast do you think you can run?'

'Faster than they can ride bicycles. What are they armed with?'

He smiles, a little grim. 'Whatever they can find. They'll be on the other side of the headland. Bring them in for breakfast.'

It's further than I thought. Bound by nothing but thistles and scrub, the sand falls away into my monstrous footsteps. After ten minutes my legs are shaking with exertion. I stop at the top of the next dune. There are four more between me and the shore. Breakers, the land mirroring the sea.

The wind changes. I hear them. Two voices, playing hide-and-seek at the easternmost point of their easternmost island.

'Tom?' The sun is already high overhead. The children are imperceptible, the sounds of them fading away. A martin dips over the marram grass. 'Iren?'

'Go away.'

I turn. Tom is a yard behind me. I never heard him come up. He is barefoot, bare-chested, with a stick in one hand. The wind catches at his coiled hair. 'I need to talk to you.'

'We don't want you here.'

'About the dog.'

'Lyu. You killed him.' His face is twisted. It is hard to tell if he is angry or sun-blind or about to cry, or some combination of all these things. His expressions are difficult, like his father's.

'I came to say that I'm sorry.'

Iren comes into sight, two dunes back. Hurrying, calling out her brother's name. *Tom-kun.* Pleading: wait for me. *Matte. Matte.*

My legs are tired from the climb. I sit down carefully on the warm sand. 'How old was Lyu?'

'Don't say his name.' His voice goes up high. I see that the shaft in his hand is not a stick at all. It is a piece of fishing equipment, metal-tipped, tridented. A harpoon or eel spear.

'Okay.'

'Ten.' The boy looks round for his sister. 'He was a good dog, but he didn't sleep too well.'

'He looked like the models they sell in Kôchi. Where did you get him?'

'My dad bought him. To protect us.' I don't ask him what

from. He is looking at my thighs. The curved smile of stitch-marks. It is wide as his head. 'He bit you bad.'

'Yes.'

'He never hurt anyone before.'

'I didn't know.'

'He must have been mad. I guess if you didn't fight him he would have bit you some more.'

'I think so.'

He sits down. The grass bows around us. 'He was a strong boy. You must be strong.'

'I'm so sorry, Tom.'

'Will you help us make his grave?'

There is nothing to bury. My ribs creak as I dig. When the hole is three feet deep Iren gets down inside, as if she is going to try it out. Tom hands her a picket painted with black prayer charac-ters. I fill the sand in around its base. Iren is buried to the waist. It is an effort for me to pull her out. She doesn't seem to mind. All the way back to the house she talks about cats.

I go upstairs to wash. The squat bath is four feet wide and four feet tall, a tub of dark slats that fills the room with the smell of wet logs. It is still too painful to fold myself inside. I sit on the stool and scrub the burial sand off my feet from the faucet by the door.

Moths bat against the window. It is the beginning of evening, balanced between twilight and dusk. The only time the bats come out this far, keener than the seabirds and after smaller prey, fluttering over the edge of the sea.

I stand up and let the shower sluice over my head. The stitches ache like bad teeth. The hair runs past my eyes. One of these days I mean to cut it. I reach back, combing its weight away, and see him.

He is standing outside, under the ginkgo tree. The porchlight is on. I can see his face looking up, lit from below. The expression there. I don't cover myself. I feel my body under his eyes. Every part of me feeling its use, before he turns away.

The clatter of the generator wakes me, the wind carrying its *put-put* from the outhouse. I sit up, feeling the lateness, wondering why I have slept so long.

There is a persimmon on the bedside table. I reach for it and something keels over behind it, awkwardly balanced. I pick it up between finger and thumb. It is a figure, a woman carved from driftwood, small as a good-luck charm. The work is simple but accurate. An expression of mine has been caught. A certain frown, centred on the middle distance. A tiny, stern Katharine. I lean by the window and eat the persimmon. Waiting to wave the children goodbye.

'Tell me something true,' I say, and he looks up from the sea as if I have made a joke. We are fishing from the quayside. People have appeared overnight. Groups of them, determinedly enjoying the emptiness of the scenery, crossing by pleasure boat from the fairground. A man with bleached teeth makes a killing from the vending stand.

'I haven't always lied.'

'I know.' I smile back at him. 'But tell me something anyway.'

'What?'

'What was your wife like?' Parrot fish graze around the jetty. The water clear as quartz.

Hikari sighs inwards. 'She was young. She came from Takamatsu. She lived here for fifteen years. After that she wanted to go back. It was her dream to start a school. She was trained as a teacher.'

'And you wouldn't go.' Somewhere a child screams with laughter.

'She left me just after Iren was born. I could never live the life she wanted.' A gilthead rises towards his bait. Hikari stares through it. 'It was my fault. I should never have married her.'

'Do you still love her?'

'Of course.' Something bites. He pulls the rod back reflexively, almost before the float dips. Reels the fish in gently, a tiny, flickering cargo of silver. 'Why were you looking for it, Katharine?'

A couple sit on rope bollards, drinking Coke, eating grilled octopus. A man and dog walk past with matching builders' bums. I wait until they're gone. 'Because I wanted it. I wasn't lying. I don't work for anyone.'

'I know.' He unhooks the fish with spare efficiency. Drops it into the bucket. I don't ask him how he knows. Whether he has gone through my belongings. It matters so little now that I feel I would be glad if he has. 'It hasn't done you much good,' he says.

'No, I have to admit it.' I reel in. Cast again. 'Maybe it was cursed while I wasn't looking.'

'You couldn't be there all the time, after all.' And he looks up at me, frowning in the sun, smiling until I smile back.

All morning he reads. I can see him from the kitchen window, alone where the dunes begin. I make drinks, whisky and ice, and go out and sit beside him.

'What are you reading?'

'A story.' He sits against a hummock of sand, nested in grass, the book on his knees. He takes the drink, nods thanks. The whisky is Japanese, cheap and rough. The water brings out its sweetness.

'I never liked stories.'

'Why?'

'No time for them.'

'Your life is full of stories.'

I smile, a little tight. 'I don't have time for those either.' Beside me, Hikari closes the book.

'This is the story of Gilgamesh. It comes from the place my grandfather came from. It is very old, five thousand years. It was already old when the *Odyssey* was written. Ancient before the Bible.'

I take it from him. The text is Japanese, the marginalia a babble of scripts. Roman, Arabic. Names I almost know. Nineveh, Ur. I settle down. Distantly, across the bay, I can see the pleasure boat heading back to Tosa. 'So what happens?'

'King Gilgamesh loses his greatest friend. For the first time he feels the fear of death. He goes looking for immortality.'

'Is that it?'

'No.' He smiles. The wind opens the pages, flits through them. 'He wrestles with lions, goes down to the underworld, meets the dead. A normal day in the office for a hero-king.'

I swill the alcohol, down to the hollowness in my stomach. 'Read me some.'

'If you like.' I hand the book back. He opens it. His voice is so quiet I have to lean towards him. His English stilted but perfect. '"A table of hard-wood was set out, and on it a bowl of carnelian filled with honey, and a bowl of lapis lazuli filled with butter.

383

These he exposed and offered to the sun, and weeping he went away again."'

The pages ripple in his hands. Time passing. The ice chimes in my glass. I watch his face while I have the chance. The hamulate strength of the profile.

"'He followed the sun's road to his rising, through the mountain. When he had gone one league the darkness became thick around him, for there was no light, he could see nothing ahead and nothing behind him. After two leagues the darkness was thick and there was no light, he could see nothing ahead and nothing behind him. After three leagues the darkness was thick, and there was no light, he could see nothing ahead and nothing behind him."'

A martin knifes through the blue air. I blink. It feels as if I have been dazed, halfway to sleeping. My head aches. Hikari's voice settles into its soft rhythm. "'After four leagues the darkness was thick and there was no light, he could see nothing ahead and nothing behind him. At the end of five leagues the darkness was thick and there was no light, he could see nothing ahead and nothing behind him."'

'All right,' I say, and my voice is unsteady. I try to shake off the unease. The headache comes back, like a symptom of sunstroke. 'You can stop now. I don't like it.'

"'At the end of six leagues the darkness was thick and there was no light, he could see nothing ahead and nothing behind him."'

'Hikari.' His name uncomfortable in my mouth. My skin prickles. The martin passes over us again. Jackknifes.

"'When he had gone seven leagues the darkness was thick and there was no light, he could see nothing ahead and nothing behind him. When he had gone eight leagues Gilgamesh gave a great cry, for the darkness was thick and he could see nothing ahead and nothing behind him."'

'Hikari.' And suddenly I am on the verge of crying. Something desperate rises up inside me. The man beside me still reading, quiet, head down.

"'After nine leagues he felt the north wind on his face, but the darkness was thick and there was no light, he could see nothing ahead and nothing behind him. After ten leagues the end was near. After eleven leagues the dawn light appeared. At the end of twelve leagues the sun streamed out."'

He opens his arms. I fall into them. He is stroking my hair. His hands go down to the ache of my bruised hips, down to the line of my cunt. In the time it takes my body to make up its mind we are already making love.

He moves inside me. Opening my shirt, spreading it under us. My wetness against his thighs. The sand is dry under my head. The rhythm of him draws me out. I shut my eyes against the pleasure of it.

He says something in my ear. I can't understand it. Even the language it is spoken in is incomprehensible. When I come I cry out against his mouth. The sea is quiet around us.

'Hikari.'

'Yes?'

It is late. His room is alien in the dark. The walls are bare; there is little furniture. A man's room. There is a house altar by the door. Gifts to its gods: a rice cake, an aubergine. I turn over onto my side. Wanting him awake again. 'Did he find it?'

'What?'

'What he was looking for.'

I listen to him smile. Hearing it in his breath. 'No.'

'Why not?'

Crickets chirr outside, the last before winter. 'He wanted something that was never meant for him. Something he couldn't have.'

'So what, he just goes home and dies? What's the point? Should he have been looking for something else?'

He says nothing, thinking. I am almost asleep when he speaks again. 'There is no point to it. It isn't that kind of story.'

For four days it rains. The forest is lush with it. The bush warblers sing all night, disoriented by the acoustics of water. The daytrippers are driven back to Tosa, leaving nothing behind but the grilled-octopus man, who shelters, hopefully, in his cabin. Tom and Iren mope inside, squabbling over the radio, desultory with homework. Hikari fishes long hours, or works the allotment. Digging for lotus root in the downpour.

I walk every day. The weather reminds me of England, and I like it for that. Under the forest pines I sit and think of my own

385

coast, its shut-up shops and shipping news. The sense of loss in its seaside towns. Testing my body a little, seeing how far it can go. Testing myself. I don't go far. The smells of rain and sex mingle on my skin and become inseparable.

It is the first of December. I come back along the beach. The children are sitting cross-legged on the porch, run-off dripping beyond them. Their father comes out with a tray of cups. He squats down and sets them out. Dozens of them, neat rows of plastic and china and glass.

'Are you having the neighbours round for tea?'

He glances up at me, embarrassed, slow with it. 'I have no neighbours.'

'I know. I didn't think you were so sociable. What is this?'

'A family game.'

'Tch!' Tom peers at me. His father fills cups with water from a jug. There is a plastic sieve by his feet. 'Don't you know?'

Hikari nods to me. Taciturn, the smile banked down inside him. 'Cover their eyes.' I close one hand over each child's face. Iren quavers with excitement. Tom shoots out his shoulders like a card-sharp. From his shirt pocket Hikari takes out a shagreen seal-case. Opens it.

Inside lie three diamonds. I lean forward. They are curiously elongated, like rice grains. Small but fine. Even in the gloom they shudder with light. He drops them, one by one, into separate glasses.

'Iren first,' he says, his voice rising. 'Slowly.' And already the children are pulling my hands away, whispering over the assembled vessels. With exaggerated care, the girl touches her breakfast cup: blue plastic, green dolphins. Her father picks it out. He holds the sieve as she pours.

Nothing collects in its mesh. Iren moans in disappointment. The stones have vanished into their hiding places. They are as invisible now as if they had dissolved, like salt.

It is a game of lost jewels. I watch the siblings play. Their faces shine with passion for it. The boy wins. He cheers himself, settling back on his haunches with an expression of thorough contentment. I help clear up. We stand over the kitchen counter, putting away glasses. From upstairs come the sounds of the children arguing over shampoo and bath space.

'They liked the game.'

Hikari grunts an acknowledgement. He is smiling, at ease. The radio is tuned to Japanese pop, music signifying nothing.

'Can I see the diamonds?'

Without looking up he takes the seal-case out of his shirt pocket and offers it to me. A fisherman with a handful of jewels. I hold them to the window light. In all three the clarity is good. Whoever bought them knew what they were looking for. The faceting is identical, possibly even worked by the same cutter. A prototype brilliant variation, mathematically inaccurate. Old, not much later than eighteenth century. The shape is not European. Indian jewels, I think. Mined before the excavations of Brazil or Africa.

I drop them into their sharkskin cavity. Hand it back. 'They're good stones. Unusual.'

'Yes.'

'They were your grandfather's.'

He looks up in surprise. I let myself laugh. 'Mankin-Mitsubishi. Three Diamonds. He named his company after them. What happened to the ten thousand coins?'

Hikari's face clears. He smiles, wry. 'Spent on drink. You know a great deal about stones.'

'It's my business. Did he go to India, your grandfather?'

'Before he came here. Yes.' I watch him watch me. Measuring me, I don't know against what or whom. He dries his hands and walks over to the bookshelves. 'Please. I want to show you something else.'

'Don't tell me there are diamonds in your Bible.'

'No.' He taps between spines. Leafs through pages. 'You asked about photographs once. Pictures of my family.'

He hands me the open book. Behind acetate is a sepia image. An old man sits in a wicker chair. His face is aquiline. A profile to cut winds on. His eyes are unsmiling. There are trees outside the room in which he waits. Tamarisks.

'Handsome. He looks like you.'

'My great-grandfather. His name was Daniel Levy.'

'Jewish.'

He nods. 'Michael, my grandfather, changed our name. He travelled in Europe. Lewis was better for business.'

387

'But he ended up here.' A bush warbler sings outside. Faint as a wind-chime.

'Many Jews were leaving Iraq at that time. Most of them came east. Asia was more welcoming to them. Without Christianity there is no anti-Semitism. Here, of course, my grandfather was a foreign devil. But then so were the Europeans and Americans. He always said that was preferable to him.'

The room in the photograph is whitewashed. Still unfinished, the floor earthen. Tools sit by the bedside table. A hammer, a level. 'Did you ever meet him? Daniel.'

'No. He married late. The granddaughter of a local rabbi. He was old when my grandfather was born. But he was a trader, like all my family. He and his brother worked together. They went to London to seek their fortunes.'

'But this is not England.'

'No.' He hesitates. 'In your country they encountered some – some difficulties. It affected both men very badly. The brother, Salman, became ill. They returned home. Salman died in an asylum when he was still young.'

He begins to take the picture away. I reach out for it. 'What about Daniel?'

He takes a breath. Reluctant now, I think, to be talking at all. 'He lived for a long time. My grandfather said he was never happy. He blamed himself for his brother's death. It preyed on his mind.'

'Wait. Please.' I hold on to the picture. Getting it clear. 'Your grandfather, Michael. He also knew about stones.'

'Yes. There was something his father and uncle had lost. Michael found it for them. It took him most of his life. He found it and took it back to Iraq before his father died.'

It is a moment before I realise what he is saying. I look up into his face. 'You're talking about the Three Brethren.'

He doesn't answer me. He is staring down at the picture. As if he is trying to see himself in the eyes of the man. The blades of his face. The hands closed together. There is a bedside table. A watch chain. A glass of tea in a tulip glass.

'What happened to it?'

Hikari shakes his head clear. He takes the book from me, returns it to the shelf, and walks away across the unlit room.

'Thank you,' I call after him. 'For showing me. It must have made Daniel very happy, what Michael did. To have the jewel again.'

'Why?' His voice is faint. He stops at the door, searching my face. I don't know what for. 'It was never something he can have wanted back.' The smell of the rain blows in. He walks out into it.

᚛

1920, a year between wars. It is almost night, the sky balanced between twilight and dusk. Daniel Levy waits in the house his son has built. He sits with his head cocked, listening to the river outside. The Europeans, digging for their past. He turns towards the window where the tamarisks are flowering.

His face is etiolated, the blood and colour lost with age. His son Michael has helped him from the bed. He can hear the boy next door. The murmur of voices. There are other people waiting there for him. Business partners. Foreigners. They have come here to arrange something. Something is expected to happen.

His hands rest on the table in front of him. He looks down. They have been disfigured with age, not only reduced but also twisted, until they have come to resemble claws. They remind him of Rachel. A beautiful jewel lies between them. Michael has put it there for him. A gift to an old man from his grown son. The heart of a story told too many times.

The Three Brethren. Daniel remembers it well enough. His mind is still good, boiled down to the hardness of facts. If he forgets the present sometimes, it is only because there is so much of the past to keep clear. In the evening light the knot blinks up at him. He blinks back. It has the face of an angel, he thinks. An angel with three eyes. Nothing human could be so beautiful.

He closes his eyes. Salman is still there behind them. Daniel recalls England. Coronation Day. It comes to him effortlessly. His brother still whole, smiling upwards. His voice, the passion in it. *Look at the sky. Look at it. We have thrown jewels up to God tonight.*

He looks down. His eyes are weeping, as they often do. It is an effort to stand. He walks to the window. There are tools on the floor. A hammer, a level. He picks up the hammer.

He is one hundred and nine years old. He leans by the window, catching his breath. The trees outside are a tenth of his age. He thinks how easy it is, to underestimate the reach of human lives. There is a strength in that. A power. The air is sweet with the smell of blossom.

He walks back to the table. When he gets there he smiles, quite suddenly, as if he has done something magnificent.

The muezzin begins. He raises the hammer.

What he thinks is his own business.

水

At night I watch him breathe. His own bulk makes it uncomfortable for him to sleep. Movement spreads from the lungs through his whole flesh, the shoulders, his cheekbones, the curve of his waist. It keeps me awake, watching him. Only in the morning do I remember dreaming of Istanbul. A calligrapher's shop window, six thousand miles away. Plastic flowers, and the great sweep of characters.

Twice a week I walk into town for supplies. There is little traffic on the coast road, only haulage trucks and the occasional vanload of surfers. I catch myself passing them with my head down, the way Hikari does. His seclusion becoming habitual in me. It is Christmas Eve before anyone stops.

I am walking back from Tosa with rice and rice wine, the weights balanced in each hand. The morning is cold and bright. An aeroplane passes overhead. I look up to follow its track, north-west towards Hiroshima, and as I do so something dark and sleek goes past on the road beside me. I have time to be surprised before there is a kick of brakes, ten yards back. The slow whine of reversed gears.

I don't look round. The vehicle pulls up alongside me. A business car with tinted glass. It keeps pace, kerb-crawling backwards. I wait for a window to roll down, a door to open, but nothing happens. I don't see anyone. It is fifty yards before it pulls away, hard, accelerating north. The sun glares off its rear window. A Tokyo number plate. I stand there long after it is out of sight.

No one is at the house. Hikari has taken the catch to Kôchi by boat, and the children are at school. The last few days before the New Year holidays. Under the stairs is a mass of fishing and navigation equipment, the smoked glass from a broken sextant, a wooden eel spear. It takes an hour to find a pair of binoculars. I go back down to the quay. The grilled-octopus man nods hello, grinning at the chance of custom. I buy a coffee. It is just past noon and I sit on the sea wall, drinking, facing inland. The binoculars focused to the coast road.

The tide goes out. The grilled-octopus man locks up and sits beside me. He talks about baseball and birdwatching. With his burn-marked hands he explains the secrets of catching octopus. I don't see anyone arrive, but when I pick up the binoculars again a figure has appeared. A silhouette against the winter light.

I focus in. There is a man in a suit standing at the shoulder of the promontory. He turns in the shuddering arena of the lenses, putting out a cigarette. Sunglasses obscure any emotion in his face. His mouth is impassive. I can't be sure if he is Japanese or not. He does nothing to show that he might have seen me. He only looks as if he is waiting for something.

It is two hours before Hikari comes back. I wait on the porch. Cold to the bone, rocking to keep warm. He sees me as he is coming down the dune path and he slows, knowing something is wrong, seeing it in my presence. He comes and sits beside me, not saying anything. His breath clouds the air, warmer than mine.

'You never asked how I found you,' I say.

Hikari blinks. His voice is gruff, covering its own surprise. 'We never talked about it.'

'Ask me.'

He shrugs. 'How did you find me?'

'I met a man in Tokyo. He knew how to access records by computer. He found your mother's death certificate. It had your address listed with it.' I stop. Not looking at his face. Not wanting to see it as I talk. 'I asked this man if anyone could trace what he had done.'

'What did he say?'

'He said that in computers, with enough money, one can see anything. He asked me if these people had money. I told him I didn't know.'

I look up. He nods at me to go on. I blurt it out. 'There was a man on the coast road today. Waiting by the headland. And this morning a car followed me back from Tosa. Not to the house, I didn't show them where I was going–'

'Enough.' He stands up and, turning away, swears in Japanese. Face wrinkled up into the words.

'I'm so sorry–'

'*Hah!*' He shouts me down. A sound without words. I flinch back from it. Hikari covers his face with his hands. When he looks down at me again he is frowning, as if he has come home and found a stranger in his house. My heart goes falling away inside me.

'Please, Hikari–'

He mutters, only to himself. Repeating a phrase in Japanese, shaking his head. I catch it the third time. *I have betrayed myself.*

'This isn't your fault.'

'No?' He turns round. Sweat has broken out on his seamed face. 'You are here because I wanted you. I let myself believe you were different from them.'

'I am.'

He walks away without answering. Under the ginkgo tree he sits down. And I follow him, knowing he doesn't want me to, unable to help myself. 'Who are they?'

His voice is dull with exhaustion. 'You think you're the only one? That no one else is as clever as you?'

'No.'

'I don't know who they are.' He looks away, smiling, wretched. 'There are many people like you. The companies who did business with my grandfather send you. All my life I have lived to avoid them. My grandfather did any work to find the jewel, anything, because of what happened to his father. He brought the Three Brethren back because it was ours, mine and my children's children. My mother promised him she would keep it, and I promised her. But these companies don't forget. You are my curse. You remember the people you have done business with. You are like flies.'

'I'm not one of them. Hikari. Look at me.'

He stares up. 'I should never have let you stay.'

'Please.'

He shakes his head. Reaches out for my face. Cups it with both hands. Later we will make love for hours. Hardly moving, the

392

dark of his room fading to daylight. The rhythm of him inside me so slow it is almost nothing. Only a closeness. I never feel it end.

He is gone when I wake. I lie still listening. I remember his warmth and the weight of his body. My body remembers it. It is late already. The house is quiet.

A seabird mewls outside. It occurs to me that Hikari was still with me as the sun came up. My thoughts follow on, one after another. Slow as breakers at the edge of sleep.

I turn my head. The house altar is gone. There is no shock, nothing so quick. There may even be a part of me which expected its absence. It is the way one turns round in a dream. Knowing something monstrous already waits.

I look round at the rest of his room. Nothing else is gone. There is not much else that could be taken. I imagine Hikari lifting the lacquered box, silently carrying it away. I get up and follow his image out.

He is less than a dream, more than an idea. On the landing a rice cake has fallen. On the third step, an aubergine. He didn't stop to pick them up. Nor do I. Distantly, it comes to me that it is Christmas Day.

The doors of the children's rooms are shut. I try Tom's, calling his name softly. No one answers. The room is full of wallpaper animals and nothing else. Light falls across their processions. They watch me go downstairs.

The house feels abandoned. My presence has no impact, it changes nothing. The rooms have become ownerless. Light falls across the empty floors. The bookshelf is stripped. The stove and mini-fridge are gone.

There is no letter for me that I can find. I begin to look harder. Scattering the insides of cupboards and drawers. The noise is out of place. It is hard to make myself stop, to hold the panic in. Iren's breakfast cup waits on the counter, blue plastic with green dolphins. I try to imagine her face, making itself keep quiet. Her eyes leaving me.

The rice wine is where I left it. I fill the cup and take it outside onto the porch. There are no chairs. I sit against the peeling wall. My hand shakes a little as I drink. There is no sound of the boat or the generator. Only the giant footfall of the Pacific Ocean going nowhere.

I say to myself, He left no message so they wouldn't find it. He left no letter because he didn't know how to say goodbye. I say, He left nothing because I am a stranger in his own house. He will never let himself love me again.

I think of his voice. His arms, the curves of them, their balance and strength. Like calligraphy. I close my eyes to think of them and when I open them again I am crying and there is nothing to be done about it. I swallow back the last of the rice wine. My throat clicks over it. The sun shimmers over the marram grass.

There is something in the grass. It is some time before I notice it. Only when I am done with myself do I look up and see it. A low square bulk against the light. I walk past the allotment and the ginkgo tree. The sand is against me. At the point where the dunes begin there is a hummock, a nest of grass. I know them. I curl myself down into their shape.

There is a box half-hidden by the scrub. An old wooden case, left in a place no one would know but me. I pull it towards me. It is dark with age, acrid with the smell of turpentine. There is a piece of paper underneath, and as I move the weight off it the wind tries to take it and I catch it first. It has already fluttered open.

Dear Katharine,

I am sorry this is all I have to give you. It belonged to my mother's father and his father before him. My mistake has been to try and keep it. It was never worth what any of us gave it.

Make a good life.

Hikari.

I open the box. It is almost empty. There is only one object inside. My head aches with the wine. I feel my life twisting down to this point.

It is a warped frame of gold. A triangle of metal, angular as a snake-head. There are vacancies where stones have been. I take it out. The weight of it catches my hand by surprise. It is a thing without beauty or purpose. It could be the skeleton of a great jewel. No one would know it but me. I sit in the shelter of the dunes and weep over Hikari and the Three Brethren.

It is noon by the time I pack. It takes me longer than it should. In the abandoned house I linger, insubstantial as a ghost. As if anyone I want would be coming back. When I'm finished I walk over to the quay. The grilled-octopus man is waiting for business. Hikari's boat still hangs at the rope bollards.

'Good morning!' The vendor shouts in enthusiastic Japanese. 'How about breakfast?'

My bag in one hand, the jewel in the other, I go over to him. 'What is there?'

'Octopus.' He smiles, bright white. 'Fresh. Good for the heart.'

I buy what he has. We stand together, tendrils splotching on the skillet between us. The man smiles and nods. As if we are talking, although we are hardly talking. Waves thud against the hull of the fishing boat.

'Has anyone been out here this morning?'

He shrugs, turning curlicues with a spatula. 'Only your boyfriend and his kids. Business will pick up after New Year.'

'You saw them?'

'Sure.'

'When?' I try and keep the emotion out of my voice. As if it matters, now; or ever did.

'Early. Your man walked into town. Came back with a car. The kids waited here. He bought them octopus before they left.' He shuffles food into a polystyrene box. Peers through the smoke. 'North. They went north. That's eight hundred yen. Half price to you.'

'What kind of car?'

'Blue Toyota, a real heap. Aren't you going with them?'

'With them?' His question catches me off guard. As if he has not asked anything, but told me something about myself.

He nods down. 'What's that you've got there?'

I look. The Three Brethren is still in my hand. Heavy as a gun. 'Gold.'

'*Eh?*' His eyebrows shoot up. The smile vanishes and he ducks inside the trailer. I wait for him to re-emerge.

'I need you to do something for me.'

'Ah.' He comes back monosyllabic with worry. I unzip my bag, take out the notebooks. They make a respectable pile on the trailer counter.

'I need you to look after these. Some friends of mine will come for them.' I put the Three Brethren on top of the books, weighing them down against the shore wind. 'Give them all this. All of it.'

395

The grilled-octopus man grimaces. 'When are they coming?'

I don't answer him. Light catches on the jewel. For a moment it is just the two of us here. Something human and something inhuman. I think of Hikari. I wonder what I am doing now. How much I will have cause to regret.

I touch it. The Three Brethren. The sun has warmed its element. I close it in my hand. An object the size of my palm. Not letting it go.

'Well? Are you leaving it or not?'

When I look up the vendor is squinting out at me uneasily. A cardboard Coca-Cola sign flaps against the trailer. I open my fist. 'I'm sorry.'

'Don't be sorry to me. Gold.' He clucks it distrustfully. 'How will I know them, these friends?'

'Ask them what they're looking for.'

'Oh. Sure then. Good luck finding your man. North, eh?'

I pick up my bag. He waves after me as I turn down the seafront. The strand is bright in the afternoon light. Somewhere a seagull begins to cry. It sounds like laughter. When I think of myself again I find I am laughing with it.

I start to walk inland. A truck clanks on the coast road. A deepwater road, this one, nothing but trucks and trailers out this far. And me. My life swings on its turning point. I say to myself, I am looking for something. Looking for someone. A love out of stones.